CRITICS RAVE ABOUT
CAROLYN JEWEL!

THE SPARE

"Creating an atmosphere rich with suspense and sexual tension, Ms. Jewel has penned a taut romantic mystery in *The Spare* that pleases on many levels…. [Readers will be] utterly enthralled with this tale of two tortured souls who eventually find solace with one another."

—*Romance Reviews Today*

"A delightful battle-of-wills romance, tinged with suspense…. Jewel handles complex plotting with ease and creates a compelling story with characters that captivate."

—*Romantic Times*

LORD RUIN

"Ms. Jewel's sensual, passionate and powerful love story keeps to the classic lines of the Regency historical while adding a fresh voice."

—*RT BOOKclub*

"Entertaining, satisfying, and sensuous."

—All About Romance

ENTER, DARKNESS

"Why did you stop?" she asked.

She was beautiful, *so* beautiful, and she did not deserve this. She thought he was going to *make* her. He was going to betray her again. He spread his fingers and traced the curve beneath her eyes. He said, "Be patient."

He needed enough blood from her to heal. Enough to give him the resources he needed. He was stronger now, but not enough. He might…might… He tilted her head upward. With the sides of his thumbs, he smoothed the line of her cheeks. She shivered, a delicate tremor. He imagined holding her, caressing, stroking while she quivered like that, nude of course, completely nude, while he tasted long and deep. He ought to feed more right now, but he didn't. He let the rush of her wash away his principles. "Let me in, Officer," he whispered. The words thrummed in his ears, in his head. "Let me into your divine self."

A DARKER CRIMSON

CAROLYN JEWEL

LOVE SPELL

NEW YORK CITY

LOVE SPELL®

November 2005

Published by

Dorchester Publishing Co., Inc.
200 Madison Avenue
New York, NY 10016

ISBN 0-505-52658-1

Printed in the United States of America.

Visit us on the web at www.dorchesterpub.com.

ACKNOWLEDGMENTS

First off, I want to thank Liz Maverick for thinking up this fabulous series and then telling me about it. Thank you Patti O'Shea for being so wonderful to work with. My thanks as well to Megan Frampton for her help and insight, and to Lisa VanAuken for the same.

I'm grateful to Jennifer Hone, M.D., for providing me with medical facts about the physiology of vampires, werewolves, anatomy and the logistics of biting. I'd say you better keep a close eye on your patients because you just never know....

To Bobby Rentfro and Deryle Davis, thanks for telling me about guns. Hopefully I haven't bobbied up the details. (If I did, it's my fault and not yours.)

Thank you Chris Keeslar for your silent agreement that I am "detail-oriented" instead of something less flattering.

Lastly, my thanks and love to my family for their patience.

Chapter One

Claudia Donovan crouched down to get a closer look at the bodies, the smell telling her it was bad—a damp smell, tangy with blood and bile. The moon hung low and pale in the sky, and darkness shrouded the freshly graded dirt. Two bodies sprawled in the shadow of a bulldozer. At one end of the lot a Dumpster overflowed with construction debris, broken sheetrock, tattered insulation and twisted re-bar. She switched on her Maglite. The beam illuminated the sheen of viscera.

Los Angeles, the City of Angels. It was earning its other nickname all over again. Crimson City. The war—oh, right, the "conflict"—between the species was spreading. This time, two adult males. The smaller one looked peaceful. Close cropped afro, square-chinned face, ebony skin, big brown eyes and a deep gash across his throat. The other one, John Doe Number Two, didn't look so peaceful. Both men looked dead.

Claudia reached for her police-issue pack and took out a pair of latex gloves. After a hesitation, she slipped them on. No sense not checking things out while she waited for the detectives and the M.E. to arrive. Considering she'd notified the L.A.P.D. fifteen minutes before she'd called the buttheads from Internal Operations, she felt confident the detectives would arrive first. They'd better. Internal Operations—unofficially Battlefield Operations or B-Ops, the city government intelligence division—was nothing but a freaking pain in the ass. No one in the L.A.P.D. liked them, least of all her. But in this case, damn it, she didn't have a choice. She had to notify B-Ops because of Korzha.

She glanced at the vampire just to make sure he was still there. He was. Now, *there* was a real piece of work. Tiberiu Korzha. He was the reputed head of the vampire family Korzha, with an army of lawyers who had so far made every prosecuting attorney in the city look like a chump. The creature stood just within sight, though much of his face remained in shadow. Mostly the P.D. dealt with rogue vamps, vampires who went outside the law and the treaty between the species or who just went flat-out insane; but Korzha had Strata +1 written all over him: He was part of their society and was as suave, rich and debonair as they came. Right now, he stood still as a statue. Claudia hoped he had control of himself. There was blood all over, including a crimson splatter on the side of the bulldozer. Spilled blood tended to make an edgy vamp edgier.

"You have anything to do with this, Korzha, or you just get lucky?" she asked.

"Lucky," he replied. But not like he meant it.

The L.A.P.D. didn't have jurisdiction to arrest him for any of the crimes of which he was suspected—racketeering, drug-trafficking, assault, forced conversion, fraud, and aiding-and-abetting all of the above—but everybody knew Tiberiu Korzha was a killer. Anyone needed a vamp taken down, Korzha was reputedly the guy to make the hit. He intrigued her. B-Ops insisted paranormal investigations belonged to them, but Claudia didn't give a rat's ass about that. There wasn't any law against the P.D. asking a vamp questions. Not yet.

Even in the dark, she took care not to meet Korzha's eyes. He'd been at her precinct for a friendly interview more than once. He liked to voodoo the ladies, give them that come-hither-for-a-mind-blowing-orgasm stare. He'd tried it once or twice with her. Damn near worked. Good-looking vamp. Weren't they all? She went back to examining the bodies. She decided Korzha must have fed on at least one of the dead guys, and that was why he wasn't twitchy.

"Lucky accident? Or lucky you got them both?" she asked, still crouched beside the bodies. The new P.D. uniforms, dark blue and body-hugging, tended to fit poorly in the crotch. She had long legs, and her uniform pants kept riding up.

"Well," the vamp said in his smooth voice. "You know what they say about luck."

Yeah right. If it weren't for bad luck . . . "Vamps don't have bad luck," she retorted. How much bad luck could you have if you lived in the Upper, were rolling in money and didn't die without a lot of help? Not much. Now, her? She had all kinds of luck, none good lately. Way too much overtime. All the cops were pulling extra shifts just to keep up. Her precinct had a pool going on total body count by end of month. She had one of the highest numbers. Halfway through the month, and they were almost there. Her pick looked pretty good.

"This guy—" She pointed to the larger body. "He

had some bad luck, I'd say." She glanced up again, kind of a sideways look so as to avoid meeting Korzha's eyes. A vamp hanging out in this neighborhood just didn't compute, not without throwing in a criminal motive or two or three. "Dollars to donuts he was looking to get made. You know anything about that?"

Korzha's teeth flashed in the dim light. "I haven't made a vampire in . . . quite a long time."

"Yeah. Right."

"The last thing this city needs is more post-human wrecks running amok."

She reached into the last of the smaller corpse's pockets. Surprise, surprise. He had no ID. "Then something's rotten in the State of Denmark, wouldn't you say?" John Doe One looked to be the younger as well as the smaller of the two bodies. Adult human male, well developed. Good nutrition. She touched his neck and found the wounds she expected. His skin was cool, with a faint sheen of something on the surface. There were two puncture wounds, and about a centimeter and a half below that a scatter line of petechiae from lower teeth pressing up, and two telltale bruises from lower canines.

Korzha hunkered down beside her, watching curiously.

"Got hungry, did you?" she asked.

She pretended she didn't notice his shoulder practically touching hers. The problem with vamps like Korzha, besides the sharp teeth and insatiable lust for human blood, was the combination of physical and supernatural charisma. Supposedly the man had been good-looking when he was human, and becoming a vamp must have tripled the effect. When the subject came up, which it did whenever he got hauled to the precinct for a little polite interrogation, most every woman agreed Korzha was a fine-looking man. *Yummy* was the adjective most often applied. Rumor was, a lot of other vamps imitated his looks. Some things, of course, couldn't be duplicated: his six-foot frame, muscled without being overdone, and a face that, when you caught him in a moment of repose, was handsome but not pretty. But the Armani suits, leather shoes, French shirts, the close shave and the perfect hair cut with a hint of sideburn trimmed to a point, razored off his neck—that look, a lot of male vamps adopted. If Korzha raked his fingers through his hair, every espresso-colored lock sprang back into place. A bit chilly, it always seemed to her, that kind of perfection. But he had a smile that could heat a person up pretty quick.

Korzha shook his head like he had a bad taste in his mouth. Somewhere in the distance a dog barked. A real dog, not a werewolf. "It wasn't me."

Claudia shrugged. "It's not like I'm a vegetarian myself. But did you *have* to kill him?"

"I didn't," he said.

"Right." She shook her head. "I swear, I don't know why I bother asking. I could have caught you with your teeth in the guy's throat and you'd be, '*Officer, I'm innocent.*'" She risked a look at the vamp. His face was expressionless, but she saw his tongue come out to wet his lower lip. She hated it when anyone—fang, dog or human—thought she was stupid. "You're one of the most freaking notorious vamps in the whole of Crimson City, Korzha. A known hitman—"

"Prove it."

"I find you standing over two dead guys, and you didn't kill anybody?"

"Officially, of course"—Korzha gave her an odd smile—"until the coroner calls it, they aren't dead."

"Stow it, fang."

Korzha laughed. "Even if I did—how would you put

it?—*take care* of these two gentlemen, Officer Donovan, you're outside your jurisdiction." Every now and then, Korzha talked like he came from someplace else. Someplace far away from the good old U.S. of A. Really, really Upper. Stood to reason. Most vampires and all the vamps from the Korzha family came from the Upper, lived in Strata +1. And it was in the nature of vamps to like the finer things. They looked it, lived it, talked it. They wouldn't interact with humans at all if they didn't need blood.

"Yeah, well. B-Ops isn't here yet," she said. Resentment gave her words an edge. B-Ops demanded they handle all paranormal incidents; like that sort of crime could only be handled by college boys and jarheads. B-Ops thought the L.A.P.D. was incompetent. From what she'd seen in her time on the force, they worked hard to compete. Nobody in the P.D. liked B-Ops; it was kind of a mutual-hatred society. Just like the rest of the city. Another serving of antipathy, please.

"Well, then," Korzha said, letting his aristocratic tones linger in the air.

"I'm the officer on the scene," she replied. Freaking vamp. Snobs, all of them. Thought they were better than everyone. "There are dead humans here. Gotta take a look. Ask a few questions. It'd be a dereliction of duty if I didn't."

"Only one of them is human," Korzha said.

He sounded serious, and Claudia thought that was a pretty interesting change of tactics. Vamps hardly ever shared information with cops. "Yeah? Which one isn't?"

"The larger."

She studied the second body for a moment. It made a far less pleasant sight than the first, which wasn't remotely pretty. Number Two's chest was torn open. Not cut; torn. It looked like someone had stuck his bare hand into the guy's ribcage, made a fist and pulled hard. A heart was balanced in the corpse's left hand and, judging from the mess in his torso, she presumed it was his. She checked her comm readout, figured she had just enough time, and dug a HemoStrip out of her backpack. "He's not a vamp or he'd be turning to dust by now, and I doubt he's a werewolf."

"Why?" asked Korzha.

"Why do I think he's not a dog?" Sheesh. Vamps could be so ignorant. But Korzha ought to know, considering the neighborhood he chose to hang out in. Lotsa wolves around here. "Easy," she said. "No sign of re-transformation. And besides, if he was a dog, his packmates would be all over this place."

The vampire didn't move. Eerie, the way his kind could be so motionless.

"Lucky us." She wiggled the HemoStrip at him. "Plenty of blood for a field sample." She collected a drop of glistening gore from the center of the chest cavity, less chance of contamination, then dropped the strip in the vial and broke the chem-release seal. "So, not a dog, not a vamp. Not a human. What the hell is he, then? A ghost?"

"A demon."

Claudia fell backward onto her butt. Something went squish under her, followed by the odor of something rotting from the inside out. "Oh, crud. This is just gross. Korzha, you made me drop the Hemo-Strip." The vampire plucked something from the ground and handed it to her. Damn preternatural vision. B-Ops got night vision contacts, but not the P.D., oh no. God forbid the first line of defense in a city about to ignite should be prepared. Not that she could blame Korzha for that. She took the HemoStrip from him. "Thanks."

"My pleasure."

She dropped the vial into a pocket to free up her hands for brushing off her backside. Thank God she still had on the gloves. Yuck. With her eyes fixed on Korzha's ear—he was a tall creature, which meant her head tipped back—she could peripherally see the line of his just-shaved cheek. She caught a whiff of sandalwood from him. Nice. "Let's pretend a minute there aren't any such things as demons," she said.

"Cut the crap, Officer." There was that voice again. Very . . . Upper. "You know damn well there are."

"How can you tell?" she asked, genuinely curious. She stripped off her gloves and shoved them in an outside pocket of her pants. "To me, these look like two regular humans who didn't deserve to die."

Korzha picked something off the seat of her pants and flung it away. "Experience."

She gave him a look. Had he, or had he not, let his hand linger on her butt? Somewhere in the back of the lot, a tomcat yowled. "Gonna explain that?" she asked. She lifted her eyebrows when he didn't, and pointed at the body. "If you're so experienced, what kind of demon is it?"

"A dead one," Korzha said.

"Everyone's a comedian," she said.

"He's Mahsei."

"Isn't that a kind of tuna fish?" She gave him a fake grin. "I got that for lunch today. Tuna salad with celery and stuff in it. Made it myself."

The vampire indicated the second body. "Considered a lesser demon. Although," he added, "I believe Mahsei are underestimated in their world."

"Har, har." Claudia turned back to the bodies. She gave John Doe Two a closer glance. Looked human to her. She really, really hated being condescended to. "Jerk," she muttered.

"I heard that."

"Oh, gee." She lifted a hand. He could be living in the Upper, relaxing amidst the best that money could buy, and instead he was out here with the freaks and losers of L.A., slumming. Feeling superior. "Sorry, Korzha. I forgot about the supernatural hearing and all that. I'll be more careful next time."

"You do that."

Claudia studied the bodies. The thing was, rumors about demons had been cropping up on the streets for some time now. Lots of dead vamps and dogs these days, too. Lots of unrest. She frowned. She wasn't about to tell Korzha that this second body bothered her. The clothes for instance: unusual fabric, and not a style she'd ever seen in Crimson City. There were no buttons on the pants, and no zipper. Instead, the pants were laced in front. She touched the corpse's chin, pulling his face around. His eyes were open. For a moment she thought he'd been blind, but it was just that his irises were so pale they looked nearly white. "No rigor yet," she said to cover her surprise. But she supposed the eyes weren't *so* unusual. She knew at least one other human with freakishly pale irises.

Korzha coughed, but she ignored him. Her mind clicked along. She didn't give a crap about contaminating the scene. B-Ops wouldn't notice, and if they did, hey, what did they expect? The P.D. was incompetent. They shoulda got to the scene sooner. "This guy . . ." She pointed to the gaping chest. "Classic rogue kill."

"You don't say?"

Claudia twisted a little to look at the vampire. His eyes glittered, but she was careful not to directly meet his gaze. Not with that vampire voodoo head stuff he liked to do. She wanted to look, but she didn't. "Look, Korzha, the P.D. isn't stupid about paranormal crimes, no matter what B-Ops likes to say." She pointed again. "Heart torn out and put in the left hand. Wasted blood as a sign of contempt. Plain as day if you know anything about rogue kills. One of these guys was here to get made, I'll guarantee that."

"If you say so."

Claudia fought back annoyance and explained. "Takedown on the first guy, all the blood drained, throat slit to be sure he isn't coming back. Then the rogue-kill here with the other. To send a message."

"Fascinating," Korzha replied.

Claudia suddenly felt the hair on her arms prickle. She glanced over her shoulder, but the construction site was empty except for herself, Korzha, the two bodies and the smell of death. "Busy vamp, aren't you, Mr. Korzha?" she asked.

"One strives not to be bored." He made a point of glancing at his Patek Philippe watch. Another affectation of the Upper. Vamps didn't need watches.

"You got some place to be?"

Korzha shrugged. "A wedding reception."

"How romantic."

She rose, and held up a hand, palm out. The howling cats started up again and she waited for a lull. "I got someplace to be, too, you know. I promised my daughter I'd make her waffles for breakfast." She checked her comm. "In three hours."

"Your daughter?" the vamp said.

Claudia knew she shouldn't smile at him, but she did anyway. "Strawberry waffles. With whipped cream on top." She pointed her forefinger downward and made a swirling motion. "You gonna mess me up and break her heart?"

"Perish the thought."

For some reason, he sounded . . . sad. Must be her imagination.

"I'm humoring you here, okay?" She checked the time on her comm. Forty-eight seconds, and she could read the test. Korzha shifted his weight, and that made her flinch. A little thrill of adrenaline rolled through her. But he didn't attack; he just checked his twenty-thousand dollar watch again. Where was everyone? She really didn't want to be alone with this vamp and a bunch of spilled blood. "What happens if I check the HemoStrip and the little arrow points to the minus?" Meaning, of course, not human.

"Nothing?" he said, with a taint of irony.

"You're a regular comedian, aren't you?" There was a moment of silence Claudia expected to be filled with a sarcastic retort. Instead, he said, "How old is your daughter?

"Ten. She's the greatest. She really is."

Man, oh, man. The guy was unfairly handsome. Hair the color of an espresso bean; straight nose, a bit flared—all the best characteristics of an Eastern European. Sensitive mouth, strong cheekbones, a hint of the Attic hordes in the shape of his eyes. Even she, trained to a certain level of immunity to preternatural charm, couldn't entirely resist.

She looked at the bodies again. "If one of them's a demon, how come they're both dead?" she asked.

"One does wonder."

She cocked her head and flicked on her Maglite again. "Now that's just weird."

"Maybe, Officer Donovan. But then, I lack your insight into the criminal mind."

"F-you, Korzha."

"Respectfully, I decline the offer."

11

Claudia rolled her eyes again. "The small guy's got a tattoo," she went on. She fixed her light on it, a pale blue swirl of interlocking lines on his exposed shoulder. "Rogues like body art. Ever seen that before?"

"No."

"Me neither." She checked her comm again. "Where the hell are the detectives?" she said under her breath. "I gave them a heads-up big enough to drive a truck through. They ought to be here." She kicked the toe of her boot into the dirt. She did *not* want to deal with B-Ops and their paperwork. Six forms for every paranormal handoff. Not to mention double pay for her daughter's babysitter whenever Claudia pulled an all-nighter. Seemed like all her overtime pay went to the IRS and the sitter. "Another freaking night totally screwed up."

Korzha seemed amused. "Perhaps your colleagues are unavoidably detained."

Claudia ignored him. "So." She narrowed her eyes and pulled out the HemoStrip. "How come you know so much about demons?"

"I make a point of keeping myself informed."

She clutched the HemoStrip but had her eyes on her time readout. Fifteen seconds. "Yeah, right."

"It's minus," Korzha said.

She flashed her light on the HemoStrip because the dim lamp at the street corner wasn't bright enough to get a decent reading. Her heart bottomed out. "Holy cripes."

"Problem, Officer?"

Hell, yes. Twelve forms! Six for Korzha and six for the nonhuman body. She thought about the bodies and the rumors of demons. The *lots* of rumors. The street lamp dimmed, buzzed, then flared before settling down to a 'faint yellowish glow. It made her feel sick, the thought of demons loose in the city. Korzha looked like a statue. "I'm just going to ask this straight out, okay?" she asked.

"I'm not going to hypnotize you," he said with a hint of exasperation. "So you can stop staring at my ear and talk to me. What offensive question do you wish to ask?"

She risked a look into his eyes. Green. Like moss. She'd always wanted green eyes, but got stuck with plain old brown. "Let's say you're right, and this is a demon. What's it doing in Los Angeles?" she asked.

He crossed his arms over his chest. "Not that we have all the time in the world for this fascinating chat, Officer, but haven't any of your forays into the B-Ops network gotten you the answer to that question?"

"I don't know what you're talking about," she said. But was it a stab in the dark, or did he really know she'd cracked B-Ops? It never paid to dismiss the improbable. It just didn't. Her chest tightened. The world was a pretty scary place. The whole damn city was on the edge of war. It was practically in the middle of one, only no one would admit it. Conflict my ass. The war between the species had already walked right in and sat down to dinner. "Does Fleur Dumont know you're negotiating with demons, Korzha?"

He laughed, only he didn't sound amused. "It's so much easier to say I'll never do it again."

"She'll have your head on a platter." The pull of his charisma tugged at her. For a guy out slumming, he kept himself pretty Upper. Right. A wedding reception. Too bad, his expensive shoes were getting dirty.

"If humans won't live up to their responsibilities here, keeping the peace and our treaty, then I'll do whatever it takes to see vamps live despite you. Despite Fleur Dumont if I have to."

"So, you think humans are killing vamps?"

"Are you?"

"You're insane, you know that?" She rolled her eyes. The lamp buzzed again, then settled down. "B-Ops is always doing sneaky shit, I'll give you that, but it's mostly died down. Everything's cool. And there are no demons here. If there were, I think we'd know." Claudia wished that had come out more like she believed it.

"How old are you?" Korzha asked. Not in a nice way. "Twenty-two? Maybe twenty-three?"

She rolled her eyes again. Twenty-five. But she knew she looked younger. "None of your damn business."

"A child. You know nothing."

Claudia bristled. "Oh, and you were how old when you got made? Thirty? Thirty-five, tops, I bet." She frowned at him. Maybe he'd been in his twenties when he was converted. It was hard to tell with some vamps, particularly when they didn't adjust well, as made vampires typically did not. And Tiberiu 'Tiber' Korzha was a made vamp; everyone knew that. "The P.D. file on you doesn't go back more than ten years, and the B-Ops file doesn't have much more."

"On the servers *you* got to," he said.

She ignored the dig, but he was right. "You can't be that old," she said.

"I stopped counting three hundred years ago."

She made a face at him. "Har, har."

A blue flash illuminated the street. No sound, just light. Typical B-Ops. Well, she wasn't going to do them any favors. "I'm stuck with these guys," she said mostly to herself. She flashed her Maglite on the demon corpse or whatever it was, but the beam sputtered once, turned yellow and went out. She stared at the cylinder with disgust. "That's what's wrong with the world today." She shook the flashlight in Korzha's face. "Brand-new batteries!"

"Tsk, tsk," the vamp said.

"Look, Korzha, I don't feel like spending the rest of my night filling out forms on you. Why don't you head off to your party, okay?" She twitched her head toward the building next door. "But if that guy's not a demon, I'm coming after you. I'll crash your reception and arrest you right in front of the happy bride and groom. That's a promise."

"How romantic, officer." He gave her a business card. "My private cell is on here. If it seems you're going to be late for your appointment, call me. I'll see you get there on time."

"Scram, would you?"

Korzha didn't waste a moment; Claudia blinked, and he was gone. Just like a vamp. She waited for the detectives or the coroner or some B-Ops bozos to announce themselves, then took a step toward the street when nobody did. The blue light faded, and she walked into a nightmare.

Chapter Two

Claudia ducked to avoid having her head burnt off by a bolt of blue fire. She made herself as small a target as she could and squinted to see who the hell had fired on her without warning. At the corner of the street, and about twenty feet away from the eerie blue glow, stood a lone figure: a man, but without any weapon that she could see. His clothes bore a striking similarity to the second corpse's, the man Korzha claimed was a demon. He wore the same tunic-shaped shirt and close-fitting pants.

She hit her comm and got a sputter of white noise. Shit. Head down, she drew her sidearm and flicked off the safety. Where the hell were the detectives? About now she'd be happy to see B-Ops. She jammed in a full clip, regular ammo, and shouted, "L.A.P.D.! Put down your weapon. Now!"

Another bolt of fire burst from the man. What the hell kind of weapon was he packing? And how had he managed to jack it up like that? Heat singed her hair and sent her heart into a tattoo against her ribs. Holy cripes, whoever he was, he meant business. Or else he was just freaking nuts. Whichever it was, she needed someplace to hide.

Cover of darkness evaporated in the bluish glow that overwhelmed the light mounted on a dented pole. Claudia fought off a wild terror. The man's sudden appearance had her rattled. Losing focus was deadly when you walked a beat in this part of the city. She was a mile from the Lower, where not even cops dared to go. She wondered if the nutcase was someone from there who didn't know he'd gone out of range. He walked toward her.

She hit her comm again and got nothing but static. Panic filled her. She held desperately to her ebbing calm. She aimed her weapon at the figure but at the last minute pulled right. There wasn't anything worse than finding out you'd killed some kid high on narco, and it happened sometimes. Mostly to new cops like her. She'd made her share of house calls to the family. She really, really hated telling some woman her baby was dead. And it didn't matter how old the deceased was; he, or she, was always somebody's baby.

Two shots, deliberately close, ought to put a dose of fear into the freak. Claudia took aim, but the air around her target shimmered. He lifted a hand and, swear to God, Claudia saw fire flickering where his eyes ought to be. Another flash of blue flame headed her way. She dove behind the Dumpster. F-this! She switched out her clip with trembling fingers. Forget vanilla ammo. She needed silver or UV. This was obviously a paranormal. She couldn't get enough air into her lungs. Where the hell was her backup?

A siren blared, too distant for her to think help might be near. Overhead the steady *thop-thop-thop* of a chopper on its nightly rounds reverberated in her ears. A bit closer, pungent sulphur curled into her nose with the fainter odor of ozone and burnt air. Not good. She tapped the comm band around her wrist. Static hiss. She palmed a fingernail-size bit of modified plastique with a detonator. Her own personal hack, this stuff. She'd probably get fired for using it. On the other hand, living long enough to get fired didn't seem like such a bad thing right now. Besides, she made the stuff on the sly for several of the beat officers. Vice and narc, too. Kept you from getting killed by a rogue vamp or some badass werewolf while you waited for B-Ops to show up. If the right guys came for cleanup they'd look the other way, and she'd be okay.

The perp moved. She saw a flash, an almost-blinding glow of energy that pulsed in her, through her, and throbbed in time with her heartbeat. Half a tick before the Dumpster imploded, she threw her explosive. She vaulted for the bulldozer. Her fingers gripped the metal edge of the bucket. The arms dipped and the whole contraption groaned like an old man struggling to rise from his overstuffed recliner. The bucket tilted down, and she dropped to the ground amid a shower of dirt. She cracked her shin on a rusted pole trapped under one of the 'dozer tracks. The plastique hadn't gone off. Given the size of the ball, there should have been a very big noise, and the perp who was after her should have been knocked flat on his ass from the concussion.

He wasn't. He walked toward her, stepping over the bodies without so much as a glance, and there freaking wasn't anywhere else for Claudia to go. The air did that queer sort of shimmering thing again, and the resulting glow was bright enough for her to read a newspaper if she wanted. She blinked once, then got a good look at him. At first, she thought she was seeing a

werewolf transformation, which would have been a relief, because that would have meant all she had to do
was change the clip in her sidearm and blow a hole in
its chest. But that wasn't it. The face went from human
to un-human in the blink of an eye. Its shoulders quivered and, like that, she faced a monster. Flames flickered in its eyes. It grinned.

Claudia went from apprehensive to terrified in an
instant. What the hell was this monster? Less than ten
feet from her, and she felt the pulse of a mental connect: a vampish sort of thing, a dark and slippery
probe in her head. They weren't even making eye contact, and this creature could touch her mind! She
shook her head and, temporarily at least, cleared her
thoughts. What the hell was it? Some kind of super-
vamp? Able to shape-shift like that? The mental-
connect thing was similar to what a vamp did, but
with a hell of a lot more range. A cross between a
vamp and a dog? How the hell did you defend against
that?

Claudia prepared to be toast. Except, two things
happened. The first was a panic-induced rush of
peace. Her years-ago decision about how she would
end her life had prepared her for this moment. She
had a will, a guardian appointed for her daughter,
Holly, and enough insurance to know Holly wouldn't
go without. She could look this monster in the eye and
feel calm. With calmness came her defense. Calm gave
her a wall, an enfolding barrier between her and the
monster.

The second thing was three Cazadores appeared on
the sidewalk.

After all these years, rogue vamps and moonmad
dogs notwithstanding, the Cazadores were still the
gang of record in the worst parts of town. One tall,

two not-so-tall, all three with illegal tazers strapped to their thighs and backs, they were looking to expand their territory, no doubt. The Lower never got smaller, only wider and uglier. The police weren't welcome there. One of the gangbangers held a Street Sweeper, modified to work like a machine gun. Nobody, but nobody, was welcome in the Lower without sanction by the Cazadores. They owned the right to illegal hunts, and they owned the midnight market. Claudia pressed herself flat to the 'dozer track. All things considered, she'd rather be killed by a Cazadore than the blue-light freak.

In the space between her breaths, she heard the distinctive *ka-schick* of an ammo clip being rammed home. She used to steal dinner every night with guys like that, and now they wanted to shoot her? The sound distracted the monster. Not much, but enough. She pitched herself sideways just as blue fire hit the bulldozer. Yellow sparks sprayed the air, showering down like biting gnats. There was a brimstone and saltpeter smell. Another miss, and that worried her. A miss just didn't sit right. If the creature didn't want to kill her, what did it want?

The Cazadores shouted. Behind them, Claudia saw, or thought she saw, a lithe shape leap from the house on one side of the lot to the back of another building. Oh, great. Just fabulous. All she needed now was some rogue vamp come to check out the proceedings. Bad enough she didn't have much chance of keeping herself alive; now she had to keep a vamp from meeting an untimely end. Protect and serve.

With a furious roar, her assailant whirled toward the street. Some kind of energy pulse burst from it. The backlash threw Claudia against the bulldozer. Her elbow hit the ledge of the tracks, and her gun arm went numb. The monster hissed and flicked its wrist in a dismissive gesture toward the three Cazadores. One of the short ones screamed, but the sound cut off and then he was gone. Just . . . gone. The tall one dropped his Street Sweeper, and just in time, too, because the weapon imploded. Laughter thundered, and at the sound the remaining Cazadores proved smarter than Claudia, because they ran like hell. Claudia lurched to her feet, but her enemy turned around before the feeling came back to her fingers. It advanced on her until they were nose to snout.

A rhino stampeded through her chest, and for a disastrous stretch of eternity, terror ruled. Then Claudia's mind divorced itself from her body. Flight wasn't possible, so fight she would. She palmed another bit of plastic explosive and transferred her weapon to her left hand. The grip felt awkward.

She had no doubt that if she fired on this lovely fellow, her gun would probably implode, too. Damn. She felt all the old attitude coming back and then some; she didn't give a damn about anybody but herself because nobody gave a rat's ass about her. No backup? No detectives, no B-Ops? Nothing but her and her wits. "You're under arrest, you freak," she said.

"Human female." It was a normal voice coming from something that looked like a monster, and that made the hair on the back of her neck stand on end.

She tossed her explosive, but, as she'd expected, the beast flicked its hand and it disappeared in a weak little *poof*. All the same, the concussion knocked her flat on her butt. Some of her calm vanished. This monster was strong. She scrambled to her feet as it advanced, and wondered what to try next. Boiling blue eyes glared at her. The thing looked like one of those snout-nosed devils perched on the walls of Notre Dame, only a lot scarier. She felt . . . well, about the only way she could describe the sensation was to say it was probing around her. Curious, that was. And then it fixed on her. She raised her weapon. Her heart went pit-a-pat because she wasn't close enough to guarantee a fatal shot, and she was pretty sure anything less would mean funeral services and "Amazing Grace" for the late Officer Claudia Donovan.

"You have courage, human," it said. Sheesh. It spoke with a British accent. The hoity-toity kind. The kind that got you killed where she came from, no questions asked. It laughed again. "Much courage, human."

"Let me go, and I'll show you some more."

"Is that a promise?" the thing sneered.

"Sure." She shrugged. "Why not?"

The monster's skin gave off the smell of sulphur and charred air. "Humans," it said, "cannot be trusted."

She glanced at the two bodies. "Wasn't any human killed your buddy over there," she said.

"The Mahsei died well."

Claudia felt her heart drop to her toes. "Mahsei?" She fought to make a plan: establish a dialogue, and maybe she wouldn't get fried. Maybe. "Is that what *you* are? A Mahsei demon?"

"Mahsei?" It sounded insulted. "Elismal, human. Elismal demon."

"Well," she said. "Okay. Elismal." Whatever that meant. "So, um, what brings you here?"

"Come to me, Claudia Donovan," it crooned. "I can make you a god. Come, and immortality is yours."

"Gee, thanks." She didn't like that the creature knew her name. How did it know her name? She shrugged. "Maybe another time." She tapped her Glock, praying the demon would take just three more steps. "I was a god last week."

The creature sneered. Its tongue flicked out over a pair of sharp upper incisors. She wondered if maybe it was some kind of vampire. Maybe it was some kind of vampire-wolf hybrid. Except that was impossible. Some rumors were just too wild to be true. It was likely a demon, like it said.

"Fool," it growled.

"Yeah, well, you aren't the first to point that out."

Another half second passed. If the demon or whatever the hell it was wanted to kill her, it wasn't going to miss this time. The chopper sounded closer, practically overhead. They must have registered the explosions. She hoped. But chances were about a zillion to one they'd see anything before she was dead. Or worse. Thanks to B-Ops, Inter-Regional Air Safety wasn't equipped to deal with paranormal manifestations. Hell, she doubted even anyone in B-Ops was equipped to deal with this fellow. Like as not, given the thing's present physical form, I.R.A.S. would mistake it for a werewolf, and that would be that. I.R.A.S. never interfered with werewolf conversions. Claudia, however, didn't intend to end up dead or worse. Not if she could help it. Behind her back, she loaded her alternate clip: bullets with enough silver to take down even a nine-foot-tall werewolf.

The monster grinned again, edging away, giving her an opening. It really did take her for a fool, because any idiot could see she was in over her head. About a thousand miles over, she'd say. The thing, the demon, super-vamp, mutant werewolf—whatever the F it was, it wasn't an idiot. It knew as well as she that the sensible thing for her to do was sprint for the apparent safety of the street and run like hell. She reconsidered her options.

Glock in hand, she found her balance, gathered her

legs under her and sprang straight toward it, yelling like some kind of demented banshee. The demon reacted a shade slower than it ought. It had expected her to run for the street. At least she was right about having surprised it. And right about ending up near enough to trap it. In fact, notwithstanding the unusual opening of her counterattack, this was a textbook werewolf liquidation. According to her purloined B-Ops Field Training Guide, this worked in every classroom simulation.

Too bad the beast wasn't surprised enough. And too bad it wasn't a werewolf. Because when she landed, her foot skidded on a sheet of waxy wrapping from a burger—some people just couldn't be bothered to dispose of their trash—and there she was: off balance and so close the thing could reach out one glittering sharp talon and touch her. Close enough for her to feel waves of white-hot hate. Close enough to see a jeering smile split its face and expose gleaming, hungry teeth, all of them sharp. Panic set in. Hers, not the demon's. The demon didn't look the least bit panicked. But then, the demon wasn't afraid because it wasn't in over its snouty little head. She got the gun up, but her aim didn't account for the recoil. Shit. The bullet slammed into the side of the construction trailer.

"Wealth," the demon said, with a gesture as if to a mountain of gold. Graceful, for a creature in monster form. "Jewels. Ten thousand times more riches than you desire," it offered.

"Nah," she said. She tightened her fingers on her Glock. The metal felt hot. She wasn't going with this thing. Not ever. No way. "If you're giving me a choice, I'd rather die."

"Love," it crooned. "Ecstasy every time you make

love. Men enslaved at your exquisite feet. A particular man, if you wish it."

"Death for me, thanks."

One demonic eyebrow lifted. "A woman, then?" it smoothly said, and it briefly changed shape into a woman. "As beautiful as you?"

She took another step forward. The backs of her knees turned to Jell-O. Almost there. No missing this time. "Could we get on with this already?"

"Give yourself to me, and I will make you the most powerful human in the Overworld. All will tremble at your feet."

"No, thanks," she said. She lifted her Glock.

The air around her shivered, pulsed, a focused cloud of deadly energy coalescing around her. She felt the monster trying to work its way into her head. *Snick.* He was in range. Her aim was perfect. Dead-on perfect. Three to four feet was more than in-range. The demon howled and loosed an attack of energy so dense the air around her steamed and sparked. She squeezed the trigger of her pistol and, swear to God, she saw her bullet come out and melt in midair. With a curse, she dropped the Glock before it burned her hand.

In a moment of crisis, instinct is a beautiful thing. There's no time for better judgment; you get whatever choice came with the moment. Claudia flexed at the hips, lofted her legs into the air and scissored. Blue energy seared the air and crackled like lightning on a power line. Heat nicked the tip of her shoulder and burned. She screamed because getting scorched freaking hurt. Her leading leg struck the demon in the kidney—if it had a kidney. It grunted, but otherwise didn't budge. Pain shot up her shin and into her knee.

The ground came up fast. She hit hard, bent arms

cushioning the impact, and kept rolling. Her hand landed on her Glock. She grabbed it by the muzzle and just about scorched her palm. Another gout of fire erupted over the ground two inches from her left foot. She tapped the release on her arm pack, and another plastique charge slid into her open palm. She prayed the damned stuff would work this time and kept her legs relaxed beneath her—no mean feat considering she'd been this frightened only once before in her life, and compared to this, thinking a vamp was going to make her was a walk in a freaking field of daisies.

The demon's reflexes made hers look like frozen tar. Being at a physical disadvantage was nothing new, not since day one at the Academy. She still compensated for her lack of brawn by training like a maniac. Not in the weight room, but in the dojo—where, in truth, she claimed only mediocre competence. Anybody could whip her in a fair fight. She'd made a point of mastering every pressure point in the book, plus she fought dirty. In close, sometimes the advantage shifted to her.

The smell of charred air increased. The hair on the back of her neck lifted. Without hesitation—that instinct thing again—she swung her upper leg in a low, sweeping semicircle. Her instep collided with the back of the demon's knee. She doubled over and punched the soft region of its inner thigh near the femoral artery, a pressure point that, properly struck, collapsed the knee. The demon's leg bobbed but immediately locked again. Blue vapor roiled above its head. Fire hissed into a pile of re-bar. The metal glowed blue, then red, then white. By now, she was convinced the demon didn't intend to kill her. Not yet, anyway. And she didn't question anymore whether the thing was a demon. It was. It had to be.

She roundhouse-kicked again, aiming for the

femoral pressure point. The demon stumbled, and then, in a flicker, stood perfectly balanced on cloven hooves. A nice touch. It roared. A scaly arm shot out, fingers going around her throat like a vise. She brought up a knee and kicked the monster in the back, a shot to the dorsal area about as effective as before. She fought off her terror and kneed the bastard again while she threw her weight down and away. Their two bodies hit the ground as she hooked her fingers in its collarbones, sliding a thumb into the soft spot over the carotid artery. They rolled in dirt and trash. The demon ended up on top, compressing her torso, suffocating her.

Its fingers tightened around her throat and her bleeding shoulder, and she felt eight individual talons slice her skin. She wasn't sure which hurt worse. Through swirling blue vapor, Claudia stared into cold, cold eyes the color of the sky at high noon. Right before the demon spoke, blue mist floating on its breath, she felt it gather itself, focusing on breaking into her head. *"You are strong for a female human,"* it said. Whether it spoke aloud, or just in her mind, she didn't know. *"Worthy."*

She couldn't speak. She couldn't breathe.

The demon found leverage. The blue vapor condensed, became a deep, uncanny hue. Claudia felt it working its way into her. Terror consumed her. The demon laughed, a joyous sound. Something maleficent slipped around her, into her, cradling her, touching her thoughts and feeding on her terror.

Claudia opened her fist. A reflection of the ball of plastique she held glinted in her foe's boiling eyes. Too bad if the explosion killed her, too; she steeled herself and tossed the tiny ball, so close she couldn't miss this time. But like her Glock, the plastique didn't work right. It sizzled and imploded, rattling the air. The sensation in her head vanished. The demon didn't. It continued to press in on her, refusing to give up. Blue vapor reappeared around its head and quickly refocused on her. Odds were slim to none that she could withstand another attack. Her heart bottomed out.

"Donovan!" someone shouted. With a rush of elation, Claudia recognized the voice: Matthew Jaise, a B-Ops battalion commander recently attached to the L.A.P.D. At freaking last!

Claudia couldn't see past the demon, which had turned its head toward the disruption. The monster hauled her to her feet, but kept a crushing grip on her throat. Air became a precious commodity. In all her time on the force she hadn't ever been happy to see B-Ops. Until now.

The demon whipped its head back to her, shoulders dipping, and Claudia's line of sight improved. Not just Jaise, thank God. There were several B-Ops commandos looking mean and armed to kill. The bunch of sanctimonious blowhards. On the bright side, she might not die today. There was that. The men moved into attack position.

"Friends of yours?" the demon asked. Its fingers loosened around her throat. Her toes touched the ground.

"Got a problem with that?" Hard-scrabble Lower echoed in her every syllable—the first time she'd ever slipped up with her speech patterns since her second term at college.

"Claudia Donovan," the demon said.

Honest to God, she still couldn't tell if it said her name out loud or just in her head. She brought up her Glock and pointed it at the demon's forehead. The weapon's grip heated, started to burn her palms. "Let me go," she said. "I won't miss at this range."

"Courage," it said, as if it were pleased. The air around them shimmered and pulsed with energy.

Claudia pulled the trigger. Her weapon kicked, flicked her wrists up. Her eardrums throbbed with the explosion. She saw the muzzle flash. But nothing happened to the demon.

"Donovan!" Commander Jaise's voice held a shrill urgency that was unusual for a guy with a rep of being cooler than a cucumber on ice. "Don't shoot again! Hold your fire, Officer! *Don't* shoot!"

The demon struck the underside of Claudia's hands, which still quivered from the shot. Her gun flew into the air. Well, okay. Not good. Like some kind of slow-motion vid, she and the demon watched the gun spiraling through in the air, all the plastic parts melting and turning edge-over-angle as if falling through water. The charred-air smell returned. The gun continued its absurd butterfly descent, and then—right between her and the demon—it twinkled once and vanished.

A burst of energy split the air and hit Claudia with enough force to send her reeling toward blackout. Only she hadn't been physically struck, since the weapon had just vanished into thin air. The demon's eyes flashed a darker crimson.

Claudia heard Jaise continue shouting, an edge of desperation in his voice now. This time, the thing was going to kill her. Which, come to think of it, probably meant she wouldn't feel a thing. But there would be that one moment of agony, and she wasn't too keen on the idea of that. So instead of waiting for B-Ops to get its act together or for the demon to crisp her into oblivion or find its way inside her head, she brought up her knee and kicked the demon in the crotch as hard as she could, hoping its anatomy was human enough for that to work. At the same time, she chopped both sides of its neck. Her hands went numb, but it let her go.

She dropped like a rock, rolling even before she landed. From the corner of her eye, Claudia saw Matthew Jaise standing with his legs spread. She didn't care if she sounded like she'd grown up in a gutter because, in point of fact, she had. "Jaise! Fry it, you fucking moron!"

The B-Ops commander imitated a block of cement. Was he insane? Arms out, he aimed his weapon. At *her*. The other B-Ops commandos were doing the same. Jaise lifted one hand, his face intent because he was listening to instructions through his comm link. The demon watched the scene play out with an amused expression. Its fangs showed—like it got a joke Claudia didn't.

Jaise closed his eyes and lowered his hand in an executioner's chop. His Magnum pointed right at Claudia's head.

"Jaise!" she shouted.

His finger squeezed the trigger.

Chapter Three

Pain boiled through Claudia. Flaming hot needles pierced her shoulder. She opened her eyes and fought to consciousness. Nothing but white. Blazing light seared her retinas, and she screwed her eyelids shut. For some minutes, the world consisted of the pain in her eyes and shoulder, and the oddness in her head that seemed to have wrapped her brain in cotton. Eventually, though, she noticed the rest of her body: aching, throbbing—not in a good way at all—but definitely there. She didn't dare move her arm for fear the pain would take off the top of her head, but she did shift her legs. Movement was good. Agonizing, but good.

She lay on a hard and unforgivingly icy surface. But for her shoulder, which felt on fire, she was cold. She groaned. She could make noise—another bodily function retained. Movement and vocalization? Good. Jeez, her head hurt. Check that. Her *brain* hurt.

She turned her head from side to side, then cracked her eyes a slit. Still white. After a moment, shades of white. Pressure in her head. Not between her ears, but down toward the base of her neck. Pressure, and an ironic sensation of comfort and pleasure and warmth—ironic, because she wasn't at all comfortable. She hoped to God she hadn't suffered some form of cognitive damage. L.A.P.D. didn't allow damaged cops on the streets, and she couldn't afford to lose her job. Her brain insisted she lay stretched out warm and comfortable, and that she ought to continue doing so for some period of time. She shivered, but her head said her body felt exactly the opposite. Warm and comfy she was not.

Sudden awareness. Startlement. And with an odd *thwip*, something felt gone, withdrawn. Or, rather, it was like an ebbing, like the tide going out, because the oddness in her head didn't go away.

Her body distracted her again. Her shoulder hurt. Recollections slipped into focus: Her falling Glock. A Magnum aimed at her head. Jaise's hand coming down, giving the kill command. Hell. She'd been shot. In the head. By B-Ops commander Matthew Jaise.

In which case, why wasn't she dead? She ought to be. Matthew Jaise had a rep in the city: tough, accurate, quick on his feet. He'd never failed a mission. Never. He didn't fail, and he didn't miss. He just didn't. Claudia saw her gun falling, imagined it striking her body, falling through her head and down into the base of her skull. No. Not the gun, something else. The demon? Behind her tightly shut eyes, she saw Jaise. All the old reactions kicked into full force. Handsome, smooth, forbidden and upper-class Matthew Jaise. Pointing a Magnum at her. Images clicked through her head. He had another rep: a hardcore Romeo—Jaise, the sex machine. Jaise the two-timer and Jaise the heartbreaker. Thank God by the time he'd gotten around to her she'd seen the damage he'd done and hadn't given him the time of day. Didn't matter how good the sex might be, she wasn't interested in adding to his legend. Holly deserved better than to have a mother who wasted her time with jerks like Matthew Jaise.

She moved her head, and nausea crashed over her. She rolled to the left and would have screamed if she hadn't been barfing. Back on her haunches, she swiped her good arm across her mouth. The earlier sense of comfort receded to nothing before flowing back, lapping at the edges of her consciousness. She fought a double set of sensations—hers and her head's. She swiveled her neck, even touched the back bulge of her skull, feeling for a wound. Nothing. No cut or bump, not even a suggestion of pain. But Jaise had shot her. She knew it. She'd seen him do it. With the memory burned into her head, that fact seemed pretty much incontrovertible. Matthew Jaise, B-Ops commander, and the man who'd spent at least three weeks asking her, with charming bluntness, to sleep with him, had shot her. More than that, actually. He'd tried to kill her.

She pressed her fingers to her temples. It wasn't like him to miss. Anger rushed through her like a tidal wave. Her head buzzed, filled with something alien. Jeez, how hard had she whacked her head?

Thwip.

She didn't usually have this much trouble maintaining mental quietude. She hung her head and concentrated on mastering her breathing. Well, whatever the hell had happened at the construction site, she wasn't dead. And neither was the demon or whatever it was. Because if Jaise and the rest of the B-Ops patrol had cleaned up after her and taken care of the demon, she wouldn't be here. Wherever *here* happened to be. No, she'd be dead or in the I.C.U., and she appeared to be neither. She lurched to her feet. Her brain felt as if it had detached itself from her spine and started bouncing off her cranium.

When her vertigo cleared, she stood clutching the edge of a white counter. She thought hard, and the pieces came together. A bathroom? Yes. She was in a bathroom. Slowly she moved her head. The worst of the nausea passed. She hit her comm band. Not even a chirp. A firewall? That wasn't something that boded well for her continued safety. Was she in prison? Fear stabbed through her. Was she about to be wiped?

She grabbed a towel from the wall rack and threw it over the puke on the floor. The toilet was white as a cloud. She must have been looking at it when she'd first opened her eyes. There was a fresh roll of toilet paper with both corners tucked into a point. The counter and sink were both carved from white marble shot through with tiny veins of gray. Prison this wasn't. Not even Jaise could afford this kind of luxury, and word was he came from money. She wondered if a vamp had her. That wasn't an idea that made much sense, but there you were. It was possible. She remembered seeing that un-human leap from building to building beside the lot just before B-Ops arrived.

She gathered in a little more resilience. She'd been worse off than this. Much, much worse. Jeez, all this white made her eyes hurt. Four cups in a soldierly row below the mirror wore little paper hats over their mouths, like they couldn't be trusted not to gobble up all the toothpaste or hand lotion. There was a toothbrush. She caught a glimpse of her reflection in the mirror. She looked like hell. Her right shoulder was bloody, her shirt a tattered mess, and her hair, which she'd let grow after keeping it so sensibly short while she was in the Academy, was singed off level with her chin.

All in all, she'd prefer to be blond. But the maintenance struck her as too much trouble, and besides, she couldn't afford a salon on her salary, so brown her hair stayed. Her eyes were still brown, and she was still shorter than she wanted to be. Oh, well. The bright side to her personal disorder was that instead of lying dead in the dirt, where, no doubt, *Los Cazadores* would have retrieved her body and sold it to some werewolf desperate for black-market human meat, she was alive in a painfully white bathroom someplace else. And that was a good thing. Never let it be said Claudia Donovan wasn't an optimist.

She turned the tap on the sink. Water streamed out in a wide, transparent rush. A quick wash of her face improved her mood if not her appearance, even if it was hard to manage with just one functioning arm. Then, she brushed her teeth. She stripped the wrapper off one of the glasses and drank about a gallon of water. For the hell of it, she let the water run. Ten, eleven, twelve . . . At thirteen, she couldn't stand the guilt. She closed the tap. Her new apartment had plumbing and faucets with an unbelievably long auto shut-off. No one was going to backhand her for letting the water run too long, but she still expected it. Holly had a choice of shower or bath and couldn't remember a time when it was different.

She retrieved her P.D.-issue pack from behind the toilet. In the medicine cabinet she found a full container of dental floss. That went into her pants pocket. Too handy to pass up that stuff. A big, lovely bottle of pain reliever. She swallowed five and put the bottle in her pack. She daubed her shoulder with QuikSeal to stop the blood oozing from her shoulder and stuffed the contents of the medicine cabinet into the many pockets of her pack. If vamps had her, she'd better not be bleeding.

She faced the shower stall. It was posh. Big enough for three people, easy, with a real glass door and a white marble surface. Through the glass she could see a bar of white soap with a convex top and rounded edges, untouched by any hand. Three bottles sat on a marble shelf, and beneath that hung a washcloth with a crease along the folded edge. There were chrome fixtures and an adjustable showerhead. Anyone who took a shower in there could stand under a spray of hot water and reach for the washcloth in leisurely fashion, make lather with the soap and then rinse it off with as much hot water as she wanted. No shut-off, she'd bet money on it. Now, *that* was decadent. Truly Upper. Living the vamp life.

With the ache in her shoulder a muffled dullness thanks to the painkillers, she gave the room a thorough look. White marble was everywhere, rarest of the rare. Before she'd got up the nerve to apply to College—she'd been secretly studying for months— during down times, she and her fellow Lowers had loved to describe the palace they'd live in when they got out and were living in luxury. Even though they'd none of them ever seen marble in their lives, a marble bathtub had made the top ten must-haves. In the Upper, they would live like vamps, girl. Oh, yes. In the Lower, if narco didn't kill you, or you didn't die in a drive-by, you either converted or you got rounded up for some rogue vamp or werewolf who paid for fresh meat. Vamps who ventured into the Lower came hungry, because they liked the edge it gave them. And the wolves just liked the chase. The City and B-Ops both denied it, but the fact was, the Lower was a favorite hunting ground for all kinds of predators. If you had the money, you got whatever you wanted. Claudia ran her fingers over the marble. Cool and smooth. To her knowledge, she was the only one of her group who had made it out. All the rest were dead.

There was no window in the bathroom. In the ceiling, she saw only a light fixture and a vent about four inches square. She considered stripping the light for the electrical wires, but decided not to, since if she was stuck here, she didn't fancy sitting in the dark. Which observation brought out the interesting fact that whoever had put her in here hadn't turned off the light and had also left her things untouched. That made the vamp idea likelier: Vamps tended to be a wasteful lot, not being particularly worried about how to pay the energy bill. Claudia considered the outlet again. Maybe later. In the last wall was the door; white, of course. It was the only way out.

She jumped up on the sink and unfastened the casing around the fan. Most bot networks worked on the simple principle that as long as a minimum threshold of juice flowed in, the bot was okay—and she knew there'd be a bot up here. All you had to do to disable a maintenance robot was reroute the circuit, and the sysoper never noticed. She checked the wiring. It was twisted pair, not fiber, which was to be expected; fibernets were for intelligence recon. She rerouted the circuit and detached the maintenance bot from its seat.

With the network wires stripped, Claudia sat cross-legged on the countertop and went to work. She re-seated the bot in a mobile cage she carried around just in case—another skill she'd decided the L.A.P.D. was better off not knowing about. Using the memory stick in her pack, only half a terabyte, but sufficient for her limited purpose, she sent a wifi-worm into the bot's flash ROM to set the device listening on the same port as her comm. She counted to ten, then rebooted. A second later, a light on her comm flashed too. Excellent. She put her headset in place and flicked down the eyepiece so she could monitor the bot's video output.

She slipped her pack back on. Her shoulder hardly hurt at all now. On a whim, what the heck, she opened the shower and took the soap, the bottles and the washcloth, plus the little plastic cap for ladies with expensive do's. At the door, she listened. There was no webcaster that she could hear. No music, no conversation. Just deep silence—a comfortable, watchful, lazy silence. She checked her thigh holster and loosened the spare Glock she carried because a girl just never could be too careful. She was glad it was still there.

Then she cracked open the door, set the reconfigured bot on the floor and sent it on its way.

Chapter Four

Claudia kept a hand close to her comm unit. It was an illegal configuration, naturally, but no self-respecting cop went with the default. Everyone assigned to a beat altered their standard-issue comms the second they were in hand; the devices came with warnings descriptive enough to make all the necessary illegal changes in about twenty minutes even if you were clueless, and she'd been doing reconfigs a whole lot deadlier than this since she was nine. After she'd snapped home the last required circuit in less than five minutes at the Academy, realizing no one else was close to being done, she'd bent over the device and re-rigged it the way it would do the most good. She prayed her assumptions then would be correct. That was what she was using to control the bot.

With her back flat against the bathroom wall, she watched her spy's data stream across her field of vision. According to the bot, it was in another room about four hundred feet square. There were no fluctuations in air pressure or temperature. Since only a fool relied on technology alone, Claudia tried to slip into what she liked to call her hyper-concentration mode, but the fuzz in her brain interfered. She must have hit her head hard. Just the thought of her last memory made her dizzy. She was lucky to be alive. Boiling blue eyes, pale as glass . . . Her heart thudded hard in her chest. *Get a grip.* With a shake of her head, she cleared out the memory and concentrated on her breath until, at last, she could focus.

There. Much, much better. She cracked the door a bit more and peeked out. Not a sound. Her nose twitched; the room smelled hollow. She sensed nothing living beyond. She tapped the spare holster tucked along the indentation of her spine, then her thigh holster. Her Glock slipped into her waiting hand. Knees bent, spare Glock ready, she stepped into the room and scooped up her bot. . . .

She stood in an empty bedroom. There wasn't a lot of furniture, just a big bed, not recently slept in judging from the fact you could bounce a Panamanian peso off the bedspread, two chairs, a webcaster black and silent, and a small refrigerator. Not even when her family was alive could Claudia have imagined anyone living in this kind of luxury. She shook off the memory.

Further investigation of the room turned up nothing but empty closets and drawers and the room service menu. The Hilton. Well, okay! Swankiest hotel in Los Angeles. Upper-upper, as they said in the Lower. And there weren't even a pair of anyone else's undies to be found. To the right was a dark wooden door. Claudia went over to it.

Concentrating on the silence, she used the tip of a finger to open the door wide enough to set down her bot. Through the narrow crack, she saw in the room beyond a blood-red carpet, a portion of a black leather couch and the edge of another webcaster. Vamp colors. Vamp posh. Then a flash of light blinded her, and even her teeth felt it. Sensation crashed through her. Something screamed. The sound keyed up into an animal howl, an inhuman noise. Then came silence, unnerving silence. Claudia pressed her back against the wall and slid down to the floor, ice sluicing along her spine.

Output streamed across her vision as she stared at the bot's transmission. Crimson droplets arced through the air. A hand, fingers dripping red, red-tinted steam and a hot, deep smell. Holy cripes! Then she felt rather than heard the implosion of mechanical parts. Her bot's data stream died.

The jolt snapped her out of her paralysis. *Protect and serve.* Right. She pushed to her feet and stepped through the door. Her pulse went into triple-time because she knew what was out there. Mayhem. Nothing alive. She slipped through the door but kept her back against the wall. She was right. There was nothing alive.

A pale man sprawled faceup on the floor, one arm twisted behind his back, the other flopped out to the side. From mid-ulna to fingers he was nothing but ashes and bits of bone already turning to dust. One leg and part of his belly had suffered a like fate. He had to be a vamp—only a vamp died like that. Her bot had caught the tail end of the vamp's demise, and in her head she could still see the body falling. She shifted to get a look at the dead fang's face. Not Korzha. The dead vamp wasn't Korzha. No time to wonder why she cared.

Her head snapped up, eyes raking the room. Blood rushed through her ears like traffic in a tunnel. She moved past the deceased vamp, sliding her gaze over the body long enough to see his gaping, empty chest and the remains of an extremely expensive suit. His heart was gone. About a foot from the ashes of his arm, what looked like a lump of desiccated charcoal smoked in a pool of crumbling ashes.

There was another body, too. A bulky man lay half on the couch, half on the floor, but he was upside-down, head and shoulders on the carpet, legs on the seat cushions. Across his chest, a half-healed scar ripened into a still-wet wound. The smell of blood, ozone and burnt air made her dizzy. She shook her head, but the sensation of fullness remained.

The vamp she didn't recognize, but she knew this man on the couch. He was a werewolf: a high beta rogue from the Middlesex clan who hunted in the Lower. Sometimes the freak paid for his meat, but most times he just took it. Uninvited. No one could prove he hunted illegally, and since he made a point of paying the Cazadores or else did a few extracurricular chores for them, the cops somehow never got notified. Brad, that was his name. If memory served, and she knew it did, Brad wasn't the sort of werewolf you could push around. The guy was an asshole dog. Whatever had got him had to have been one mean son of a bitch, because his sort was hard to kill.

A salver sat on the coffee table near Brad's body. It held rare lamb and still-bloody beef tips; untouched. There was coffee in a pewter pot—the polite beverage to offer when entertaining those of the preternatural persuasion. Shards from a shattered porcelain saucer appeared to be the only damage in the room—aside from the bodies, of course. Claudia glanced at the suite phone and shook her head. Given the circumstances, calling anywhere on an unsecured line was suicidal: For sure there was fiber VoIP to the phone, and every word would end up on a B-Ops server.

Claudia shook her head again. Vamps and werewolves were like the Bloods and the Crips. The Hatfields and the McCoys. The Lower and the Upper. Tomaytoes and Tomahtoes. What were they doing together? She stared at Brad. Even though she thought nobody deserved to die, she couldn't summon much pity, except for his folks. She hoped she wasn't the one who had to do the notification. Out loud, she said, "What the hell kind of meeting were you boys having?"

Nobody answered. But since there were real live demons in Crimson City now, she had a kind of sickening feeling she knew.

Two more bodies lay near the windows in a brilliant pool of light from a wall lamp. The first body was naked, perfectly naked. There wasn't a mark on him. Claudia caught her breath because, Jeez Louise, he was beautiful. White-blond hair fell away from his face, and even from here she could count the ridges of his abs. He was her age, she thought: twenty-five or -six, tops. He had hardly any body hair, none on his face or chest. His eyes were closed, his face turned toward the light. He looked too healthy and pink to be a vamp. Most fangs took on a faintly chalky complexion unless they'd just fed. Possibly he was a werewolf. Likely, in fact. He must have healed faster than the late, unlamented Brad. Which meant two things: He was an alpha dog, and he might not be dead.

She moved closer to get a better look at the other body. Her heart raced. This one was B-Ops. A dark-haired man, dressed completely in black. Black cargo pants, black boots, black tee-shirt with sleeves that ended just above the bulges of his biceps—B-Ops for sure. A sick sort of thrill shot through her when she got close enough to see the man's face. Matthew Jaise.

Holy cripes, Matthew Jaise.

"Hey!" she called out. "Jaise. You all right?"

She got no response, from either of the two men. She hit her comm band again. Nothing but static. Damn. She needed a medic. Fast.

She approached the bodies, her fingers curled on her Glock trigger. There was no sign of a wound on either. The naked man had no scars, which made Claudia wonder if he was a werewolf after all, because all but the newest of them had more than a few scars. If he was strong enough to have healed before Brad, then he ought to have a few scars on that perfect body of his. And there was no sign of death agony. In fact, except for the part about not breathing, he looked like he was simply sleeping.

On the far side of Jaise's torso, near the window, a bit of metal glittered. Claudia moved closer. The fuzziness in her head thickened, almost as if someone were stirring up a pond so she couldn't see the bottom. With effort, she blocked the sensation. Light glinted off the metal. Heart sinking into her toes, she recognized at last what it was: the remains of a silver-coated bullet. Several more melted bullets spattered the floor.

The demon had been here. Now that she was close to the bullets, the air reeked of saltpeter. Dollars to doughnuts, it had been the same monster who nearly killed her. Jeez. He'd killed four people like it was nothing—two paranormal, possibly three, and one human. Quite possibly, this gorgeous wolf had died of fright. That happened sometimes. She crouched between the two bodies and touched Jaise's throat, two fingers to his pulse point. "Please don't be dead," she whispered. "Don't be dead. I want you to tell me what the hell happened here."

Thank God. She felt a nice even pulse thumping slowly against her fingers. But then, Jaise was fit. Forty bpm wouldn't surprise her in the least. There was no need for CPR.

She did the same to the other man. To her surprise, a pulse fluttered against her fingertips. His skin was warm. She shoved her Glock into her boot-top and ripped through her PD pack for the epiStart.

The first dose, administered cutaneously by a patch two finger-breadths above his mid-sternum, had no effect. She used her teeth to rip open the second pack. In reaching to apply the patch, her bare hand brushed his skin. Static electricity zipped through her. The fuzziness in her head cleared. She felt as if she'd been sucked down to the very bottom of a well and thrown out the other side.

The epiStart fell from her mouth and landed on the floor. Claudia stared at the body. It hadn't moved, not one atom, but sure as flies buzz, this guy wasn't anything like dead. She had her fingers around the butt of her Glock, but before she could get a solid grip, an arm shot out and had her by the throat. His eyes opened. Blue eyes—brilliant, boiling blue. Her head felt full, her heart felt like a lump of coal. A presence leapt into being in her mind, dark, malevolent and unmistakably alien. Shit. She was a complete loser. A genuine moron. The beast had been there the entire time, and she had never even realized that fuzzy cotton-wool feeling in her head was it.

The demon laughed with velvet delight.

"If you want to possess me," she said, "or do any of that weird-ass demon crap, you gotta kill me first."

She'd said it before and meant every word: She'd rather die than be anything but human.

She didn't doubt her captor one bit when he replied in a voice full of malefic laughter, "I'm more than happy to kill you, human."

Chapter Five

The demon laughed, then said something low and soft—not words, just a series of syllables that made no sense to Claudia. The room flickered. The white walls disappeared, the wooden furniture vanished, and the window frame just wasn't there anymore. Instead of a hotel room, she saw gilded pillars and flashes of gold, bronze, cobalt, ruby, topaz and citrine against sandy stone walls. And then she saw nothing but boiling blue eyes.

Desperate, she lifted a hand and reached to strike her captor's *chun gun*, the pressure point at the middle of his nose. His head snapped back. The room flickered like the shutter of an old-fashioned camera firing through shots, and Claudia's head pounded. Images flashed behind her eyes: hotel, stone columns; hotel, stone columns. She shook her head and tried to wait it out.

At last her vision stabilized, and when it did, the columned room was gone and the hotel remained. The demon still gripped her throat, but he wasn't in her head anymore. He grinned. "We'll kill you if we must. Is it necessary?"

Claudia shook her head. The demon let go of her throat. She fell back in agony, but the pressure on her windpipe was abruptly eased. She let air fill her lungs, a huge, grateful inhalation, and then realized she couldn't move from the shoulders down. She could breathe, which was good, and despite not being able to move her limbs, she could feel them. That was a reason to be optimistic. Then movement caught the edge of her attention, and when she looked, her blood turned to ice.

The dead werewolf. Brad.

Oh, cripes.

First an arm twitched, then a leg. Like some sort of macabre puppet show, the werewolf corpse lifted its head from the floor. The upper body still sprawled, still looked grotesquely dead, on a patterned rug with fringe on the short sides. The vamp, thank God, wasn't moving; his body continued slowly turning to ash. But the werewolf got to its feet, wavered and then took a step. The chest wound gaped wider. Pink lung tissue flapped on one side. The beast lurched toward her, and rather than squared-off doorways and the flat ceilings of the hotel behind him she saw arched doorways and a vaulted ceiling. Tapestries draped the walls and rippled in an unfelt wind. Then the hotel was back.

"There is no time to waste, *en*-Aslet," the werewolf said with a sepulchral hiss. Its chest wound gaped wider.

"Prepare, Faullk," the naked demon replied, not taking his eyes from Claudia.

The dead werewolf shuddered, and the air around it turned to mist. Then, before Claudia's disbelieving eyes, the mist solidified. The werewolf's body collapsed, falling to the floor like a rag doll thrown away in a fit of rage; the mist took on human shape, shimmered, flexed and became the form of a man. He bowed to the naked demon, covering a clenched fist with his hand. He wasn't a giant, but was tall enough to be impressive. "*En*-Aslet," he said.

"What the hell do you guys want?" Claudia gasped, turning her head back to the demon. Her belly felt like a block of granite. Whatever was going to happen here wasn't going to be good. Odds were, she'd end up like the vamp. If she was lucky. If not, the werewolf's gaping chest might be closer to her fate.

The blue-eyed demon regarded her, eyes like ice. She felt a vibration through her body, and a resonance that built in her head. His features were Nordic. Delicate, fine-boned, cold and pale as snow. She felt a weird twitch inside her.

"Well?" she asked, pathetically proud she didn't sound as frightened as she felt.

"It does not matter to you, human female."

She tried to move her arms again, but it was still no go. It was the same for her legs. The Police Academy four-hour course on sexual assaults by paranormal creatures focused on citizen-victims, the blunt reality was that officers on the street were just as vulnerable to assault—a statistic everyone knew and no one publicly admitted. Male and female both could be victims, but overwhelmingly, as with similar human-on-human assaults, male paranormals assaulted female humans. Claudia wracked her mind for anything that might help her in this situation and came up blank. She just hoped to hell she lived through it.

She turned her head toward Jaise and got the shock of her life. The commander's eyes were open, and he blinked once. "You okay?" she whispered.

Jaise blinked again.

"I can't move," she said. "Can you?"

His pale gray eyes stayed steady. "No," he replied. But he could say no more, as Faullk, the second demon, the one who'd emerged from the werewolf corpse, joined them.

The demon knelt to one side of the Nordic beauty he'd called *en*-Aslet, though Claudia suspected from the way he'd pronounced *en* that the word was a sort of honorific prefix. Faullk motioned with his hands, and a box of chased gold, about a cubic foot all told, appeared on the floor.

"It'll be all right," Jaise said.

Claudia appreciated his attempt to reassure her, but she didn't see how things could be all right. Not unless B-Ops came crashing through the door right about now—and nothing like that happened. The demon Aslet moved between her and Jaise. He bent over her. Close, and then closer yet he moved. *This is it*, she thought. A lock of white-blond hair fell over his shoulder. *The end.* The vibration in her head increased, and her stomach pitched and rolled. The resonance came from Aslet, the blue-eyed demon; a low hum, syllables, louder in her head until the noise was unbearable.

"*En*-Aslet," the other demon said. It sounded worried, urgent.

Aslet nodded, breathing hard.

Faullk, the smaller demon, sat on his haunches on the other side of Jaise, hands on thighs, eyes closed, concentrating. The resonance in Claudia's head became unbearable. The sensation spread from her head to the rest of her body. She closed her eyes and saw red behind the lids, bright as new blood, cold as the demon's icy beauty. Aslet touched her upper chest with the tips of two fingers. When she looked at him, she saw his mouth moving and knew he must be speaking, but the words made no sense. Not English, not Spanish, not Chinese or Russian or Hmong, Tagalog or Vietnamese or any of the hundreds of languages spoken in Crimson City. She heard a thud and forced herself to look. Thank God, she saw nothing threatening. Jaise watched her calmly.

"You all right?" she whispered again. Slowly he nodded.

The demon Faullk held the box he'd summoned, opened it reverently and took out a small, curved knife. The blade glittered gold, a brilliant deep gold, a color you just didn't see outside of a museum. Absurdly, Claudia thought that a gold knife, however beautiful, wasn't going to be a very effective weapon. All the same, she didn't fancy being stabbed with it. Better a quick death from a sharp steel knife. She swallowed hard, remembering the dead werewolf's gaping chest.

From the box, Faullk also produced a golden cup, the color of very old gold, soft and mellow, rich in tone, in shade and material a match for his blade. He set the cup at Aslet's knees. Figures carved in the bowl of the chalice danced in a chain, hands linked. Claudia wanted to look more closely at the vessel, but when she tried to move, she couldn't. Her heart pounded and her stomach threatened to turn inside out. Certainty grew. The demons intended to kill her and Jaise. One look into the blue-eyed Aslet's face confirmed that the outcome of this wasn't going to be pleasant. Well, she wasn't ready to die just yet.

"Let us go," Claudia said. She was prepared to tell whatever lie seemed like it would work. "There's no point in killing us. We'll do whatever you want. Isn't that right, Commander?"

"Silence, human," Aslet snapped. He lifted Jaise's arm and stretched it out, palm upward. Faullk extended his knife and put the blade in Aslet's other hand. The demon spoke in a low, soft voice, a chant almost. None of the words made sense. He lifted the knife and held it crossways to Matthew Jaise's arm. He turned the blade perpendicular to the skin of Jaise's forearm. A red line appeared. Jaise didn't even flinch. Maybe, like her, he couldn't. The B-Ops commander's gray eyes held hers and never once wavered. Crimson trickled down his arm and dripped into the chalice, a thin stream of blood. The demon finally released his arm.

Next, Aslet reached for her. Claudia resisted, but her body refused to obey. The noise in her head increased, buzzed painfully. Aslet's blue eyes shimmered. He held her arm as he had Jaise's, upward, palm out. A curious satisfaction settled over him. Faullk moved close, the chalice in his hand. Aslet put the point of his knife to Claudia's arm and cut. A pinprick of pain swelled and intensified until she wanted to scream.

Something warm trickled down her arm. From the corner of her eye, she saw Jaise's body. It was motionless. His eyes had fluttered closed. She knew the moment her blood hit the chalice and mixed with his. Lost—she felt lost. Tears welled up behind her eyes. They were going to die, and she had no reason to think they would die quickly.

She watched as the demons' golden knife reappeared in her line of sight. Aslet dipped the dagger into the chalice. When he drew it out, the blade shone crimson wet. He pressed the hilt to his forehead and then handed the knife to Faullk. Jaise's eyes snapped open when his pants were unfastened by Faullk as if the demon weren't good with zippers and snaps. Jaise's hip was exposed. She and Jaise were going to die now; Claudia knew it. *A gut wound,* said a clinical voice in the back of her head. A painful and slow way to die. These two could keep her and Jaise alive for hours that way.

Claudia met Jaise's gaze. He was awake.

It must be true he had ice in his veins, because he didn't look afraid. Claudia wished she had even a quarter of his courage.

The resonance in her brain went off again, a hum of darkness and utter black. She twisted her head, eyes following the dagger. With a deftness that suggested practice, Faullk cut the skin just above Jaise's hip bone, tracing a swirling line that spiraled and interlocked inward and outward in infinite dimensions. Aslet drew in a sharp breath when Faullk finally lifted the knife away. Faullk dipped the blade into the chalice again, and Claudia swore she felt her body react; a weird kind of leap toward Jaise.

Her eyes met Aslet's. The demon said her name, the sound tolling like a bell rung in the dead of night. Like iron filings drawn by a magnet, the blood on the demons' dagger flowed down the blade and into the cut on Jaise's hip. Again, the knife transferred hands. Aslet dipped the blade into the chalice, but this time when he withdrew it, he touched the tip, not the hilt, to a spot just above the bridge of his nose. A dot of red was left behind. He knelt at Claudia's side and deftly unfastened the belt of her pants. His fingers exposed her hip and slipped beneath her underwear. Her belly flip-flopped, but all the demon did was expose her hip, nothing more. The knife flashed, and she tensed, expecting the worst.

The moment the blade touched her skin, she felt cold as ice and hot as fire. The knife cut, but even though she reacted to the pain, her body's reflexive flinch existed only in her head. She couldn't move. Aslet worked precisely; she could feel the care he took with an inward, circular interlinking motion. Something cold flowed into her, entering from her hip. Aslet's face appeared in her line of sight. Close. His white-blond hair fell forward, framing his face.

"Claudia Donovan," the demon said. "I am called *en*-Aslet of the Elismal demons." The words echoed in her head. With the tip of the dagger he touched her just above the bridge of her nose. He did the same to the B-Ops commander. "*Nir*-Jaise." He bowed. "I am called Aslet of the Elismal demons."

Then the other demon, Faullk, knelt. Both chanted, and Claudia didn't understand a word of it, except that it sounded increasingly dark, something from a nightmare. Faullk sat straight.

Aslet stretched out his arm until the fingertips of his left hand rested beneath Faullk's sternum. Claudia saw the smaller demon tense. Aslet's pale blue eyes flashed. And then, so fast that she could hardly follow what happened, his hand plunged inward, upward and to the left. In the blink of an eye, he held Faullk's heart in his clenched hand. Faullk stayed upright for two breaths. A cloud of crimson mist dissipated in the air above them as his body toppled forward.

"It is done," Aslet said. His dagger clattered to the ground, and his face appeared above hers. The fingers of his hand touched the mark incised on her hip. Burning cold spread from her hip, inward. Inside her. "Claudia Donovan. It is done," he said. And like that, the vise that had immobilized her vanished.

Jaise sat up, head bent between his upraised knees. Like her, he was probably fighting off nausea and dizziness. Aslet continued to sit without moving. Claudia sat up, gyrating as she managed to get her pants up and fastened. Her head felt filled with cotton, woozy, and she felt sick. Her hip hurt where he'd cut her. What the hell had he done to her? "You okay, Jaise?" she asked.

Jaise raised his head and looked at her with his freaky pale gray eyes. "I am now."

Aslet simply sat as still as stone. The demon's head was cocked, as if he was listening. But to what?

Chapter Six

Claudia couldn't hear anything, but she felt Aslet's interest become a cautious anxiety. Next to her, Jaise flexed his arm and let out a low sound of pain. Aslet flowed to his feet in a motion so smooth she almost couldn't follow it. She watched him dress quickly in loose black clothes. When he was done, but for the fire flickering in his eyes the demon could have passed for human.

Strange doubled sensations in her head made it hard for her to ground herself. Claudia wobbled, woozy and sick to her stomach. Somewhere, people were moving. A soft stealthy shuffle whooshed in and out of her head. One minute she felt it, the next, nothing. Underneath it all she felt a sense of urgency that didn't belong to her. *We must leave. Now. Danger.*

A gun cocked, a sound she knew well enough to cause her some fear. Aslet barked a word she didn't understand and signaled with one hand, and the shatterproof glass vanished from one of the windows. Cold air rushed in. Anxious—the demon was anxious, but he wasn't afraid. In the meantime, Jaise had managed to lurch to his feet. His pants gaped open. His tee-shirt fit like a second skin, and Claudia had a flash of bare belly before he managed to zip his pants.

Claudia jumped as the butt end of a police baton hit the suite door three times. A voice called, "Open up! This is Internal Operations. You are under investigation. Failure to open this door may result in severe criminal and civil penalties, up to and including imprisonment in a Federal Detainment Center."

Aslet made another motion with his hand. The door vanished in a flash of blinding blue light, leaving an astonished commando with his baton lifted to strike a door that no longer existed. Claudia broke for the doorway, but her legs refused to cooperate. Her head objected to the attempt, too—and what the hell was with that?

The commando with the baton gestured to the soldiers behind him and stepped in, sweeping the room with his weapon—a textbook entry. Behind him, three operatives moved in. They wouldn't be stupid enough to cover only one entrance; no doubt the entire building was under surveillance. Claudia was pretty sure one of the men was a werewolf and having trouble holding back the transformation. A woman spoke into her comm unit while her eyes flicked around the room, stopping on the bodies.

Schick-tak. The sound of a clip loading into a semi-automatic weapon sent Claudia's heart pounding. Someone shouted. Claudia smelled their fear and felt Aslet's disdain—and underneath that, his elation. He savored the mayhem and sneered at them all. A red dot appeared on Claudia's chest, a sniper's sights. The dot moved and then disappeared. No doubt because it was focused on the demon's head. Or maybe hers.

"Got him!" someone said.

"You're too far away, asshole!" someone else shouted. "Get in range. Get in range!"

The demon spoke another word. Heat flashed all around, and the bedroom door blew off its hinges. The heat almost melted Claudia's eyebrows. The red dot reappeared on a side wall and then winked out. Shit. Plainly, B-Ops really didn't know the correct range. Not a good indication that they could handle this situation.

Claudia kicked out and connected with the back of the demon's knee. He anticipated her, though, and shifted just enough that she missed. The kick would have collapsed his left leg. Instead, her head flashed with pain. Aslet's emotions remained constant. There was no increase in anxiety, no fear.

Jaise got her arm in a viselike grip. "Explanations later, Officer," he said in her ear. "Trust me, we don't want to be here when our boy gets started."

Behind him Aslet laughed, all cold and icy delight.

A chair erupted into flames. Choking smoke billowed toward the ceiling and water whooshed from the sprinklers. Claudia blinked against the flashing strobe that accompanied the emergency alarm. While the B-Ops team was distracted by the fire blossoming toward them, Jaise stepped onto the balcony. Claudia followed.

"They're gonna jump!" someone shouted.

"Move and you're dead!"

Claudia stood in crisp air, looking at a bright moon, round as a platter and pale white. A sharp wind blew against her face. Damn, but Strata +1 was freaking high in the air. Claudia's legs trembled. She wasn't going to fall, but she felt like it. Jaise's dark hair swept across his cheek. *Click.* Behind her, somebody chambered a bullet. A flood of sensation overwhelmed her. She felt sick to her stomach, and her head throbbed. Jaise reached up, grabbed the railing on the balcony above and pulled himself up. He had hold of her wrist, and she felt her legs lose contact with the ground. She screamed. The B-Ops commandos shouted over each other.

"They're getting away!"

"Fire!"

"Watch the monster!"

"They're compromised, soldier! Shoot to kill."

"Motherfucker!"

"Shoot to kill!"

Too late. Jaise yanked on her arm and hauled her up to the balcony above. Claudia's stomach flipped inside out. Wind whipped her hair, shrieked in her ears and tugged at her body. The ground was a hell of a long way down. She teetered at the railing, too dizzy to stop herself from falling. Jaise caught her and pulled hard. The sky around them flashed with bluish light. She heard screams from the floor below. Jaise got her turned around in time to see the window in front of them vanish. It wavered and then shimmered into a heap of sand at their feet.

A backwash of warmth caught her face, and Claudia took a last gasp of air. Jaise charged through the opening, dragging her along as if her weight weren't anything. His body felt hot. They bowled through the suite. She smelled saltpeter again, and the scent of burning carpet. They went into the corridor. At one end of the hall the arrival bell dinged in a bank of chrome-plated elevators. At the other, an EXIT sign glowed green. B-Ops soldiers swarmed the hallway. More came out of the elevator. The air shimmered again, and the demon Aslet appeared.

"Shit," Jaise said. Still holding her, he faced the EXIT sign. Boots thundered down the hallway above. The service exit door flew open, and B-Ops commandos poured through. Jaise ducked into an alcove, pulling her with him, and just in time, too.

The demon lifted his hand, and the front three commandos vanished. Another gesture, another guttural word, and the second rank disappeared, too. The third wave moved into position. Claudia felt the flood of energy leave the demon and take care of them, and half a beat later, the exit door bounced once and closed. No one else came through.

Claudia smelled saltpeter again. Jaise moved so fast she lost track of him for a moment. He flashed through the stairwell door as if it weren't there. She got her legs under her and, with Jaise, flew down the steps like her life depended on it. Probably it did. The demon followed. From the floor above, more commandos pounded down the stairwell, all of them under the mistaken impression that six feet was a safe range. It wasn't. One motion of the demon's hand, a flash of heat, and they vanished in an explosion of brilliant blue.

Jaise gripped Claudia's hand, and they descended forty flights of stairs as if strolling through the park. At the bottom, her thigh muscles screamed in protest. As for B-Ops, someone must have figured out they'd mistaken safe range, because though she could hear the sound of pursuit, it was from a lot farther away.

At the street-level exit, Jaise lifted a leg and kicked the door. It crashed open. The bottom stairwell felt hot. By the time the door rebounded, the alarm was screeching and they were through, outside, in the paling dark of pre-dawn.

"Come on, Donovan," he said. His voice sounded

different, but considering she'd never been in an operation with him, and certainly not one that went so wrong, maybe it was his tense voice.

He hauled her into the street and, hand in the middle of her back, pushed her along. "Pretend we're lovers out for a stroll," he said. His fingers landed on her side, right underneath her breast. She slapped his hand.

"What the hell is going on, Jaise?"

"Classified, Officer. Not for L.A.P.D. to know."

"How come they were shooting at you?"

He gave her a look. The pupils of his eyes were huge, the gray irises a narrow ring. "Standard operating procedure, Officer," he said. "For all they know, I've been compromised by the demon. That goes for you, too."

An image of the golden knife flashed into her head. "*Have* we been compromised?"

He let out a bark of a laugh. "No."

"Well, what the hell did that thing do to us?"

"Classified information, Officer."

She rolled her eyes. "Okay, how about this one: How long have demons been getting into Crimson City?"

He reached into a pocket of his pants and pulled out a pair of sunglasses. Below his shirtsleeve, muscle bunched and flexed. He slipped on the shades and walked faster. Claudia hurried to keep pace. "Longer than anyone thinks," he said.

"Are your guys going to manage that freak back there?"

"Probably not," he said.

"That's not reassuring."

Jaise gave her a look.

"Where are we going?" she asked.

Jaise sidestepped a tipped-over garbage can. "Somewhere safe. Until I can prove I'm not compromised, we need to stay the hell away from B-Ops. And the cops."

They left the downtown for a seedier section of L.A. Back to the Lower and the narrow streets, dirty gutters and overflowing trash cans of her youth. Most of the street lamps were broken or constantly dimmed from the rewired power grid connection. Jaise navigated the dark like it was midday. Night-vision contacts. Had to be. He wrapped his fingers around her wrist. The sensation in her head just about dropped her to her knees. Her stomach dry heaved. He waited until she'd finished, then pulled her back to the street. "What the hell was that?" she asked.

"Residual effect," Jaise said.

"How come you're not puking?"

He shrugged. "I'm bigger than you are. More lean body mass. Defuses the effect of a demonic ritual. You're smaller, so you feel it more." He glanced around the street. "Come on."

They set off purposefully, striding into an area where the homeless sagged in doorways or under cardboard boxes. Whores paraded in skin-tight shirts and skirts that looked more like somebody's sparkly hanky. One of them had two prominent bite marks on her throat. She watched Jaise speculatively. "What'd'ya do?" she called out to Claudia. "Make that fine man mad at you?" Claudia ignored her and kept walking.

But eventually, she got tired of wondering. "Where are we going?" she asked again.

"I told you. Someplace safe," he said. It was his tense voice. He gripped her arm and kept her moving.

"I was only asking." She inched toward the street. If anybody jumped them, the street was a safer place to be than the sidewalk. She ignored her nausea and the tension between her and Jaise that felt like a rubber band stretching tighter and tighter. From the corner of her eye, she caught a blur of motion. What now?

"Someplace safe," he repeated.

Twenty seconds later, all hell broke loose.

Chapter Seven

The air shimmered, heated and then, like that, Aslet stood before them, blocking their way. His eyes glittered their usual hot blue. Before either Claudia or Jaise could react, a squadron of B-Ops commandos swarmed around the corner behind them. More streamed from behind cars parked on the street. Claudia tugged on her wrist, trying to break his grip, but Jaise tightened his fingers.

Someone with a bullhorn said, "Lay down your weapons. Get on the ground, arms up, face down. If you do not comply, all necessary force will be used to subdue you."

Three commandos went down on one knee. *Schick-tak*. They had automatic weapons, and were poised and ready to kill. The demon lifted a hand, focusing on the middle of the three. Claudia felt a whisper from Aslet, and then, astonishingly the middle man whirled and shot the man to his right. The one on the other side fired at her. The center man screamed in agony and dropped his weapon. A moment later, his gun imploded.

Jaise nearly pulled Claudia's arm from the socket as they fled, and she just did her best to keep up. Several commandos detached from the group in the street and followed. Another blur of motion appeared in the corner of her eye, something tracking them faster than she could see. To her knowledge, only a vamp moved that fast. Overhead, she heard a copter. Jaise moved fast. Really fast. To the rear, something exploded, and before they'd gone ten more steps, she smelled smoke and burning plastic. Automatic-weapon-fire rang out. Chaos reigned behind them. Utter chaos.

Jaise continued at a relentless pace. Claudia was in damn good shape, but the speed taxed her. Jaise's longer legs meant she ran two steps for every one of his. Her breath labored in her ears, and her side started to ache. She could do a sub-six-minute mile, but not for much longer than a couple of miles. Her legs were almost out. But eventually the sounds of pursuit faded and Jaise slowed. Even the sirens had faded. She was still catching that blur of motion in her peripheral vision. She wondered if Jaise knew they were being followed. She didn't have the breath to tell him. They came to a stop in front of an abandoned building, decrepit and decaying. She put her head down and sucked in breaths. Her legs, already stressed from a descent of forty flights of stairs, shook. Even the condemned sign was falling apart, here. Claudia had about five seconds to look around and figure out where they were. Then the blur materialized.

Oh, great. Just freaking great. A pair of moss-green eyes met hers, and she could swear they sneered even better than his mouth. This wasn't just any vamp, but

Tiber freaking Korzha. What had he come for? Was he watching out for his bloodthirsty group of criminal vamps?

She didn't have time to find out. Jaise moved around the side of the building, pulled her through a broken chain-link fence and slipped through a cracked door. Claudia stumbled in the sudden dark. The smell just about killed her: werewolf musk mixed with piss and the damp smell of vomit and rats. Somewhere deep inside the building, a tomcat yowled. The hair on the back of her neck lifted. Who'd have believed things could get any worse?

"Jaise. Hey!" She tugged her hand, but his fingers held tight. "Look, Jaise, I know you have that B-Ops secret training going for you, but trust me, we really don't want to be unprotected in what is obviously one of the shoddier werewolf dens around town."

"You are not unprotected," he replied.

"Right. Well, see, the thing is, in case you didn't notice—Oh, yech." Her foot skidded in something smelly and soft. Jaise pulled on her hand. He still wore his sunglasses, and he didn't seem to be having any trouble seeing. "Look, the moon was full. I'm pretty sure of that. Honestly, you do not want to confront any doggie desperate enough to live here. Really, you don't. I'm not so sure even you are a match for one of these bad dogs."

He turned, and Claudia, not expecting the motion, stumbled into him. His arm slid around her waist and he pulled her closer. Heat roiled through her, and, oh, for cripe's sake, he had a hard-on. "You are not unprotected," he repeated.

"Well, it sure as hell feels like it." She pushed away from him, away from the insistent pressure of his erection. In the distance, something crashed, wood broke.

Rats skittered in every direction. Claudia's temples pulsed. Shit. Her heart raced. "They're here. They know we're here. Wolves. Shit." She scrambled for her police pack. "You armed, Jaise? Just let me get the wolf gun out, and we'll have a chance." A slim chance. But slim was better than none.

"I'll protect you," he said.

"Gee, thanks." She gritted her teeth. From the corner of her eye she saw a blur. Korzha again. Was that good or bad? Who knew with him? Probably bad. With her luck, he was the kind of sicko freak who liked to watch a werewolf conversion.

Jaise pulled her to a wooden door, bent on its hinges. Through the cracks, she could see a sterile glow. Electric light. If they were really, really lucky, the light was from a homeless person and not doggies. Of course, it was possible there were rogue vamps on the other side. Normally, that would be unlikely, considering a vamp's natural predilection for the finer areas, but if Tiber Korzha hung out here, maybe it *was* rogue vamps. Pick your damn poison. Fang or dog, they both had sharp teeth.

On this side of the wall, a naked bulb illuminated the corridor. Enough to light the passageway for about three square feet. Jaise turned to speak to her. He still wore his sunglasses. "Open the door."

"We're not alone, Jaise," she whispered. Her stomach felt taut and sour, and her pulse pounded like a pile driver going full steam in her head. She didn't care that it was ridiculous to whisper, since vamps would hear her from about fifty yards out and werewolves would have smelled them long ago.

"I know that." He went back to watching the corridor. "Open the door."

"Are you insane? You have no idea who or what's on

the other side. *You* open it, you're so freaking anxious to get fried or eaten or converted."

He pushed her toward the door. "Open it," he repeated.

She touched the wooden surface. Heat rippled through her palm, sharp, and then cold. She snatched back her hand like she'd been shocked, even though that wasn't it, not really. She shook her hand and gingerly moved her numb fingers. "What the hell was that?"

"Open it."

"Look, just because you're B-Ops doesn't mean you get to jerk me around. I don't work for you. Obviously, whoever's on the other side has himself connected to the power grid. Illegal as hell, I know, but there you go. Let's go that way." She pointed to where the corridor turned sharp left.

His jaw clenched. "Open the door."

"How about we don't, and I get to live to see another day?"

He turned his head. "Open the fucking door, Donovan."

The sunglasses hid his eyes, but there wasn't any mistaking his fury. Claudia could hear noises upstairs. Feet pounding.

"They're coming after us." Jaise touched the door. Blue sparks flew up from either side of his palm. "Fuck!" He snatched back his hand. With pain etched on his face, he said, "Whatever happens, I will protect you." His voice slid down a notch. "You have my promise. I can't do this myself." He bit off each word. He pushed her, hard, and said, "Open the door, goddammit."

She slammed into the door. Heat zinged through her, and for a crazy moment she thought she felt the

68

door shudder. Her head pulsed, and then pain blossomed there. She caromed back and would have hit the corridor wall and probably broken her neck if Jaise hadn't caught her. Nevertheless, when he let her go, she slid to a hard landing on her backside. From over her head, Jaise said something that sounded like it wasn't very nice.

A little wobbly, she stood. "What'd you do that for, you mor—"

"Fuck!" Jaise reached into his front pocket and pulled out a Swiss Army knife. He popped a blade and extended his arm, palm up.

Interesting, Claudia thought through her dizziness—*a lefty.* He touched the point of the dagger to his palm and cut. Blood pooled in his hand, a tiny lake that didn't trickle out like regular blood should have. "What the hell are you doing?"

"Trust me, Donovan. There's no other way. You have to open this door." He lifted his head. The light from the bulb above glinted off the black lenses of his sunglasses and made it look like there was fire behind his eyes. He made a fist of his cut palm. Quick as a blink, he grabbed her, pinning her by tucking her upper arm under his armpit. One-handed, he pushed up her sleeve and put the point of his dagger to one of the blue veins in the crook of her elbow.

She tried to pull away, but couldn't. He pressed the point of the blade to her skin. Her voice slid up half an octave. *Okay,* she shrieked. "What the F do you think you're doing?"

"That was a demon back there," he said, as if that explained everything. "If you want to live through this, hold still." He tightened his grip and slit the vein. Not a hole, a slit. Blood ran down the side of her arm. Holy cripes, she was going to die; he was going to let her bleed to death right here, and she'd end up wolf meat or vampire bait. He put his hand over the cut, pressing his bloody palm over her skin.

Cold flashed through her. His blood. That was his blood going into her. She lifted her eyes and, swear to God, she saw fire inside Jaise's eyes. He took a deep breath, and just like that she could feel him in her head. In her body. His breath came fast—deep and hard and fast. Jaise reached for her. Her temples throbbed, her body felt full, and she wondered if her head was going to explode. Mist rose around them, and she could smell the heat, and the desert and air so sharp it hurt to breathe, and she fell into him.

Someone shouted. Claudia pried open her eyes and for one disconcerting moment saw Tiber Korzha through Jaise's sight. She saw the vamp through Jaise. He wasn't normal, Claudia thought. Jaise was not a normal man. In a flash, Korzha launched himself toward them. Jaise muttered something, threw up a hand, and a faint smell of ozone drifted in the air. Korzha went flying backward.

Dimly, Claudia heard voices shouting. B-Ops and the police this time. The good old L.A.P.D. Jaise vaulted toward Korzha like he'd thrown himself headfirst down the hallway. He landed like a dancer, light and perfectly balanced. She remembered hearing he'd been a gymnast in college. Pac-Ten champion at Cal Berkeley, she'd heard. Still, that kind of preternatural grace always made you wonder. Lots of vamps trying to pass claimed they were gymnasts or dancers. Although, of course, if Jaise was a vamp, he'd hidden it well from a hell of a lot of people.

She turned her head. Six B-Ops commandos moved down the corridor. The saltpetre smell sharpened. The commando in front slipped and went down. Claudia's head cleared. The rest rushed on, weapons raised, until suddenly they were shouting and throwing the guns away as if they'd been burned. Korzha dropped straight down from the ceiling. Claudia caught a glimpse of enraged green eyes in a vamp-pale face.

One of the commandos panicked and took a shot at the vamp with a conventional weapon. At the vamp! The freaking idiot, one bullet wasn't going to kill Korzha, so that was a total waste of ammo. Korzha made like a whirling dervish amid B-Ops, scattering them. Claudia didn't see what happened next. Jaise slammed her against the door, trapping her between his chest and the wooden door. He howled in pain. Behind her, along her back, wherever she touched the surface, she felt electric sparks. The air shimmered. Ozone coalesced around her head. A black-clad figure appeared next to her, hunkered down in a crouch. Light glinted off his pale hair. Aslet? The demon Aslet. He held something in his arms. Someone. A child. A girl about ten years old. Claudia's world came to a stop.

The demon had her daughter.

She strained past Jaise, toward the demon, stretching out her arm. Her voice shattered. "Holly!"

Aslet stood, calm in the chaos exploding around them. With a smug grin, he hugged Holly to him, one hand to the back of the child's head, keeping her face against his chest. In the light, his eyes caught a flare, and for a disturbing moment flames danced in his pale blue irises.

"Donovan," Jaise barked. "Open the goddamn door or your daughter dies right now."

One of the commandos aimed his weapon at Jaise, who ducked and loosened his hold on her. Claudia's hands shook and she couldn't get a grip on the handle. From the corner of her eye, she saw one of the commandos take aim at Korzha. In frustration, she slammed both her palms against the door. From over her shoulder, she watched the vampire blur. The commando attacking him dropped to the ground, dead or out cold, she didn't want to know which. And then the door gave way. It just freaking dissolved, she swore that was what happened, and she fell.

Aslet leapt for the door, Holly in his arms. With a roar, Jaise threw himself over Claudia as she went through. The last thing she saw of Crimson City was Tiberiu Korzha making the same leap, and four B-Ops commandos in pursuit. Korzha looked pissed off, she thought; then she didn't see a damn thing.

Chapter Eight

Something pulled at her. Claudia felt her body slowly stretch. Just when she thought she'd break in two, she snapped forward and screamed from the tearing, searing pain. Behind her, the air felt thick. A high-pitched buzz shattered her ears. She didn't hear the sound of splintering wood or feel the door breaking under the impacts of their bodies. She felt no scrapes, no blows against her back. She didn't feel anything at all except the prickling electricity that threatened to tear her apart.

Thwump.

Jaise held her tight. He shouted in triumph. Cold surrounded her, filled her belly. They hit the ground hard. Her spine slammed against the contents of her backpack—there would be painful bruises later. Air came out of her lungs in a whoosh. Bright light stabbed her eyes. Jaise threw back his head and yowled like a tom interrupted mid-mating. When they landed, he didn't seem to be caught off guard or disoriented or struggling to breathe like she was. He fell on top of her and caught his weight on his hands.

Claudia fought for air, trying to get her bearings. The light and the air and . . . just everything was all wrong. Jaise rolled them away from the door, wrapping his arms around her as if he expected the fires of hell to descend on them. Her pack ended up skewed sideways, pulling the straps hard into her armpits. With one hand, Claudia fumbled for the fastening of her pack and her weapon. Her heart pounded like a jackhammer; her legs were still in the doorway and pain shimmered through her from her feet to her head.

Aslet, holding Holly, appeared through the wood like a ghost in a bad horror movie. He came *through* the door. To her still-woozy eyes, their two bodies seemed to slow, elongate as they emerged from the wood, and then snap back to normal. Four B-Ops commandos came through after them. Claudia saw Korzha vault into the room, too. The vampire hit the ground rolling. She put her hands against Jaise's shoulders and pushed. For God's sake, if there were dogs here, she didn't want to be trapped underneath anything when they attacked. She pulled her legs toward her torso, and the pain in her body stopped.

But the horror had just begun. For an eternity burned into her head, the four B-Ops commandos stumbled, mouths open in screams of agony. Aslet looked on, arms folded across Holly's back, holding the girl tight, a palm cupping her head. The child's sneaker-clad feet swung free on either side of his body. One of the commandos took a step, then a second. Another clawed at his own chest. Claudia heard a wet sort of pop. Before her eyes, all three men vanished in a puff of crimson mist. The third flickered through the various stages of a werewolf metamorphosis, but in no progressive order and so fast she could hardly see, and then he, too, just dissolved. Red mist settled on the stone floor. An iron scent hung in the air: a smell of hemoglobin, tart and musky. None of the deaths took more than a second or two.

Korzha didn't vanish. At the end of his roll, he landed on his feet, facing the door. Surprise was etched on his face, while Jaise's howl of protest lingered in the air. Like Claudia, the vampire had watched what happened to the commandos with revulsion. His mouth drew back in a rictus grin that exposed a pair of razor-sharp upper canines, white as freaking snow. Quicker than she could follow, he dodged a knife that seemed to come from nowhere—or, rather, from somewhere to one side of her and Jaise. Claudia couldn't see, what with Jaise still looming over her. The air pulsed, pressing in on her eardrums.

"No!" Jaise shouted. He leapt to his feet. Holly's head hung limp, and with Aslet's sudden reaction to Jaise's cry, one arm slipped free and dangled. "Not here!"

Now, why did his accent sound strange? It wasn't normal anymore, but more British, Continental. It was the kind of accent certain people liked to affect until they realized they sounded like jackasses. Only, this was convincing. The accent was a lot like Aslet's.

Moonlight spilled through a window set high in the wall. Slivers of reddish-white light made the mist on the ground sparkle like holiday glitter. The air didn't feel right, and Claudia couldn't place that either. It was . . . paler air, if that made any sense. She heard noises, but couldn't identify them. Moving. People moving. Not dogs. Dogs would howl, claws would scrape the floor.

Claudia rolled to her knees, shook the cobwebs out of her head and tried to stand on legs that felt like limp celery. Another knife flashed through the air. With a blur of his hand, Korzha caught it. He held the blade between thumb and forefinger. The changed quality of the light—slightly blue, Claudia thought—brought out the pallor in his cheeks. But Claudia only wanted one thing right now, and that was her daughter. She lunged for Aslet and Holly. The pale-haired demon's eyes flashed orange-red. Jaise put out a hand, but she ducked under his arm and dove for the demon.

Unfortunately, Korzha caught her by the wrist and brought her up short. She whirled toward him, but her efforts to free herself were about as effective as pushing at a boulder. Like a lightning flash in the sky, Claudia suddenly remembered that a vamp who hadn't fed recently enough to maintain a healthy color had to be considered dangerous. Bad things happened to humans when vamps got hungry. She snarled, "Let go, fang."

Korzha stood still as a statue, unruffled and relaxed, his fingers curled around her wrist. Behind him, Jaise roared with inchoate anger. "Consider what you're attacking, Officer," the vampire warned her over the sound.

"Let me go," she growled. She fought him like a cornered cat, but to no avail. Korzha dodged every blow, and his grip was relentless. "That thing's got my daughter!" she cried at last.

The vampire leaned close. "Officer." His calm voice cut through her panic. He nodded toward Aslet. "That thing is a demon. If you want your daughter to live, don't piss him off until we know what's going on." He grabbed her by the shoulders. "I will watch out for her." His gaze held hers. "You have my word of honor, yes?" She jerked on her arm, but that did no good. "I won't let go until I know you aren't going to do something stupid."

"That's my daughter," she repeated.

"My word of honor," Korzha said.

Claudia pulled in a deep breath and looked at the door they'd come through. It wasn't broken in the least. Her pulse roared through her, about as controlled as a winter blizzard. They were in a huge square room, with a tall ceiling and a wide, short window high in one wall. The room was all in gold stone, with squares of sandy-gold stone covering the walls and floor. At head level on the wall, metal-cage sconces emitted a bluish light. Opposite the door they'd come through, stone steps led up to another door.

A stranger stood on the opposite side of the room from her and Jaise. He was tall and bare-chested, with chestnut hair held back by a silver clip. He wore pants that laced. The ties flapped unfastened at his crotch, exposing skin and, about an inch below his navel, the band of the form-fitting garment underneath was partially folded under. He stood on a tasseled rug about four-by-six, woven in magenta, ocher and brilliant yellow. In a face of masculine roundness, with full cheeks narrowing to a pointed chin, his brown eyes were so pale they looked transparent. A woman crouched at his feet, holding a torn garment to her chest. She watched the new arrivals with desperate, desolate eyes. As a cop, Claudia had seen that look too often not to recognize it for what it was: the hollow look of someone who'd passed beyond the worst and couldn't imagine why she was still alive. Shock. Complete disassociation. Claudia was pretty sure the woman was human.

"Surely, Commander," Korzha said, "it is not necessary to involve women and children." The knife he'd caught appeared in his hand again. His fingers moved and the blade flashed upward, end over end. As it fell back down, he caught it by the hilt. The corners of his mouth tilted up. "Why not give Officer Donovan back her daughter and send her and the other woman home?"

"I do what's best for my people," Jaise replied. He crossed his arms over his chest.

Well, there you go, Claudia thought. A good commander stood up for his men. Matthew Jaise might have his personality flaws, but she'd never heard anyone deny his ability to lead. "And what's best for my people is that Claudia Donovan stays here."

Korzha squared his shoulders. Despite his expensive suit and drop-dead good-looks, he managed to look menacing. One eyebrow arched. "I did not agree to involve humans. The whole point, if you recall, was to avoid human involvement entirely. We had an agreement, Jaise. You assured me you were trustworthy."

"You will get what I promised."

"You can't trust him," the woman cried. Her voice cracked on the last syllable. "You can't trust any of them. They lie. They always lie." At first, Claudia thought she meant Korzha. God knew vamps weren't to be trusted. But after a few moments, she wasn't so sure.

The man at the woman's side said something in a low voice that made her cringe. He reached down and tangled his fingers in her hair, pulling hard. Her torn shirt slipped off her shoulder, and Claudia felt a chill upon seeing the tiny pattern etched into the woman's skin—just like the one she'd seen on the body back in the construction lot. A bit smaller, maybe, but it had the same internally interlocking pattern. The same mark she and Jaise now had.

She noticed three more tall men. They stood at the edge of what appeared to be an indoor camp of some days' duration. Leather satchels lay on the ground, and blankets were spread over rugs as brightly colored as the blankets. The remains of a recent meal were near a neat fire. All three men had startlingly pale eyes that were nearly transparent. They were on their feet now. Alert. Aware.

Four healthy, hale men living in a condemned building struck Claudia as odd. What were they doing here, besides the obvious occupation of rape? An answer popped into her head: guards. These men were guarding the room. All of them were tall, all of them powerfully built. One nodded toward the red mist on the floor. "One of them was not human," he said.

Claudia's ribs hurt something fierce, and now that her body was backing down from its state of high alert, she was feeling the pain. Since Korzha had at last let her go, she sidled toward Aslet and Holly. What the hell were these men guarding?

Claudia walked to Aslet, and with trembling fingers touched her daughter's cheek. Her skin felt warm, and thank God, Holly was breathing. Claudia held out her arms, but Aslet tightened his grip. "What happened to her?" she asked. Holly's head lolled. The girl was out cold. Her breathing was regular, a gentle expansion of the ribs, but was she drugged or hurt? Claudia looked at Jaise. "We've got to get her to a hospital."

"She'll come around soon," the B-Ops commander said.

"What the hell does that mean? And besides, how do you know?" She stared into Jaise's eyes. They were such a pale gray, like mist seen through dawnlight. She didn't smell werewolf anymore, but somehow she didn't think these guys were vamps—although, come to think of it, Korzha's presence kind of argued for that species identification. Korzha hadn't gone up in crimson mist like the others. Rogues didn't always get along. They tended to be maladjusted, frequently had a tenuous hold on their sanity. Maybe Korzha had some serious opposition among the others. That would make an interesting note for the files.

She stared at Matthew Jaise. "You're a vamp," she accused. But that didn't sit right. What could he be, if he wasn't a vamp? "I never guessed."

Jaise's mouth twitched and showed white, even teeth. Plenty of vamps filed their fangs. "I am not a vampire," he said.

The four guards stood without moving, all in various attitudes of cautious relaxation, the brown-eyed one with his hand still tangled in the human woman's hair. They didn't look homeless. None of them. They weren't human bums at any rate. *Not human*, she thought. She eyed the woman again. Now, she, she'd bet was human. The men, though, weren't were-wolves. They weren't vamps, rogue or otherwise.

"What the hell are you?" she asked. But she already knew. They were like Aslet. Jaise and the rest were like Aslet. Demons. They had to be demons. Holy cripes. Demons in Crimson City.

"You're not stupid," Jaise said, and this time he sounded like he used to. "You tell me."

"Demons," Claudia whispered.

"Oh my God," she heard the woman whisper. "Oh my God, you're a cop."

She looked at the woman. "Yes, ma'am."

"He did it," the woman said in a wondering, desperate voice. "You opened the portal."

"So?"

The brown-eyed demon let go of the woman. With a swift motion, he retied his pants and now stood, hands free. Ready for anything. "Eventually," the woman said, "the portal kills us. It'll kill you, too. Don't listen to anything he says." The demon at her side reached down and closed his fingers over her shoulder until tears sprang to the woman's eyes. "You're going to die just like the rest of us!" she cried.

Jaise walked to Aslet and stroked Holly's cheek. Claudia's heart thudded. Her child stirred. "Yes," he said. "Demons." He lifted his eyes. "She is safe," he said. "As long as you cooperate, she is safe."

"Take me and let her go."

"I have you both. What do you Overworlders like to say?" He tipped his head and laughed. "Two birds in the hand?"

"No," she whispered. "You can't do this. You can't."

Jaise bent and retrieved the knife that someone had thrown at Korzha, and tapped the flat of the blade against his open palm. "Only Aslet is able to perform the spell that allows you to open the portal. It works only on humans and, I'm sorry, none live very long." He looked at the white-haired demon. "Aslet is young. His mother was Bak-Faru demon. He is very strong, but unpredictable." With a sigh, he faced Claudia again, speaking in his refined voice, which she now realized was his natural one. He crossed to her and put a hand on her shoulder. "The human woman is right. You will not live long. Three weeks. Perhaps a month."

"Don't touch me," Claudia said. She glanced again at the woman with the desolate eyes. Was that going to be her in a few days? Her skin flashed hot all over, then cold and clammy, like melting snow.

Jaise tilted his head and stroked Claudia's throat.

Her skin crawled. She'd thought about going to bed with him. She'd actually been tempted when he got around to her. Seriously tempted. Probably, she'd eventually have said yes. It was possible. She'd done dumber things. His lip curled. "I will enjoy mating with you, Claudia Donovan. We will do so soon."

Louder, he said, "I have need of them all. The humans and the vampire." He rested his palm on Claudia's throat. His thumb slid up the side of her neck, pressing the soft skin there. "Vampire," he said, without looking away from her. "We have much to talk about." He fit his palm to the curve of her throat. Cold raced through her. Claudia tried to shake off his hand, but didn't succeed. Her arm throbbed where he'd cut her. Inside her body the cold continued to spread.

"You broke your word," Korzha replied.

"You are here," Jaise said, lifting both hands palms up. "You will meet with the Council as we agreed. In the meantime, you are free to deal with the rogue. As agreed."

"Korzha," Claudia said, "Fleur is going to have your freaking head for this."

The vampire smiled at her, but his gorgeous eyes were dead. "So much easier to apologize, yes? I assure you she will accept my apology when she understands the alternative is worse."

Jaise stripped off his black shirt and dropped it to the ground. He pulled his cell phone from a pants pocket and threw it on the ground. The casing had melted. He bent over one of the satchels near the guards and pulled out clothes like the others wore. Given his distraction, Claudia decided to risk reaching behind her to unsnap her Glock from her holster. The metal felt warm. She wasn't sure what she'd do even if she got it out, but the shape and weight felt comforting. Just having it on her hand made her feel better.

From the corner of her eye, Claudia saw the other woman back away from the brown-eyed demon, toward the door they'd come through. Deliberately, Claudia refused to make eye contact. If the woman wanted to make a run for the door, Claudia wasn't going to stop her, but she wasn't going to endanger Holly, either.

Tiberiu Korzha lifted his head. Claudia held her breath. Was the vampire going to betray her? He gave no sign of definite understanding, no sign of his intentions, but she figured he knew what was up, because she could see his eyes narrow. Cripes, Korzha was seriously handsome. No wonder all the women in the department got flustered when he was around. She wasn't the promiscuous type. She didn't sleep around. In fact, she hadn't slept with anyone in ages, which was part of the reason Jaise had tempted her so. She cleared her throat, and kept her hands behind her. The muzzle of her Glock pressed against her spine and burned her through her shirt.

"Jaise," she asked. "Where are we?"

He turned to look at her, throwing his comm unit on the floor to join his pants, cell phone and car keys. His irises thinned, became so pale she thought she must be able to see through to the other side. "Home," he said.

"Home where?" The escaping woman was about three feet behind her. "Home," Claudia repeated for the sake of distracting Jaise. She had to pray the other demons were similarly engaged. "Home like Beverly Hills? Or home like somewhere in France?"

Jaise let out a breath. "Biirkma city."

"Never heard of it," she said. She shifted to block

his view of the door. "Is that anywhere near Van Nuys? The Valley? No? North of the city, maybe?"

One of the demons started laughing. But another had at last noticed the woman.

"What's so funny?" Claudia asked. She balanced her weight on the balls of her feet and prepared to throw herself at Aslet. If there was going to be trouble, she wanted to be near Holly, and that meant taking out the platinum-blond freak.

But the woman caught her off guard, completely sucker-punched her. She wasn't trying to escape, at least not yet. She got behind Claudia and instead of lunging for the door, grabbed her around the knees. Claudia fell forward and got her hands out just in time to prevent her head from hitting the floor with an unpleasant crack. The woman smelled of sex and old sweat and fear, and she was a hell of a lot stronger than she looked. The brown-eyed demon let out a screech that just about shattered Claudia's eardrums.

"Go," the woman cried. "We have to go now while there's still a chance. Come on. I can't anymore. It won't work, it won't work without you. You're the only one who can open the portal. You have to be touching the portal or it won't open."

Claudia fought a wave of dizziness. She turned herself over, scrambling to her feet. The woman released her legs, grabbed her by the arm and hurled her toward the door. Claudia's booted feet slid on the stone floor, and she lost her balance. Aslet, with Holly in his arms, looked over his shoulder just as she hit the ground. She rolled again and sprang toward him.

But, from behind, the woman got an arm around Claudia's throat, cutting off her breath. Claudia grasped the woman's forearm, pulling down, trying to ease the pressure. Someone said a guttural word, but

Jaise roared a denial. She heard a thunk. Something hit the door. The planks rattled in the frame. Off balance, Claudia threw out her other hand, slapping the surface behind her. The feeling in her arm disappeared. Pain rushed through the rest of her body, agonizing pain. But then she felt a quiver, a sense of elongation. Her hand disappeared up to her wrist, then up to her elbow. She smelled the derelict basement with its werewolf musk. She threw her hand forward, out of and away from the door, and stretched toward Aslet. "Holly!" she cried.

The brown-eyed demon leapt forward and, in one bound had the woman by the elbow, hauling her back. Claudia felt her air cut off as she was dragged. But the woman kicked out and clipped the demon in the gut. He went down. In one motion, the woman took Claudia's gun and pressed the barrel to her temple. "Come with me," she swore, "or you're dead right now."

"Not without my daughter," Claudia replied.

The woman laughed. Claudia felt the arm around her throat tense. Her Glock's trigger clicked. She closed her eyes. . . .

Nothing happened.

She was facing out, facing Aslet and Jaise and the others. She couldn't breathe, and in another few moments it wouldn't matter that her gun had misfired. The brown-eyed demon approached.

The woman screamed and dragged Claudia back toward the door. They tripped and went down in a heap. Claudia jackknifed and slid sideways like a crab. Her leg slammed into the door and went through the wood like it was water. She screamed in pain. Near her, she saw the woman's eyes go wide. The brown-eyed demon roared and lunged for the portal. Claudia watched him put a hand on the surface and keep going. His arm disappeared and then his shoulder; then he slid through and was gone. One of the other demons grabbed the woman and hauled her back.

Jaise pulled Claudia to her feet and toward him. The moment she lost contact with the door, the buzzing, dizzying hum in her head ceased. Steam rose from her gun where it lay on the ground. She lunged for the weapon, brought it up and pointed it at Jaise. "Give me back my daughter. Now," she demanded of Aslet.

Aslet shook his head, amused. "She belongs here," he said.

"The hell she does." She glared at the demon. "Give her to me, or this freak's dead."

Aslet only laughed.

Claudia squeezed the trigger. Nothing happened. She lowered her sights, aiming for Jaise's chest, and pulled the trigger again. In the blink of an eye, the metal turned white hot, searing her hand. She screamed and dropped it. The weapon sizzled as it hit the ground. All the synthetic parts went up in smoke. The metal parts collapsed in, distorting like a Dalí clock bending in time and space.

In the meantime, Jaise strode to the sobbing woman captive and reached for her. With a snap that reverberated in Claudia's head, he broke her neck. The woman's body hit the ground and didn't move.

Jaise hauled Claudia away from the door. "Overworld technology doesn't work here," he said. He ripped off her comm and pressed one of the buttons. The circuit imploded. "You see?" He threw the unit on the ground. "Your technology is useless here. We are in Orcus, Claudia Donovan. My world, not yours. Our world," he said. "Our rules, not yours." He stared at her, and she could swear she saw flames in his eyes. "Overworlders cannot live in the demon world. If you were not bound to the Elismal demons, you would be dead, like the others." He nodded toward the door they'd come through, and to the red mist on the ground.

"Korzha's not dead."

"Some might say," the vampire spoke up, "that is a misstatement, Officer."

"Only demons and half-demons can live in Orcus. Humans must be bound as you are, or they die. Your daughter can live here because she is half-demon," Jaise said.

Claudia felt a surge of anger. "Like hell."

"Aslet is right. She belongs here." Jaise let go of her and pressed his palms together. He touched the tips of his fingers to his forehead. Her skin flushed hot, as if someone had opened and then closed an oven nearby. The demon opened his eyes. After a moment he said, "I am called Jaise. I am an Elismal demon." He held out his hands at waist level, as if anyone should have known that.

"I figured out you aren't human," Claudia snapped. "Duh."

"Aslet," Jaise said, turning to his cohort. "Take the human child to Biirkma palace—"

"No!" Claudia darted toward Holly. Her voice sounded shrill, high and thin. "Jaise, no! Please. What are you doing?" Jaise had her arm in a tight grip. She whirled and struck at him, leaning all her weight in the other direction. Her heart slammed against her ribs. "Holly!" Aslet turned and headed for the other door with the child in his arms. Claudia's breath stopped. Her world stopped. "Holly!"

Jaise twisted her arm, wrenching her shoulder in its socket so that the pain sent her to her knees. Claudia stared at the erstwhile B-Ops commander. "No," she said through the pain. "For God's sake, Jaise, where is he taking her?"

"Claudia Donovan," Jaise said in an amused voice. "You have nothing to fear. Aslet will keep her safe. Unless I tell him otherwise."

Claudia turned to Jaise again and said, "Hurt her, and I swear I'll hunt you down and tear out your freaking eyeballs."

Jaise laughed and stepped close. "You could try." His fingers brushed the line of her cheekbones. Her stomach bottomed out. "But we are in the demon world now, Claudia Donovan, and you and your child will never leave it without me."

Aslet disappeared. Along with her daughter.

Chapter Nine

In the velvet night of Orcus, a red-tinged moon filled the sky. Stars shimmered like diamonds scattered across the heavens by a careless god. Korzha was for a moment taken back to a time when walking in the dark of night meant a heavenly vault that took your breath and reminded even an immortal that life sometimes required passionate embrace. The air had a peculiar taste, a sharper scent that was cleaner and older. A resonance echoed through him. Familiarity. Recognition. Not only demons were here in the city of Biirkma.

The air around him pulsed, and he smelled that peculiar burnt scent that had so tickled his senses at the construction site, that he'd let Officer Donovan see him there. He turned to look around and, half a heartbeat later, Donovan collapsed. One of the demons bent over her. Jaise shouted. Korzha made the mistake—a rare one for him—of assuming the attack had been aimed at her. He reacted on instinct. After centuries of indolence, centuries under a diminishing sky, old habits, original habits, weren't so far away. He still could not stand to see a woman hurt, particularly one whom he'd already failed by not protecting her daughter as promised.

Because of his previous dealings with Jaise, he knew more about demons than just about anyone in Crimson City, but he had a great deal more to learn. One thing he did know was that in addition to being extremely long-lived, upwards of several hundred years, demons approached sex—"mating" was their preferred term—in a manner that to humans seemed highly casual. For a demon, mating was like food, and they were a hungry lot. For all that Donovan was a cop, she seemed too delicate to withstand the sustained sexual attentions of demons. She played tough, talked tough, but underneath she was decent, and that made her vulnerable. What a pity, he thought. She'd never see her daughter again. This was his fault. His.

That was when the equivalent of a freight train hit him between the shoulder blades. He felt the nerve-slivering pain of bones breaking, puncturing internal organs. Even if he'd possessed the robust strength of the recently fed, he'd have had a time recovering from the blow. Something that felt like an electric eel climbed upward from the locus of the impact and sizzled in his head. He struggled to keep his feet as his injuries spread, and the new demon who'd appeared, whose lust for Officer Donovan broadcast itself even now, put rough hands on her. Korzha's last thoughts were that he pitied the woman. Behind the demon who held Donovan, Jaise said something low and guttural. Then light flashed, pain burst through Korzha, and he lost consciousness.

When he next opened his eyes, it was to a windowless room with but one door and no window. His internal clock seemed to function here in Orcus. If that was a correct assumption, at least one night had passed since he'd followed Donovan through the portal. He tended to wake early and always had. Over the centuries, his rising time had increased perhaps a second or two a year, and eventually that meant he rose to sunset rather than full dark. The receding sun echoed in his bones.

The injuries he'd suffered were healed, but they'd been extensive, and he was correspondingly hungry. For now, he had to tuck away the hunger and take stock of his predicament. The room was too large to be a jail and too clean to be a dungeon—he'd been in his share of both. The pallet on which he lay provided no protection from the frigid stones beneath. On the other hand, there was no smell of staleness or unwashed fabric. No fleas, no ticks, no lice. No vermin of any sort. Just cold, bare walls. In another corner were the necessary fixtures for a human, pleasantries for a vampire: shower, toilet, sink. But nothing else.

He closed his eyes and let his senses drift. Demons did not feel so different from humans, and not all were as insistent as the ones who'd been at the portal. Of course, some of them were more insistent. Wherever he was locked away, demons weren't far. Nor were humans near. The veil between the worlds was supposed to be sealed, but, as Jaise had claimed, demons had found a way through, one that involved humans. He wondered what, exactly, they'd done to Donovan to enable her to open the portal. He wondered too if Officer Donovan was still alive. He hoped he was wrong about her fate. Her death would be intolerable. A woman and a child? It was intolerable to have such blood on his hands.

As for being locked away, he doubted the door

would withstand his concerted effort to defeat it. Of course, it wouldn't be easy, either. A layer of what he could only characterize as a sort of electrified oil coated the lock, and defied his attempts to engage the tumblers from this distance. He did prefer the elegance of moving the parts without physical effort, but sometimes need dictated action. With the growing fullness of night, trenchant hunger licked at him, ate at his belly, whispered to be fed. But just as he prepared for a brute-force attack, the door opened. Korzha flowed to his feet, and the demon Jaise walked in.

Here in Orcus, the arrogance of Jaise's face suited him. In Crimson City, the expression had made him appear careless, though he hadn't been careless at all. Jaise's hair gleamed with bronze highlights amid dark honey. "Vampire," he said.

"Demon," Tiberiu replied, with a chill that any member of family Korzha would have known meant trouble. He brushed off his sleeve. In his human life he'd had more than one moment like this. He'd had many as he solidified his position with king and country and more again as a vampire in control of Family Korzha. In the last three hundred years no one had questioned his rank or status, yet the politics of establishing one's standing came back to him like a favorite dog.

Jaise was nearly his height, but broader through the torso. Even here in Orcus, where demons naturally made no attempt to hide their nature, at first and even second glance he might easily pass for human. But red flickered behind his translucent gray eyes. Even a dog or a fang, as the paranormal were called in Crimson City, might have been fooled. He had warm skin, all the scents of a living body, a beating heart, blood in veins and arteries, peristalsis, muscle, sinew and cartilage. Yes, he was warm—perhaps too warm. For a human, he'd be in a constant state of fever. But here the demon did not hide his un-human nature. And with Jaise so near, Korzha felt the difference between human and demon in his bones.

The demon put his hands on his hips. "My regrets, vampire, on your accommodations."

Korzha cocked his head. He might, probably could, reach the door before Jaise could react. The question was whether he wanted to. "This is temporary, yes?" he said. One did not treat Tiberiu Korzha as if he were due anything but the utmost respect. Jaise nodded, smiling oh so slightly. "Then I will overlook the affront to my dignity. Instead, we will discuss my safe departure from the lovely city of Biirkma."

"As you know," Jaise said, "without the council's agreement, our terms are not official."

Korzha crossed one arm over his chest and propped his elbow on his fist, settling his free hand near his mouth, as if he needed to think. He ran the pad of his thumb over the tip of a fang. Ruthlessly he tamped down his hunger. "You insist demons keep their promises. Perhaps that is so. Unfortunately," he said so softly that Jaise moved forward to hear—a step further from the door. "Unfortunately, *demon*, without honor, there is no trust. You have not acted with honor. Therefore, I cannot trust you."

"My promise is enough, vampire."

"Our agreement is null and void, and became so the moment you tried to kill me."

"It was an accident." Jaise lifted his hands. "I meant to hit the demon who touched Claudia Donovan without my permission."

"How clumsy of you. And how distressing for me to learn so late of your deficiencies. I'll meet with your Council, Jaise, but the terms we negotiate will be a little changed. There must be compensation for my increased risk. Your lack of honor, demon," he explained. "And yet more risk in allying Family Korzha with someone who cannot punish when he means it." He smiled and let his fangs show. "I have not made such a mistake in over five hundred years. It will not happen again."

Jaise's eyes flickered red, obliterating all trace of gray. "You are here, vampire. In the Underworld. As I promised. That is no accident." It was a threat, and a reminder.

"I hope it was not." Korzha had the satisfaction of knowing he'd unsettled the demon. "Let's move on, shall we? Tell me about the rogue."

"I have told you all you need to know."

"So you say." Korzha pressed his palms together and, for a moment, touched the sides of his index fingers lightly against his lips. "But you lack honor, so, alas, I must ask you now for a gesture of good faith."

Jaise's eyes flared again. "I am *Nir* of the Elismal demon, vampire. I have promised the Elismal demons will protect you and your Family Korzha. In return for your intervention and influence with the other vampires."

"Perhaps the Dumonts would be willing to negotiate with you." Korzha let the corner of his mouth twitch. Jaise wanted *his* demons—not some other branch—firmly ensconced in the political structures of Crimson City, and where better to start than with the wealth and power of the vampires? "Fleur Dumont is quite beautiful. I'm sure you'll enjoy coming to terms with her."

"What do you want?" Jaise asked.

"Personal protection."

"Agreed. I will keep you safe, vampire."

"Not you. Aslet."

Jaise scowled, but he nodded.

"And I want Officer Donovan and her daughter freed. Now." The words came out far more strongly than he meant. Absurd as it was for a vampire as old and jaded as himself, the light in Donovan's face when she talked about her daughter had touched something in Korzha he thought died more than five hundred years ago. And there was the not inconsequential matter of his having given her his word. "Send them back to Crimson City."

The demon shook his head. "We risked too much to bring you to Orcus. Humans will be watching the portal more closely than ever. And now that only Claudia Donovan can reliably open the portal, we will not open it again until we're ready." He scowled. "She will die soon, vampire. The Elismal can do nothing to prevent that." He paused. "Take your rogue, vampire, be satisfied with that."

Chapter Ten

Claudia pulled the insides out of a ballpoint pen she found in one of the side pockets of her pants and, with the prong from her badge, a credit card and some nail clippers, fashioned a reasonable lockpick. The door came open after a broken fingernail that hurt like a mother and twenty minutes of frustrating, sweaty work. There wasn't anyone in the hallway outside. It was time to find Holly.

She walked boldly down the hall. A glance or two out the windows confirmed the palace was large. It looked to be mid-morning: blue sky stretched all the way from the horizon to infinity. In L.A., buildings went up. Here, it seemed as if they sprawled low to the ground. She wasn't going to find her daughter easily in this complex, but find her she would. First she planned a recon, then, the serious attempt. But she'd take her child as soon as she could. She'd seen enough of the palace on the way from the portal to get a general sense of the layout. They had her on the top floor.

Instead of traversing the interior hall, where inevitably she'd run into some demon who knew she wasn't supposed to be walking around, she quickly found a window near a drainage pipe, cracked it open and hauled herself onto the roof. Courtyards and colonnades connected a series of square buildings. The few individuals she saw out and about she pegged for guards or servants, judging from the combination of clothes, activity and the fact that all those without shoes were cleaning or carrying something. Above her, the sun beat down from a pristine blue sky without even a hint of smog.

Well. Everyone knew if you wanted to find a prisoner, you should follow the guards, so that's what she did. She kept her head down and waited, tracking the movements of the guards and waiting for a change of shift. At roughly eleven o'clock, judging from the position of the sun in the morning sky, guards emerged from a square at the corner of the building to her left. She followed the line of the roof to the building opposite. The tiles made for uncertain footing. Twice she barked her shin. But she also decided the men she was following were guards: They got to wear shoes. She hunkered down and waited some more. She ignored the hollowness in her stomach. Another shift change came about two. The next change would be around five. Then she was going in.

The sun blazed overhead, and she moved into the shadow of projecting decorative stonework. A little water wouldn't be amiss. Too bad she didn't have any. Arms wrapped around her knees, she wondered what had happened to Korzha. Was he somewhere here? Jaise had blasted him something fierce. This time of day, the vampire wouldn't be up and about. If he was even still alive. It saddened her, the idea that he might not be.

The sun sank lower in the sky, cooling her, but it also brought out more demons. More guards. More servants. When the shadows lengthened, around five o'clock, Claudia guessed, she loosened her legs, swung her arms a few times and worked her way down. As she reached ground level, she tucked herself into a niche and waited. The single guard at the door was getting antsy. He wore a set of padded armlets and greaves, but other than that, he was bare-chested. Thinking about his upcoming meal probably. She counted to three thousand before she walked up to him.

"Hey, there." She stuck out a hand. The demon stared at her like she'd spoken Hindi. "Claudia Donovan, L.A.P.D. How ya doing tonight? Everything going okay?"

The guard's eyes opened wide. "Human female," he said.

"*Nir*-Jaise told me I could see my daughter. Didn't he tell you?"

"No."

"She's here, right?" Claudia's heart beat triple-time; she knew from the guard's expression that she was. A little social engineering, and she might even get her out. Then she'd race for the portal and home.

She caught the guard eyeing her body and smiled. "Come on . . ." she said, stepping close. She touched the tip of her finger to his chest. "I don't want to get you in trouble or anything, but I can make it worth your while. A big, handsome guy like you? Mmm." The guard's eyes went wider. He grabbed her around the waist and growled. A girl couldn't be in Orcus long before she realized just how highly sexed demons were. It didn't take much to distract this one's thoughts south of his brain.

"Now," he said. "We mate now."

"Hey, sure." She pressed her pelvis against him. "It'd be a lot better if I wasn't worrying about my daughter, though. You know?"

The demon dipped his head and bit her shoulder. Hard enough to hurt. She needed to get him alone, so that nobody saw her hitting *kyung dong mak*, the pressure point on the side of his neck. Properly done, she'd cut off the blood supply to his brain, and he'd pass out long enough for her to get past him.

The guard spoke, but he wore a look on his face like he was going to humor her while his buddy snuck up from behind. Claudia reacted on instinct. She punched the guard in the solar plexus. Hard. The demon went down. She dropped with him, using her momentum to drive her fist into his crotch. Behind her, she smelled the air starting to burn. She whirled. Another demon. She dove for his knees.

He spoke a single word, and suddenly she was moving through air like it was soup. Her foe's eyes flared red with rage. When she landed, he spoke in a low voice, a guttural chant. She remembered it too well. Sounds like that meant trouble. The air around him quivered and took on a blue glow. He meant to kill her, or to try to kill her. His eyes were red as blood, flickering with fire.

She tried to kick him but couldn't. She hadn't expected to succeed, and now she just hoped she wasn't about to get killed. The first guard was on his feet, crouching to dive at her. The other guard gestured. The air got hotter. It seared her lungs. Her muscles contracted, all of them at once. She would have screamed with pain if she could have. From her left, a troop of demons rushed forward, led—oh, damn—by Jaise. A flash blinded her, and she screwed her eyes closed. When she opened them again, Jaise stood over her. "Claudia Donovan," he said.

Her head felt like it was on fire. She sat up. Every muscle in her body screamed. "I want my daughter."

He crossed his arms over his chest. "You deserve to die for this disobedience." He gestured to someone behind him. A female demon with iron-gray hair appeared in Claudia's field of vision. "*Nin*-Siath," Jaise said. Politely, too, like the demon female was someone important.

"This is the human female?" the demoness asked. When Jaise nodded, she made a "come along" gesture with her fingers.

"I'm not going anywhere without my daughter," Claudia said.

"Cooperate, Claudia Donovan." That was Jaise's voice. "Or I promise you will never see your child again."

Her blood chilled at the threat.

"Such a thing is not necessary," Siath said. The demoness spoke boldly, no bowing or toadying to Jaise. Claudia almost liked her for facing him down like that. The demoness crossed her arms over her chest and stared at Jaise. "Come, Claudia Donovan. You and I will walk and speak of your daughter."

Claudia tried to stand, but it made her shriek with pain. She worked out a massive kink in her thigh. Hell, her whole body was one massive muscle cramp. The female demon helped her to her feet, then offered a shoulder to help her stand upright.

"*Nin*-Siath. Do you think I cannot handle this female?" Jaise called.

Siath's eyes turned yellow-orange. "We are fortunate that all is not lost because you failed to keep her from this. You will be heard when the time comes and not before. Do not doubt, *Nir* Jaise, that I will reward your assistance. As promised."

Jaise bowed. "*Nin*-Siath."

Siath held her tight, giving Claudia no choice but to follow as best she could. They worked their way along a corridor like little old ladies setting out for more blue hair dye. Still clinging to the demoness's arm, Claudia managed to limp along the colonnade she'd stared at all afternoon. Her head pounded, and her muscles were only slowly loosening up.

"You are foolish," Siath said. "Very foolish."

"I wanted to see my daughter." Claudia stopped walking as they reached a small courtyard, hoping to work out a cramp in her calf.

The demoness Siath turned. Crinkles gathered in the corners of her pale yellow eyes. "She is safe for now, human female. I will see to that."

"Everyone keeps saying that"—Claudia shrugged—"but I can't see her. *I want to see her.*" Tears blocked her throat. Fear for Holly. Hopelessness. Anger. "Don't you have any feelings? Or do you demons just hate and nothing else? You must have children of your own." She could hardly move, but her mouth didn't seem to have any trouble. "Do you even care what happens to them? Because where I come from, we care about our children."

"We care," the demoness said.

"How would you feel if your child was taken from you and nobody let you see her?"

The demoness faced Claudia, arms crossed over her chest. Red flashed in her yellow eyes. "Are all humans as foolish as you?" she asked. "You do not understand that demons sense others. We always know each other. We know who is near, what they are. We know when a human is near. You cannot hide here. Not even on the roof. You were clever to watch for the guards to change. Very clever. But you would not have been able to take your daughter tonight or any other night. You would not have gotten anywhere. You have been allowed to do all that you have done this day." She walked down the corridor and Claudia hobbled to keep up.

"I just want her, that's all. Can't you understand?"

"When humans sealed the portal, one of my sons was trapped in the Overworld. My first." Siath touched the center of her forehead. "As dear to my heart and body as any of my children. I do not hate you because my first son is lost to me."

Claudia leaned against a sandy-gold column and massaged her shoulder. The pain in the demoness's eyes and voice twisted in her chest, twinning the pain she herself lived and breathed since Holly was taken. "What happened to him?" she asked.

The demoness tilted her head, considering. Red still flickered in her eyes. "Until Jaise returned, I did not know if my son was alive." Siath briefly left her to walk to a fountain in the center courtyard, then returned with a cup of water which she put in Claudia's hands. "Drink."

Claudia touched the demoness's arm before taking the water from her. "I'm glad you found him."

"My son is your daughter's father," the demoness said.

Claudia almost choked on the water. When she had her breath back, she said, "No, he isn't. Holly's father was from the Lower, just like me."

"My son Garath is a dark demon, Claudia Donovan. If he did not want you to know what he is, then you would not have known."

Claudia leaned her head against the column and stared at the ribbed arch overhead. She couldn't get her mind around the truth about Holly's father. Better not think about that at all. She wished she had a computer and decent web access, because she'd get her butt in a chair and search *political structure of Orcus* so she'd have a clue about what was going on here. With a computer in front of her she was pretty damn competent. Without one, well, trying to figure out how to connect the dots was a whole lot harder. She felt utterly lost. With a sideways look at the demoness, she said, "You found out Jaise was getting into Crimson City and you sent him to find your son, am I right?"

"That is so."

She thought about the portal. The only demons to come through were Jaise and Aslet, and she knew for a fact Aslet was not Holly's father. "Your son didn't come back with Jaise and Aslet. Why not?"

Siath smiled gently. "This is between demons. But, Garath sent me my granddaughter. Your daughter is demon, and should know what that means for her."

Claudia could hardly speak over the pounding of her heart. "You can't have her. You can't. She's my daughter. And, no disrespect to your son, but my daughter's gone ten years without a father. As far as I'm concerned, she can go another ten without him."

"I cannot say what was in Garath's heart, Claudia Donovan, but I wish to know my granddaughter. Will you deny me that?"

Claudia straightened. "Have you told her already?" The demoness shook her head. "I want to be there when you do. I want to tell her myself."

"Very well."

"When?"

"After Jaise addresses the Council, when matters are settled." Siath shook her head. "He is Elismal, but strong. Few will oppose him. The Council is likely to allow Jaise what he proposes."

"Killing humans, you mean?"

"There are worse demons than *Nir*-Jaise to come to the Overworld." Siath stared into Claudia's face. In the semidark of the corridor, her eyes glowed a soft yellow. "Now a healer must see you."

"I'll be fine." Claudia rubbed her other shoulder, but it was her head that hurt.

Siath frowned. "You are ill with the bond." She motioned to the marks underneath Claudia's clothes.

"I'll be fine once I get home."

The demoness regarded her steadily. She touched Claudia's forehead and shook her head.

"Well, the end justifies the means, right?" Claudia asked bitterly. "Because the Council will give Jaise what he wants."

She pushed off the column and did her best to keep up when Siath started walking again. The sun had set by the time they came upon a second courtyard. On three sides, archways led to the interior of the palace. Above, a brilliant orange-red moon lit the sky. The fourth side of the courtyard was an exterior wall. Here, a steady stream of demons walked, a handful of them females but all brightly dressed and escorted by barefoot servants. They walked the outermost corridor and vanished into the building.

Siath spoke again. "*Nir*-Jaise is right about many things, Claudia Donovan. An alliance with vampires will give demons a legitimate presence in the Overworld."

"What about Korzha?"

"Tonight there will be a Council meeting," Siath said. "Among other things, we will speak of you, the vampire and the Overworld."

"The vampire? What about Korzha?" Claudia shook off her interest. Her legs protested—hell, her entire body protested—and her head felt like it was going to explode. The little catch in her chest surprised her. But he was from home. Hearing of Tiberiu Korzha was like being in a foreign country and hearing someone speaking English. And he had promised to help her in that brief exchange by the portal. Perhaps that was why he'd been hurt. "He's alive?"

"Yes. Though he has made *Nir*-Jaise very angry."

"I thought Jaise killed him."

Siath hesitated. "Many wish he had."

On the opposite side of the courtyard, a demon near the entrance to the arched corridor roared, a loud, piercing call. The nearest guards straightened. Half a dozen or more jumped from their perches atop the exterior wall and landed in the center of the courtyard, heads lifted. One or two flickered between humanoid form and other, more monstrous shapes. Another howl shattered the night, and the sound raised the hair on Claudia's arms. Moon-mad wolf, she thought, intensified a thousand times.

The air shimmered, and then came a concentrated flash of light, as if someone had suddenly turned on the noontime sun. Claudia flinched and turned her face from the glare. It faded. Adrenaline pulsed through her. The demoness Siath grabbed Claudia's shoulder and pushed her down, hard. Claudia's forearm scraped the flagstones. The guards in the center of the courtyard howled but stood their ground.

A single demon emerged from the shadows of the arched walkway, alone, with no escort. There were no toadying servants at his heels. When he passed a wall sconce, light reflected off his black hair, which was very long and tied back from his face so that it hung straight down the middle of his naked back. Siath continued to hold Claudia's shoulder, but she did not object when Claudia stood. The black-haired demon looked to be a head taller than most other demons. He moved like he knew his precise center of balance, too. He had a dancer's grace, was controlled and seemingly ever-ready for a burst of motion.

Instead of continuing inside the palace as the other demons had done, this demon came to a full stop. He stared into the courtyard where Siath and Claudia waited. Siath, who had turned her back on him in order to pull Claudia away from the building, whirled and crouched as if prepared to flee. Claudia heard her draw in a sharp breath. The guards stiffened.

"What?" Claudia whispered. "What is it?"

"Bak-Faru," Siath replied.

The black-haired demon walked into the moonlit night and stared. Right at Claudia. A shiver ran down her spine. He wasn't wearing a shirt. He wasn't muscle-bound, but Claudia couldn't look at him without thinking of the hours in the gym it took to get ripped like that. The demon continued crossing the courtyard, walking in a trail of moonlight. One of the narrow plaits that held back his hair fell over his shoulder. Twined in the black-as-pitch braid was a thin platinum thread. Siath quivered but stepped in front of her. Claudia stared at the demoness's back. Protecting her? The other demon was still far away.

"Hey," Claudia said.

"He is very strong in power." Siath said. "Very strong."

"Stronger than you?"

Siath glanced at her. "He is Bak-Faru."

"What does that mean—Bak-Faru?"

"He is dark. A *dark* demon." Claudia would have stepped from behind Siath, but the demoness grabbed her arm and stopped her. Siath's palm felt hot. "If he addresses us, say nothing to him. Do nothing. Do not even breathe." The demoness sucked in air, a hiss of fear.

"What?"

Siath's voice shook. "He hides nothing," she said in a low, urgent voice. "Among Bak-Faru, this one is strong. Very powerful. Dangerous." She rocked her shoulders as the demon continued in his slow approach. Now and again he lifted a hand. One by one, the guards in the courtyard disappeared. And now there was no doubt where he was headed. Siath drew herself up.

Cornered meat, Claudia thought. She was no better than a hapless human citizen cornered by a hungry dog or a starving vamp. Siath stood fast even though the male demon had blithely dispatched the guards.

The Bak-Faru walked to within a foot of them and came to a halt. From behind Siath, Claudia waited for him to lift a hand and vanish her into oblivion. His eyes were an eerily pale lilac in an Aztec face. What scared her, what scared her more than guards who vanished without a trace, was that, put the guy in regular clothes, fix the freaky hairstyle, and he'd completely pass for human. She felt dizzy. Fluttery. Like she was at a party and the best-looking man in the room was staring at her. A gorgeous killer.

The demon studied Claudia so openly that she felt her cheeks flush. His gaze started out chilly and ended as hostile, but despite all that hatred she couldn't mistake the sexual interest in his perusal of her. The demon tilted his head to one side, as if listening to something only he could hear. Awareness sparkled in his eyes. Claudia could not look away from him. He nodded to her, put his palm over his fist and bowed once.

"*Nir,*" Siath said. She too bowed, hand over fist, but to waist level.

"Not *Nir,* grandmother," the demon said in a voice

all black smoke and velvet. He smiled, and dimples appeared in his cheeks.

Siath straightened, though her palm remained clasped over her fist. She stood tall. "May a grandmother ask why a Bak-Faru comes to Biirkma palace?"

Lilac eyes swept over Claudia, studying her. The sensation of fullness in Claudia's head surged to life. She recognized it as what she'd felt in her head since the hotel in Crimson City. Almost. But this was different somehow, a different shape, a darker density. Something else. *Desire.* How sick was that? Claudia Donovan, who in Crimson City often went weeks and weeks without even thinking about sex, was consumed by the thought of making love to a demon. Siath gave Claudia a sharp look, and there was more than enough light to see a cunning flicker enter the demoness's yellow eyes.

"Grandmother," the black-haired demon said. He sounded like a sweet old lady's favorite nephew. "The Bak-Faru hear that demons may soon be in the Overworld again."

Siath bowed. "That is so."

"Then the Bak-Faru have much to say."

"The Bak-Faru oppose the Council. I think there will be little to say."

"Grandmother, the Bak-Faru are led by the Bak-Faru." The demon faced Claudia, devouring her with his ludicrously pastel eyes. "A human female," he said.

"She belongs to *Nir*-Jaise," Siath replied. She sounded out of breath.

The statement distracted the demon. He turned his head, and Claudia read surprise in the curve of his mouth. "Grandmother," he said with a nod at Claudia. "Her bond is dark."

Siath bowed waist-level, saying nothing.

The Bak-Faru's lilac eyes hardened. "No Elismal has the power for this bond."

Siath bowed again. "It is not my concern if the Bak-Faru are careless with their spells. Aslet knows how to bind humans."

"Who else?"

"Only Aslet. But what matters except that this one can open the portal?"

The Bak-Faru stepped close—too close, within a foot of her—and Claudia found herself mesmerized by the lilac pools of his eyes, the thick and dark-as-soot lashes. She saw—felt?—something like regret in his eyes. "You will die from this bond. Soon," the Bak-Faru said. "The Elismal who did this is strong, but not Bak-Faru." He reached for Claudia, resting a hand on her shoulder. One finger slid over the nape of her neck. She shivered at the contact, dizzy. "If you were demon, I would mate with you, female."

She touched his chest—an instinct, really. She didn't know why she touched him, but she did. His skin was warm and smooth, a layer of silk over muscle. He looked at her and, swear to God, she felt a spark pass between them. The demon sucked in a breath and took a step closer. Claudia snatched away her hand.

"The vishtau?" Siath said.

The lilac-eyed demon growled. The sound rumbled in Claudia's chest. "I refuse." His eyes shot to Siath. "I refuse this." He touched the underside of Claudia's chin and slowly smiled. Dimples flashed in his cheeks. "When you die, I will rejoice."

Chapter Eleven

Korzha clung to the outside walls of Biirkma Palace as he moved into the streets of the demon city, keeping to the shadows of eaves and roofs. He knew the general direction of the rogue he'd come here to take, but, first things first. He needed information and a meal. There wasn't any way in hell he could deal with the rogue in his current condition. Drained by healing himself from the attack at the portal, his body felt like it had been days now, months, years, a century since he last fed.

Ancient habits came back with a sharp sense of having—how perverse—come home. In L.A. he did not hunt, and he hadn't realized how much he missed the pursuit. He found the city center by following the glow of light, the sounds, the flow of traffic. Satisfy this need first—hunger, burning hunger—then he would search for the vampire he'd felt since he first set foot in Biirkma. Tiberiu lurked in courtyards and streets and waited for someone who suited his needs. He found one quite soon: an attractive female, alone

110

and whose mind he could touch without difficulty. Very nice.

Slinking, slithering, he lurked in the shadows while the demon world walked past, unaware of the monster in their midst. He knew now how to hide himself from them. In L.A., when he'd followed the pair of half-demons Mika and Conor he'd not known precisely how. He did now. Demons, while impressive and even frankly dangerous, were not, it seemed, invincible. They were every bit as susceptible to mental persuasion as humans, though in variable degrees. Certain demons he touched with difficulty; a few he could not touch at all. Some were highly susceptible even from the distance he kept. When his chosen prey would have turned to a populated street, he urged her otherwise—a light touch, a gentle suggestion:

Not that way.

Take the narrow street.

The darker street is so much quieter.

Hunger urged him on, and he needed every ounce of his restraint not to throw himself on her too soon. At last, she did turn. He slid behind her. The noise from the main square faded and became a hum where before it had been a din of conversation, of shutters opening and closing, of laughter and movement along the stone streets. He moved toward her. Closer. Nearer. In the shadows, closer yet. His mental touch became a caress and then an embrace. By the time he revealed himself, by the time he stood, in fact and in deed, with her in his arms, she relaxed against him and lifted her face to his. She was warmer than a human. Feverish. He enjoyed the mental connection, vampire to demon—a first for him. She was pretty, with thick, blond hair like straw and eyes of tourmaline, but paler, more like a memory of tourmaline held to the light. A kiss. Their tongues touched. Almost, he lost control. His hands were moving. He nuzzled her throat. Hunger. Raging hunger. When he fed, her blood was warm. Hot. Too hot. He took more than he intended and came away unsatisfied even as she slipped bonelessly to the ground.

Unsated.

He touched her head and wiped away all memory of their encounter. What, he wondered, would demons think of the marks on her neck when she woke? An interesting thought. Given the length of time the other vampire had been here, had they developed a myth to account for such a presence? Were demons long-lived enough to recall everything about the races of the Overworld? That was another interesting question. The rogue had been here a very long time. The rogue must know Korzha was here, too; he must be able to feel Korzha just as Korzha felt him. The tie of their blood and creation linked them forever.

Korzha pondered the nature of Orcus as he worked his way farther from the palace. Cloaked though he was, Korzha could not mingle with demons as he could with humans. His Overworld clothes marked him as foreign on sight. Next time, with something local to wear, he might be able to pass in two worlds. It was risky, but possible. But since he was unable to walk in the open market as at home, he avoided the most crowded streets.

Eventually he came upon an outdoor kitchen erected in a wide alley with walls covered by a flowering vine of murky sweetness. He crouched on a rooftop and watched from the shadows. Demons stood holding buns or other pastries he didn't recognize. The smells of savory meats competed with the blossoms. Several demons held small cups of a liquid that smelled like fruit. All of them were males, all were blustery and full of spit and venom. Chances were good, Korzha decided, that whatever they were drinking wasn't as mild as it smelled. A knot of half a dozen young males bragged to each other of the exploits they intended, full of alcohol and bravado.

He chose his second victim from among them—a male in his early twenties with an undercurrent of humanity about him. He had a richer scent than the others, a mind less foreign, and, to be sure, he was more inebriated. Korzha's hunger flared, and he almost missed a crucial remark: The men were heading for someplace they called "the snare."

Korzha laughed to himself when he edged closer and let his mind touch the one he'd chosen. Vampire myth did exist in Orcus. With a twist. These males were bound for the demonic snare—a morass of magic where Jaise had claimed the rogue was trapped. According to Korzha's information, when the rogue, already many years insane, escaped into the Underworld, it raged among them like vampires of human lore; wily, cunning and able to elude even the demons' senses. Interestingly, or so Jaise claimed, a demon couldn't be made vampire in the way a human could. Instead, demons taken by the rogue found themselves cut off from all demonkind. Few survived such an encounter. The rogue, frustrated in his futile attempt to create a vampire family of his own in Orcus, began to kill, and did so liberally until a particularly powerful demon encircled it with the demonic equivalent of an electric fence. They'd decided to leave it there, trapped in a prison keyed to its physical body. Because the snare was magically keyed to the vampire, anything else could, theoretically, enter and exit the snare at will, but the reality was that precious few of the demons who went in ever came out. By now, most of them knew better. But, every generation had its skeptics.

For these young demons, if they were not brave and valiant facing the monster, the beast inside the snare would take their blood and eat their bones. Their worlds were not so different, then, if young demons took deadly risks to prove their valor. When the demons had drunk down their courage, Korzha followed them and with the gentlest of touches convinced his choice to leave the others.

The young male wasn't full demon; Korzha knew the instant its blood flooded him. It was part human. Only part. A suggestion of human, but the genetic cross was there. In the end, the male demon made a more satisfactory meal than the female, but still Korzha was unsated. His lingering injuries continued healing, slowly, drawing from him what little strength he'd regained after his first victim. He remained empty inside. He might have sought a third, but as he was stepping out of the cloistered square where he'd left his lovely prey stripped of all memory, he felt the unmistakable slide of night toward sunrise. On silent feet he followed the others to the snare. It was easy to follow drunken minds.

The rogue's prison turned out to be an entire area of the city, lifeless of energy and sense. He would have noticed it even if the young males had not stopped, even if Jaise had not told him where it was and what to expect. Silence rose between the demons, in high contrast with their earlier raucous braggadocio. Korzha moved closer and felt a mind inside. Insane. Beyond insane. The males, minus their part-human companion, stood at the threshold of shadow. One of them, wearing a gem-encrusted vest of yellow and purple, egged on his friends. Korzha felt the muffled pull of the vampire trapped within. The first demon, the one in the vest, stepped into the shadow. His friends waited outside. Perhaps two minutes later, the demon's upper body emerged from the darkness. He opened his mouth for what Korzha was certain was to be a taunt, but just before the sound would have come out, his body jerked back into the void.

Demons, it seemed, could be as stupidly brave as humans. The friends charged through. From the snare, Korzha felt skittering madness. He perched on the eave of the house opposite the shadow and contemplated his next action. Dawn approached, perhaps half an hour away, and he was not at full strength. Nor did he have any of the protections of Los Angeles. No sunscreen, no stimulants to keep him alert and alive through the daylight hours. To face the thing lurking in there with sunrise approaching was madness.

Korzha headed back to the palace.

The snare was not far from the portal, perhaps a mile distant. Roofs made for a convenient road above the street and provided a clear view of the palace. He slipped away and then up, clinging to walls beneath eaves and to the shadows of dormer windows, attics and garrets as he worked his way back to his cell. He felt the pull of humanity when he was scaling the wall to his room, his fingers unerringly finding the notches and seams in the wall. Unquestionably it was the draw of blood and pulse, full on, like a light switch flipped in the dark. He slid up the window and flowed into his room, his hunger surging.

It was Jaise who waited for him. The demon lifted a hand and motioned with his fingers. The room flashed once with a blue light, then settled into a persistent glow more than sufficiently bright for Korzha's eyesight. The game began immediately.

"Vampire."

"Demon."

"I've brought you a gesture of good faith." Jaise's gray eyes flashed red. "A human female."

The smell of blood coursing through a body—a human body, fully human—invaded Korzha, sharp and clear, like a blow in its intensity. The woman stood behind Jaise, out of direct sight, but Korzha quivered in hunger like a cat facing a bird in a cage. Her mind felt too disordered to be Donovan's. A pity. The truth was, since their encounter at the construction site, when he'd already been hungry and out of sorts because of the spilled blood, he'd been fantasizing about how lovely it would be to feed on her. It was a game he liked to play, imagining which human he'd most like to bite. Officer Donovan headed the list.

Jaise pulled his offering forward. The familiarity of the woman disoriented Korzha. It wasn't Officer Donovan. His disappointment in that surprised him. The woman with Jaise was shorter than Donovan by a good four inches, and blond instead of brunette. Her clothes were ragged, her hair unkempt, but the suit wasn't off-the-rack and the haircut had been skilled enough to hold its shape.

"Well," the woman said in a creaky voice—unused to speaking or strained by overuse? "If it isn't L.A.'s bad-boy vamp, Tiberiu Korzha."

"Laura," he said, aware of Jaise's intense regard. He refused to show the depth of his shock at putting a name to this captive. "Delighted to see you again."

Laura Masters was a Los Angeles City Council member. She had been missing long enough that even B-Ops couldn't control the rumors about her disap-

pearance. She wasn't popular among the city's paranormals. Once, just for show and, frankly, because he
could, Korzha had pissed off the entire vampire Primary Assembly by getting his picture taken with her at
a fund-raiser. He wouldn't have minded taking her to
bed, but that, alas, was not to be. Word on the street
was that she believed every word of every hate-filled
speech she gave. And, in point of fact, as he'd discovered, she did believe them. Worse, she represented a
growing minority in the city government. A powerful
minority, reelected by a resounding margin last year.
Vamps were the primary target of Masters's signature
bitterness, but the dogs hardly fared better. Parasites,
she called them all. Parasites who ought to be wiped
off the face of the earth. Her abhorrence of the supernatural was legendary. More than one attempt had
been made on her life or that of her longtime partner.
A rogue vampire had managed the most spectacular
failure, which meant vamps were first in line for suspi-
cion when she vanished.

Rumors about her disappearance centered on
paranormal-inspired murder. Korzha's reputation being what it was, and considering his public pursuit of
her, his name had been whispered most often in connection with the talk of her death. Since the day Masters vanished, her partner, a woman, had accused
Family Korzha of murdering her—a not-too-subtle ac-
cusation of Korzha himself. If Family Korzha hadn't
killed her, she told anyone who would listen, then
they'd sponsored the hit. Until now, Korzha hadn't
been sure it wasn't true. Though if it was, he had to
wonder why whoever was responsible hadn't hired
him. He'd have done the job right.

Very little of the woman's elegance remained. Her
blouse was a tattered mess and exposed a portion of a

swirling, interlocking blue tattoo on a pale strip of her shoulder. Her skirt had once been pink but now looked to be a shade of ash, spattered with old blood. She wore no shoes. Her feet looked red and chapped. Her physical beauty remained undiminished, but a hint of madness glittered in her eyes, and when, instinctively, hungrily—he was still so hungry—he reached for her mind—a stroke, a gentle call— madness pirouetted there, too. She drew in a breath and turned her face to his. She wasn't completely gone yet, but there was little left of the whipcord intelligence he'd grudgingly admired in Crimson City. She was a shell of that woman now.

"Feed," Jaise said.

Korzha faced Laura Masters again, breathing in. *Gladly,* he thought. *Oh, gladly.* Her blood called to him, not in a whisper but in a torrent of beating heart and heat. She smelled human, and inside he was hollow. Demon blood left him wanting, feeling worse than hungry. He needed to fill his emptiness. Korzha turned his head to Jaise, but the smell of Masters, the pulse of her heartbeat, all of her drummed in his body and through him. What it cost to look away from her nearly sent him to his knees.

Jaise crossed his arms over his chest. The light—it was impossible to tell from which direction it came— reflected off his hair. And then he added a stipulation: "Until there is no more to take, drink. Until she becomes like you, vampire."

Yes, Korzha thought. *Yes.* He trembled. He craved, yearned for, starved for everything there was before him. But with a wrench that felt like the extraction of his soul, he put away the hunger. He and Masters agreed on at least one thing: Made vamps were dangerous. "That is not advisable, Jaise."

The demon leaned against the wall and, with one finger of his hand, swung the door to the hallway closed. In the gloom, Masters blinked. Korzha could smell her fear. He could take some blood, he thought. He could have some. Just a bit. He could slake some of his thirst. Just enough to dampen his quivering need. But he fought his desire.

"She is of no use to us anymore," Jaise said. "But, I think, vampire, there is a way she could be. You can help with that."

Korzha said nothing.

"No," Masters said. She stared at Korzha. "Fucking demons." Her voice cracked. "Bastard fang."

"Humans are weak." Jaise went on as if the Councilwoman hadn't spoken. "The strongest among them lasted only a month from the time Aslet bound them. As vampire, she would be stronger than she is now. She will not die. She might be very useful. Maybe strong enough to open the portal again."

"How did you get humans into Orcus?" Korzha asked.

Jaise's smile sent a chill racing down Korzha's spine. "A rauthima summons."

"Which is?"

The demon's lip curled and his arctic gray eyes darted to his captive. "A rauthima summoning brings a demon to the Overworld against his will. He is stolen from his home, from the arms of his loved ones to service a human's desire. No matter that he is not willing. Nothing can stop it. As soon as he reaches completion, as soon as those who summoned him are done compelling him to mate, he is banished from the Overworld. But there is nothing that says he cannot bring his summoners back with him." Jaise grabbed Masters's chin and stared into her face. Flames leapt in his eyes. "They thought they could control whatever demon they called. Is that not so, human?"

"I didn't know what she was going to do," Masters moaned. "We thought it was a game. I thought it was all in fun."

"Is that so?"

"Yes."

Jaise's fingers tightened. "You were wrong, weren't you?"

"Yes." Her voice was broken.

"You could *not* control the demon you called," Jaise said. He released her, giving her a push. "Aslet is young, but he is very, very strong." He shrugged and looked at Korzha. "Aslet brought them back to Orcus with him. It is unfortunate, however"—he cocked his head toward Masters—"that humans die so easily, after they are bound by the spell that allows them to exist here."

"Vampires can also die," Korzha remarked.

"Yes, yes." The demon's mouth twitched. "But you don't die easily. You know that, Korzha. We both know that. You're fucking immortal."

"I won't make her." Korzha didn't look at Laura again. Smelling her, hearing the beat of her heart was torture.

"If you refuse," Jaise said, as if Korzha hadn't just done so, "I will have no further use for her. I will give her to my guards." Masters made a small sound. The corner of the demon's mouth curled. "She will die, yes, but I think it will take a long time. Very long."

Jaise cocked his head, staring past Korzha's shoulder until Korzha had to look. Laura Masters, he saw, gazed at Jaise, her eyes wide with horror. All the color had drained from her face. "Unpleasant," the demon said. "Painful. You see she understands. She knows what this means for her. She saw what happened to the others when they became useless. Yes, it will be a very long time before she dies."

Korzha's belly quivered. He understood Jaise better and better. He was cunning. Ruthless. Deadly. The injury outside the portal had been about many things. Jaise had known he would rise hungry, desperately hungry after healing. Chances were good he'd also known that demon blood wouldn't satisfy a vampire's hunger.

Korzha smelled Masters. Her life. Deep, rich, edged with madness. He hadn't been this hungry since the early days of his conversion, when he knew nothing, when he bumbled through his new existence with all the sophistication of a newborn lamb.

Jaise laughed. "An easy decision, vampire." He pushed away from the wall and tapped his chest over his heart. "I know your nature." His eyebrows drew together. "Why resist? I have made it easy for you, Tiberiu Korzha. Is not my gesture of good faith what you desire? You are hungry. Here is a human. Feed. All I ask is that you make her vampire. Then I will bind Aslet to you."

Korzha shook his head, "I will not make another vampire."

"No!" Laura spoke at the same time, and her voice collapsed into a sob.

Korzha looked at her, then wished he hadn't. The councilwoman's eyes were hopeless. Desperate. As desperate as he himself was. Hunger made his voice sharp. Did she think it was nothing for him to refuse in his present state? "Save your breath, Masters, I've already told him no."

She shook her head. "You heard him. I'm no good to them anymore." With a sinking heart, he understood he'd mistaken her objection. "I can't open the portal anymore. Not reliably." Her voice broke. Twice she tried to speak and couldn't. She walked within arm's reach of him and smiled a death's-head of a grimace. "I've seen what the guards do when they don't need us anymore."

Sweet Life, he could taste her now, the tang of blood and heat. "No. You'll turn rogue, Laura. This I guarantee."

"Do it," she whispered. Her eyes locked onto his, pleading. Her fingers curled around his wrist, warm and surprisingly strong. "You have to."

Korzha stretched out a hand, intending to move her away, but at the last, didn't dare touch her. His hunger was too demanding. "You don't know what you're asking."

The woman's tongue darted out, wet her lower lip. "You're a monster, Korzha," she said with a dry giggle. Her human smell filled him, made him ache. With eyes that shifted between madness and sanity, she pinned him like a moth to corkboard. She whispered, "A monster, Korzha. And you know what monsters do?"

He shook his head, though he knew quite well what she thought.

She went up on tiptoe and put her mouth by his ear. "Monsters kill." Her voice dropped again, a trembly whisper, warm against his ear. "And I want this. Now. Not later. Not like . . . that." Her eyes glittered. "Please." Laura grabbed handfuls of his coat and embraced him, whispering so softly that only he could hear. "Don't you dare convert me. I don't want to be like you. I want to die human, and I don't ever want to come back."

She wanted this. She wanted him because of what he was, because of what a vamp could do for her. And he was hungry. His fingers tightened around hers. "Laura, I can't."

"Either he'll find another way, or he'll give me to the guards. He'll do it, you know. He will. No matter what, I'm dead." She walked past him to the pallet, and he turned with her. She lay down, tugging on his wrist, stretching out her neck. "Does this make it easier?" She tugged again. "Come on, Tiber. I know just how you like it. You know you want it."

Trembling, shaking with hunger, his body followed hers. He put his hands on either side of her rib cage, but kept himself from touching her. Did she really want to die? He remembered the woman at the portal and what the guard who'd escaped into Crimson City had been doing to her. "Laura . . ."

"Don't you get it?" Masters said, looking deep into his eyes. "I'm already dead. I've been dead since he brought us here." She pulled him closer. "Tiberiu," she whispered. "You can make it so I won't even feel it happen. If you don't . . ." Her voice broke. "Oh, God, Tiberiu, if you don't. I've heard them scream, the other women. They scream for hours. Hours." Her voice broke. "Please. You have to. They're waiting for me, did you know that? They know I'm next. So, you have to do what monsters do best." She closed her eyes and turned her head. "Just don't let me come back. That's all I ask."

He knew she was right about what would happen to her if he refused. Jaise would give her to his demons and she would die a far more horrible death. No matter what he did, he was damned. Adjusting her head and neck, he found the soft hollow where her blood called to him. She didn't resist. His teeth broke her skin, and dark crimson blood flowed into him. Her body tensed, then relaxed. She tasted of life, warm and

123

tangy and salty and like the sun. As Korzha raced along the edge of his hunger, he fell into the sensual rhythm of feeding. He reached for her mind, touched and soothed. Reassured her. His lingering injuries healed, her warmth pulsing through, gushing into him. Her madness danced in his head, twirling at the borders of his own stretched sanity. Beneath him, Masters stirred, and so did his sex. Feeding was always like this for him. Insistent erection. Sensual, sexual—the act itself was a craving that demanded completion.

If he wanted sex, he could have it now. He knew she didn't like men, but Masters wasn't likely to object. To feed and have sex with a beautiful woman was a reason to continue in the world—he'd always felt that. In the back of his head, he sensed an electric shiver, a quivering probe, alien, unwanted. The demon! With a mental roar, he threw the intruder out and shut down to everything except the body beneath him that gave him life and a recollection of long ago: warm sun on his naked, mortal back.

Masters had her hands on his shoulders, her fingers hooked in the fabric of his coat, still in the reflexive clench of the initial pain. He'd admired her before, and why not? A connoisseur could admire something he knew he'd never have, and Laura Masters, who went home every night to a woman's soft curves, had disappointed more men than just him. The thrum of her heart raced through him, and his sexual response increased. He was hard as a rock, his balls tight, aching for him to plunge himself into her. He could do just that. And the little quiver of knowing he wasn't going to stop himself from draining her this time sharpened his arousal.

No, nothing could stop him from taking what he wanted. All that and more, beyond more. Her heartbeat drummed, matched his. He wanted himself free of his pants and over her, taking, tasting, drawing her life into him. Filling himself with her life and her scent and everything. Off the edge, falling, spiraling, turning. His body went taut when he came to the point where he could leave her alive. Her pulse pounded in his ears, her life whorling into him. Close. Very close. Everything. Everything except sex. There would be no sweet completion for them, because she wouldn't want it.

Her palms slid off his back.

It was over.

There was nothing more. The last whisper of her mortal life faded and cemented in blood his place among the damned. He'd not killed like this in far too long. How could he have forgotten the ecstasy of it? He had owed her the end she wanted. It was the least he could do. And now she was gone. In a blur of motion, of preternatural strength, he reached for Jaise, grabbed him by the throat. His grip was gentle, but there wasn't any doubt that if he'd wanted, the demon would be dead.

Jaise just smiled.

"I ought to kill you right now," Korzha said. He itched to tighten his fingers. The moment of hesitation cost him.

The demon chanted something in a low voice. Too sudden even for Korzha's reflexes, a bolt of energy sizzled through his body and blew him across the room. He hit the wall, reeling toward blackout, in agony as his bones broke and his internal organs burst. The healing began immediately, but it was excruciating. Jaise was chanting again, so despite the pain, Korzha moved straight up. He could see Jaise by the door, not quite sure where he'd gone. Laura Masters lay on the pallet, motionless. Eyes closed. Dead.

More fire burned through Korzha's thigh. It wasn't real fire or he'd have been seriously injured enough to put his existence in doubt. The pain was intense. Enough, he decided. More than enough of these games. Jaise needed to know with what and whom he was dealing. Korzha snarled and launched himself toward the demon. Killing Jaise with his bare hands would be a pleasure. But Jaise was speaking again. Another flash of blue fire erupted from the demon. Korzha shot upward.

He stayed on the ceiling, no longer bothering to hold back instincts suppressed since he'd left Romania. He moved fast enough that the demon lost track of him. At his speed, even at such close range, the demon's defenses amounted to too little, too late. Korzha swung his arm in a sharp arc and slashed the demon's shoulder at the same time as he plunged his mind into Jaise's. This would be a warning not to trifle with him.

Jaise's shriek of pain bounced off the walls. The demon may have infiltrated B-Ops, but the very nature of vamps and Crimson City meant he was most familiar with weaker specimens. Vamps of significant power rarely embroiled themselves with the cops or B-Ops. B-Ops thought they knew the power of all vampires, but humans had no idea what they were up against. Neither did these demons.

In the same motion that left the gaping slash on Jaise's shoulder, Korzha threw himself backward, retiring to a high corner. He laughed, a roar of adrenaline and delighted satisfaction. The door crashed open and three new demons appeared, one in monstrous form. The room shook. All around, the air shimmered and turned hot. Korzha snarled again and dropped from his high corner. One of the demons was mentally susceptible, so Korzha killed it with nothing more than fear.

Landing on the ground, he gripped the monstrous demon by the throat. The other demon he kicked in the head. It crumpled against the wall, unconscious. Six more demons crowded into the room, most in human shape, but not all. Korzha lifted the demon he held and grinned. "Call them off," he said to Jaise, "Or this one dies."

Jaise threw up a hand, and the others fell back. "All but you," he said, indicating the tallest of his minions. He stood aside to let the others leave, then gestured to the tall demon who moved unhesitatingly to examine his bleeding shoulder. Jaise looked only slightly less murderous than before. "Release him, Tiberiu Korzha," he said.

"Fuck you," Korzha replied. He opened his fingers. The demon he held fell to his knees, taking in great gulps of air. "A lesson for you, Jaise. Play nice, and chances are good I'll play nice, too. Put my back to the wall," he said, "and I'll retaliate."

"They have sworn to protect me," Jaise said. The demon at Jaise's side began to chant, sounds that had so far proven an infallible precursor to an attack. Korzha tensed. "Hold, vampire," Jaise said. The tall demon looked up, and Korzha read alarm in his eyes, smelled it in his body. "He means no harm. He is a healer."

"Take me to Officer Donovan," Korzha ordered. "Now." He watched as a soft glow came from the healer's hand; a green-tinged mist formed in the air and slowly dissipated. Jaise's wounds sealed themselves. The healer stepped back from Jaise and bowed, keeping a cautious eye on Korzha, who said, "Let's get the woman's daughter. We're going the hell back to Los Angeles. Now."

Chapter Twelve

The attack took Korzha by surprise. His head snapped back with the vicious onslaught of another being slipping inside him, taking over. His lips drew back, and a sibilant growl rolled from his throat. The skin across his back rippled. The spot where Jaise had been standing was empty, but that didn't matter; Korzha knew where the demon was, and it took everything in him to stop Jaise from taking over completely. Even so, it was a close thing. If Korzha had been at full strength, Jaise wouldn't have succeeded. But he wasn't at full strength. His body wasn't healing quickly, and the mental skirmish with Jaise had weakened him further. Possession. With Jaise indwelling, Korzha was a spectator in his own body.

An escort of four demons accompanied Korzha/Jaise through Biirkma city. One of them carried Masters's body, wrapped in a dark blanket. Yet another demon had been sent to fetch Aslet and Donovan. They all moved at a quick pace, without stopping or slowing, and every demon they met hurried to get out of the way. Jaise lifted a hand—Korzha's hand. They walked faster, practically running now. Korzha knew where Jaise was headed: the portal. The closer they got, the more he felt the pull of the snared rogue vampire. Madness. Skittering madness in the shadows.

One effect of Jaise's possession was the way in which the demon's perceptions seeped into his. He sensed the four guards in a different way than before. All four were Elismal—information that leaked to him from Jaise. Unlike Jaise, these demons were not powerful. Jaise held them in a deal of contempt. Another discovery of Korzha's was that no matter how closely Jaise had studied vamps while in B-Ops, the fact was, the demon wasn't prepared for the reality of vampire physiology. There was a very real difference between book-learning and hard experience. Indwelling wasn't the same as being. Only a vamp knew what it meant to be a vamp.

At the threshold of the portal room, before he was far enough past the door to see, Korzha felt a subtle change in the air, a disturbance of the magic, a pulsing that unsettled the demons. The demon carrying Masters's body put the corpse near the portal. They did not have to wait long for Aslet and Donovan to arrive. The humanness of her, everything about her made his senses flare. But he was an onlooker only. Jaise processed the information and interpreted for himself, leaving Korzha isolated from action.

The tow-haired demon was Elismal. Strong, like Jaise. More than a match for Jaise. He was a demon to be watched, a rival. The guards at the portal, more powerful than the four Elismal with him, came to Korzha's attention. Was it only forty-eight hours since they'd come through from L.A.? It felt like forty-eight years.

Aslet held Officer Donovan by the elbow. She wore her clothes from L.A., except they'd taken her shoes. She looked healthy enough; she stood without wavering, her back straight. Perhaps her skin was a bit pale. Her eyes were shadowed with purple, but there was no madness there, though strain showed. Korzha felt all the demons' attraction to her. The greed, the lust. He wondered how she was managing the demons and their sexual avarice.

Donovan tried to jerk free of Aslet. "Freak," she said to the white-haired demon. "Let go of me."

Aslet's hand tightened on her elbow. With her free hand she grabbed his forearm and pressed her thumb into the soft tissue there. The demon's hand popped open. Fury pulled at Aslet's mouth, but he stayed silent. The guards all flinched, one taking a step toward Donovan. For a moment Korzha thought she was about to pay for making Aslet let go.

She looked at him, met his gaze squarely. "Korzha," She said. She let out a breath, looked disappointed. "I should have known."

Jaise spoke from Korzha's body. "Prepare, Aslet."

The blond demon bowed and bent to grab the leather satchel on the floor. He took out the clothes Jaise had worn in Crimson City. The guards had cooked their dinner, and one of them was cleaning up. The others spoke amongst themselves. Jaise leaned Korzha's shoulder on the entrance door. "Sit down, Donovan," he said.

She did so. "I'm not leaving here without Holly, Korzha," she said.

Jaise's anger flashed. "You're not leaving here at all."

Aslet stripped off his clothes. Donovan, sitting with a straight line of sight to the demon, turned the color of a tomato and scooted back. Jaise had lived among humans long enough to understand their tendency for sexual repression; he took it as a sign of inferiority.

In her haste to avoid watching Aslet strip naked, Donovan bumped into Master's body. The wrapping parted, and a pale arm flopped out. She looked down and, very much to her credit, all she did was draw breath, though her skin went several shades paler. "Holy cripes," she whispered. The cop in her came out. She squatted at the body's side and twitched the blanket open. She craned her neck toward Korzha, her eyes big as quarters. "Laura Masters?"

Korzha had a sense of not quite doom, but the word sufficed for the moment.

She turned to him. The wounds on the body told a clear enough story about what had happened, but to Korzha's surprise, Claudia looked thoughtful. She took a step toward him. "Unfortunate woman, wouldn't you say, fang?"

"Not particularly," said Jaise.

Korzha's hunger flared. But Jaise didn't know what that meant, because he had no context. The demon knew human hunger, not a vampire's need.

Aslet put on Jaise's B-Ops gear: black shirt, black pants, boots. He fished out a pair of dark glasses and hooked them into the collar of his shirt. A set of car keys went into a pocket. He produced from the satchel the melted cell phone, a shoulder holster, and a gun, which he slipped into the holster. He stood by Donovan, smiling, taunting in silence. Korzha felt a pulse of energy flow from Aslet. The demon morphed. Except for the eyes, which remained blue as a boiling sky, he was Jaise, the very image of him.

"So, Aslet," Donovan said with remarkable poise. "You been passing for Jaise? Taking turns, are you?"

"When necessary," the demon agreed.

"You taking Korzha with you?" Donovan jerked her thumb in his direction and snorted. "Because if you are, man, you cannot trust him. Never, ever trust a vamp. Isn't that the B-Ops motto? You're a freak and a mole, so you would know, right?"

Aslet lifted a hand and struck her full in the face. She staggered back, but caught her balance so quickly she must have expected the attack. One of the guards leapt at her. Korzha roared, a sound that echoed off the walls. In the face of his rage, Jaise retreated, was pushed back. Korzha flew straight up. All the demons looked surprised; they knew Jaise indwelled.

While Jaise struggled to regain command of the body, Donovan reached for her comm band, abandoned here since their arrival in Orcus. In the time it took Korzha to cling to the ceiling and swing down to kick one of the guards on the point of his chin, she'd bent over Masters's body and snapped the unit onto the corpse's arm, then clapped a hand to her cheek as if in agony.

Korzha's fury at the attack on Donovan inevitably faded, and Jaise surged back, encircling Korzha's will. Enfolding him. He dropped to the floor while Aslet slung Masters's body over his shoulder.

"You're a cop," Jaise said to Donovan, Korzha's voice still resonating with rage. "What do you think the P.D. will say when they find this body looking the way it does?"

She returned his gaze coolly. "I think they'll call Internal Operations." She shrugged. "SOP when all evidence points to a vampire kill."

The demon inside Korzha grinned. "And what will happen on the street when word gets out Laura Masters was killed by a fang?"

"War," she said. "All-out war."

"Four hours," Jaise said to Aslet through Korzha's mouth. Then, to Claudia, he said, "Open the portal, Officer Donovan."

Chapter Thirteen

Claudia shuddered with the pain of holding open the portal. Korzha had a merciless grip on her arm, keeping her there while Aslet, looking eerily like Jaise, went through into Crimson City, the body of Laura Masters with her comm unit on the arm slung over his shoulder. On one side of her was the dilapidated corridor in L.A., on the other, Orcus, Korzha and her daughter. She threw back her head and screamed because she felt her body ripping apart.

Korzha pulled her back to the Orcus side of the portal. Her legs quivered under her, but she stared at the vampire, heart and body pounding from the effect of standing in the portal. She wobbled on her legs, disoriented and feeling somehow thinner, less substantial than before she went into the portal. The vampire, the traitor, had retreated from her, and now he leaned a shoulder on the doorframe surrounding the portal. "Officer Donovan," he said. Fucking Upper voice.

He still wore Armani, still looked elegant and not

the least bit human. Aslet was in L.A., passing for human and inciting a war. Korzha, the freaking vamp who'd provided the body, seemed less human than ever, paler than a normal person, with more presence than a normal person. With a wave, he dismissed all but the original portal guards.

Those guards settled against the wall. One of them picked up a cup and dice. Another of the guards threw down a coin, then the other two did likewise. Korzha pushed off the door and walked toward her. Her heart sped up. *Never trust a vamp. Never.* He settled himself on one of the rugs like he'd been doing it all his life. Claudia frowned. Definitely this was Korzha. Definitely it was the vampire, but different from the Crimson City vampire. "What happened to your hair, Korzha?" she asked.

His hair hung in curls to his shoulders. She'd have killed for hair like that. She'd also have killed for eyes like his. Big, and green like wet moss. Not long lashes, but really, really thick. Really pretty eyes. Even for a vamp.

"My appearance, Officer, is none of your affair." But he ran his fingers through his hair, she noticed. The curls tangled a bit, and when they settled around his face again he looked like he'd just come inside from a windy day. And he needed a shave, because his face held a hint of five-o'clock shadow. Just a hint. The long hair made him look younger, and the not-just-shaved jaw took away some of the cold haughtiness. It was a shame for a guy like that to have been taken out of the human gene pool.

"I thought you were one of those vamps who got all gussied up before you got made," she said. She concentrated on his chin. It was pretty typical among people who decided to convert: a flurry of dieting, working out, surgery if it was in the budget, a visit to the spa and then they'd get made.

"Evidently not." His eyes flickered oddly. "Sit, Officer." He held out a hand.

She thought about refusing, but then she'd have to spend the next four hours on her feet just to piss off the bastard. Wasn't worth the aching feet. She sat on the rug, but as far from him as she could. He stared at her. Something wasn't right, and it wasn't his appearance. She just couldn't put a finger on what it was. It bothered her. "How come your good buddy Jaise isn't here?" she asked.

Korzha smiled. "He's not so far away." Behind them, one of the guards shouted. Dice rattled again in their cup. "Why so quiet, Officer?"

"You're the errand boy, fang. I'll save my breath for Jaise."

Korzha's expression went blank, as if he could not imagine anyone speaking to him so bluntly. Too freaking bad if his feelings were hurt. His eyes flared and, with a leap of reddish light in them, Claudia felt heat sliding along her, into her. The vampire leaned toward her, his voice turned low and dark. "Aslet bound you to Orcus and the Elismal. You cannot change that until you die."

She sneered. "You're fraternizing with the enemy, Korzha. If they told you pigs could fly, would you believe them?"

"This world is in your blood. That is Orcus you feel in your head. And now me." Claudia saw fire in his eyes. The back of her head felt hot.

"Don't." She lifted her hands and tried to push him away. The pressure in her mind increased. Her head felt thick, and she couldn't tell if she was talking or just thinking.

"We need you," the vampire said. "They need us. Both." His voice fell, low and soft. "You are tied to demons, Claudia Donovan. Because of you, demons will again walk in the Overworld. Accept what you cannot change."

"No."

"What is the alternative?"

More shouts rose from the guards, groans as a roll went badly for most.

"I'm not going to talk philosophy with you, Korzha. I want Holly back. That's all the philosophy I know."

Korzha smiled, and the chill in the curve of his mouth made Claudia's heart sink like a stone to the bottom of the ocean. "In due course," he said. Something about his voice sounded funny, like it wasn't really him talking. "In due course, you will know your place among demons."

"Somehow I think I won't like it much." She felt pressure on her hip. A filament of flame coursed through her. Hot. Burning hot. Her head felt like it was on fire. The heat in her head increased, and her hip felt dipped in lava. She tried to turn her head, but couldn't. She felt like she was standing in the portal again. The thought of moving sent spasms of agony through her. Claudia heard someone scream. A roar sounded in her head. The noise deafened her. Her blood boiled, every inch of her body alight. Someone screamed again. It sounded like a woman. It sounded like her. Someone was holding her down, stopping her from moving, but there wasn't anyone touching her.

Like that, the sensation stopped. Pins and needles prickled across her skin, dying electricity after a short.

"You see?" Korzha said. Through the fog of receding pain, he sounded like Jaise. Why was that?

She opened her eyes and saw the vamp leaning over

her. His eyes didn't seem right. *He* didn't seem right. A vamp like Korzha didn't get emotional and petty. Korzha was a killer who didn't lose his cool, ever. But she'd seen him attack Aslet, clinging to the ceiling, doing things only a vamp could do. It had to be Korzha.

The vampire sat cross-legged and picked up Claudia's pack, left behind in the confusion of their first arrival in the demon world. "I would like to show you Orcus," he said. "Will you think it as beautiful as I do, I wonder?" He grabbed the top loop of the pack. "All the same," he said, "a home you cannot leave is a prison."

Claudia shook her head. "Why do you care so much about demons? From what I've seen, they weren't locked away without reason."

"Mistreat a dog, Claudia Donovan, and you should not be surprised if one day the dog bites you." He watched her with his big, green eyes, gorgeous vamp eyes that settled on her with an intensity that made her blink. "You never think to stop the human who acts on his hatred."

"You forget I'm a cop. I do that all freaking day."

He let her pack dangle on his index finger. "Humans fear vampires. You also fear werewolves, but . . . I think humans fear vampires more. Do you agree, Claudia?"

"Depends," she said. "On whether it's a full moon."

Korzha laughed. "Demons want to come to the Overworld, to live peacefully with vampires and werewolves. With humans, too. They wish not to be imprisoned. Their children have no future if demons remain imprisoned here. Surely you, of all people, understand that. Together, demons and vampires can convince humans there is no danger."

"Yeah, Korzha, sure." She let out a quick breath.

"And now, how 'bout a round of Kumbyah? Humans and demons just don't mix. Like fangs and humans don't mix. Have you seen the trouble we've had lately? It ain't gonna work and there's no point pretending it ever will."

Korzha scowled. Claudia had the impression he didn't mean it for her. "Better the Elismal than the Bak-Faru."

"Demons are demons," Claudia said. But she'd seen a Bak-Faru with her own eyes, and she wasn't so sure.

Korzha laughed, and the sound unsettled her. "Few demons can stand against a Bak-Faru. Few demons can, and no humans. But the Bak-Faru have come to Biirkma City for the first time since the portal was sealed. They have been trying for many, many years to return to the Overworld. They know. They know the portal has been breached."

"These Bak-Faru, they're not very nice, are they?"

His voice dropped to a lower register. "We must convince the Council to move on the Overworld before you become useless and die. Before the Bak-Faru learn how the portal can be opened. They will learn. The Bak-Faru do not follow the Council, and they have magic no other demon dares use." His mouth curled on one side. "Humans break promises all the time. You think nothing of not keeping your word. So, understand this about demons: *Our* promises must always be kept. Always. Help me, or instead of the Elismal the Bak-Faru will rule your world."

A chill worked its icy way along her spine. "Korzha?" Claudia whispered.

He lifted a hand. "Break your word to a demon, you will be glad to die and lucky to die quickly. Do you understand?"

"Yes."

He met her gaze, and she could have sworn she was looking at someone else. Korzha—or whatever the hell was sitting across from her—moved toward her. The lump in her throat turned to lead. He touched her chin. "She looks so much like you, Claudia. Don't you agree? All the beauty of her mother."

Claudia's world depended on every word Korzha said.

"I don't want to hurt you, Claudia Donovan. But if I must . . . You will not live much longer here. This is so. Time runs short for us all. If the Council does not move now, you will not see your world or your daughter again. And that is a promise that will be kept. I want your help. Cooperate with me, and I will let you see your daughter before you die."

Claudia realized she wasn't talking to Korzha anymore. The freaking demon was inside him. She'd been an idiot not to understand sooner. "What is if you want from me, Jaise?"

"To know if you can become vampire and still open the portal."

Chapter Fourteen

Officer Donovan stared into his eyes, and Korzha knew she was unaware of the danger she was in. She knew about Jaise and still didn't understand. The scent of her rose sharp in Korzha's nostrils, living and warm, and Jaise took in the information too, classifying the constituent pieces as a human might; ignoring what he didn't understand. An attractive woman, a vampire's sharper-than-human sense of smell, ignorance of a vampire's mental reach, ignorance of true need.

Jaise was hungry, but only that. Just hungry. Jaise's frame of reference for sensing others was limited to demons. An assessment of power and rank was natural for him, but that was all. He disregarded what did not relate to his hierarchy of power. Jaise felt Claudia's bond with demons, the bond Aslet had created, that uneasy edge of darkness, in a way Korzha never had. But the demon didn't know what to do with the unaccustomed flow of her thoughts. One thing came clear in her emotions, overwhelming everything else: anguish. Overwhelming anguish over the loss of her daughter. Physically, she hid it well. Mentally, not at all.

Korzha's hunger affected the demon, fascinated him, but Jaise didn't know what it meant. The demon found Donovan an object of extreme sexual interest and ignored Korzha's other attraction. Perhaps that was best. Korzha thought so.

He tilted his head and had the odd sensation of seeing and feeling Donovan with the demon's perceptions: attractive, a desirable partner. Jaise found her more than a little attractive. Hell, yes. Korzha did, too. She was a gorgeous woman for a beat cop in his quarter of the city. It was intriguing, too, that she had a daughter. That made her less typical than the typical Crimson City blue-hat. How many female officers in their early twenties had school-age children? Answer: None. How many teenaged mothers rose above the demands of parenthood and made their lives a success? Not many. How long had it been since a human woman had intrigued him to this extent? Eons. Centuries. Since she'd been assigned to the precinct in his neighborhood, he'd always thought she was one of the less transparent humans. In his experience, most young cops were either fanatics about power or, more frequently, they simply believed the Protect and Serve nonsense. Korzha was curious. Very curious. And so was Jaise. She would be good to mate with.

The demon laughed, a welling up of inward amusement. One thing he understood quite plainly was the duality of indwelling. Korzha struggled to understand how and in what ways Jaise controlled him. And he waited to see what his vampiric nature would do to the demon. In the background, one of the guards crowed over a dice win; the others protested.

Korzha studied Donovan. Both he and Jaise did. Her

eyes were brown. Plain brown. A dark, deep color, not pale like demon eyes. This difference in pigment saturation between human and demon aroused Jaise. He found her eyes compelling, arousingly different. She swallowed hard. Pretty eyes, he thought. Different eyes. Human eyes. Human emotion. There was no aura of rank and power to sense. To a demon male, a human woman was exotic in her complete lack of demonic energy. There could be no question of his dominance, because a human had no power to oppose his.

She had a pretty face, a lovely face and a prettier body. Her legs were long and sleek, just as he preferred. Korzha did like females with long legs. He'd like to see her in high heels and a dress. Something expensive. Something to cling to all her curves. He'd show her off in Strata +1. A human trophy in witness of his power.

Among male vamps, most typically among the warrior class, a woman like this lent cachet to one's reputation. Walk into a Strata +1 party with a beautiful, intelligent human female on your arm, and every male vamp in the room knew you walked a wicked edge and wished he had the balls to do the same. A few of the women ended up made, which wasn't always unmitigated disaster unless she went rogue. Even the uptight vamps of Family Dumont understood the lure of humans and the edge of bloodlust. Sometimes a human got converted. It happened.

What most appealed to him was that she wasn't ten pounds underweight like so many women who aspired to beauty. Jaise's desire surged, a bubbling up of demonic sexual impulses; a desire to mate with this dark-eyed human female. Under the circumstances, sex with Donovan was almost certainly unavoidable.

"I'm sorry," Korzha managed to say. His voice was

soft and regretful. She gave a restricted shake of her head.

Korzha didn't doubt that if Jaise wanted Donovan dead, he could permanently end her life in a hundred different ways. But what Jaise really wanted was what he hadn't gotten with Laura Masters. The problem was, the demon had just realized he didn't know how to convert a human. For that, he would need to cede some control to Korzha, leaving them at an impasse of sorts. Inside Korzha's head, the demon laughed, and his amusement was clear in Korzha's voice. "Converting you is a rather neat solution to the problem of human fragility. Wouldn't you say?"

Donovan's eyes opened wide, the irises like bittersweet chocolate. *Jesu*, but he'd like to be looking into those eyes while he caressed her, touched her, bit her deep and hard, brought her under his mastery. He caught himself. That was Jaise. Pulling his strings, taking the thread of his body's sexual attraction and using it, twisting it, amplifying it.

Korzha laughed crazily, overwhelmed, and along the peaks and valleys of the sound he felt Jaise's delight. They both wanted her. He was surprised to sense that in L.A., Donovan had turned the demon down quite firmly. Good judgment, he thought. A woman of discernment. She was much prettier than he'd thought the first time he saw her in the precinct, and he'd taken a second look then. Sex with a human came fraught with complications, and despite his appearances in the society pages, he'd avoided such complications for some time. Mostly. Now and again he indulged. He wished he'd thought to indulge with Donovan. She would have been worth the risk.

"What's going to happen?" she asked.

He stroked her temple with the tip of a forefinger

and pressed the pad of his finger on the pulse point. A conundrum of irony. Jaise needed to give over some control to Korzha if he was going to force him to convert Donovan. Korzha didn't want Jaise to understand how a conversion was done, but he needed to feed in order to regain his strength and force the demon out.

Korzha stepped close, practically touching her while Jaise raged inside him, impatient, aroused. The demon wanted Donovan converted, but he wanted sex, too. Sex with a human female. Sex with Donovan, whose earlier refusals still rankled. He wanted sex with a female with dark eyes and a tender body. The hell of it was that so did Korzha, separate and apart from Jaise. Separate from his urgent hunger, Korzha wanted her, and it was a strange feeling for him to resist something he wanted. He could plunge his teeth into her now. Right now. Take everything from her. Every hope she had for her human life. *"I won't convert her,"* he managed to say through gritted teeth.

"She will die if you don't," Jaise responded.

Donovan's eyebrows drew together. "Korzha?" she asked

He shook his head, and Jaise made him pay for that: A flash of heat seared through his body from the inside out.

Donovan grabbed his arm. "You okay?"

"I . . . won't."

"Why not just do what he wants?" she asked. She seemed surprised, and that pissed him off. Did she think him without scruples of any kind? "What difference does it make to you?"

Fighting Jaise with all his strength, he said, "A lion in a zoo no longer hunts. There's no need. In the wild, he must hunt or he dies. Crimson City is one huge zoo, and the lions who live there are practically tame."

"What are you talking about?"

"You're human, Donovan." He put his hands on her shoulders, and her humanness seeped into him, flowed into both him and Jaise. The demon wanted to bite. To fuck. To satisfy the demand of his cock. "You live with vampires and you don't understand the first thing about us." Korzha said. "You've never seen what we real vamps do. You think we're like lions at the zoo." He looked away and then back. His body quivered. His hand went to her cheek, and the demon's senses were concentrating on her: the softness of her skin, her curves, her lush, dark eyes. The demon lusted after this body, this woman. So did the vampire.

"He promised," Donovan said.

"What if he's lying?"

"Demons can't lie. Can they?"

"Who told you that? Of course they can lie."

"Are you lying now?"

Jaise howled. He wanted Donovan—now, this moment. Korzha quivered with a double anticipation, Jaise's and his own. The demon urged him forward, and Korzha wasn't exactly resistant. He slid an arm around Claudia Donovan's waist. She tensed, but with a hitch of breath moved toward him. Emotions in conflict came at him like a flood. Fear. Trepidation. Determination. His own contradictory feelings swirled in the mix. Arousal. Reluctance. The impulse to feed. The need. The pull of her warmth, the blood beneath her skin. He drew her closer, and she stepped into the curve of his arms.

He grabbed her hand and kissed her palm. She tried to pull back, but he didn't let go. She gazed at him from beneath her lashes. His tongue traced a swirl on her palm, then moved downward to her wrist. Eyes closed now, he pressed his mouth to the inner surface of her wrist. A normal kiss. For now. Jaise amplified the sensation for him.

"Korzha?" she whispered. He lifted his head and looked into her chocolate eyes. Her teeth pressed into her lower lip when, with Jaise's impulses, he loosened the belt at her waist.

"I'm sorry," he said again.

"It's all right. I know it isn't you." She drew a breath. "Let's just get this over with, okay?"

His arm tightened around her, and she flinched. "Will it hurt?" Her brown eyes fixed on him. Did she have to look so trusting? His control slipped a little further.

"Claudia," he said softly. "No. I won't let him hurt you." Maybe he should forget his scruples and give everyone what they wanted. Whatever sick game Jaise wanted to play, the truth was that feeding from Donovan would be inevitable and natural. The fact was, vampires fed from humans, and Korzha was hungry. If he was going to best Jaise, he needed to feed. What choice, really, did any of them have? He heard the policewoman's heart beating in her chest when he kissed her wrist again, maybe a little harder than a normal kiss.

"Mm," he said, low and growly, and it was mostly him.

Jaise had relented. Backed away. Was present, participating, was in control but not controlling.

"What the hell are you doing?"

Korzha's teeth slid into her wrist. She gasped, but he held her tight against the reflexive recoil. The moment absorbed him completely. In this moment there existed only the sensation of his mouth, the brush of his tongue against her wrist, the salty taste of human skin. Blood. The sweep of her lashes against her cheeks, the heat of her skin beneath his fingers. He wanted her desperately. His cock ached with longing, his belly quivered. Her pulse beat in his ears. Her blood flowed into his body, and he healed. Strength returned—not in a rush, because he'd started at the relatively blood-poor wrist, but an inexorable remediation nonetheless.

His fingers remained around her arm when he lifted his head. He left his eyes closed, too, but when he did open them, he smiled and licked the tip of his fang. He felt more himself with every second that passed. Donovan stared at her wrist, at the two still-bleeding punctures in her skin. He could feel her trembling and savored the reaction. "Holy shit," she whispered.

Strength and health came back. Still holding her, he watched her face, and damn if he didn't decide her eyes weren't plain brown at all. Chocolate eyes, they were dark in her face, bright in the whites of her eyes. Such lovely, alien, other eyes. He grabbed her head, holding her so she had to look at him.

Her eyes widened, and Korzha saw understanding dawn. He would have laughed if it weren't so fucking pitiful. "You don't want this any more than I do. Do you?" she asked.

"No. I don't." She was beautiful, beautiful, *so* beautiful, and she did not deserve this. She thought he was going to make her. He was going to betray her. He spread his fingers and traced the curve beneath her eyes, and wished like hell the circumstances were anything but these. While Jaise raged at his dawdling, Korzha said, "*Be patient.*"

"There's got to be something we can do," Claudia said.

He needed enough blood from her to heal. Enough to give him the resources to evict Jaise. Hell. He tested his physical state. He was stronger now, but not enough. He might . . . might . . . He pushed Jaise back. He got himself into the forefront. But only barely. Possibly not for long. He didn't understand enough about an indwelling demon to be sure that was enough. He did know that Jaise was still in control.

Quiet did not mean weak. The demon was still in charge. Korzha tilted Donovan's head upward. With the sides of his thumbs, he smoothed the line of her cheeks. She shivered, a delicate tremor. He imagined holding her, caressing, stroking while she quivered like that, nude of course, completely nude, while he tasted long and deep. "Let me in, Officer," he whispered. The words thrummed in his ears, in his head. "Let me into your divine self."

With a quick step forward, he closed all distance between them and slid his fingers upward over her body, then down her back.

"Can *he* see?" she asked.

"Yes. And he thinks the same thing I do."

"Oh. Yeah?" Her bravado was so touchingly human.

"Yes. He thinks you are beautiful and he's right." His hand skimmed the underside of her breast through her uniform shirt. "He wants you very much." He bent his head and flicked his tongue across the pulse at the juncture of her neck and shoulder, the hollow there, below the veins and arteries. He felt her reaction all the way down to his toes, and with that, he felt his own anticipation of sating himself at her throat. "He's eager for you." There was no point in mentioning that so was he. She swallowed, and he watched the play of skin along her throat. "Intoxicating," he whispered. Wasn't that the truth? He whispered again, but he wasn't talking to her this time, but to Jaise, who wanted to spoil everything with precipitous curiosity.

"Be patient. She'll agree to whatever we want."

Korzha slipped his hand past the waistband of her pants. Heat from her body warmed his palms.

"Korzha," she said. Her cheeks were flushed. "The guards? We're not alone."

"This is a night of apologies for me. I'm sorry," he murmured. At least he could keep her back to the portal guards. He didn't yet have the strength to keep Jaise from objecting, but he ignored the demon's complaints. "Oh, man, oh, man. I can see fire in your eyes. He's really in there." She tried to back away, but with a growl that wasn't him at all, he moved forward and slipped an arm around her waist.

"Officer Donovan," he said. In his head, Jaise demanded he lay her back and thrust into her now. Right now. He resisted the demon's impulse. The connection between them narrowed and gained focus. He loved this, the fey closeness with a human woman, warm and soft in his arms. He loved their confusion about whether he was speaking out loud or just sending the words straight into their heads. And at the borders of his mind, Jaise's arousal twinned with his. The demon wasn't thinking about much except sex.

Korzha trailed a hand upward, along her belly, pausing at her navel. He felt a tripling of minds now: his, Jaise's and hers. She felt his desire for her, and behind that a flicker of something else. Someone else. Because of the mental connection, she felt Jaise, too. The fear in her grew, but she tamped it down, and, with Jaise less resistant to restraint, Korzha reached for her mind, taking himself deeper into her head, soothing, distracting her.

"Fuck you, Jaise," she said.

He drew away, just a bit, and settled his mouth by her ear, nuzzling, breathing in the scent so close to the surface of her skin. He kissed her throat once, just once. The pad of his finger slipped over the dampness his mouth left behind. He drew her earlobe into his mouth. Her body tensed, a surge of fear because she'd caught the sharp blade of his anticipation and the demon's. He held her head to prevent the instinctive jerk back when he used the side of his canine to prick her skin. He licked away the welling blood. Hunger raged up, a lion's roar, the beast coming to life. Her blood had a delicious tang, and a faint taste of something unique. Darkness? Jaise quivered in Korzha's head, curious, eager, impatient.

"You'll spoil everything, Jaise," Korzha hissed.

He balanced at the abyss of capitulation, to Jaise's impulse to lay her down and drive his cock into her. Korzha's command over her thoughts and reactions was nearly complete, and he was absolutely merciless in intensifying her sensations. He wished like hell he'd moved on her in L.A., because she would have been worth breaking taboo. She was worth a world of trouble. He fit one palm behind her neck, bringing her toward him, tasting her. At the very edge of his conscious control, he said, and he must have said it in her head, "Now. Yes. Now."

Then he laughed, and it was a bizarre, crazy sort of laugh that sounded more like Jaise than him.

"I don't think so," she said. And then the heel of her hand came up, his hand still wrapped around hers. She struck hard at the underside of his nose, driving her hand upward. He felt bones break, shattering inward. And then he didn't feel anything, because that's what happens in a mortal death.

Chapter Fifteen

"So, what happened?"

Tiberiu Korzha stood by the window, leaning against the sill in a suit that would probably cost Claudia four months of her salary. One deep brown ringlet of hair curled around his ear, and he looked like himself. Just a vampire and nothing else except really, really good.

"You mean after I killed you?" she asked. They were back at Biirkma Palace under something she supposed was the demonic equivalent of house arrest. Who knew demons didn't react well to being trapped inside someone when they died? Jaise was decidedly not himself when he finally dis-possessed Korzha. And then, when Korzha came back to life sometime afterward, the vampire lit into the demon with a ferocity that scared the hell out of her, even as she admired the sheer dominance of his attack. He'd been pretty freaking pissed off. She wanted to make sure he wasn't still pissed off.

"Yes," he said a bit too calmly. "After you killed

me." If the vamp was angry, he didn't show it. He *looked* perfectly calm. But considering she'd just recently offed him, she didn't think it wise to conclude his expression matched his mood. "After you killed me and before I rose, what happened?"

Well, how about that? He sounded concerned for her. If so, that was unexpectedly sweet. But she still didn't trust him. "One of the other demons had a knife, so I got my hands on that. And after that they were too afraid to do anything."

"It was four against one, Officer. Why would they be afraid of a human with a knife?"

"I kind of told them I'd make sure you stayed dead if they tried anything." She smiled tentatively. "I think they were afraid Jaise would die, too."

"Believe me, that I recall." He smiled. Sort of, and he still managed to take her breath. "A vampire does not easily forget when a beautiful woman threatens to take his heart."

"You heard that?"

"I felt the damn knife in my ribs."

"I wouldn't have. Not unless I had to." She shook her head and risked a another small grin. "Sorry, but I don't sleep with possessed vampires, fang—and things sure looked headed in that direction." His eyes lit with a wicked light that reminded her she had two puncture marks on her wrist. He'd bitten her, taken her blood.

"But you would with one who is not?" At that she rolled her eyes. Would she?

"Hell, no," she said. One thing she knew for sure, Tiberiu Korzha was a hell of a bigger temptation than Matthew Jaise had ever been.

"Claudia," he said, suddenly serious. "I would not have allowed Jaise to have sex with you. Never."

"You're a vamp. How am I supposed to know what you will or won't do?"

The vamp gave her a low bow, and way he moved, all uptight and mocking, made Claudia feel like complete shit. "Thank you for such a creative solution to the problem."

"You're very welcome, Tiber." She tried to imitate the airport intercom voice, with only limited success. "If you liked that, you'll be thrilled to know I have another creative solution to run past you."

"Does it involve my death?"

She grinned at him. He smiled back, and her heart skipped a beat. Maybe two beats. "Nope."

Korzha tilted his head. "Most human women wouldn't have thought to temporarily neutralize a vampire by killing him."

"Oh. Well. You know. I was desperate."

"Or would have been able to do so," he added. He touched his nose. "You pack a hell of a punch."

"You were distracted."

He looked at her with almost no change of expression. "To put it mildly."

"Also, awhile back I downloaded the Army Field Manual on combat training. Good supplement to my martial arts." She did two half-hearted karate chops. The Jet Li imitation felt lame, and now Korzha wasn't smiling anymore. Maybe he *was* pissed off. "So, wanna hear my plan?"

Instead of answering her, he ran both hands through his hair, then shook his head to keep the front curls from falling into his eyes. He did that one more time, and she felt the urge to look right into those green eyes and dare doing whatever he asked. She dug into her pants pocket and pulled out a battered scrunchie. "If your hair bugs you that much, take this. It's green," she said, tossing it to him. "Matches those killer eyes."

He caught the scrunchie midair and closed his fist around it. "Thank you." He gathered his curls into a ponytail. Voila. Instant bohemian. He looked better than she'd ever seen him. "What is it? This wonderful plan of yours?"

"You don't have to die, you just have to *make* me."

Korzha stared at her, and Claudia saw refusal in the set of his mouth. "No, I don't have to make you," he said. "More to the point, I won't."

"I can't get Holly back if you don't." She took a step toward him. Even from a distance of several feet, his eyes mesmerized her. He didn't move, but he looked tormented. She didn't think he intended the effect. He raked his fingers through his hair, and she got distracted. The weird thing was, he felt closer than he was. They stood at least six, maybe seven or eight feet apart. But he felt closer. A whole lot closer. She stared into his gorgeous eyes and wondered whether, if she could read his mind, she'd want to. "With luck it won't be necessary, but we need to be prepared just in case. *You* need to be prepared."

"No."

With eyes like his, with her having this dysfunction of her sense of personal space, looking at him just wasn't safe. She looked anyway. He didn't say anything, and something about his expression sent her heart plunging. It was the kind of feeling that cops on a scene sometimes got right before they opened a door. "Why not? Everybody knows that for the right price you'd make the Pope."

He sneered. "I have standards, Donovan."

"I used to have those, too," she retorted. "Knowing

what's right and what's not, those lines you just don't cross. You know?" She swallowed hard. "But you don't. There isn't any line *you* won't cross. I mean, you cross them all the time. Biting people and all that. Being a killer."

"Believe what you will." His eyes shuttered and Claudia felt like a complete jerk.

"Since they took Holly—" She licked her lips. "I don't want to outlive my daughter. No parent should outlive her children." She let out a breath. She'd forgotten about the fact that she was dying here, slowly but surely. "Well, I guess I won't."

"She's half-demon, Donovan. It's quite likely your daughter will live long past her generational cohorts. And besides"—he gave her a sad look—"let a few hundred years go by, and you'll hardly remember your children."

She let her hands dangle at her sides. "Like you know anything about that."

She blinked, and the vampire was next to her. He was right in her face, standing there with one arm on the wall above her shoulder. Her heart nearly jumped out of her chest. "Holy— Give me a heart attack, why don't you?"

The vampire leaned close. His shirt whisked against the inside of his coat. White canines showed between his lips. "Converting a human is against the law. You know that. If you wanted to get made you shouldn't have killed me at the portal."

"You weren't going to make me." She wondered which held her tighter, his gorgeous voice or his seductive eyes.

"It was a hell of a lot more likely then than it is now."

"Look, all we have to do is tell the Council that you

will. You might not even have to. Forget Jaise, Korzha. If we do this my way, you don't need him. We make our deal directly with the Council. We agree to convert me into a vamp who can open the portal for them without all that inconvenient dying, and in return, I don't die, *and* I get Holly back. Wait, it gets better, I swear. This is the best part, fang. You get a sanctioned alliance with the demons, and with me in control of the portal, the only ones who make it into Crimson City are the ones under your direct command."

Korzha was quiet for a very long time. "You are one hell of a woman, Donovan." His face went completely and deadly still. But his eyes glittered. "A very long time ago, I won my independence. I will not now tolerate being manipulated. Not even by you. I will *not* make another vampire."

"Why not? Vamps like you go around biting people all the time." She put her hands on his face. A slight roughness on his cheeks, but cool skin. "Despite the laws, vamps bite people all the time. Here I am telling you no limits. No stopping point. I'm not going to file a complaint afterward. What's the problem? You get performance anxiety or something?"

His teeth flashed. "I resent being treated like an animal. A performing bear."

"I don't mean it like that."

"Yes, you do."

"I've read your file, Korzha. You hit the society pages about as often as you end up on the blotter. You got caught fang-deep in Senator Baker's daughter. Salvatore Giamani testified you hit his Persian connection and had a drink afterward. How come I fall below your standard?"

"*She* was biting *me*, Officer, and there were seven witnesses who directly contradicted Giamani."

"Where there's smoke there's fire, fang. You're a bad man."

"No."

"They want to keep my daughter here, the demons do. She'll grow up without me, Korzha. I'm her mother. I don't want to leave her. She's only ten." She swallowed the lump in her throat. "Who else is going to love her no matter what?"

Korzha closed his eyes and whispered, *"Draga inama."*

Her breath caught and rattled on the way out. Her chest felt tight, like there wasn't enough room for her lungs to expand. She felt the force of his thoughts around her, calling to her. "Stop that," she whispered. "Stop it."

"Why, when you won't stop torturing me?"

"Don't you get it, Korzha? I'm going to die like all the others Aslet has made open the portal. If you think I'm going to leave Holly here at the mercy of these freaks, you're crazy. And if you don't help me, I'll make my own damn deal and you can stay here and rot for all I care."

He had only one hand on the wall now. The other swung free. He leaned in closer, pressing her against the wall. His clothes rustled, but she didn't hear any breath coming from him. "You have no idea what you're asking."

"I bet you say that to all the girls."

"My little vampire-hater." He put a cool palm to her cheek. "Making a vampire isn't just a matter of a bite or two. I'll feed from you until you're weak and can't resist even if you want to. Except you'll want me. You'll want what only I can give you. I'll put my cock, hard and warm with your blood, inside you and make you dizzy with pleasure. And when there's biting? When I feed, too? It feels good for humans, having sex with a vampire who knows what he's doing. I assure you, I know what I'm doing."

"What the hell difference does it make what it feels like, Korzha?" She threw back her head and stared at the ceiling. It wasn't safe to look at him. His eyes weren't safe for her at all. "Give me a hundred orgasms, and I still only want my daughter back."

"Enough to become a monster like me?"

She didn't even hesitate. She whipped her head back to look at him. "You're not a monster. But if it made me one, I'd still do it."

The vampire moved, stepping in front of her to capture her chin between his forefinger and thumb. His voice sent a shiver through her. "Here in Orcus, the civility—if that's what we want to call it—of Crimson City is gone. It's back to the old ways. Tradition, dear heart." He touched the pulse of her throat, pressing gently. "All the ancient lusts and perversions denied us at home are permitted here. Here you're just meat. A meal."

She looked at him, and wondered why she didn't feel threatened when, plainly, that's what he'd meant to do. "Crimson City's no safer."

"Here, I can take you if I want you."

She was breathless. "Then do it."

"Maybe I will." He brought his mouth close to hers. In her head she felt a tiny pulse, a touch. His eyes fluttered closed. At the last minute he pushed up her chin and dipped his head to her throat. Claudia's breath froze in her chest. The vampire didn't so much insert himself in her thoughts as take control of her heart, replacing the sliver of fear she felt with desire, with a longing to be held by him, with a longing to surrender. His lips touched her throat. His tongue touched, lingered. *Come to me*, he said, *ravishing Claudia*.

She twisted her body toward him, but he let her go. Electricity crackled between them even so. She could feel the pull. Jeez, his eyes were brutally green. Devour-me green. "I'm not an idiot," she said. "I know I have two, maybe three weeks left before I die. I know this place is killing me."

Korzha nodded.

"I don't think anything pleasant happens to humans who can't open the portal anymore, and I don't want to be near a demon when that happens to me." Claudia felt his mental presence in her head. He wasn't trying to touch her thoughts, not deliberately, she realized; she just felt his intense interest. She bit her lower lip. "You don't fool me, Korzha. You're not a monster. I know you killed Masters. Who else would leave fang marks like that? But you didn't do her just because you felt like it. I'm asking you, Tiberiu, begging you." She swiped at her face and felt tears. "If I had a choice, I'd tell you to keep your fucking fangs to yourself. But there isn't one. Not for me."

Korzha was silent. Claudia waited.

"What a monumental joke this might turn out to be," he said at last.

"Not to me."

He chewed on his lower lip. A pinpoint of crimson appeared and vanished. "If you're looking to be a vampire for other reasons . . . It won't make you any happier. It won't make you belong—"

"Don't you get it? I'm not looking to belong."

"Are you sure?" he asked.

"This is about my daughter and nothing else."

He put a hand on the wall, back above her shoulder. "There are always other choices," he said.

"Like what?" She started to cry in earnest. "There aren't any choices for me. I don't have time."

"Sometimes death is better."

Claudia freaked out. "Fuck you, Korzha. I don't give a shit what happens to me." She grabbed his coat. "It's Holly who has to get out of here. I'm not letting her grow up with freaks like these. God, they think she's one of them, but she's not. She's mine. My daughter, and that makes her human."

"If you don't adjust, you'll go rogue. You're a cop. You know what that means. You've seen it."

"I only care about what I have to do right now to get Holly home." She let him go. "Nothing else."

"If I make you," he said, "chances are you'll go rogue. You'll become dangerous and bitter. You'll be a risk to everyone in Orcus or in Crimson City. You'll be a danger even to your daughter. It has happened in the past. It happens nine times out of ten when someone converts for the wrong reasons. You'll be no better than an animal, a killer."

"You didn't turn rogue. I won't either. I promise."

"Oh, dear-heart. You cannot know." He kissed her forehead, a touch of shocking tenderness. "I was made against my will, and I very nearly did not survive what I became."

"You're okay now."

"I was made a very long time ago. You've seen what happens to a vampire who can't embrace what he has become."

"You promised you'd help me get her back. You gave me your word of honor. Well, this is the only way I can see you keeping that promise."

With his lips above her skin, leaning against her hard, pinning her to the wall, he said, "Madness."

"Please. Please, you have to. I think it's the only way we're going to get out of here."

The sheer quietness of his body reminded her he wasn't human. When it came right down to it, Korzha had more in common with demons than he did with her, even if she had sensed odd moments of unexpected kindness. "On one condition," he finally said. Her heart about flew out of her chest.

"Anything."

"If you go rogue, I'll hunt you down and kill you. And that's a promise I will not fail to keep." He stared into her eyes.

"Deal."

The vampire put his hand on her throat, sorrow emanating from him. "At least you will not live to regret your choice for long."

Chapter Sixteen

Korzha rested a hand against the small of Claudia Donovan's back. She glanced at him, but didn't shudder at the contact, and that was something. He didn't want her to cringe from his touch. Especially not when, before much longer, he'd be making his first vampire in a new century. Donovan's plan was risky—any plan involving demons was risky—but he recognized her desperation and respected her self-sacrifice. It was something he himself would never do.

Their timing was good. Jaise was before the Council now, seeking approval for his plan to establish a permanent demon presence in L.A.—and without him! This was yet more evidence of Jaise's lack of honor. Korzha and Claudia managed to wangle their way into the Council Chamber and request permission to address Jaise and the demon councilors. Korzha let himself relax, not touching Donovan's mind but absorbing the essence of her all the same. She smelled of fear, trepidation, but most of all, determination. Considering how little he'd actually fed from her, the strength of his mental connection to her surprised him. Not only could he feel her emotional state; he sensed as well the bond the demons had created with her—like a dark thread twining through her human nature.

The chamberlain sneered at them, but no matter his feelings on the subject of non-demons, he led them into the Council Chamber.

If he did make Claudia, and she turned rogue—something Korzha believed was more likely than not—he intended to see to her eventual merciful death. Perhaps a shot of UV, if he could get his hands on some. He'd sit vigil for her, waiting for her to rise, because he didn't want her to face the reality of a transformation she didn't embrace. Not alone and not ever. For a time, she would be his. Fully his. He would be her master even when and if she turned rogue.

A vampire was by nature a killer, no matter how often the Primary Assembly claimed otherwise. What natural killer didn't anticipate the very thing that defined him? Blood and that sweet, final echo of a heartbeat. What a pity if she had to be destroyed afterward. Under the right circumstances, she might be able to make the adjustment. Conversion didn't have to be violent, as it had been for him. He could make her loss of humanity a slow, sensual descent into darkness. She wouldn't even know it was happening. He could sate himself on her blood, enjoy her body, embrace the fragility of her mortal life until he took it all within himself. Oh, indeed. He'd bring her home, and convert her in the luxury and privacy of his home. He could take all night to make her. In his belly, he felt a quiver of anticipation at the thought; a heroin addict looking forward to a long-delayed fix.

The chamberlain paused at a high, narrow door. Korzha and Donovan stood at the threshold of a great hall straight from the Middle Ages. Vaulted ceilings, massive walls, stone floors. Narrow, deep windows, pointed at the top. Tapestries covered the walls, brilliantly woven scenes of demons hunting, dancing, dining, sitting in council. The air in the chamber hall crackled with tension, a feeling he remembered from his last days of mortal life. No ordinary meeting, this. Political lives were at stake. The four demons who made up the Council sat on a dais at the end of the hall. The tapestry behind the Council depicted a human king kneeling before a Demon Council, about to offer his crown. From the Council members, Korzha sensed caution as he and Claudia entered the hall. He was getting better and better at reading demons and better yet at cloaking himself from them. If he had to, he could probably cloak Donovan, too. At least for a short time.

He let his senses expand. The demons were agitated, in part because of Donovan. A human felt so different from their usual experience, she unsettled them a good deal. More, she represented at one and the same time the enemy who had imprisoned them in Orcus and the savior who might break them free. As for him, they didn't know what to make of him. Certainly he did not upset the demons the way Donovan did. Yet another presence charged the room, too: a vivid darkness, a chthonic pulsing energy. Most of the demons, Korzha realized, were far from calm. The darkness made them edgy, ill at ease. He turned his head, marking the exits. Every one of them was guarded or blocked. Up, then. If disaster struck, he would go upward to safety.

From the dais at the far end of the room, a female demon with gray hair beckoned them forward. To one side of the Council, a stout demon sat at a low table, bent over a sheet of paper, a black stylus in his left hand. To his right sat a squat black bottle.

With his fingertips light against Donovan's back, Korzha walked her into the Council hall. He made no effort to mask himself. Better the demons not know he could mask his presence from them. A few probed at him, and he let them touch enough to satisfy their curiosity before he turned them away. It didn't matter. Donovan interested them far more. As more and more demons took note of her, their level of sexual interest rose. Dark energy gathered like lightning captured in a jar.

Behind the dais and along the perimeter walls, guards stood, legs spread, arms crossed, faces blank. Each wore a sword at his hip, ceremonial no doubt, though he noted that more than one guard had the centered balance of a warrior. He'd be foolish to think they didn't know how to wield a sword, not with those wary eyes that scanned and assessed. These were soldiers, of this he had no doubt.

One of the Council members gestured to them to come closer. Korzha left his hand in the small of Donovan's back, as if he were her escort showing her off at a fancy ball. The notion made him wonder what she'd look like in a dress. Damn good, he thought.

He and Donovan stopped before the dais, between two groups of demons who sat on rugs spread out for some ten feet around. A third demon knelt on bare stone, head bowed, separate from the two groups. To the left, Jaise and Aslet sat at the head of perhaps ten demons. Supplicants. From Aslet, Korzha felt discontent. The pale-haired demon sat straight, hands clenched at his sides, in contrast to Jaise, who sat cross-legged and radiated mere caution. The demons to the right were something else again. From them emanated the darkness that permeated the chamber and had the others as jumpy as dogs in a room full of fangs.

A mere seven demons, and a squadron of demon guards was on edge? All seven were formidable and as tall or taller than Korzha himself. They were barechested and sleek-muscled, and knelt with backs straight, hands on their thighs. Thin braids that began at their temples and tied at their napes fastened their waist-length hair away from their faces. Each had a narrow strip of metallic thread plaited in one of the braids. One of them, the most physically striking of the seven, had black hair and lilac eyes, and he watched Donovan like she was the only woman left in the world. He radiated desire like heat from an oven. The demon wanted Donovan so fiercely it was a wonder he didn't go up in flames. Hell, it was a wonder the whole damn room didn't. Even Donovan herself felt it. The flush of blood to the surface of her skin roused Korzha's hunger, but nothing he couldn't control.

Korzha and she took their places between the two groups of demons, and slightly behind the one sitting alone. She sat to Korzha's right, away from Jaise, deliberately sitting so the Elismal demon could not really see her. A flutter of reaction went through the room. Demons shifted, stared, twitched, and a few made low sounds, purrs of anticipation. If any demons needed to be convinced of the necessity of opening the portal, the effect Donovan had on them put that to rest. As vampires were creatures of blood and the night, so demons were creatures of heat and emotion; they thrived in the presence of humans.

At the dais, the gray-haired female lifted a hand. All

conversation in the room ceased. She had yellow eyes, the color of faded citrines. "Continue, *en*-Aslet. We listen," she said.

"*Nin*-Siath," Aslet replied, bowing low, hand clenched over a fist. "We should go to the Kiverian." He raised his voice. "The Kiverian remember how to fight. The Setonian, too. And the Nitah. We should not waste time with Overworld alliances. We should act as one. When Overworlders sealed the portal, they showed us no mercy; we owe them none in return."

"*En*-Aslet speaks wisely," said the demon on Siath's right.

Siath lifted a hand. "Calmness, *en*-Tanith. Calmness." She directed her attention to the lone demon. He lifted his head and made the fist-clasp obeisance. "Success?" Siath asked, leaning forward with fire in her yellow eyes.

"*Nin*-Siath, esteemed Council, we have not yet found the amulet. But—"

"If you do not have the amulet, then you have failed," Siath said sharply.

"*Nin*. We will find it. We—"

Tanith leaned toward the other demon, who trembled in his kneeling position. "Time grows short, and you have not yet kept your promise."

"Amulet or not, we must act," Siath said. "To delay courts disaster." Her attention returned to Aslet. "Why not seek both?" she asked. "Fight and negotiate." Her eyes flicked between Donovan and the demons before the Council. The long-haired demons put their heads close together and began an urgent discussion. Jaise and his faction did the same.

One of those on the dais nodded to the guard nearest the dais. "General?" he asked.

The general dipped his head in a bow, then stood,

arms crossed over his chest. "Council, I hear you. If the portal is opened," he said, raising his voice to instant silence. He glanced at the long-haired demons. "*If* the Bak-Faru join us and *if* the portal is open, two months."

Jaise bowed his head and was acknowledged. "All demons respect the Bak-Faru, but long ago they refused the authority of this Council. They have always acted for their interests first. The Council should not open negotiations with the Bak-Faru. It is not necessary. The Elismal will open the portal. With an alliance with vampires, and soon with werewolves, the Overworld is ours again." He bowed to the dais. "We will fight when and if necessary." The noise level rose.

"When we find the amulet—," the lone demon said.

Siath's raised hand cut off the interruption. "Address the Council when you have come to tell us the amulet has been found. Until then, we do not hear you."

"Overworlders cannot be trusted," Aslet said. "We must fight. We must crush them. Humans, vampires, werewolves—we must crush them all."

"You underestimate them," Jaise said in a voice like the edge of a blade. "We fight, yes, but we must conquer from within, too. Make them weak inside and out. Make sure they do not try to close the portal ever again."

The demon with lilac eyes spoke up. "The Bak-Faru intend to fight."

Another of the Bak-Faru nodded. "We promise warriors," he said.

Tanith smiled. "This is most excellent." The other Council members nodded in approval, too, except the female, Siath.

"Warriors who fight for the Bak-Faru?" Siath asked,

tapping her finger on the tabletop. "Or who seek to help all of Orcus?"

The demon with lilac eyes left off staring at Donovan. He clasped a hand over his fist and bowed in the direction of the dais. "*Nin*-Siath. Council. One hundred Bak-Faru will enter the Overworld."

A murmur rose from the dais, from Jaise and his demons and from the guards. The stout demon, the scribe, dipped his stylus into the inkwell and began filling another page.

The councillor next to Tanith blanched. His pale eyes skimmed the seated Bak-Faru. "One hundred? Of what strength?"

The black-haired Bak-Faru indicated his companions. "One hundred warriors no less strong than the weakest among us here."

"That is good," Tanith said. His eyes were pure fire. "Very good."

The scribe dipped his stylus in the bottle and wrote without looking up.

"All the same," said Siath, glancing around the room with her citrine eyes, "we will now hear what the human and vampire have to say." She looked at them directly for the first time. "We hear you," she said.

Donovan correctly interpreted the invitation to speak. She swallowed once, coughed and began. She sounded confident, but Korzha felt emotion pour from her. He didn't doubt for a moment the demons felt it, too. The tension in the room ratcheted up, particularly the sexual tension from the black-haired Bak-Faru. The intensity of the demon's interest made Korzha's skin prickle. And, to be honest, to feel a certain sense of angry possession. Donovan was with him. He'd fed from her, tasted her blood. She was, in a way, promised to him. Her life was his.

As for Donovan, though she could not in the multi-layered way he did sense the simmering emotions in the room, she felt enough. More than once her eyes darted to the lilac-eyed demon. But her nerves made her all the more convincing. The demons seemed to recognize the pattern of her feelings and listened on two planes: the verbal and the emotional. She set out her offer logically, the scribe's pen flying across the page. She had, she said, convinced Korzha to make her vampire as Jaise desired, on two conditions. Her daughter must be returned safe, sound and healthy to Crimson City and remain safe and protected there. Korzha was to have his alliance in the Overworld. Once she saw for herself that her daughter was safe, then, and only then, would she allow Korzha to convert her. She would give her direct and binding promise to open the portal for any demon under treaty with Korzha.

"Vampire?" Siath said to Korzha.

Korzha bowed. He lifted his eyes to her and found the demoness considering Donovan. "I would agree to these terms."

Siath glanced at the other three demons seated on the dais. They put their heads together and conferred for several minutes. Jaise stared hard at Donovan, and Korzha reached out and took her hand. Her fingers curled around his, warm. The Council had more conditions and stipulations to accept or renegotiate. Aslet's plan for direct and immediate conquest would be implemented if Jaise failed; they would ally with the Bak-Faru. Until then, the Council accepted the promises of the human and vampire. Donovan stuck to her essential points. Korzha would have his alliance. Her conversion would take place in Crimson City when she saw that Holly was safe. Only then would she aid the demons in opening the portal as long and as often as she remained able.

"We agree," Siath said at last, looking at Korzha. "Vampire, the Council approves your alliance"—she hesitated, consulting the document the scribe had handed over, and said—"The Council approves your alliance with the Elismal."

Korzha nodded and turned the motion into a bow, in part to hide a smile of satisfaction. Donovan's negotiations impressed him. His alliance was now a sword with an even deadlier blade for vampires to wield if an inter-species war did break out in Crimson City. If Fleur Dumont chose not to support him, she'd be looking at a Bak-Faru invasion. "You will not regret your wisdom."

After another conference, Siath turned her attention to Jaise. "You will return the child and the vampire to the Overworld under the permanent protection of the Elismal. Is this agreed, *Nir*-Jaise?"

He clasped a hand over his fist. "It is agreed, *Nin*."

The scribe brought the document to Jaise who touched his finger to it. "Jaise of the Elismal," the demon Siath said. "It is done."

Tanith took the document from the scribe, spoke a word and touched his finger to the page. Pale mist rose from the sheet of paper. One by one the other councillors did the same. "Claudia Donovan, Tiberiu Korzha," the female said when she, too, had brushed her fingertip over the page. "It is done."

Jaise straightened from his bow and rose. "Council. I will take them to the portal now."

Donovan's shoulders slumped. Her relief engulfed Korzha like a wave. Without thinking, he put a hand on her shoulder. He heard her whisper, "Holly. Sweetpea, we're going home."

The lilac-eyed demon stood. The air around him

jumped and quivered. He stared past Korzha at Donovan. She caught her breath and flinched as if struck.

"I will not permit this," the Bak-Faru said. His voice was sharp, rang like a hammer striking iron. Silence followed, thick as the quivering, burning air around the demon. Korzha scanned the exits again. There was still no fast way out except up. Out a window if need be. Donovan started to shake.

Several guards broke rank. The other six Bak-Faru also stood, taking up positions behind the other. One of them said something indecipherable. A sharp and acrid smell floated on the air. Guards from either side of the room crouched and flowed toward the Bak-Faru. The scribe's stylus shot off the dais and *tika-tak, tika-tak* rolled along the stone floor until it came to an abrupt stop at the edge of the rugs. Crimson ink sprayed outward in a fine mist. The stylus vanished, and so did the nearest guards.

Jaise shouted. His Elismal came to their feet.

The black-haired demon's eyes glowed red. He faced Jaise and spoke—a single sound, a low syllable redolent of darkness, of the absence of life. The air closed in on everyone in the room, a vacuum of sensation. Like rings of water moving outward from the center of an impact, the Council chamber flooded with light—searing light. Korzha instinctively threw his arms around Donovan. Demons roared. The yellow-eyed demoness stood, both hands on the table. Every demon was on its feet. When the light faded, when the sound was a dark and maleficent whisper, Jaise remained on the ground and didn't move.

The demon with lilac eyes walked unmolested toward the Council, a path that brought him nearer to Korzha and Donovan. Two more Bak-Faru followed behind him. Bodyguards. The hush was intense. No one moved but the three Bak-Faru. The one with the lilac eyes bowed to Aslet and then to the Council hand over clenched fist. And when he straightened, he smiled. Dimples appeared in his cheeks, charming. Aslet stood his ground but looked wary. And no one, not even one of the guards, intervened.

"Council. *Nir*-Aslet," the black-haired demon said. "The Bak-Faru will fight in the Overworld with or without the rest of you." He turned to Donovan again. His dimples were gone, his smile dry like desert sand. "The vishtau," he whispered. The physical heat of his body felt alive, dancing around the demon. "I deny you, *tes*. I deny you, human." Yet he faced the room, sending a lilac glare over every demon present. "Let her die from the bond, or by my own hand and no other. Interfere, be you demon or vampire, and you will find the Bak-Faru an implacable enemy."

Korzha prepared to launch into the air with Donovan, but in the instant before his feet left the ground, the black-haired Bak-Faru focused glittering purple eyes on them and let loose with a concussion of energy that tossed the vampire and Donovan to the floor in a tangle of bodies. The purple-eyed one flowed toward them and gripped Donovan's arm hard enough to pull her to her feet. Korzha lunged for her, but the Bak-Faru clamped an arm around her and levered it so that one good twitch would break her neck. The demon smiled and said, "I *will* kill her, Overworlder."

Donovan braced herself against the demon's body, trying to relieve the awkward pressure of his grip. "Don't be an idiot, fang," she said when their eyes met. "One vampire against a few hundred demons . . ." The

Bak-Faru shifted his weight, and Donovan went up on tip-toe. "Go," she said in a choked voice.

Another of the Bak-Faru flicked a wrist, and a spinning disk exploded into Korzha's chest.

Chapter Seventeen

Claudia watched the moon. Crimson-tinged and hanging low in the sky, it filled the window where she stood. One thing was certain: moonrise in Orcus was spectacular. Her head ached, her mouth felt dry. It was four days since Holly had been taken. Her daughter had been within her grasp, had been moments away from being back in her arms, but now . . .

She had a new and bitter understanding of demons. Jaise's promises had died with him and Aslet had no interest in seeing Claudia made a vampire. He agreed with the other Bak-Faru that she should open the portal once more, to send through the Elismal, the Bak-Faru and as many demons as agreed to join them in a direct assault. After that, she should be allowed to die. In the Overworld, with the help of the Bak-Faru, the Elismal would bond as many humans as necessary in order to keep the gate open. Dead, that was what they wanted of her. They were going to keep her daughter, and turn her into one of them.

The only one who'd come off well from the entire

debacle was Korzha, if *well* wasn't an overstatement. He still had his alliance with the Elismal because the agreement had been with Jaise as *Nir*. Aslet, and all the Elismal, were bound to see that promise kept. If Korzha was still alive, he had managed to keep his demon alliance. That was *if* he was still alive. She wasn't sure what happened to him after Jaise was killed. She knew the Bak-Faru had tried to kill him, too. The flash of light in the room had blinded her.

Sighing, she pressed her head to the windowpane and wondered if she would ever see her daughter again. And, though her heart chilled to think of it, she wondered if Holly was even alive.

It was four stories to the ground. Not much chance of escaping out the window, and the door lock had defeated any pick she'd managed to fashion. She would never survive a jump, and there wasn't any ledge. She'd already tried several times to reach the roof, but she might as well try to fly, for all the good it did her. Flying was about the only way she'd leave this place without a demon.

As she looked out the window, a shadow crossed the expanse of courtyard below, and vanished into the blackness. Somewhere out there was her daughter. She pressed her fingers against her eyes. Was Holly crying? Had they hurt her? Her chest tightened with unbearable, unfathomable pain.

Behind her, the door hinges creaked, and a shaft of light expanded on the window, blotting out a slice of the moon. A surge of adrenaline sent Claudia's heart winging to her throat. She faced the door but kept her back to the wall. A shape filled the doorway. Wide shoulders, narrow waist. Male, unquestionably. The figure was tall and broad-shouldered. In the light, she couldn't make out the color of his hair or eyes. That it might be Aslet made her sick to her stomach. She didn't want to be what she'd seen of the other human women here. Korzha had done Laura Masters a favor. Claudia was sorry he wasn't around to do the same for her.

Whoever it was, stepped inside. Claudia's stomach bottomed out. The figure lifted a hand and the room lightened appreciably. She looked into a still-darkened corner, shading her eyes from the sudden brightness. After a bit, she adjusted and could look without squinting. There wasn't any improvement in seeing better where she'd been imprisoned: a dismal room, as gloomy as it had looked in the previous dimness. The silence unnerved her.

"Who is it? What do you want?" she asked. Maybe, just maybe, she'd try to escape. The door was open, and she didn't have much to lose anymore.

But . . . it was the Bak-Faru demon. The one with lilac eyes. The one who couldn't wait for her to die. The one who'd killed Jaise and whose companions had frightened the pants off a hallful of demons. He sure as hell scared her. Of all the demons she'd seen in Orcus, his appearance was by far the most unusual, what with that black-as-midnight hair and purple eyes. God knows he'd never blend into a crowd looking like that. Platinum threads glittered in his hair. His pastel eyes didn't make him any less threatening.

The demon closed the door and crossed his arms over his chest. "A human female," he said. He took a step toward her and stopped. He drew a sharp breath, as if shocked or surprised or angry. "This cannot be so," he said. "Not with a human female."

Cripes, his voice sent shivers rolling up and down her spine. Claudia felt a little dizzy, being this close to him. Her head pulsed. Had he come to kill her? No other reason came to mind. *Improvise,* she thought.

Keep him off balance. She wrapped her palm over her fist and bowed—pretty deep, so there was no question of her not giving him all due respect. "Good evening. Um . . ." *Quick, quick*, had she ever heard his name? Her skin felt hot. And her belly, too, all shivery. "Demon . . . of the . . . Bak-Faru."

He looked at her like she was a particularly clever poodle. He wasn't wearing a shirt, which disconcerted her. Not that it was cold or anything, though it wasn't warm. A low-body-fat demon, this one. His dimples appeared, and she was pretty sure that meant trouble. He'd been smiling like that right before he killed Jaise. He leaned toward her, so close she felt the warmth of his breath. "The vampire," he said in a slow, easy tone, "hides from *Nir*-Aslet and the others."

Korzha was alive! Thank God. "Can you blame him?" she asked. "I'd hide from you too, if I could."

He nodded toward the ceiling. "He cannot hide himself from me." The demon looked her up and down and shook his head. "I do not like human women. I do not like you or your dark eyes."

She smiled and said in a friendly voice, polite as she could be, "I don't like demons. Sorry about that."

His lilac eyes flickered red, then settled back into their soft and pale shade of purple. What gorgeous eyes. Like his hair, eyelashes black as soot. She wondered why she wasn't dead yet, and while she was wondering about that, the demon, standing less than arm's length from her, stretched out a hand. She tensed, but all he did was touch a fingertip just below the inside corner of her eye.

"Your eyes are too dark. This is not good for a demon male to see in his mate." With a shake of his head, he drew a line from the inner corner of her eye to her temple. "*Tes*," he whispered. "I do not like human women, but even so, I will mate with you tonight."

Her first thought was foreign to her, and astonishingly carnal. She wanted to mate with him. Her second was that she must be freaking insane to want anything to do with him. The demon moved closer, and sensation hit her like a ton of bricks. She sucked in a breath. Her belly shivered as if he were already touching her. She would have edged away, but the wall was against her back. "Why bother?" she asked. Jeez, he was handsome. An exotic mix of imperial beauty and golden skin. "If you don't like human women I mean."

"*Tes.*"

"Um." She swallowed. "That's Claudia."

"This is your name?" He tipped his head to one side. "Claudia?" Unexpected curves interrupted the sharp planes of his face. He had a soft, full mouth, slanting cheeks, a nose that hooked just the tiniest bit. Thank God, she thought, thank God he hadn't brought his Bak-Faru friends. She wished like hell Korzha were here.

"Yes. My name is Claudia. Claudia Donovan."

"Claudia Donovan." The syllables shimmered on the air, floated between them. His eyes flickered again. The heat in the room increased another fifty degrees. "Claudia-*tes*, I deny you."

He sounded cold and desolate. Desperately alone. He threw back his head and let out a long, low moan of despair and wrath. Cold heat whirled outward from him and through her. "Please," she said. "Just leave me alone."

"You understand nothing of demons." He drew a breath and lifted a hand. Lilac mist formed in the air, caught fire and danced around them both. "This is what I feel for you."

He wasn't touching her, but she sure as hell felt his desire, and behind that, his anguish. He loved what he was: a Bak-Faru demon. He loved his world and his people. Nature demanded he desire her, and so he did. Without limit. Claudia couldn't help herself; she touched his bare chest. His sexual response to her grew. She didn't understand why he hated and desired her, or when the heat and cold in her would ever stop. The demon hated with exquisite passion, and wanted with sublime need.

"Claudia-*tes*," he said. His voice went soft and tender. "I will mate with you now."

"No." Her head was quite clear about that. But every bone in her body said yes, like it wasn't even connected to her brain.

"*Tes*." His voice, all shadows and black velvet, put some horrifyingly explicit thoughts in her head, and when he leaned forward to touch a fingertip to her forehead, all she could do was stare at the planes of his cheek. Something flowed between them, from him to her. Darkness clung to him like vines to a wall—and power, too. He'd killed Jaise. Easily. And in a hall full of demons, no one, not even the leaders, had dared move against him. A sliver of cold rippled through Claudia at the spot where his finger touched, right there, between her eyebrows. Watching his mouth curve was like watching the sun rise on a cold morning. The air shimmered around him. This kind of beauty in a man ought to be criminal. He turned his head to one side, watching the nearby burning air.

In profile, his face lost its hint of gentleness but none of its beauty. The very top of his cheek slanted outward, his skin like taut silk over the bone, but then curved to the hollow of his lower face. That Aztec face, blended with something else. His eyes, such a pure and icy color, met hers. Claudia felt his surge of lust, a rumbling, growling purr, and all of it resonating in her too. In human mythology, demons were notorious for their libido. A convenient displacement, she'd always thought, for normal sexual longings most humans elected to deny. Well, all of her sexual longing had just been displaced to these six-plus feet of lilac-eyed demon. The way he consumed her terrified her.

He drew in a sharp breath. He stepped close and put his hands on her waist, up high, near her ribs. His head dipped until his lips hovered just inches over hers. The demon was quite a bit taller than she. If he played basketball, he'd be a power forward. Her hands ended up on his shoulders. Heat radiated off him like he was on fire inside.

"Aslet does not have the power to properly create this bond." His fingers moved slowly over her back, over the marks on her arms. "You will die because he tried to do what only we Bak-Faru can." He scowled. "But still, I have this"—he tapped her forehead. "The vishtau. With you. A human." He seemed perplexed.

"The vishtau." She repeated the words. Any meaning seemed to race around her head, refusing to be caught. "What does that mean?"

"Come, *tes*," he whispered. His thumbs lifted, brushing the bottom swell of her breasts. "We will mate."

Her breath caught. She was horrifyingly close to letting him do whatever the hell he wanted, as long as he came inside of her. The feelings weren't normal—not for her—but there they were, calling to her, pulling at her, demanding. She managed to make a face like she hadn't quite heard him. Except she knew that he wanted her, that he intended to have sex with her, and that she wanted him in the same way.

"*Tes*," she repeated in a conversational tone. Cripes,

she could hardly concentrate. The backs of her knees felt watery, and her hands were still on his heated skin. "Why do you keep calling me that?"

He smiled and slid his hands up her rib cage, under her armpits as if he intended to pick her up. His beauty stunned her again. Such a soft and tender mouth. Gentle, she thought. A gentle mouth on a dangerous monster. "This word is very old. An ancient word used between vishtau mates. It means . . ." He frowned, trying to find the right word. "*Beloved*." He brushed his thumbs over the tips of her breasts. She felt her body react to the touch, tighten and tingle. "Claudia-*tes*, beloved vishtau mate, I wish to mate with you now."

Then his mouth touched hers, and pretty much she forgot everything but the demon. Heat rippled through her, between them. Soft lips, gentle lips. His chest pressed against hers, not hard, but solid. Insistent. She managed to lift one hand. Her palm pressed flat against his bare torso. Cripes, she'd forgotten he was naked from the waist up. Smooth skin, muscle and sinew. So warm.

"Claudia-*tes*." The demon breathed her name. His breath warmed her cheek. He put his hands on either side of her waist again and pulled her hard against him. She did not want this, but she had no control over the sensations raging through her. And she felt damp heat between her legs, an aching need for sex with him. Just him. She felt as if her mind were losing control. Abdicating control to her body and to lilac fire.

He stroked her, so soft and slow she thought she might float away. It was as if he'd got hold of her thoughts and could twist them any way he wanted. *Thwip*. Like a key in a lock. Her body reacted, ignoring her brain. She wanted him so badly, she'd do about anything for him. Anything at all, as long as he mated with her. She had an image of his golden body poised over hers, moving, sliding, thrusting, his lilac eyes caressing her.

With a soft sigh, the demon froze. His eyes met hers, and she believed the tenderness she saw there was real. Nobody could fake that. Could they? "You are mine, human. Tonight must be."

God, what a fantastic voice, low and seductive. His lower body pressed against her, close enough that she felt his erection. Everything about him was sublimely sexual. He backed away, toward the pallet, bringing her with him and there released her. While she stood, dizzy from the sensations that expanded in her, he stripped. Underneath his slate-gray pants he wore a pair of shape-hugging thigh-length shorts. Her breath caught. His erection bulged against the fabric. Like a dancer, with a graceful flex of the long muscles of his legs, he slipped his hands under the waistband and extended the material out to ease his turgid penis free. He lifted one leg, then the other and slid the shorts off. "Come," he said—so softly, all smoke and black velvet.

In the back of her head, Claudia was more afraid than she'd ever been in her life. Ever since she'd got Holly out of the Lower and made a new life for them, she'd been in control of what happened. She alone decided whether she acted on her desires, however poor her choice of partners. That was her decision, no one else's. Hers. And now what she wanted didn't matter. Her mind was subject to her body.

Her attention focused on him, on his golden-skinned muscle and sinew, and she was splendidly and impressively aroused. The demon radiated warmth, a wonderful, welcoming warmth, and Claudia realized she felt cold. All her life she'd been cold, and only he

could make her warm. And the worst part, the very
worst part, was that she knew she didn't want him.
Not rationally. Having sex with him felt like she was
cheating on someone—a ridiculous thought, since
there wasn't anyone to cheat on. She had no one to
love, no one who loved her. Did she? Her body wanted
the demon more than her head objected. He had to
have sex with her. He had to. She had to.

His eyes were like pools of sky at thirty thousand
feet. Her body ached for his. She didn't like him, but
perversely, inexorably, she wanted the act. She knew
he felt the same way. He didn't like her either, but his
body demanded. Their bodies demanded.

"Come," he whispered, and she stepped close. His
fingers slid beneath her shirt to just above her belly
button, then downward. Heat radiated from the pads
of his fingers. He would soon be inside her. She would
die if she didn't have him inside her.

"Claudia Donovan," he said in his dark voice. "*Tes*,"
he murmured. "Mate with me now, Claudia Donovan."

She stared at the demon, forcing her eyes to focus.
His gaze pinned her. A silky shiver went through her
core. *Mate?* Jeez, she felt cold inside. A picture formed
behind her eyes—of his hands on her, his head bending over her, his body, sleek and powerful, flexing and
moving, working itself inside her. God, yes, that was
what she wanted. "Mate?" she said with the very last
shred of her resistance. "No. No, I don't think that's a
good idea at all."

But here she was, inches from him, her hands on his
bare chest, her fingers moving over his nipples, feeling
them peak under her touches, shaking with need for
him. Against her stomach, in her head, she felt the
pressure of his erection, and more, his curiosity about
her, about what it would feel like to mate with her, a

human. If her impressions were to be believed, he hadn't had any satisfactory couplings with human women. She shook her head. The thoughts weren't hers, but they were in her head, shared with him. He could see her, wanted to taste her, was aroused by the shape of her breasts, by her shoulders, stomach, legs. Overwhelming desire—more than enough for them both. She did want to touch him, to caress him, to have her hands on his buttocks, palms sliding along the backs of his thighs. She needed his body.

He made a low sound, a purring growl. Like that, they were on the pallet, and his body moved over hers. His fingers worked at her pants and slid them down. She wiggled her hips to help him. Her hands moved downward, slipping along the muscles and bones of his back. Inside her was the swirling sensation of desire. His? Hers? That desire increased, the duality of wanting and not wanting. As if he knew, a smile covered his face, wild and dark, and in his eyes, pale purple swirling like specks of arctic cold. "We must, *tes*."

She felt the answering darkness in her reaching for him—a pull, as if something inside her were him already. His fingers flexed on her skin in a light touch, delicate, at odds with the hatred also raging through him. He shuddered once, and his skin rippled. His nature opened up to hers, and he became what he felt. And she embraced a demon of dark heat and darker fire. He scorched her very soul, pulled her toward him. Compulsion, black and hot and overwhelming. He pushed up her shirt and touched the bare skin just below her bra.

"I am Bak-Faru," he said. "I am called Lath. I am named Ur-Kashev-Ghan. And you are my vishtau-mate."

She thought about scooting away, but the pull between them defied her. Inside her head, desire pulsed. Not hers or his, theirs.

"I give you my name, Ur-Kashev-Ghan, because you have my heart and my life," he whispered. He worked at her shirt, her bra. Her breath vanished when he covered her breasts with his bare hands. A reverence. "Give me your heart, Claudia. What are you named?"

She shook her head. His hands were on her—touching, molding, melting her. Tears welled up in her throat, in her chest, but none of that could stop her need. Or his. Between them, that need grew, candesced, entangled and became irreducible. The last of her clothes came off.

He ran his hands along her waist and then trailed one along her flank. "*Tes*. What are you named?" he repeated.

"Claudia Donovan."

"We have the vishtau." He hauled himself atop her, his body naked and ready. "The vampire must not touch you as I do. Never. You are mine," he growled. "I do not want you. I know you do not want me, but I must . . . we must . . . *You are mine.*"

She opened herself to him and he growled. And then, then he was at her entrance, seeking, nuzzling at her, sliding his cock inside her, and she was wet and hot, ready for him and only him.

His beautiful smile appeared; dimples, too. "This is good, *tes*. You are beautiful, and you hold me well. You give me delight." Claudia flew to the sizzling edge of a passion so deep she didn't know if she could survive it. His cock was hard, and he filled her more than she could stand. She didn't want him. She didn't want this, but heat poured from his body, and she thought she'd die from needing it so badly. Her mind whirled along with his, both of them dark and insatiable.

Quickly, too quickly, they moved toward an abyss. He was hard inside her, and this was wrong. She did not want this. Her body rocketed toward pleasure while she tried to pretend it wasn't happening, but she saw the planes and edges of his face, breathed in his scent, reacted to the touch of this demon who made her desperate for him.

She held him as he continued thrusting, and he was just absolutely the most perfect thing in her world. He kissed her, tenderly and then passionately, and mindlessly. His ponytail fell over his shoulder, brushing her skin. She held him, stroked his body, arched toward him, mindless with need. Their need. Fast. Hard. Incredible. He hated her, hated her kind, but he saw to her pleasure first, made certain of that, and she peaked and shattered.

His lilac eyes held her, caressed her, touched her. Lath lived in her head and made her want him. His hips flexed against her, the rhythm of his thrusting increased. His face tensed, flames shadowed his eyes, and he let out a low growl that rose in pitch. Beneath her hands, his back bowed, and his sex was deep, deep inside her. Cold. His ejaculate felt cold. He kept his arms straight, his hips tight against her pelvis. "When you die, *tes*, my tears will fall on your grave," he said.

She tried to move away from him, and this time, her legs obeyed. But the swirling inside filled her and took him with her. His breath came fast at first, then slower and softer. One last touch, he gave a stroke along her cheek. He withdrew. How alone she felt.

Now that he was done, his hatred of humans raged through him, warred with the tenebrous heat that coursed through them both. He dressed with the same heart-wrenching grace as before and left without a word. But in her head, Claudia felt him. She would never be free of him.

After Lath left, she gathered her clothes and dressed herself. She curled up on the pallet, eyes closed tight. A classic reaction, her head told her. But all the reading and lectures in the world on such paranormal assault hadn't prepared her for the reality of intercourse with a creature who made her want him even when she didn't. She'd rather have Korzha any day. Korzha didn't want her either, but he'd never leave her feeling like this. He'd convince her sex with him was exactly what she'd been missing her whole life.

Hours later, a lifetime later, the window inched open. Air flowed through the opening, and something moved with it, silent as falling snow. But she knew him. The shift in the stillness of the air was the reason. She knew he was there. Korzha. Not Lath.

She gave no sign of being awake. All the better if he thought she was asleep. For a while, the quiet deafened her. Behind her closed eyes, she tried to guess what he was doing.

At last, he spoke. "Oh dear-heart," he whispered. "I am so sorry."

Chapter Eighteen

"I know you're not asleep," Korzha said. A note of anger underlay his words. "Who was it?"

Without turning over, Officer Donovan said, "I don't know what you're talking about."

"Don't lie to me. I can smell it," he said. Her mind was closed to him, and that made his heart ache. He would *not* feel for her. Did not want to. "This room reeks of sex." His voice trembled and the betrayal of his control shocked him.

Humans always misjudged a vampire's ability to see and sense. Always. A child had more hope of gulling a vigilant parent than a human had of fooling a vampire. Claudia squeezed her eyes tightly closed, and her breathing went shallow. God, she just did not know she couldn't fool him. Not about this.

"What difference does it make?" she said. Did she think he felt nothing? "Go away," she said.

Her voice came out lifeless, and Korzha wanted to weep the tears that ought to be hers. He reached for her mind again—a light touch that sent her sitting bolt upright, ready to battle. She was a warrior to be admired.

The first thing he did was look at her eyes. There was no hint of madness, only hopelessness. "Don't you dare try any of that voodoo head stuff on me, Korzha," she said. She teetered on the edge of hysteria. He could smell the tears coming. "Just don't, okay?"

Like that, he was at her side, kneeling, close enough to touch, but not touching. He was done with humans. Done. In all things emotional, he'd been done with them for longer than she'd been alive. But he wanted to make everything all right. This was his fault. His alone. She should not feel so dear to him.

She pushed at his body. "Get away from me."

"Are you hurt?" The demon's scent rose to him. Sweat. Heat. Lust.

She let out a sharp puff of air. "Not so you can see."

He took her face between his hands and tipped her head toward his. Their eyes met, and he almost couldn't stand to look. She radiated despair, a quiet closing of a door in her mind. The smell of sex and sweat, hers and the demon's, became sharper. He ought to have known this would happen. He knew enough of demons and their nature that he ought to have known she wouldn't be safe. He should have come after her right away, healed or not. While Jaise was alive, the other demons hadn't dared. But now, a different demon had touched her, had put himself into her body and left her like this. Anger rose in him, fury. He, Tiberiu Korzha, had touched her, caressed her, fed from her and marked her as his. She trusted him enough to agree to a permanent connection between them—vampire and vampire-maker. If she hadn't trusted him, she would have made her own deal with the demon Council. Now he wanted to kill whoever had done this to her.

"Go away," she whispered.

"I should have come sooner."

"Why? What do you care? The deal's off. There's no point in converting me now." She swallowed hard. "I'm going to die, so nothing you do or don't do makes a hell of a lot of difference."

He used a thumb to wipe away a tear she didn't realize she'd shed. He lifted his hand from her face and stared at the drop of water balanced on the side of his thumb. His tongue flicked out and caught it. There was a lovely taste of salt. "This is my fault," he said.

She laughed bitterly. "How do you figure that, Korzha?"

"If I hadn't let you see me that night, you'd never have come to investigate. You'd never have been anywhere near Jaise or any other demon."

"If you hadn't let me see you, I'd be in Crimson City taping up posters with my daughter's face on them. I'd be just as bad off as I am now; so, you know, fangs, really—don't sweat it."

"I let myself get caught up with half-demons in the city." God, no. This was not the time to speak of Mika and Conor. She didn't know, and it wasn't important. "We leave now," he said.

She resisted the pull of his hand on her wrists. "I'm not going anywhere without Holly."

"I'll take care of that." He let her go and rose. "We're going now."

"Where?" She pushed to her feet. He knew from the way she stood that she was sore between her legs, and damp with the demon's seed. "Why?"

Korzha whirled on her, and Donovan, whom he'd

rarely seen back down from anyone or anything, took a step away. He didn't let her see the extent of his anger. With some effort he suppressed his reaction, but anguish bubbled up. "I do not countenance any creature who does what happened here tonight. I will not stand by and let it happen again. I promise you, I will get you and your daughter to the portal. The rest is up to you." He had to fight back his desire to do more.

Her lip curled. "What about the Elismal?"

"What about them?"

She shrugged. "Nothing, I guess."

He bit back his retort. Darkness impinged on his senses. Demons were coming. Elismal—he recognized their arrogant overconfidence. And something else. Something darker and separate. The thing that had assaulted Donovan. It was heading this way, too. In a flash, Korzha was outside the window, clinging to the wall, hand outstretched. "Move it, Donovan. They're coming. *He's* coming for you again."

"It's no good," she said. "Demons can sense me. Take me with you and we'll both end up dead."

"No, we won't. I can shield us both." He stretched out his hand to her again. "Now, come on," he said.

The door flew off its hinges. Donovan threw herself at the window, grasping for his hand. From over her shoulder, Korzha saw Aslet and three other demons rush in. The air wailed in his ears, a hurricane of motion. Aslet opened his mouth to speak, his hand pointed at Donovan's back, but the word didn't reach Korzha's ears because he snatched at Donovan's collar and hauled her up and out. Her feet left the ground, and, when she was out the window, her legs swung wide and threw him off balance. He tilted precariously. Donovan rocked her hips toward the wall, keeping her legs moving, an instinctive reaction. It worked—her center of balance shifted, and Korzha recovered.

He reached the rooftop just as Aslet and another demon with a thatch of dark blond hair did, too, exiting a nearby stairwell. Emotions flashed through Korzha. Not Donovan's. Not Aslet's, whose mind Korzha recognized without much difficulty. No, these were the emotions of another demon. One dark and strong enough to broadcast his emotions directly into any receptive mind. One who knew. He knew Korzha was taking Donovan away from him. Korzha could feel the demon's emotions: rage, fear, jealousy. And, oddly enough, concern for Donovan's safety. And a direct challenge to Korzha's link with her.

The blond demon split off to the right, Aslet to the left, both trying to head them off. Korzha reached an attic projection and poised on it. Donovan got her arms around his neck. He cloaked himself and her as dozens of demon guards suddenly took to the air. They'd learned their lesson after the debacle in the Council room. There was no simply going upward to safety this time. Korzha breathed in Donovan's scent. The monster in him was aroused by the smell of her blood, the heat of her body. Acrid sweat. Stale sex. He got an arm tighter around her and plunged off the side of the palace. Wind whistled past his ears. He braced himself for landing, cradling Donovan and absorbing the bump. He turned her toward him, and she put her arms around his shoulders, holding tight because he raced across the courtyard and leapt for the wall, away from the palace and into Biirkma.

Downhill, along the city's narrow streets he raced, turning corners at a dizzying speed. Demons screeched overhead. Korzha got brief impressions of his surroundings. Every now and then he saw someone disappear into a house. Doors slammed, windows banged closed. Far away the air shrieked, bodies hurtling through the night at top speed.

He kept moving. Away from the palace. In the dimness of the moonlight, Biirkma's impression of age reminded him of his first sight of London, the city to which he'd headed after he first left Romania. Biirkma possessed a similar grandeur, though here the buildings were of stone undarkened by the smoke from thousands of fires. And the air smelled different, cleaner, sharper. Older. The position of the moon matched his internal clock. Late night, heading toward morning. Not much time. Below, animals barked, yowled in protest and then quieted, their cries cut off.

Korzha leapt onto another roof as a howl split the air. The sound sent ice shivering down his back. He knew without doubt it was the demon who'd killed Jaise, the Bak-Faru who'd stared at Donovan like he couldn't decide whether to kill her or lay her flat on her back. Apparently, he'd made his decision, whether Donovan wanted him or not. The demon's rage and jealously filled Korzha's head. Donovan's arms tightened around him as he leapt from roof to roof. At last, he was out of range.

He plunged downward again, into a street so narrow that moonlight did nothing for shadows blacker than black. He set Donovan down and pressed his back to the vine-covered wall. She did likewise. Crushed blossoms gave off an oversweet smell. Her breath came too fast, too human. With luck, the flowers would mask her scent. How did humans survive to dominate Earth when they had so little physically at their command?

Across the street and under the glow of a fuzzy blue

lantern was a door painted the color of old egg yolk. There was no one inside the house beyond. Korzha touched Donovan's arm, signaling that the door would be their destination when the street cleared. She nodded. Overhead, red tinged the crescent center of the moon, the craters and crevices so clear he wanted to reach up and touch them.

The street where they'd come to a stop exited onto a wider avenue where demons walked in greater numbers. Some looked around. A few broke into a run. Others dashed into buildings like they were taking cover from a blizzard. A covered sedan chair carried by two bare-chested demons appeared. The owner's head popped out once, a pair of pale yellow eyes scanning the alley.

"Shit," Korzha muttered. He willed the demoness to see nothing, to sense nothing but demons on the wing.

The sedan-chair curtain flicked back, about its bearers trotted away. Korzha motioned with one hand, and *snick*—across the street, the yellow door swung open. Korzha grabbed Donovan's wrist, swung her into his arms and leapt, catlike, across the avenue. He slipped inside and closed the door after him. The bolt slid home. He waited for Donovan's eyes to adjust to the light. As in every demon home he'd seen, lights came on with the first movement, glowing blue.

"Someone lives here," she said.

It was a cozy room with a low wooden table, rugs, two piles of pillows, and cupboards lining the walls. Wood and stone. Nothing synthetic. "But they are not at home," Korzha said. He turned to the cupboards and started opening them. "It's why I chose this house."

"Well, yeah, but—What are you doing?"

He pulled open another cupboard and rifled the

contents. It distracted her, focused her on right now instead of what had happened. Good. That was what he wanted. "Looking for something more comfortable to wear."

"What for?"

"If we're going to pass, for however brief a glimpse, we'll have to dress the part." He looked her up and down.

"Pass?"

"Dear heart. *Draga inima.*" He put a hand over his chest. "While I find your current attire *très charmante*, it lacks local flavor."

"Creep," she said, but not with much feeling. "None of that vampire voodoo head stuff on me."

"Forgive me," he said. He hadn't meant to, but honestly, reaching for her that way, with his psyche, was his nature. Now that he'd fed from her enough to forge a surprisingly strong connection, such a reaction was instinct.

"I am *not* going to let you bite me," she said.

"No time for intimacies, I'm afraid," he replied with a laugh. He found a cupboard with clothing in it and dumped the contents on the table. When he looked up, he caught a furrow between Donovan's eyebrows. "What?"

"I mean it."

"I'm sure you do," he said.

"Well?"

"Officer Donovan." He sat on the floor and selected clothes that looked a reasonable fit for him. He shoved the rest toward her. "You are so engagingly . . . human."

She snatched something from a peg by the door. When she turned back to him, the leather straps of a knife and sheath dangled from one hand. His eyebrows lifted. "Protection," she said. "A girl's got to have some protection."

He nodded. "Good. Fine. Now please find something that looks like it might fit you, Donovan. You need to at least try to pass for a demon. It's not that hard."

"Right." With the sheath dangling over her arm, she knelt to look through the clothes. Korzha made small talk.

"My sort has had to pass for human if we wished to continue in our lives in Crimson City," he said.

She held a pair of trousers to her hips, but snorted. "Your sort," she echoed.

"*My sort*," he said, "want only to assure ourselves we will not be hunted down for the mere fact of our existence."

Officer Donovan rolled her eyes. "Is that someone's bleeding heart I hear? A killer's bleeding heart?"

Korzha's eyebrow quirked, but he didn't say anything. He didn't defend himself. She could say anything, think anything if it helped to keep her mind off what had happened to her. Life, but he was jealous. Deep in his bones, he was jealous that another creature had dared touch what was his by tradition. And such fierceness for a human. If Claudia Donovan were a vampire, she'd be running one of the four families one day.

"Today, right now, if you want to live, you better be a killer too, yes?" he asked. She pricked up her ears, and he knew he'd let his old voice come back, the old-Europe voice. Orcus seemed to be reverting him in more than one way. "You'll have to pass here, Officer, at least from a distance. I can only cloak your humanity so much. The sooner you learn to deny what you are, the better for everyone—I assure you of that." He plucked a shirt from the pile on the table. "And your daughter is alive. Do not give up hope. Do try not to get yourself killed in some moment of grief." It was his biggest fear.

"I'll manage," was all she said.

He allowed himself a moment of bitterness, thinking back to her earlier accusations. "As if," he said, "you've ever pretended to be something you're not."

She laughed, a cold and sad sound. "Korzha," she said. "You have no freaking idea how long I've been 'passing.'"

What could she know about that? "Humans are so infernally naive. There ought to be a law to protect you from your own stupidity," he said.

Hand over her chest, she replied, "My own bleeding heart says I have a right to my stupid opinion and that I will defend to the death your right to have one, too." She grinned at him. "See? Ain't equality grand?"

"How grateful I am," he said with a laugh. "Where would I be without you?" He put both his hands on the table and leaned toward her. Seeing her smile was good. He kept back a grin of his own.

"I told you," she said. Her dark-chocolate eyes widened—eyes that a demon adored, that a demon had stared into while making love to her. He fought his anger. "None of that voodoo head stuff you freaks do."

"I'm doing what I must," he said.

"Fang, I can't tell you how sick and tired I am of hearing about what other freaks *must* do. Particularly, when I don't want to do whatever it is they think they *must* do."

That didn't stop him from touching her mind. "I am

trying to keep you from getting killed. Your pathetically short mortal life, the one for which you are so grateful, could be considerably shortened at any time."

Eyes wide, Donovan backed away from him.

Chapter Nineteen

Korzha laughed. He took a step toward her. "I'm not going to bite you, if that's what you're thinking," he said.

"I wasn't."

"Liar. But know this. I can survive here indefinitely without you, Officer. You can't. Even the weakest demon will know what you are. Without me, you won't last five minutes." He felt a need to challenge her, to know, really know, if she was as resilient as his connection with her suggested. It seemed she was. Donovan faced him down.

"Maybe so. But without me, fang, you can't get back through the portal. So you better hope I live long enough to get us through."

He turned away from the table, away from the lure of her blood and her body and mind, and his completely inappropriate admiration of her. He couldn't even remember the last time he'd admired a human or a vampire, for that matter. He often appreciated them. His lawyers he appreciated for their legal skill. Human women he appreciated for their beauty. Female vampires he appreciated for their grace. But he admired Claudia Donovan, a human woman who fucking hated vampires and reminded him that he'd once been human himself. The creature he'd become whispered that he should take her. Right now. Oh, how he wanted to finish what he'd started with her. "What a joy you must be to friends and family," he said wryly.

Donovan sat down on the pillows. Hard. All that toughness, and she continually spoiled things by letting softness show.

"Look, Korzha," she said. "Can we maybe start over? I'm not even sure what happened to me. Or how the hell we got here. I'm not Miss Congeniality. I never have been. If it was *your* daughter who was missing, I don't think you'd be so freaking easy to get along with either. So if you'll just back off, I'll try to do the same, all right?"

He knew she wasn't trying to mess with his head, not on purpose anyway, but that's what she was doing to him. Tiberiu Korzha did not get involved with humans. Not like this. Not anymore. He stared at her, but she must have decided she had nothing to lose by staring back. He hadn't fed from her deeply enough to feel a connection like this, this physical, sensual tug. Her eyes were ravishing, he thought—irises of deep, bittersweet chocolate, with long, thick lashes. A man would die to have those eyes watching him with passion. Korzha imagined the sensation of his teeth gliding through her skin upon request, and only just managed to pull himself out of his reverie. He nodded. "Agreed."

"Thank you," she said. After a bit, she asked, "Can you really shield us from demons?"

"Yes, but not without effort. And perhaps not infallibly." With a shake of his head, he focused on their present difficulties, but, shit, he could still feel her. Doubtless, she felt him, too.

"No more time for idle chitchat, I'm afraid. Dress, and I promise you we will talk later. Questions will be asked. And some may even be answered."

She looked at him. "The only thing I want is Holly."

He was moved. "I swear upon my honor we will not leave Orcus without your daughter." He picked up the knife she'd taken off the wall and set on the table. He handed it to her. "Don't forget your protection."

"I'd prefer my Glock. That's protection a girl can trust." She slid the blade out of the sheath. The metal glittered blue-black. She blinked. "Wow. Cool."

He tossed a satchel at her feet. "Start filling it with anything you think might keep you and your daughter alive. And be careful," he added. "That thing's sharp."

But of course she touched the blade. And of course she cut her finger because the dark knife was wickedly sharp. Her shoulders jerked. "Rats," she said.

The smell of blood stopped him dead. Hunger burned his mind. Donovan put her nicked finger in her mouth, and the smell thankfully dampened.

"You could kill somebody with this," she said around her finger.

Korzha stared at her mouth. "In Orcus, Officer Donovan, you will find that, except for another demon, such a blade may be all that kills our horrible friends."

Without another word, the policewoman grabbed the clothing she'd selected and went into another room to change. Korzha shucked his Overworld clothes. Soon he was wearing a pair of light, close-fitting trousers of tolerable fit, and a sand-colored shirt that was a less tolerable fit. He stuffed his suit in the back of a cupboard. He found a pair of leather boots that fit reasonably well and put them on. His Mezlan Oxfords went into the cupboard, too. Alas. But they were nothing he couldn't afford to replace.

Donovan tromped back into the room with her old clothes stuffed under her arm. She'd found a pair of sandals two sizes too big and looked to have hacked several inches off the bottom of the pants. Despite the tight laces up her groin—how was he not to think of unlacing her?—the waist sagged below her navel. Her L.A.P.D. shirt hadn't done her any sort of justice, but this new shirt did. Waist-length, exposed navel and all, it had a high collar and a vee opening that gaped invitingly over her curves. She looked damn good to him. She had her dagger sheath tied around her thigh under an unwieldy length of belt that flapped uselessly from the belt's buckle.

"Good girl," he said. Too bad they weren't on familiar enough terms for him to put her on the table, unlace her pants and make love to her. Yet another pity in a growing list of them.

"Drop dead, Korzha." She grabbed the empty satchel he'd given her and started opening cupboards and drawers, looking for useful items to steal.

"I meant that," he said, "in the very nicest way. A compliment. And, please, you must call me Tiberiu. Or Tiber." He thickened his accent. "Which you prefer, yes?"

She gave him the finger. But he smiled at her, and she spoiled the effect of her defiance by laughing. "Do you know how to use a pump?" he asked. He threw two leather skins at her and pointed to a lever that worked a well. "Fill them. You'll need water."

She saluted. "Yes, sir." But she didn't move.

"Do it."

"Yes, sir," she muttered. But still she didn't move.

"Just do it."

"Fuck you, sir," she said under her breath. But at last she picked up the skins and went to the pump.

"I heard that."

This time, she just mouthed the retort, pumping herself water.

Korzha rifled the rest of the house while she ransacked the pantry. When she was finished, he said, "Let's go."

"Just a minute." She laid the excess length of her belt on the table and knelt on the floor. With the heel of her palm on the belt, she leaned back to get tension. Her shirt rose up, exposing her soft, human skin. Korzha stared at her stomach. It didn't pay to get involved with humans. It just didn't. It seemed to him that he felt the connection with her more intensely than any bite justified. But this had been a connection of spectacular intensity. He'd been leagues deep in her. Fathoms. She was *his*.

When the belt was taut, she sliced through the leather. Her blade went through like a hot knife through butter. "Much better." She slid the knife back into its sheath and grinned at him. She had a nice smile. It'd be good to see it more often. "I'll go anywhere with you, Kemo Sabe," she said. She held out a hand and gave him another smile that wasn't much of a smile. He helped her up. "As long as it includes getting Holly," she added.

Korzha picked up the remnant of the belt and considered its cleanly cut edge. He must be out of his mind to involve himself here. This couldn't end except with his teeth in her. He dropped the scrap of leather. At least the sex would be good. His eyes shifted, taking in the room, sensing outward. He heard the demons call again, too far away for Donovan to hear. "They're closing in on us now."

"Have you got a plan, or are we improvising?" she asked.

His mouth twitched. "I have a plan."

"Well." She shrugged. "Okay."

It would be dangerous. Very. But these were parlous times indeed. "I want us out of the city for a while. Let them wonder if somehow we've made it back through the portal. In the meantime, we'll circle around and come at Holly from another direction." She looked worried, and he took pity on her. "We'll be out of the city one or two nights. No more than three."

"I don't get you, Korzha. Why are you helping me?" Her eyes narrowed. "What's in it for you, fang?"

"I gave you my word about your daughter," he said softly.

"So?"

"Family Korzha survives because everyone knows I never break my word. Not in public and not in private."

"That's it? You make one stupid promise in the heat of the moment and now you have to help me no matter what?"

"Oh, no," he said. "I am not a kind man. Do not think otherwise of me."

She picked up one of the satchels. "If you're not careful, fang, you're going to blow your cover. There's gonna be a big headline in *The Post* when we get back. Tiberiu Korzha Reveals Self as Big Fat Softie."

He grinned. "My lawyers are far meaner than I, Officer Donovan, and I rely on them utterly to protect my reputation. Now, are you ready? Or do you have a better idea?"

"Not really." She took a breath and then made a face at him. "I'm ready, Freddie."

Korzha felt Donovan watch him. She expected him to go out the door, but he didn't. Instead, he opened the room's single window—it was in back—and heaved himself out and up. A moment later, his upside-down head stared in at her. He waggled his fingers. She slung her satchel across her shoulders, put her hands in his and climbed out. For a moment she dangled face out over the street. He hauled her up and onto the roof. She practically somersaulted over him, he pulled up so hard. But, for a human, she had good reflexes and recovered well. She lay on the tiles, staring up at the sky. "Jeez," she whispered. "The moon sure is beautiful."

He looked. She was right. He rolled over her, snaked a hand around her waist and stared into her eyes. The back of his head tingled, and something stirred in him. Called to him. It was a very human moment, actually. One he hadn't felt in a long time. He wanted to kiss her—softly, sensually. And then he wanted to fuck her silly, he reminded himself.

"Korzha?" she said.

The sound of his name broke the moment. He got to his feet and held out a hand. "Yes?"

She slapped her palm against his. "He's coming. Now."

Fire erupted far above, over their heads. A signal? A high, keening scream broke out, a wail of rage. In the street below, all noise ceased. Doors slammed. Windows clanged shut. The demons of Biirkma were terrified.

Korzha hauled Donovan up, got an arm around her, and she held on for dear life as he ran. Given that the pursuers were in the air, he thought it foolish to fly himself and make an open target. Instead, he cannonballed across the rooftops, keeping low and in the shadows, leaping the gaping chasms of the streets, inexorably heading west, toward the moon. Fast. Faster yet. Their only hope was to flee beyond the pursuing demon's ability to sense Donovan.

Eventually, he succeeded. All Korzha's speed and cleverness were enough. Barely. But even when he'd outrun the demons, he continued to zigzag until he reached the last houses before the city wall, at which point he moved along the rooftops searching for the house from which he sensed the least energy. *There.* Ahead. Perfect.

The house was tucked against a part of the wall that was disintegrating into rubble. Beyond lay an expanse of rolling earth. At the horizon, black mountains peppered with white lifted toward the sky. With a pulse of thought, Korzha silenced the dog that raced, maddened, in the house's tiny interior courtyard. The animal was a dog in the way a mastiff compared to a Chihuahua. The thing looked like a cross between a mountain lion and a wolf. With the size of an Irish wolfhound and a close, curly coat and pointed, tufted ears that quickly broadened at the base, it wasn't like any domesticated dog from L.A.

Sleep. Deep, canine sleep, he demanded of it. The creature whined once and settled to the ground.

With his mouth by Donovan's ear, Korzha whispered, "Stay here. I'll be right back." He was going to look around.

She was riveted by the dog. As well she should be. Something that size looked more than capable of taking down a human. "Scout's honor?" she asked.

"Scout's honor." He cocked his head, jumped down and walked to a side building that looked like a garage. It wasn't. He went in and a few minutes later came out leading a horse. It was a pure-blooded Friesian, unless he missed his guess; and he knew he didn't. It was subtly altered, though, from the medieval horse of his memory. He kept reaching up to stroke its nose. Pointing to the mountains, he said, "That direction. West. Then southwest, around the city we go. Out of range of demon senses."

"How?" She looked at the horse.

He nodded. "We ride."

"Why can't we fly? I've seen you fly."

Korzha shook his head. "No. They'll be looking for us in the air. Keeping to the ground is the only thing that's kept us alive so far."

"Oh." She eyed the horse again.

"Yes. 'Oh.'" He laughed.

"I never pulled horse duty on the force, Korzha," she said after a moment. "I don't know how to ride one of these things."

He shook his head again. "You better hope you're a fast learner, because I am not carrying you the whole way." He laughed again and vaulted onto the beast, and held out a hand. It had been years since he'd been on a horse, and yet he felt right at home even without a saddle.

"Show-off," she said.

He waggled his fingers. "Afraid?"

She glared at him and put her hand in his. "Not on your life."

"Good girl." He pulled her up, and with an embarrassing degree of bumbling, they got her astride in front of him. He breathed in. She smelled and felt warm. She had a fantastic ass, too, right against his crotch.

Donovan glanced over her shoulder. "We better ride like hell."

Chapter Twenty

They took cover from the dawn in a cave formed of an outcropping of gleaming black rock. Korzha grabbed Claudia's hand, and she slid off the horse with the fervent wish that she would never have to get on one again. Not a wish likely to come true. Korzha whispered something to the horse and let it go. Already, the sky was turning to charcoal, and around the edges of the night the promise of dawn tinged the sky. Korzha dove straight for the opening. As he passed her, a flash of pale-reddish moonlight lit his face. His skin was tight over his cheeks, and his eyes seemed set deeper in his head than she recalled. She wondered what he'd been doing since Jaise was killed. How badly had the Bak-Faru's attack wounded him?

She followed, not having much choice since Korzha had a death grip on her hand. She stumbled now and again as they ran, more frequently when they reached the back of the cave where no moonlight penetrated. They turned a corner, and Claudia found herself in complete blackness. She smacked into Korzha's back.

He didn't budge. It was like walking into a Mack truck.

"We'll rest here," he said. From the sounds, she guessed he slung his satchel off his shoulder. She heard him lay out a blanket. "Stay in here, Officer." His voice echoed in her head and bounced off the walls too, giving it a doubly hollow sound. She still felt the off-kilter sense of his presence. He was too close. Deliciously, awfully close.

"Okay." The air felt cooler here than outside, and she was pretty sure she heard rustling overhead. Bats. Had to be bats. Right?

"I can't guarantee your safety if you leave my side." He turned while he spoke, which she knew because of the directional change of his voice. "Go to sleep, Officer Donovan."

"I can't see a thing," She said. Keeping the panic from her voice took just about everything she had. She hated the dark. But she'd fooled him in that, because he only sighed.

"I sometimes forget humans do not see as we do."

"Yeah, well, I'm limited," she said. The events of her time in Orcus were catching up with her. Pretty much, she wanted to puke. Or to go sit someplace where she could see her hands in front of her face.

Korzha made a noise and, a moment later, her satchel or something hit the ground with a soft thud. There came the sound of another blanket snapping, then wavering to the ground. Was it the darkness that made him feel so insistently present? She sighed, took a guess at where the second blanket had landed, and sat down—in dirt. A miss. But not by much.

She scooted onto the blanket. He'd cleared away the largest of the rocks, leaving a layer of what felt like cold sand covering the ground. Still, it was a more comfortable surface than one might hope to find in a cave, she guessed. She'd never been in a cave before. She managed to locate her satchel without smacking into the freaking vampire she had for company. Leather pack on her lap, she started feeling around inside.

"What are you doing?" Korzha asked.

By feel, she found one of the water skins, got it open and took a swig. "I'm thirsty. And hungry," she said. A heartbeat passed. The vampire's ability to be silent unnerved her. Every other creature breathed now and again. She never heard him do that. And she jumped when he spoke.

"So am I," he said.

Her hand froze somewhere near the middle of her bag. One wry rejoinder from him, and she was reminded in a flash that not only was Korzha not human, but that even among vamps he wasn't well-behaved. Just how hungry was he? Cripes. He could do whatever the hell he wanted to her here. "Not on your life, Korzha."

He laughed. "It's *your* thirst that's important right now, not mine. But, Officer Donovan, much as it may surprise you, the truth is that I haven't drunk illegally in years. Until Masters, I hadn't killed an innocent human in even longer . . ." His voice went soft again, like he was remembering something that saddened him. "She was the first in a very long time."

Claudia rested her head on her knees. "Killing a human is a Class One paranormal felony," she said. Korzha didn't really talk too much about himself, but she had a feeling there were circumstances she didn't know about. "That makes you subject to the no-strikes law, presumption of intent, no pleading out, no appeals. If you're convicted, it's straight to the Lompoc

Federal Detainment Center for Paranormal Offenders for you."

"You going to arrest me, Officer?" In the dark, his voice sounded sexy. Wouldn't it be something to have a man with a voice like that be interested in her?

With a soft laugh, she said, "I don't think the penal code applies in Orcus."

"Does it matter?"

Moved, and surprisingly so, she reached toward the sound, searching for the creature whose desolate voice tugged at her heart. Her fingers landed on his hip, right by his crotch. Oops. In the darkness, his hand closed around hers, moving it away. "For what it's worth, Korzha, I think you're okay. For a vamp." They'd been off-and-on allies, and she was getting a better sense of who he was. Imagine that. Why, she was practically friends with a fang. It was always better to judge a person by his actions, not rumors.

"And you're tolerable. For a human."

She squeezed his hand. "Gee, thanks."

"You're safe from me," he said. "For now."

Funny thing was, she believed him. She felt like he was beginning to care for her. A vamp. Was the feeling due to sincerity on his part, or vamp voodoo? Whatever the reason, she believed him. "Thanks," she said.

"You're welcome."

She slid her fingers free of his hand and, a moment later, pulled out one of several rectangles she'd taken for stale bread. Most of the food she'd found at the demon house was too strange to meddle with. She'd grabbed some bread, something that looked enough like cheese to take a risk and some apple-looking fruit. The rectangle was a bit mushed, but not much worse for wear, all things considered. "Not too many places to go shopping around here. Is food going to be a problem?" she asked.

He didn't answer right away. "Not for me. We'll manage."

She sniffed the rectangles. Didn't smell like much. She bit off a corner. Not bread, but sort of crackerish. When she'd eaten half, she remembered her manners and said, "Sawdust flavor. Yum. Want some?"

"No, thank you."

"Vamps eat all the time," She didn't know why, but she'd seen it. Talking to him about this sure felt strange, especially in the dark. Normal people made sounds. They breathed, remember. She couldn't quite shake the feeling there wasn't anybody there, that she was just talking to herself. Which made her a real loony-toon. Except, she *felt* him. "I see vamps eat regular food, I mean," she clarified.

"It helps us to pass, Officer." His voice had a husky edge that appealed to her far more than felt safe. "And it's fashionable. Very retro. Like back when a few of us were alive. When we were human." He sounded bitter.

"Oh." Well. Still, if it was crazy to trust him, so be it. It wasn't like she had much choice. It was just too bad he was a vamp. She felt a connection, a sadness. And it wasn't the weird fuck-me connection she'd had with Lath. She shivered. Better not to think about that.

"Human food has no nutritional value for us," he reminded her.

She took a bite, and another mouthful of sawdust went down her throat. "So, how do you get by, if you don't eat and you don't drink illegally?"

He made an odd noise. "You should know this, Officer. In the Upper, there are blood banks."

"Yeah, I know. Just seems kind of . . . boring."

"It is." She heard his amusement, and that made her feel good: making him laugh a little. "However, for the old-fashioned among us, there are plenty willing in our fair city."

She ate the last of the rectangle and forced it down. "Well, I'm not willing. Not anymore. No offense, Korzha, I want to be perfectly clear."

"Duly noted."

In the pack, searching for more rectangles, her fingers bumped against something cold and metallic. She grabbed it: a mini mag-light that must have fallen out of one of the pockets of her uniform pants. "Ah-ha!"

"What?" Korzha's voice rose from ground level, which Claudia presumed meant he'd laid down. Damn. She hadn't heard him do that.

"My sister used to call me a pack rat. She always complained I carry around too much stuff." Her heart shrank in her chest. "She had no idea what you have to do when you're a mom. Extra everything, emergency everything. I swear, Korzha, if you're ever going to be lost in the boonies with someone, make sure it's some kid's mother."

"My lucky day," he said.

"I'll take care of you. Never fear. If your face gets dirty, I'll bet there's a moist towelette in here somewhere."

"And who takes care of you? In Crimson City."

She laughed. "Me, that's who. I do everything. The cooking, the cleaning and the laundry. I see homework gets done, I play crazy eights 'til I'm crazy myself, *and* I pay the bills. Just call me super mom. Well," she whispered, when the lump in her throat was gone. "Well, anyway, I've saved the day, Korzha. *Fiat lux.*" She pushed the mag-light switch. Nothing happened. "Rats."

She yelped when Korzha snatched the mag-light from her hands. The whole thing was pretty unexpected, because she hadn't heard him move. For a petrifying moment she thought he was attacking her, and it was too late to get her knife. He threw the mag-light hard against the cave wall, which she knew because she heard the swish of his arm moving and then the metallic clunk and tinkle of the device smashing. "Hey!" she cried.

Halfway through the exclamation, fear romping through her chest like a stampeding rhino, the flashlight exploded. Or, more accurately, the batteries imploded. The air where the light had been blazed with a bluish glow bright enough for Claudia to see their blankets, packs and Korzha staring at her with glittering green eyes. In the flash of light he looked more handsome than any man had a right. Shit. She looked away. The metal barrel of the mag-light dripped down the black wall like wax down a burning candle.

"Idiot," Korzha said. "You could have been killed. Overworld technology won't work here. Did you pay any attention to what happened back at the portal? *Nothing* from the Overworld works here."

"Not really," she admitted, more sharply than she should have. What the hell was she thinking? Falling for a vampire defined suicidal. "I was too busy trying to figure out how to make Jaise give back my daughter."

Korzha went silent for a count of ten. "My apologies. That moment must have been terrible." His voice sounded strangled.

The rhino continued its rampage in her chest. Korzha lay back, hands beneath his head. Blue light flickered on the wall, showing his face. Despite his voice, he looked calm. Claudia's control crumbled like a sand castle under a wave.

"Take a deep breath," the vampire said.

"You don't get it, do you, Korzha? When you have a kid, nothing's ever the same. You're never safe again."

In the blue light, the vampire's teeth flashed. "Lie down," he said. "Go to sleep."

"Go to hell," she whispered.

He said, "What happened to your sister?"

"She died."

"I'm sorry."

"Except for Holly, everyone I've ever loved is dead. It's not that big a deal. No one who stays in the Lower lives very long," she said acidly.

"I'm sorry."

"That's just the way it is."

"Why didn't *you* die?" he asked after a moment.

"I didn't want Holly growing up like me." Claudia sat, arms wrapped around her upraised knees. "I was fifteen when she was born—Yeah, I know, but it's none of your damn business. I thought I was in love. Shit." She shook her head. "He wasn't. Obviously, I guess. He was a fucking demon. But I don't care. Holly saved my life. She really did. Turned me around. I made them let me stay in school, and I worked like burning cripes, and I got into college. You have no idea what it's like when you want something everyone says you can't have and can't do, so, hey, why try? It was a waste of time and money, right? But I did it. And after that, they couldn't tell me I didn't belong. And they can't say Holly doesn't belong, because she does. I'm a regular person now." She felt a moment of embarrassment for her outburst. He didn't seem to mind.

"Why a cop?" he asked.

"In the Lower," she said, stretching out on the blanket, "mean life expectancy of a human female is twenty years, six months. I'm twenty-five now, so, to be honest, I figure I chose pretty well." But the last few words came out as a choked sob, an ocean pooling in her eyes. Tears flowed like a salt river because she wasn't even going to live to twenty-six, and what would Holly do without her? Korzha's arms slid around her, beneath her arms, enfolding her, and she didn't even think how crazy it was to have a vamp so close. "I just want her back," she said.

One of his hands stroked her back. "I know."

"I want my daughter back," she repeated. She put her arms around him. Tears poured down her face. "I just want her safe. I don't even care what happens to me, as long as she can live and have a good life."

"We'll get her," he said. The burning wall flickered and dimmed. After a bit, as the pace of her tears slowed, his fingertip touched her cheek. She turned her face toward him. First came one finger, a light brush beneath her eye, then the sides of three. She wanted him to kiss her. He had a gorgeous mouth. A to-die-for mouth. He was probably a great kisser. With a mouth like his, that full lower lip, he had to be. To her surprise, he tenderly licked away the damp of her tears. It was an odd and peaceful moment. Her last glimpse of Korzha before the battery light on the wall disappeared was his tongue slipping along his fingers, tasting her sorrow.

Then the dark was unrelenting, the silence fathoms deep. Exhaustion pulled at Claudia's eyelids, but her nerves felt too jacked up for her to give in and sleep. When she got bored staring into the blackness, she curled against Korzha and lay staring up into inky black.

Very faintly, she could feel a bizarre sensation in the base of her skull. It was familiar. Not the kinky, sexy mind thing with Korzha—what the hell had the demons done to her? And what had they done to Holly? The thought numbed her. And then she slept, with nothing but nightmares for company.

A touch, feather-light along her cheek, a tender stroke, woke her. Or seemed to. She stirred under the caress. Someone whispered her name. In her head, she saw Lath as he'd looked standing naked in her cell. Her first thought, her very first unwilling thought was that she'd never seen a more beautiful man in her life. His black hair gleamed blue along the two braids and in the shadows of his ponytail. Black as a crow. Black as pitch. And his eyes—such a pale, pale lilac. He had a mouth a woman would die to kiss. Oh, but it was Korzha she wanted to kiss. Her body softened for him, ached. Lath cupped her cheek in his hand. In the back of her head, the tiny part that was still herself thought, *He isn't really here. He can't be.*

"*Tes,*" he said, in a low, soft voice. "Claudia-*tes.* Come back to me. Mate with me again."

Fear chilled her insides. She wanted to; she wanted him with such fierceness she could feel tears welling up in her eyes. And Korzha wasn't here this time to help her remember that she and the demon didn't belong together. His darkness thrust inside her, filling her, threatening to take everything until there wasn't anything left of her soul. Where was Korzha to save her?

"I miss you," Lath said in her dream. His body was muscled, unforgiving in its strength. She felt like he'd given her sunlight again. Far back in their depths, lilac and a winter's noon sky, she caught the reflection of a pale crimson moon. "I'm nothing without you," he said. In her sleep, she frowned. "Come back to me. You are my vishtau mate, *tes.* I will give you anything you want."

Chapter Twenty-one

All sense of time left her when she opened her eyes.
She might have been asleep ten minutes or ten hours.
She felt different, though. Not Claudia. Not Officer
Donovan. Not exhausted, either, so she must have gotten some sleep. Her hand, she realized, rested on the
mark Aslet had cut on her hip. Odd that it wasn't a
bloody sore or scabbing over or doing any of the unpleasant things a healing wound generally did. She
traced the raised twists and turns of the mark.
Smooth. Cold. Her fingertip warmed, though.

Korzha lay beside her, unmoving. Not just beside
her, next to her. One of his arms was draped over her
waist. While she'd slept, he'd turned his body toward
her as if seeking warmth. She shifted away. In the
dark, she retied her thigh sheath, which had come undone. Her arms hurt, an intramuscular ache. There
was no appreciable change in the darkness that she
could see. Her chest felt constricted, and she had to
pee. If she stared into the black for even one more
minute she'd go insane. Freaking insane. She sat up.

Oh, cripes. Her legs shrieked with soreness from overexertion.

Stealthy as a mouse creeping past a cat—well, a mouse with muscles full of lactic acid—she moved forward until she found the rock wall. When she hit the spot where her mag-light had melted, she continued right and retraced their path into the cave. A bat winged past her head, heading home. She fought back a shriek, more rhinos stomping in her chest. Around the corner, she could see a shift in light coming from the opening.

It was still daylight. From the mouth of the cave, a fading blue sky had started its slow transition to dark. The moon hung above, a pale bittersweet orange, not so red as last night, a sliver less full than before. She took a deep breath. The first order of business was to take care of her pressing biological needs, and the second was to work out some of her muscle aches. First things first.

She spent ten minutes pacing, getting the blood circulating through her body. Then, at the mouth of the cave, she started a series of slow stretches while she faced the foreign moon.

What happened to your sister?

She died.

Yeah. Tears welled up, but Claudia was years past crying.

What wouldn't she give to feel her mother touch her cheek? *Claudia, you worry so. Go to sleep. The dark won't hurt you. I won't let monsters under your bed.* Claudia had said those very same words to Holly. And it had been a lie. The dark *was* dangerous, and there *were* monsters. And she was so far from home that she might never get back.

She worked out the worst of the kinks in her body.

She moved through the poomse forms that got her mind off everything except her breathing, and the sky darkened and the moon turned a fat golden red. She didn't need anything right now. Nothing at all.

She finished the last form and realized that for several minutes the back of her head had been tingling. Now the sensation took on insistence, a demand that she pay attention. Lath was looking for her. A plethora of emotions from him reverberated through her body. Faint, though; he wasn't near. Her body remembered his, longed for him. He longed for her, too. *Vishtau*. The word echoed in her head but slipped away without meaning, without true definition. The word made her long to see Lath and his lilac eyes. Even though she fought the reaction, the longing blossomed. Her body ached with the tension of want.

Behind her closed eyes, she was back in Crimson City watching Aslet's hand disappear into the other demon's chest, watching the crimson mist of blood. That ritual had put her under a sentence of death. She saw Lath. Felt him. Felt his need for her. She wanted to go back to him, the monster, the killer. She wanted to belong to him. To be in his arms. She hurt with the physical longing.

Behind her, she heard movement, but she felt the vampire first, heard his deliberate sound, a shoe kicking a pebble. She craned her neck to see. Korzha stood within arm's reach. If he'd wanted to, he could have killed her. Broken her neck. Immobilized her and held her down while he fed. But he wouldn't do that to her. Not without an invitation. She shook her head. His eyes were green. Not pale, but a deep and mossy green. No one had ever accused any Korzha of making an unattractive vampire. Physical beauty must be on the list of requirements for the family.

"What the hell is with you?" he asked.

She wasn't sure if he'd spoken or not. She shook her head because she didn't have breath.

"I can *feel* you," he said. His mouth went taut, lips pressed together. "You might as well have a sign over your head that says, *I need to get laid.*" He hesitated, his eyes looking into her soul. "I never felt that from you in Crimson City. Not like this. Why here?"

Claudia stared at him. At the moment, there wasn't any mistaking what he was. "I want . . ." What did she want? A tear slid down her cheek. She didn't want to be alone with the ghost of Lath's hands on her, the thrust of his sex in her. "He . . . did something to me. He's doing it now, and I don't know how to make it stop."

Korzha's hard expression melted away. "Oh, dearheart." He dropped to his knees behind her, put his arms around her and drew her against his chest. His body wasn't warm, and there wasn't any smell of sweat. "What did he do?" he whispered.

"He had sex with me." She trembled and shut away the feeling in darkness. "Lath," she said. "A dark demon. Bak-Faru." Inside her, desire whirled. She was losing control. "The one with black hair. His name is Lath."

The vampire pressed his chin to her shoulder. She felt his cheek brush hers. His presence enfolded her, made her feel safe, took the edge off her shivering lust. She hung her head, and Korzha pressed his lips to the side of her neck. She felt no teeth, just his soft mouth.

"He's in my head, Korzha. Right now. I must be sick or something. I want him again. Right now, and I don't know how to make it stop."

Korzha's mouth slid off her neck and traced a slow, desultory line along her shoulder, then the back of her neck. It traversed her sensitive nape beneath her hair. Her breath caught in her throat. His fingers delved to her stomach, then along the ridge of her pelvis to the line of her underwear; then they stopped. "Officer Donovan," he said. His hips pressed against her backside, a slow, slow press of his erection against her. "I know you want to have sex with him. I can feel it. But you do not want him."

Claudia shook her head.

"Since he is not here, he cannot have you. And perhaps I can help." She knew, just knew from the tone of his voice that he felt what raged inside her. He was drawn to her, to the heat she couldn't control. Maybe to more. Inside, desire pooled between her legs. But for whom?

"He kept touching me and . . . and I . . . I felt like this. Like I do right now. I didn't want to, but I had to. I had to let him." She drew in a breath, but still felt like she couldn't breathe. The air was heavy, and when Korzha's cheek brushed hers again, the contact felt like an electric shock. She pressed back against him.

Korzha slid his hands underneath her shirt, cool palms against the burning skin of her back. She waited, holding her breath to see what he'd do next. His palms slid around and up, across her stomach. How strange that his hands weren't warm. They weren't cold, but weren't warm either. Not damp with lust. Not dry, but cool. Assured. The tips of his fingers brushed the bottom swell of one breast. He did something with his other hand, and with a soft snap, her bra came loose. Claudia sucked in a breath. Her body became a tumult of perceptions as his fingers slid upward and both hands cupped her naked breasts. She strained against his palms, seeking his touch, begging for more. She wanted him; he drove away thoughts of Lath.

"Very nice, Officer Donovan," the vampire whispered. "Very, very nice." She shuddered when his lips brushed the back of her neck, but, "No biting," he murmured. "I promise you."

"I don't think . . ."

"Let's not think. Either of us," he said.

She reached up and behind herself, touching his head. He adjusted to the change in her position. His hands slid down, underneath her breasts, and just held her. Such strong hands he had, and really, it was astonishing how warm she felt, how much heat pooled where he touched, and even more so when he gently pinched her nipples. She about melted. And he was there to sop her up. The touch of his mind came gently, a touch edged with desire that drew her into the reactions of her own body and redoubled them into a heady mix. He was as caught up by whatever was happening to her, as taken over, as she was. She didn't have time to wonder why.

He shifted his head, got his mouth near her ear. His tongue flicked out, wet her earlobe, and then he nipped. Not a bite; there was no blood drawn. She didn't feel the warmth of breath on her, but it was okay. The thought of Korzha holding her like this emptied her of any other thought. This was what she'd wanted. She got her hand lower down, over his belly. He flexed his hips back enough to allow her hand between them. Her fingers settled on his erection. It wasn't possible to be close enough. She had to have him inside her.

He whispered, "If you still want pleasure, if you need pleasure now, I can give you that. Let me give you that."

Jesus. What was she thinking? She leaned forward, sliding out of his grasp. His hands slipped around to her back, but he left his palm on her bare skin. Her desire wasn't all gone. Whatever Lath had done to her, the demon wasn't responsible for her physical state now. The truth was, she was attracted to Korzha. This freaking vampire. More than a little. Maybe a lot. And not just when she was drugged with paranormal passion, or because he was gorgeous. The thought that she was legitimately attracted to a vampire was scarier than anything that happened with Lath. Korzha moved his hand along her back, fingertips tracing the bumps of her spine. She couldn't. She couldn't. Not with a vamp. Not of her own free will. Not on purpose. Oh, but couldn't she with Korzha?

Claudia hung her head and concentrated on putting her clothes to rights. "You broke my bra," she said. Her fingers shook. Rats. Oh, just rats. Her skin still tingled with his touch. She wasn't small enough to even think of going without.

"There's nothing wrong with having sex, you know." He sounded tense. "It is an enjoyable way to pass time."

She pulled her bra out from under her shirt and assessed the damage. Pass the time? "Yeah, well."

"You wanted me. Or are you going to deny what you felt? I made us both feel good, and you know it."

"I don't have sex every time I feel the urge." Why not with Korzha? Why not? It would be her choice.

"Maybe you should," he said.

She glanced over her shoulder at him and then returned to rescuing her bra. "I don't have sex with vampires, okay? Or werewolves." She choked back tears. But why not? Why not let Korzha hold her? "In fact, I hardly ever have sex at all."

Korzha stretched out, elbow on the ground, head on his hand, staring at her.

On the third try, her fingers cooperated and tied a knot in the broken bra strap. A vampire. She had let a vampire take her in his arms. "What kind of idiot throws herself at a vamp? Might as well offer you my throat now."

"Mm. Yes, you could," he said. He seemed torn between amused and annoyed.

She slid her bra under her clothes and managed to contort herself into it. She stood without his help, and he still stared at her. Hard. Her face heated. "Cut out that voodoo head stuff, would you?"

"Voodoo head stuff?" During the day, Korzha's hair had slipped loose from the scrunchie, and the effect was unfortunate, considering that Claudia would rather be immune to his looks. "Dear-heart, what on earth are you talking about?"

"You know what I mean. That stuff you do when you want someone to do something with you."

He stood up, rolling his eyes. "Do something? Did you think we were doing something?"

"You had your hands up my shirt, you perv."

"And you had your hands on my cock." He took a step toward her. "My hands were up your shirt, not down your pants."

"That's—"

Korzha sneered. "What you just felt was all natural, and you know it. Don't cheat yourself—or me—by pretending it wasn't, or do I need to explain the birds and the bees to you? I have a penis in fine working order I assure you—"

"Could you be a little cruder?"

"Yes. But I won't." He continued to glare. "I apologize, Officer, for daring to lay a vampiric hand on you.

But I won't apologize for enjoying it. Nor for your enjoyment, either. Or for wanting to make love to a beautiful woman, even if she is human."

She drew in a breath. Oh, jeez. She felt more rhinos in her chest. "I didn't mean that," she said.

"Yes, you did. I know what was in your head just now. And I know what you were feeling when my vile unhuman hands were all over you." He threw an arm in the air. "I fucking felt you like a truck running over me. I assure you, the moment got away from us both. That's it. Face it."

"Look, Korzha—"

"You talk too damned much," he said, turning back to the cave. "We need to get going."

"Fine," she said to his back. "Let's go."

He faced her again. "Officer Donovan," he said softly. He wasn't sneering anymore. He wore an oddly plaintive expression, and for some silly reason, that made her heart feel too big for her chest. "Is this necessary? All this protestation?"

"No. You're right. I know you're right," she said. Shit. "I am such a loser. My life just totally sucks." She gave a half-sob "I've screwed up every relationship I've ever had. All freaking three of them."

Korzha held out his arms and she walked right into them. "Hush, dear-heart," he said.

"Let's go." But her words came out muffled by the lump in her throat. Something tickled her cheek, and she wiped at it. Oh, great. Just great. Tears. And she was legitimately attracted to a vampire.

"If you'd like, we can go," he said. But his voice was all soft, a mellow invitation to take up where they'd left off.

"No," she said. "I'd probably screw that up, too. And then you'd hate me, and I don't want that." She looked at him, and her body tingled with the shivery wraith of his touch, as if he still stroked her. And he knew it.

"But, it would be nice for a while, yes? Very nice." They stared at each other. She understood, at last, what he seemed to already know. They were going to end up having sex. If Lath did that to her even once more, she'd be all over Korzha. That freaky mind thing pulled him in too, and it wasn't his fault he was affected. They both were. It intensified feelings they had for each other anyway. What's more, he now knew she understood.

"Oh, yes," he said, lengthening his vowels. "Let's. Let's be lovers while we can. For as long as it lasts." He seemed pleased.

"Look," she said. "Look, um, let's just cross that bridge when we get there."

His eyes gleamed. "Here is the chasm. Right in front of us." He smiled, the expression mirroring the softness in his voice. "I would adore taking you to bed. With or without the biting." Even more softly, he said, "Biting or not—which do you prefer?"

She said, "Go to hell." But she didn't mean it anymore, and he knew that too.

He grinned. "Dear-heart, we're already there."

"Can't we just get out of here?"

With a shrug, he said, "Let's do that, too."

Chapter Twenty-two

Korzha recited all the curses he knew. He started in Romany, then Romanian and Hungarian, then threw in High German and Middle English, moved on to Russian and Latin, and progressed through the Romance languages French, Italian, Spanish, visited a few of the Gallic ones he'd picked up and ended with English. None of it did any good. Even the old favorites diverted him for only a moment. He cursed himself, he cursed Orcus, he cursed demons. He cursed Jaise and Aslet and Lath and all the Bak-Faru. He didn't curse Donovan, because that only made things worse—too many of the curses had a sexual element. He was frustrated enough without being reminded.

They'd been traveling for what felt like a night and a half but was more like four hours, when Donovan called a break. He'd have loved to take to the sky, except every half hour or so he felt or heard distant demons on the wing. They were patrolling.

It was going on thirty hours since he'd last fed. He

did not feel a dire hunger yet, but hours of closeness to a human hadn't kept his mind off his need. Unfortunately, they continued doubled up on the horse. She wasn't a horsewoman, and probably wouldn't ever be. More than once he'd been tempted to risk flying just to end his torture. But then he'd catch the shadowed darkness of demons overhead, searching.

The enforced contact put all manner of temptations not just within reach but in his grasp—if not directly in contact with him. It'd be better for him, he thought, if for ten or twenty or thirty minutes they could just let their bodies do the communicating. Maybe even better for her, too. They could work out a little mutual aggression, explore the frustration and simply get it over with. He wished like hell he didn't want to protect her, too. That kind of involvement with a human never came to a good end. For the human.

All things considered, a few minutes of respite between them seemed a splendid idea.

He directed the horses toward an outcropping of black rock and dismounted. "We haven't much time," he said, striding away from her. She slid down, stomach scraping the horse's back, hands clinging until her feet hit the ground. She backed away and stared at the horse. Korzha faced her, admiring her behind and feeling like a jerk for his sullen behavior. She must be sore, he thought, and too proud to say so. He put his hands on his hips, trying to decide if he was irritated or felt sorry for her. She turned around.

"Unlike you," she said, looking him up and down, "I need bathroom breaks."

"One of the many limitations of humanity." He gave her an amused grin, and was appalled to find himself considering, *seriously* considering, what he would do about her. Oh, fuck. He was thinking about the future, but more disturbing was that he was actually thinking of a future that included her.

"Oh, yeah?" she said, in that tough-girl voice that seemed to make his heart melt every time he heard it. She took a hobbling step away from the horse. "You're just jealous."

He wouldn't make her, not now that her deal with Jaise was off. All the same, his body reacted to the idea even though nobody knew better than him the risks—for all concerned—of a vampire going rogue. God knows he wouldn't mind having sex with her. Not at all. He watched her. Who was he kidding? He was dying to make love to her. It was all he could think of lately. Such a lovely body, athletic, sleekly muscled. And the mental connection that came with having bitten her once already would make sex all the more delicious. He did his best to shut off his feelings, but it didn't do any good. He still wanted her.

She passed him, and he refused to look at her; though, damn, he could feel her. Nose in the air, she headed for what her human senses would consider far enough away to be private. It was unlikely she'd go far enough for him not to know what she was doing. He pulled the pack with most of their things off the horse and whispered to the animal. *Don't go far. Rest.* He knew it would do as he commanded.

Donovan marched around the side of a boulder to take care of her business. He knew exactly when she heaped dirt over the hole she dug. He leaned against the other side of the boulder and opened his senses. She rummaged in her satchel and took out her water. Soon after that, he smelled the scent of baked grain—she'd taken out one of the packets of bread. To be fair, and all things considered, excluding what had happened at the cave, they got along well. For a vampire-hating cop, she wasn't bad. And here in Orcus, she was a desperate mother. He could do little but admire her resolve, grieve for her anguish and wish she'd go to bed with him. Wouldn't that be nice?

His thoughts drifted back to sex and, specifically, sex with Officer Claudia Donovan. Current circumstances favored him. They were stuck together for at least the time it took to circle around the city, with no privacy from each other. He'd not spent this much time in the company of a single human in more years than he could count. They might have tacitly agreed not to talk about what had happened during their earlier encounter, but he couldn't stop thinking about his hands on her and the desire that radiated from her and into him. He could feel her now: firm breasts, soft skin, the feel of her nipples coming to a peak under his palms, the rush of blood to his cock, the human scent of her, blood scent, heartbeat, pulse. Sweet Life, he really, really wanted to fuck her.

On the other side of the boulder, he heard her whisper, "Go to hell, Tiberiu Korzha."

As long as she went with him, he was amenable.

A strange animal yowl split the air, a distant coughing. Aside from bats, it was the first indication he'd heard of wildlife. With the back of his head against the boulder, he watched the moon and stars, and the sight took him back to the centuries before electric lights had obscured the night sky. The yowls continued, closer now. He blocked the sound out, closing his eyes and imagined himself looking into Donovan's dark brown eyes as he entered her, feeling that slide into female warmth and damp. Heaven. She had eyes to drown in, he thought. They could have sex without biting. Although, sharing blood would be nice. So really nice.

The yowl sounded even closer. He heard another dry, animal cough, but from above him this time. How had something gotten above him without his hearing? He heard steps on the huge boulder behind him. He opened his eyes.

Pad, pad. Pad, pad. Those were not the steps of a bipedal creature. He tracked the sound without moving. It was heading away from him. Toward Donovan with her human warmth and smell. Then he heard another sound and a chill went through him. There were two of them, cunning predators who'd gotten upwind. Dread turned to ashes in his mouth as he launched himself into action.

Around the boulder, in front of him, lit by the moonlight and facing Donovan head-on, stood a feral version of the "dog" he'd lulled to sleep before they left Biirkma. This one's eyes glittered and its mouth drew back, exposing a set of long, razor-sharp teeth. Its broad ears rotated. Unlike the domesticated one, he couldn't reach its mind. The creature was feral, too intent on hunger and hunting. Donovan stood, her satchel at her feet. She had her knife in her hand.

Overhead, a pebble skittered—the dog's mate. The thing in front of Donovan snarled and took a step toward her. Its glowing red eyes glanced upward. There were two, this dog in front, and one behind and above on the boulder. Teeth like that, long and sharp, teeth like Korzha's own, were for killing. The creature on high shifted, adjusting to the other's movement. Warm-blooded creatures. Donovan balanced herself, as yet unaware of her dual danger.

"Above and behind, Donovan," Korzha called. She twitched in acknowledgment of his warning. But he was too late. Too late.

The creature facing her went belly-down, a low

growl rolling from its open mouth. Claws scrabbled on rock like fingernails down a chalkboard as the second beast crouched. The one on the ground leapt. Its teeth flashed, and that was all Korzha saw before the one above descended. Korzha threw himself forward as Donovan's knife flashed. The second creature landed a hair-breadth from him. It was larger than the one Donovan knifed, broader through the chest and much heavier.

Korzha roared, a sound calculated to frighten. Both animals started, and that provided critical seconds. Donovan's knife glinted in the moonlight, then disappeared into the female's body again. For a human she was fast, and she'd judged her blows exquisitely, her expression intent and grimly focused. She looked like a woman who'd fought for her life more than once. She could take care of herself.

Korzha's inattention to his own situation cost him, because the male now faced him, hackles raised. The male was faster than he expected. Stronger, too. It jumped at him. If he went up, ducked or dodged, the thing would have a clear line to Donovan. He stayed where he was. The male hit him like a wrecking ball. A set of heavy jaws closed on Korzha's upper arm, teeth rending. Pain exploded everywhere. He dropped to the ground, rolled, and got a hand in the creature's jaws and pried his arm free. With another roar, he got the thing's head back, exposing its throat. He caught blood-scent, warm and liquid. His own.

The female took another blow from Donovan, a kick in an attempt to keep it from lunging at him. Donovan had injured it badly. White-faced in the darkness, she tightened her fingers around the hilt of her knife and hurled herself after the beast, who was trying to protect her mate. Two females protecting their males, Korzha fancied. That was how he'd like it to be—if only she were like him. He howled, and felt his sinews stretch with the effort of keeping his grip on the male.

Donovan dove, straddled the female, grabbed it under the muzzle and slit its throat. Life spilled out in a gush of blood. The female flailed once and went limp. Chest heaving, eyes wide, Claudia stared at Korzha.

"Kill it. Break its neck," she said. Dirt smeared her face, and her sleeve was torn.

"Not yet." His mouth thinned. Already his injuries were sapping his strength. "Turn your back," he ordered. He didn't want her to see this.

"Are you crazy?"

"This thing now or you later. You decide," he roared. His lips drew back, exposing his fangs. He strained to pull the creature's head upward. His injured arm was numb. "Turn your back!"

She hesitated a moment longer, then faced away. "What if there are more of those things?" she asked. She ripped off her sleeve.

He didn't answer. A bitter, chalky taste rose in his mouth, coated his throat as he fed. Bile rose when the creature's blood hit his stomach. Still, it was better than nothing, as a man dying of thirst might say of his own sweat. When he had taken all that he could stand, he broke the thing's neck and let the carcass fall. Donovan, her back to him, stared at the ground. A scratch pinkened the back of her neck.

Korzha shuddered. The brackish taste spread through him. A trickle of black oozed at his feet, reached a dip in the ground and pooled: blood from the creature Donovan had killed. He watched the pool grow and quiver at an edge until the pressure breached cohesion and the liquid oozed forward.

"Shall we go now?" Korzha stepped toward her. He

gripped his upper arm with one hand. He'd been bitten to the bone, and despite having fed on the animal, he was healing slowly. Too slowly. Maybe even not at all.

She looked at the bodies of the two dead creatures, then retrieved her satchel to pull out an extra shirt. He grabbed her hand.

"Not necessary," he said.

"Your face is filthy dirty."

"So is yours."

"Yeah, but on me it looks great, right?" Her eyes moved over him with a motherly eye. "Let me get the gunk off you at least."

Korzha nodded. He stood still while she used the hemmed edge of the shirt to dab at the blood on his face.

"No moist towelette?"

"So sue me." She turned the fabric over and swabbed the sheen from his forehead. "Looking kind of gray, my man," she said.

"Dinner was not to my taste."

She grimaced. "Sorry about that." She put away the cloth and, as she wiped her hands on her thighs, looked at him guiltily. Or so he fancied. "Remember, I offered to share my sawdust bars with you."

He laughed. "Not to my taste either."

She shook her head. "Well, what is, for cripe's sake?"

Their eyes met. He realized she'd forgotten what he was. He couldn't help it; he smiled. Humans could be *so* naive, and this lapse of hers was rather flattering. Lovely Claudia. Sweet Claudia. She could almost think of him as human. "*You* are," he said. The hungry wolf to Little Red Riding Hood.

"Right." She folded the shirt and jammed it back in the satchel. "Okay. We ought to get going, I guess."

He nodded. "Thank you," he said. "For coming to my assistance." When she shrugged, he walked to where they'd originally stopped. The horse still stamped and flicked its tail there, and he soothed it of its fright and disquiet. The muscles of his legs felt thin, not fully under his command. He wondered if the dog creature's blood had poisoned him. "Clean your knife, Officer."

While he gathered his things, she hunkered down and searched again in her satchel. Korzha's stomach clenched. The animal's blood was worse than any non-human blood he'd ever had, including demon. His knees didn't feel like water anymore, but his injuries weren't healing either. Hunger called to him, whispering to be sated. He held on to the horse and watched Donovan use the shirt to clean off her knife. It was a damn good thing they were riding instead of relying on him to get them back to Biirkma. He felt like he'd been left in the sun without PABA. Some of the blood had coagulated, and she had to work at the last of it. The knife finally went back into the sheath. She stood and tapped it.

"My new best friend," she said. She looked Korzha up and down. "You gonna be okay?"

"We ought to go before more of them show up," was his only answer.

Claudia gave him a grin, obviously pleased with herself for having survived such an encounter. "We're not there yet?" she asked.

A hint of humor filled her eyes. It was almost as appealing as her smell, the remembered taste of her. He hoped to hell they made it somewhere safe before he jumped her.

Chapter Twenty-three

As they rode, Korzha's sleeve darkened. Before long, even Claudia smelled blood. The scent made the horse uneasy, with the unfortunate result that the vampire was forced to hold onto her tight, which had to hurt. He refused to talk about his injury, just insisted he'd be fine by next nightfall. Which wouldn't do either him or Claudia any good if anything else caught up with them before then.

Her stomach clenched. Korzha *had* to be all right. Without him, she'd never get Holly. She'd never find her way out of this wasteland, and chances were even slimmer she'd make it to the portal. "Liar," she said.

He didn't reply.

"You better not die on me," she said. She made her voice light, a playful warning, like she didn't mean it. All in fun, right? Her situation wasn't dire at all.

"That is unlikely."

She shook her head. " 'Never trust a vamp.' That's what the instructors back in the Academy said. You're all out for yourselves." Her voice dropped to a whis-

239

per. "If you had any sense at all, you'd trade me back to Aslet or those Bak-Faru guys in return for safe passage to L.A."

"Never." His arm tightened around her waist, and they rode in silence with just the sound of hooves and the occasional snort from the horse. They weren't in a desert, but the ground was barren except for scraggly brush that grew in clumps. The sky was enormous, bigger than life, with stars so bright they took Claudia's breath.

"I don't know about this place," she said, to break the silence.

"Meaning?"

"All this open space makes me nervous. I'm used to the city. People. Noise. Everything and everybody close together."

"Surely you've been out of the city?" he asked. His voice sounded strange to her. Like he had to work at keeping his pain under control.

"Nope." She kept her back straight because she didn't want to bump his wound. He kept his good arm around her waist, but she didn't lean against him like she had before.

"The beach? Skiing at Mammoth? Yosemite? Disneyland?"

She sighed. "Korzha, unless you've been dirt poor, you just don't get it. You can't."

"What don't I get?"

"When my folks were alive, my mom worked three jobs, and my dad—well, he wanted to be a cop, but he was a janitor at the Arena. Mom got killed in a drive-by. Wrong place, wrong time. Not long after that, my dad got caught in a sweep. A vamp."

"Your father's a vamp?"

"No." She drew a breath. "He was rounded up and

sold to a vamp. A rogue." She felt him react, and she hurried on. Hardly anyone wanted to believe what went on in the Lower. And the ones who knew, didn't admit it. Which was Korzha? "I'm going to take Holly to Disneyland, though. I'll have three weeks vacation in six months, and I'm going to take her. We're going to have a blast."

He leaned against her back. "What did you do for fun when you were her age? Anything?"

"Stole stuff, mostly." She laughed softly. "Jacked up the ticket machine at the movieplex to see if we could get free tickets. Modified comm units. You'd be surprised what you can get for some of those. Kind of my specialty. I was in demand."

"You were a truant?"

"No way," she said in a low voice. "No way. I had to get the grades and test scores for college because I didn't want to end up like everyone else I knew. And then with Holly . . . She's the best thing that ever happened to me." Her voice fell. "The best."

"And how did everyone else end up?" He asked. She was used to his arm around her, but Korzha was holding her pretty tight now.

"OD. Gun to the head. Or meat for an illegal hunt. I got out, paid for courtesy of illegal comm-unit mods. I got my AA. Straight A's, and they had to let me into college."

"Why a cop?" he asked again.

"Because they were hiring, and the benefits are good. I have to have medical and dental for Holly. Orthodontia is in our future. Insurance, in case something happens to me. In two years I'll be fully vested in my retirement accounts, and then I'm going to apply to law school. I want to go to school and be a DA. Maybe a PA. It's been an education, being a cop, Korzha. Life on the other side, you might say. But there's always progress to be made. None of that's going to happen now." Korzha pulled her tighter against him, but she didn't mind at all; he didn't mean anything by it. She knew that now. "We have a lot in common," she guessed. "I was a regular criminal in the making, and you are—"

"Shit," he said.

"What?"

The horse started dancing around as if the ground were hot under its hooves. The sound of wings beating in the air made Claudia look over her shoulder. Two black shapes hung in the air, low and moving fast in their direction.

"We might outpace them," Korzha said. But before any more words were out of his mouth, a burst of wind stirred up a choking dust. "Is it Lath?" he asked.

"If it was Lath, I think I'd feel it."

The two demons were overhead now. A shrill cry ripped through the sky. One swooped down; the other held back, watching for any feint. The air from the downdraft of their wings beat against Claudia and Korzha's heads and pounded in her ears. The horse was tired, but a spurt of speed got them a short distance ahead before its energy petered out. With a sinking heart, Claudia realized there wasn't a chance of outrunning them, and there was no defensible position in sight. One of the demons landed in front of them, wings beating so hard the horse reared. Claudia held on for dear life.

Both creatures had started in a gargoyle shape, but only one kept the form. The other morphed into a biped, a woman. She looked primed for action.

Of the two, Claudia judged her the more formidable. The demoness stood, legs spread, knees slightly bent, waiting, perfectly balanced. She kept her eyes on

Claudia and put her hands on either side of her mouth. "Claudia Donovan," she called out.

The other demon circled above. Korzha's arm tightened around Claudia, also controlling the prancing horse.

"You belong to the Bak-Faru called Lath," the demoness said. The sound of the dark demon's name prickled the hair on the back of Claudia's arms. "He wishes you back with him."

"Sure, he wants me back. To make certain I die," she said.

The flying gargoyle barked another word and the horse shuddered under them. The air shimmered. Korzha grabbed her around the waist and vaulted upward. The gargoyle swooped in and rammed him so hard in the back that Claudia heard them both grunt from the contact. Korzha's arms popped open, and Claudia fell, spiraling toward the ground.

Both demons screeched, drowning out her shrill cry. The gargoyle dove for Claudia. But it was Korzha who caught her. Their landing was hard. The gargoyle followed, wings beating. Korzha hauled himself and Claudia up and pushed her behind him. There wasn't time for panic. Of course, there was no way she could be more panicked than she already was. Shit. She smelled blood, Korzha's blood. He wasn't in any shape to take on two demons. Not if he was going to win.

"You can't take them both, Korzha," She got the black-bladed knife in her hand and pressed her back against his. "Not in your condition."

"I'm not that far gone," he said.

"Right." She hoped he hadn't broken anything in the fall, but they'd hit awfully hard and her own ribs were bruised. "But, fang, I have an edge you don't."

"Oh, do tell, human."

She glanced at the demoness and decided it didn't matter if she told. "They won't kill me because they need me for the portal. You, they'll kill."

"They can try."

"You're immortal, fang, not invincible."

He nodded, conceding the point. "Together, then?"

"The gargoyle first." She felt Korzha nod in acceptance. A wind came from nowhere, stirring the dirt into dozens of tiny whirlwinds. "I need to be in close," she reminded him.

"I've seen you fight."

The gargoyle padded forward and snarled, a combination of rabid werewolf and cornered cat. A hint of reddish-orange flickered in its eggshell eyes. With her left hand, Claudia tapped Korzha's leg to signal she'd attack.

Korzha nodded again. She glanced back to remind herself he wasn't at anything like full strength, and then she turned her attention to her foe. She moved forward, knife extended, and hoping this was the right decision. Korzha shadowed her. Claudia frowned because he held his injured arm close to his body. The female shrieked. The wind picked up, carrying debris. Claudia squinted to keep the dirt out of her eyes.

Korzha feinted right; the gargoyle tracked the blur, snapped its teeth on air, then overadjusted. When the blur stopped, Korzha was underneath the gargoyle with his hands under its forelegs and his fingers clasped over the back of its human neck. Claudia rushed in, striking her thumb hard against the underside of the monster's nose in the *inn jung* pressure point. Simple but effective. Pain cut off the howl of protest from the creature. Claudia raised her knife to its belly, and that brought the demoness's attack to a halt; the wind died.

"Don't kill it," Korzha said. His voice rasped, like sandpaper over green wood.

By now the pressure of her thumb had had its intended effect on the other demon. It kicked once more, then lay still. Claudia paused with her knife inches from the gargoyle's belly, but eased up on the pressure.

Korzha adjusted his hold on the gargoyle, too. "Are we in agreement," he asked the monster, "that if you cease to struggle, Officer Donovan won't use her knife on you and I won't break your neck?" The gargoyle nodded, an infinitesimally small motion because of Claudia's thumb.

"Officer Donovan," Korzha said. "We're in its world. Its home. This demon hasn't done anything but defend its home from invaders. Let's let him go—if we think we can trust him."

Claudia stared down at the vampire and couldn't hold back a grin. Good cop, bad cop? In L.A., she never got to be the bad cop. This was going to be fun. "Have you gone fricking nuts? Do you think demons care about honor?" she asked. "About trust, or giving or keeping their word?"

"Yes."

"Oh, for cripe's sake." She rolled her eyes. "What are we going to do? Sit here hoping until the sun comes up?"

The demoness called from where she was, "I can wait, Claudia Donovan."

Korzha tightened his grip on the captured demon. He called out to both of his foes: "The human is bad-tempered. But she won't kill you if you make me a promise. Understand?"

The gargoyle started to morph, but Claudia pushed up on its nose. It yelped once. Silver mist rose between them. "None of that monkey business," she said. "Not if you value your life. I'm not as tolerant as my vampire buddy here." She pressed her blade closer to its throat. "Korzha, I'm getting tired." She twitched her knife. "What do you want it to promise?"

"To take his lady friend home straightaway."

"Well?" she asked the gargoyle, watching its eyes. "I'm feeling darned impatient. You promise?"

"Yes," it said.

"Well," she said, "I'm not so sure. Why should they get to go home?"

"Cut them some slack, Donovan," Korzha said.

"Okay." She shrugged. "I guess."

A gout of silver mist formed over the gargoyle's head. "Tiberiu Korzha, it is done."

Claudia lowered her knife several inches below the monster's underbelly, and twisted to stare with narrowed eyes at the demoness. "Lath did some of that demon crap on you, didn't he? Don't bother answering. I know he did. I'll let him go with his balls intact if you make me a promise."

"What promise, Claudia Donovan?" the demoness asked.

"Bring me my daughter."

"I cannot do that." She lifted her hands. "I am forbidden."

"Is she all right?"

"Yes."

"All right, then—promise me demons won't hurt her. Strike that. Promise me you'll watch over her. Keep her safe."

Korzha shook his head. A drop of condensation from the silver mist rolled down his cheek, looking remarkably like sweat. Except vampires never perspired. "Officer Donovan," he said. "Can we get on with this?"

"Promise me," she said to the female.

The demoness bowed her head in acknowledgment. "Donovan!"

"Claudia Donovan," the demoness said, "I must keep my promise to your vishtau mate, and I must have my mate safe. The Bak-Faru called Lath wishes you to know he hopes you are safe. He wishes you to know he desires to be with you again." She smiled. "He wishes to assure you he will protect you from Aslet. And from the vampire."

"Tell him I said thanks but no thanks."

"Siath watches over your daughter, she will protect her."

The gargoyle squirmed in Korzha's grasp, and Claudia gave it a hard look. "Cut it out," she said.

"Officer Donovan," Korzha said.

Claudia looked the demoness right in the eye. "Tell Lath to leave me the freaking hell alone."

"He cannot do that. But now you must release my mate. Unharmed."

She pretended to think about it. "Go ahead, fang," she said to Korzha.

The vampire loosened his grip on the demon. The moment it was free, it morphed into another form—that of a handsome man. He walked to his mate, and an instant later the two were winging away in the air.

Claudia shaded her eyes and looked after them. "Cute couple, don't you think?"

To her surprise, Korzha laughed out loud. Claudia was so shocked she gave herself whiplash looking at him. Wow. Korzha was seriously handsome when he laughed. Now, why the hell had she gone and noticed that?

Chapter Twenty-four

Without the horse, Korzha had no choice but to take to the air with Donovan in his arms. Flying took more energy than he wanted to expend, not to mention increasing their chances of being found again. But what else could he do? Walking wasn't an alternative.

More than once, he stopped. His stated excuse was to give Donovan the opportunity to tend to her human needs, which she did. But in reality, he needed to rest. At each stop, he sank into a motionless crouch while he waited, conserving his energy and willing himself to heal. At the first and every stop thereafter, Donovan ate and repacked the satchels, redistributing the weight more evenly between them. After the third time, he stopped wondering if she was trying to give him more time to rest; he knew she was.

He didn't complain. In truth, his body ached from the weight of carrying her, hungered from the exertion and the drain of his body which was trying to heal. He ignored his hunger—an unpleasant effort, but happily still possible. He wasn't starving. Not yet. Daylight whirled closer, and with the promise of dawn came a creeping dread that he might sink into a permanent stupor. He flew lower and slower.

Biirkma at first reappeared as a charcoal smudge against the rising dark of the horizon, but eventually the smudge took shape against the inkiness of night. The palace lay northwest, and they alit to the south, at an outer edge of the city wall close to where he'd intended to end up. Korzha saw little choice except to keep Claudia with him when he went after Holly. In order to cloak her, she needed to be close by. Demons would find her if he left her unattended in the city. Leaving her unprotected in the country felt nearly as risky and, unacceptably to him, increased the chances of their being caught. Since he wasn't at all certain that he could cloak Holly's half-demon nature once he had her, all three of them needed a straight shot to the portal.

Now Donovan paced, pausing now and again to shake out her legs or windmill her arms. She never seemed to notice the attention he paid her body, particularly to the curve of her backside. Did she not notice, or did she choose to ignore? He wondered which. At the moment, he was too tired to care. He just watched and admired. She put her hands to her hips and her head down, pacing like a sprinter in the minutes before the five-hundred-meter race. He could feel her mental preparation for going into the city.

He stood, and Donovan stopped pacing. Without comment, she bent for the satchels and slung them across her chest. Now began the most dangerous part of their dangerous plan: making their way back to the palace with him cloaking them both, staying low, roof-level if practical, street-level if necessary. The air if disaster came. His injuries meant he had to reach deep for physical and mental strength. His body felt the hum of the demons; he felt the tug of Donovan in his head. She walked to him, and he took her in his arms. He leapt from the wall to the top of the nearest house. In silent agreement, he put her down and they carefully walked the roofs.

They'd been prowling the rooftops for twenty minutes when an ear-splitting shriek shattered the air. Korzha saw immediately the sound had nothing to do with them, but Donovan cried out and clapped her hands to her head. She slipped, and the heel of her leading leg went *flak-aclak-aclak* along the tiles, heading straight for the edge and a drop to the street below. Korzha dove after her, reaching for her wrist. On her belly, she stopped the slide by jamming her foot against a stone gutter. Korzha hauled her up, ignoring the pain in his bitten arm and the smell of blood seeping from her scraped leg.

On the rooftop, she got her legs under her and crouched so that when he grabbed her, she fit against his chest. But his injuries made his grip awkward and insecure. She twisted against him, trying to settle herself, but jarred his injured arm. Agony exploded in him. His mental control slipped, exposing them to demon senses.

From the west, blue light flashed. Demons launched into the air, and Korzha swore. With an inarticulate shout of apology, Claudia got the straps of the satchels over her head and let them spiral down to the street below. There wasn't anything in them they couldn't do without, and he could make better time without the burden.

The demon pursuers moved fast, and more joined them. A flood of winged and airborne creatures rose from the distant palace. On their present course, the demons would corner them in ten minutes, probably less. Korzha dropped to street level and veered away, back toward the portal. Donovan tightened her arms around him. There was nothing else to do, really. They were near enough to the snare with its imprisoned rogue that the vibration made his head ache. Donovan tightened her hold on him.

Behind him, the air heated. Wind whipped his hair. The ground shuddered. More demons joined the chase. Some were close enough now that their clothes identified them as guards from the palace. The pursuers stayed airborne, but others also poured from alleys and streets. He soared away from the palace. The demons had a visual on them, and Korzha decided he'd be better off putting his resources into speed.

The demons were herding them northwest, so Korzha, contrary creature that he was, cut due east. A ball of fire exploded five yards ahead of them. Heat singed his face as he blew past. Behind him, fire billowed, cutting off any retreat. His body reacted to the danger, and he found a reservoir of strength. He would *not* allow harm to come to Claudia. Three snarling demons landed in the street ahead—not Bak-Faru, but something close, something nearly as malign. *Trapped*. Above, demons on the wing hovered; behind, fire; ahead, more demons. To the right, another malign presence lurked, and with that, a desperate plan took form. He wasn't cloaking them now, and he opened himself wider. Behind them, an explosion rocked the ground.

Korzha bolted left again. Turn left, he told himself; then right, then right again. Away from the hum of the trapped vampire, toward the trap itself. He put Donovan down, and they ran at top speed down a street so narrow the overhanging buildings blocked the sky.

And then he cloaked them. A roar went up when he and Claudia essentially vanished from the demons' senses. He tucked Donovan in close and backtracked to the snare. Near where they'd "vanished," light flashed in the air. The ground shuddered under their feet.

"Go!" Korzha roared. The snare was the only place the demons couldn't sense them, and with any luck their pursuers would never think to look there. Donovan flinched but plunged ahead. Korzha leapt after her. He felt a flicker of something as they passed through a shadow and then there was nothing—no sound, no trembling ground, no shrieking demons. He kept them cloaked because there was another danger here.

"What is this place?" Donovan whispered.

"A prison." He stood tall, and she stepped closer, pressing herself to his side. She gave no objection when he slid an arm around her waist.

She shot him a panicked look. "Are we going to be able to get out?"

"Probably." He hoped so. According to Jaise, only the rogue was trapped here. He hoped that was true.

Her mouth opened, but whatever Claudia was going to say, something changed her mind. "Prison," she repeated. "What for?"

"A vampire."

Her head turned and she caught his eye. "You?"

"No." He pulled her from the edge of the snare, further into the dark. "From the point of view of demon senses, this place is a dead zone. But just in case, let's not be standing here if any of those demons figure out we came in here."

She walked with him deeper into shadow. Jaise's description of the snare was accurate, and the abandoned homes and streets felt dead to Korzha, too. Some moonlight shone on the streets, casting an eerie haze in every direction as if light came through only to warp endlessly off each surface. The light reflected the red tinge of the moon and refracted into crimson mist overhead.

"The trapped vampire in here," he said in a low voice, "has been in Orcus since before the portal was sealed. How long it's been in here—that, I do not know." He considered what more to tell her. "It's rogue. I suspect it is now beyond recovery."

"And you're after it?"

"Yes."

"How do you know it's rogue?"

Another decision. He ought to say nothing; this was vampire politics and vampire law. He chose to be honest. "It was rogue years ago when I chased it and then lost the trail."

She tightened her fingers around his hand and exerted just enough pressure to make him look at her. A shaft of orange-tinted light arced over her head and vanished, refracted from somewhere. "Maybe those demons would have been a better choice."

"One vamp," he said lightly. "Not a thousand demons. When it finds us, I'll take care of it. I promise."

"I sure hope so." They turned and looked around.

"All the same, keep that knife of yours at hand. Don't hesitate to use it."

"Trust me, I won't."

Inside, the snare was larger than he'd expected, a bending of dimension perhaps, encompassing a square mile or more. Which meant that, if they were lucky, the rogue would not know right away where they were. Korzha led them past buildings closed up tight or else wide open to the elements. Vines obscured many of the windows, covered the walls and roofs. They walked a street of nothing but modest homes, empty. This was a ghost town of reduplicated emptiness.

Donovan had her knife out, tightening and untightening her fingers around its hilt. Crimson-tinged light hit the blade, looking more than a little like blood. Their feet kicked up dust as they walked. Korzha found it comforting to think that nothing had walked here recently—more comforting that he didn't sense anything. There was no life here but Donovan. They passed stone buildings, stone roofs. The snare was a cold and desolate place with no animals, no dogs, no cats, no rats. Farther away, miles and miles away, he smelled the city of demons living close by, heard the sounds of activity. If he turned, the faraway glow of life lit the sky. So it was possible to see out, but not to see inside. In size, Biirkma was nothing on the scale of Crimson City, but it buzzed with life in stark contrast to this desolation. They passed a wagon, empty, one wheel tilting at an odd angle. But there were no sounds but their own.

Dawn approached, pulling at Korzha's bones in a way he hadn't felt since his early days of immortal life. There, at the edges of his perception in the snare, he felt quivering, a strumming wire of awareness plucked softly. "Hurry," he said.

He ran uphill along the widening street, pulling Donovan with him, heading for larger, lavish houses of carved stone and curly-topped columns but just as empty as the houses behind. He stopped at a door with stone carvings of the surrounding murky-sweet vines. Thick stone. Deep. Cold. It went down deep. He reached for the door's locking mechanism and missed it. He focused himself, and then the parts slid and the door swung inward as the first rays of dawn crested the hill. Sunlight hit the top of the trap and veered off. The mist overhead turned a richer red: crimson, scarlet and maroon without an appreciable increase in visibility. He crossed the threshold and pulled Donovan after him. He needed darkness. Coolness. Retreat. Surely as did did the rogue.

Inside, he slammed the door and picked up a pot abandoned on a stone plinth. A weak bluish glow came from the cutwork in its front, providing a bit of light. Demon magic was still extant here.

"Thanks," Donovan said. He didn't need the light, but she did. Darkness terrified her; he'd learned that at the cave. She took the lamp by the handle that stuck out from the side opposite the cutwork, and looked around. "Where are we?"

He shrugged, and she didn't pursue the subject. He walked quickly to stone steps leading downward, feeling his way. Nothing lived here, not so much as a beetle. The air smelled stale, and a layer of dust coated the floor. On their entrance, lights appeared at the tops of the walls. But the quivering in his head increased, a thrum of awareness: The rogue knew, and was outraged that dawn pulled him to sleep.

Squares of black stone lined the floor, cool and hard against his boots. Korzha moved without sound, but Donovan's sandals shushed in the dust thick on the floor. The deeper they went, the closer dawn came, the less he felt the thrum of the rogue's awareness. A mosaic of garden scenes decorated the walls: a couple dining outside in full moonlight; children playing with a green ball, a male demon lifting his delighted child into the air while two more waited their turn. Korzha wasn't surprised when Donovan stopped to study the panel. Overhead the ceiling was painted twilight blue.

The corridor met a transverse passage, larger and wider than the first. He opened a door with a painted crimson moon above its glowing transom. The moment the door opened, light suffused the room.

"Wow," said Donovan.

He didn't realize at first that it was the luxury of the room that impressed her. But when he saw her face, awe shone from her eyes. He went straight for a nest of pillows in one corner, pushed aside a gauze flap and collapsed. His senses moved out, not in his control anymore. He wished the day would take him over, that he would fall into sleep. Thank God, Donovan didn't object to his mental push for her to follow. But if the rogue came, he would know. He would need to be ready.

She put her lamp on a table near the bed and stared at him while he sank into the pillows. She wasn't even half acclimated to this night schedule, and exhaustion pulled at her; he could feel it. Yet she'd not complained, not once, despite being human. A remarkable woman she was. Pale light flickered over the bed, as if a breeze had swept the room. He lay with his injured arm over his chest, the other at his side, watching her. Dark lashes brushed her cheeks. "You okay, Korzha?" she asked.

"Go to sleep, Claudia."

Her eyes drifted shut where she stood.

No doubt about it, she was thinner than when they'd first ended up in Orcus. And like him, she was gray with exhaustion. He still wanted to sleep with her, to keep her safe with him forever and ever. To finish what he'd begun. *Claudia. Dear-heart.* It was a strange welling emotion in his soul. He'd found his other half and just his luck, she hated vampires.

She joined him on the pillows. Her soft body was so

warm. He wrapped his arms around her, curving himself around her warmth. Sweet Life, he thought, let me not wake to irrational hunger. His body went still. He could sleep here a whole year; he really could. He felt Donovan's thoughts drift off, and the blue light faded. By the time the room was dark, she was asleep and didn't notice either the darkness or that she was sleeping in the arms of a vampire. Korzha followed her into slumber.

In his sleep—restless sleep, a sleep that didn't heal—Korzha felt not the rogue but Claudia Donovan. He appeared in her dreams without knowing he did until he was there, present in her sleeping mind. It was a thing that sometimes happened with humans, in the days when he'd pursued relationships with them that included biting. She was dreaming about home. It was before Jaise. Before everything had changed. Holly was laughing while Claudia cooked dinner. Any minute, the sitter was due to arrive. Holly had a book report due in the morning, and she was forbidden to watch TV or surf the net until the report was done.

Holly thought their apartment was too small. She didn't remember living on the streets in the Lower or, later, in their off-campus studio. All she knew was that most of her friends lived in a place twice the size of this apartment. To officer Donovan they were living in luxury. Holly had her own bedroom, all to herself. So did Claudia. No one shared anything except the bathroom. Holly had a mom who loved her and was proud of her, who watched her daughter play soccer on a grass field.

Korzha awoke with a start, sitting up. A soft bluish glow appeared through the gauze flaps draped over the pillows which had shifted, tumbling into softness around and beneath him. His stomach quivered, an unsettling roil that became near-nausea, but he felt hunger—burning, scouring hunger. At his side, Donovan slept. His arm wasn't even close to healed. He pushed up on his good elbow and bent over her. Sensitive to his presence, her eyes opened.

"Good evening, Officer Donovan," he said.

"Jeez, fang! Are you trying to scare me to death?"

"No such luck," he said.

She grabbed a pillow and hit him with it. His arm felt like it would come off—pain all the way through the top of his head. Donovan rolled to her feet and headed for the bathroom, open to view here in the demon fashion. It was of gleaming black stone, obsidian. At one end was a black stall with gold knobs and no door. She faced him. "You know," she said, "I thought technology didn't work here. How come there's all this modern plumbing?"

"There's a cistern at the top of the hill that feeds the plumbing system. Nothing any feudal lord from Camelot couldn't have managed."

She touched the black walls. "And the lights?"

Korzha stared from his nest of pillows. She smelled alive. But his hunger could be controlled. "I don't know, Donovan. Perhaps, the magic that keeps the vampire in, traps this magic too."

Even from the distance between then, she looked like hell. Pale. Tired. Worried. "You can call me Claudia," she said.

He felt a little jolt. "Such intimacy, Officer?"

"Be a jerk about it, then." She turned her back on him. For the count of twenty, he heard nothing but her breathing. She made no move toward the shower or anything else. Then she said, "You okay? For real. Are you going to be all right?"

He closed his eyes. Her voice sounded . . . bruised.

"Yes," he said. "Now do your business. I won't look. Scout's hon—" He sat bolt upright.

"What? What is it, Korzha?"

"He's here."

The rogue. And he was mindless with hunger. Inhuman. Un-vampire.

"Get away, Donovan." Korzha gestured. "Back into a corner. If I can't manage it, aim for the throat then take its heart to be sure." His words were lost in the sound of the door smashing open. He felt Donovan's fear and heard her scrambling backward. Whether she'd heard him or not, she had the sense to retreat. But he heard the sound of her knife sliding from its sheath. Brave woman.

What came in resembled a human in proportion and shape, but there the resemblance ended. Korzha's heart shriveled. Any hope the rogue could be recovered vanished. Insanity burned in its eyes. They were gleaming, cunning green eyes that sent a chill through Korzha to think how long this vamp had been insane. Isolated in the snare, starving and confined to infrequent feeding on demons foolish enough to venture in, on the edge when he'd gotten trapped here, the years had sapped the vampire of the last of its mind.

Clothing purloined from demon victims adorned his body in a motley array of colors and shapes. Too-short pants, crookedly laced, and on his feet leather boots, splitting at the sides. Thin arms, the joints huge, sprouted from a bright purple-and-yellow vest to which a few gems still clung. Black hair hung to the creature's shoulders, but the curls were a disreputable mess. The rogue's skin clung so tightly to his bones that each sinew and muscle stood out in high relief. At first and then second glance, the face was skeletal, the eye sockets deep receptacles for burning green eyes.

Korzha touched the rogue's mind. There was nothing recognizable, nothing at all. A hiss slithered from the rogue's mouth and, beneath that, a low rumble. The vampire had been so long in Orcus that his mimicry of a demon's growl was pitch perfect. His eyes skittered around the room, and his upper body twitched, a clonic tic of the shoulder that rolled down first one arm and then the other. His focus darted to Donovan and back to Korzha, Donovan and back.

Korzha lifted his hands. "Vasile," he said.

The rumbling hiss increased. "Vasile," it echoed in an an imitation of Korzha's voice, pitch and timbre without flaw. The rogue's arms twitched, one, then the other. Then, in a different voice, in perfect Romanian, it said a word, venomous and low: *"Vampyr."*

The rogue leapt, intending to go past Korzha, in a frenzy to get to Donovan. Korzha blocked him. His injured arm took the brunt of the collision. A sharp fingernail raked his cheek, deep and tearing. His elbow dug into Vasile's ribs, and the rogue caromed off, flying across the room with unexpected speed because his body weighed practically nothing. Korzha went after him, attacking, keeping himself between Vasile and Donovan. Korzha was prepared to die in the battle.

Vasile fought with the madness of years of isolation, with the insanity of unending hunger. He wanted Donovan. *Blood. Hunger. Vampire. Woman.* The stream of thought came in Romanian, the language of their nativity, of their human lives. *Sânge. Foame. Vampyr. Femeie.* Another attack, arms and legs swinging, fingernails deadly sharp. Korzha ducked, and Vasile screeched and twisted in midair. He flew at Korzha in a rage, arms twitching.

Korzha had no choice. None. Vasile could not be permitted to live. He should never have been made. It was a mistake that had defined their lives for eternity. Korzha waited for Vasile to dive at Donovan and when he did, he moved in and up. He delivered a slash to the throat, deep as forever. Vasile dropped to the ground at Claudia's feet, body twitching. His head didn't move, and the eyes stared upward. Animation seeped away. Gone, his fire of insanity had come to an end. Easily, finally.

Korzha didn't give himself time to think. Act now or all would be lost. The boy was lost forever. Forever. Long ago, he'd been lost forever. He plunged his hand inward, through Vasile's paper-thin skin, past the gap in the rib cage and to the left. He took the heart that should have beaten its last long ago and perhaps been buried with a body ancient and white-haired, next to a beloved wife with children mourning their father. Instead, Vasile had had none of that, only a slow and inexorable descent into madness. The head came next. A slash through bone and cartilage, and vertebrae and spinal cord separated.

Korzha dropped to his knees and bowed his head. Vasile's body quivered once. The process of disintegration to ash rippled through the corpse so quickly there wasn't time to say good-bye. The thought that only madness held Vasile together came and refused to leave him. Now that his madness was ended, so did the body. Nothing was left of his son. Blood, a single drop, dripped from Korzha's gashed cheek and dripped on the ashes. A hiss, a wisp of smoke rose up, and with it the acrid scent of destruction.

He felt Donovan move, knew every motion she made, but only as he was aware of the room, the background. He didn't allow the sensations to move beyond that. She joined him, crouching at his side with a cobalt blue jar about the size of her two fists. A roselike scent came from it. She'd emptied it and done a hasty clean-out of the inside. Without saying a word, she scooped the ashes into the jar. It was a human gesture and, for all that, remarkably touching.

When she was done and the jar was stoppered, her hand slipped over his uninjured cheek. "Korzha," she said.

He turned his head to her. There was no horror in her eyes. She knew. And his heart was lost to her right then, forever.

"Tiber," she said. She took his hand and tugged. "Come on."

Chapter Twenty-five

The first thing Claudia did after she started the water in the shower—it came on just like magic—was to help Korzha remove his clothes. She did her best not to look, or maybe it was fairer to say she did her best not to admire what she saw. They peeled off his tunic and tossed it to the floor, and he stood motionless while she unlaced his pants. Oh, my. He went commando-style. When his pants dropped and he stepped free, she reached up and pulled the scrunchie from his hair. She let it drop to the floor. With a gentle push, she got him under the stream of water.

His fingers curled around her wrist. "Come with me," he said.

She stared at him, right into his beautiful but desolate green eyes. She couldn't. She wanted to, but what would follow didn't bear thinking on. Yet, how could she leave him alone in such grief?

"Please," he said in a soft voice. His forefinger circled on the inside of her wrist.

Curls fell to his shoulders. Sparkling drops of water

covered his body. He dragged the fingers of his other hand through his hair, slicking away the moisture. A few drops clung to his eyelashes. His espresso-bean curls stayed back from his face. Beads of water clung to the gaping edge of his slashed cheek, and, at the worst spot, a red-tinged rivulet coursed down his skin.

The look in his eyes broke her heart. Before she could change her mind, she slipped out of her clothes. He made room for her. She faced him, and words just spilled from her mouth. "I didn't know. Korzha, I didn't know. You should have told me. I'm sorry."

"Hush, dear-heart," he said. "*Draga. Draga inima.*"

Tears streamed down her face, and the vampire reached for her, embraced her, comforted her when their roles ought to be reversed. She rested her cheek against his chest. Her breath hitched. His son. Mad. Ruined. "I'm so sorry."

"This was tragedy of my own devise," he said, in a voice pitched low but at her ear so that she heard him perfectly. "My daughter—she married at sixteen, which was quite usual in my country. She died in childbirth soon after. The child, too. My wife the year after. Vasile hadn't married. I thought . . ." He rested his chin on her head. "I waited until he was your age. Twenty-five. And then I made him. He was not ready. He did not want it."

"I'm sorry," she said.

"Today I have undone my mistake." He stroked her hair. "There is no more to say of it."

He shifted until the water beat down on them both. The hot stream felt good. Perfect. There seemed no need to worry about an auto shut-off. She could stand here forever if she wanted. Perfect. She closed off everything except the heat and warmth, but the truth was, the skin on the nape of her neck prickled with awareness of Korzha. Eventually, she pushed away from him and bent to the jars at the edge of the shower. She opened each until she found what she figured was probably soap. Sometimes it was best to pretend everything was fine even when it wasn't.

When she faced him, he cocked his head. The guy wasn't human, she reminded herself. Korzha was taller than she was, so when she reached for his hair, she had to rise on her toes. He set his hands around her waist, helping her keep her balance. He looked gaunt, she thought. And his wounds weren't anywhere near healed, though he gave no sign of being in pain. How could he not be? His upper arm was a mass of angry crimson punctures—deep wounds, probably to the bone. If it weren't for him, she'd be dead. Probably several times over.

Taking care to avoid the injuries, she soaped his arm, first one, then the other. His face, his upper body—it was nice, touching him like this. Arousal trickled through her and the defined, specific and sensual task of washing him kept her focus on the physical and away from emotion. His skin was clean and clear, pale over the kind of lean body she'd always liked in men. But there wasn't any lack of muscle. His wasn't the kind of body that was built in the gym; it came from the kind of specific activity that made a fencer's body different from a sprinter's, different from dancer's, different from anything else.

She used the soap, the shampoo and the oil, too, because it smelled so good. He stretched like a cat in the sun, keeping his body in the hot spray, keeping close to her, offering her whatever part of him needed washing next. A floral scent filled the air, drifting with the shower mist: not roses, but similar—a dryer, sweeter scent than the roses back home. Water and steam warmed his skin, she could feel the difference in his surface temperature. His erection strained upward from a tangle of dark hair. Thick and turgid. She wanted to touch it. She put the pads of her fingers on his stomach, just above the tip of his sex.

"Do you think we should?" she asked.

He laughed. "Should what?" He looked wary, too, despite his laughter.

"Do it."

"Fucking is nice," he said with a wicked smile. "But I'd like to make love."

More than anything she wanted that, for him to hold her in his arms. "Okay," she said. And her mind felt gloriously free of any push. This was what she desired.

His hand went around her waist, fingers splaying. Water sprayed down, heating them both. Korzha touched her body. *Yes.* She stared into his green eyes. Not lilac. She wanted to drown in those green eyes that would never, ever lie to her. Never compel her. Heedless of the water hitting his face, he said, "Are you sure?"

Korzha's eyes held hers, dark green and, at the moment, glittering like moss at the far end of dawn. His fingers pressed into the skin of her back, slipping along the wetness.

"Yes," she said.

"Fucking or making love?"

Water beat down on them both, and in her belly, desire rippled out in concentric waves. "Korzha . . . ," she said, helpless.

"Fucking or making love?" he asked softly. "Which would you prefer?"

"A little meaningless sex wouldn't be so bad," she said. She didn't feel in any position to promise her heart to this man. But the longing to have him in her arms, to kiss him and stroke him, welled up, overwhelming her. And then there was the errant thought that sex with Tiberiu Korzha couldn't possibly be meaningless. She fisted her hands and rested them against his chest.

He searched among the bottles and jars for the soap, and dipped his fingers in the container. A whiff of the roselike scent floated on the steam. He washed her hair. His fingers massaged her scalp, scrubbing. Eyes closed, she let him turn her around to rinse away the lather. He used a little of the oil to untangle her hair. Every now and then their bodies came into contact, his swollen sex touched her hip or her back, or his thigh brushed against hers. Each contact sent a fresh gout of desire shivering through her. Claudia put her palms against the wall of the shower and let her head hang down, willing the water to wash away all coherence.

The scent of flowers came to her again as Korzha made more lather. His hands slipped on the hot skin of her upper shoulders, pushing her wet hair off her neck. She drew in a breath as his palms moved along the curve of her back and down to her hips. Like water to a parched man, cool to a burning body; every inch of her quivered in the wake of his touch. His fingers slid up the inside of her thighs and to her nether hair, soaping, rinsing. Eventually, he put his head by her ear and said, "Time to dry off, Officer Donovan."

He stepped out of the shower. Claudia watched the flex of muscle along his flanks, the taut sinews as he reached for one of the towels on the bench. With his good arm, he took her hand and helped her out. She was naked, and he was looking at her. His free hand came up and drew the damp hair from her face.

But his attention focused lower. He looked for a long time. His eyes glittered like gemstones. He touched the interlocking lines carved into her hip, and Claudia felt a spark from him to her flowing through it. It was interest, blunt male interest. With a short grunt, he took a step forward. Underlying his interest, threatening to overwhelm, lurked a stark hunger, viciously suppressed. Despite having fed on the wolflike creature the previous night, despite a day's sleep, his face was ashen, the skin tighter than ever against his cheeks, clinging to his skull.

"That thing's blood wasn't enough for you, was it?" she asked. "It wasn't good."

He wrapped a towel around her, shoulders and all. "You smell like flowers."

Since her arms were trapped underneath the towel, she nodded toward the soldierly line of jars. Hunger gleamed in his eyes, but she said, "Answer me, Korzha."

"No. It was not good for me." He grinned, but his mouth stretched tight. He didn't seem to care that he was naked. Or that water dripped off his body. Or that she was looking at him. Trying not to look at him, but looking, definitely looking.

"You're beautiful," she said. And wasn't that the truth? "Really beautiful."

"Tasted like crap," he said at the same time.

Claudia hurried to talk over her previous words. "What about demons?" she asked.

"What about them?" Holy cripes, he was naked. And he was going to make love to her. He was, wasn't he?

"Do they taste like crap, too?" Her clothes lay in a neat pile on a stone bench. Her sheathed knife lay on top, holding down the pile. He smiled, but underneath, his hunger still burned; she could feel it.

"I don't know," he said. "I've never eaten one."

"You know what I mean. Is demon blood good?"

His smile disappeared. "Not particularly."

"How 'not particularly'?"

He stared at the towel around her. "Particularly bad."

"And . . . how long can you go without?" she asked.

"Without sex? Indefinitely, I'm afraid."

Claudia went to her clothes and adjusted her towel to more safely cover her. She picked up her knife and, facing him, slid the black blade free of its sheath. A drop of water from her wet hair fell on it.

"If you try to use that on me," Korzha said, "it's only fair to warn you I've never been much for your strict anti-vampire self-defense statutes."

"How long, Korzha?" She faced him. "In your condition. How long can you starve before you're compromised?" They weren't far apart, physically. Three or four feet at most. She held the blade point down over her extended arm and then did what Aslet had done, sliding the point into the swell of a vein. She grimaced. A well of blood appeared in the fold of her elbow. She watched it flow, then looked up.

Tiberiu stood motionless. His eyes glittered, and she watched the green disappear as his pupils dilated. He lifted his head, catching the scent of her blood. His mouth thinned, drew back, exposed the white of his teeth. His hunger was a palpable thing. It gleamed in his eyes, drew his body taut. The air turned thick as mud.

"Fuck you, Donovan," he whispered. "If you don't mean that, fuck you."

"Don't waste it," she whispered, stepping toward him.

"That's not enough." His eyes glittered with fever. "Not nearly enough."

"It's a start."

And like that, he was there: a blink and the distance was covered and his hand cupped her elbow. He lifted her arm and at the same time lowered his head. She braced herself for pain, but his tongue lapped at the nick. A shudder rolled through him. His fingers tightened around her arm.

She closed her eyes. "Do it, Korzha."

He laughed and stepped closer, snaking an arm around her waist. "When I don't intend for my hapless victim to die, I prefer the carotid." He drew a finger down her throat. "But this will do. Thank you."

She felt his lips brush her skin, his tongue tracing a whorl in the bend of her elbow. She recognized his mental touch. His hunger pulsed through her. "Korzha," she said.

He looked up at her in awe. "You are a thing of beauty, Claudia. Have I failed to tell you that?"

"Would you just bite me already?"

"Dear-heart, of course." He gripped her arm, making a tourniquet of his fingers. A moment later, she felt his other hand at the back of the towel, pulling it away from her body. It fell to the floor. Cool air flowed over her, raising gooseflesh. Her breath hitched. The spell of their contact swept her along in a current of warmth. When he lifted his head, the gash on his cheek had thinned and faded from angry red to a heated pink.

He seemed not to notice any change. His tongue appeared between his lips to lick a drop of blood away. The motion revealed a flash of sharp white canine. He pulled her close. The hunger in him surged. She felt him edging away from his habitual control. Wildness twitched in his eyes, around the corners of his mouth, and sent a ripple of fear through her. His hand on the nape of her neck kept her close, kept her on her feet. He put his mouth by her ear. "I can taste the demon in you," he hissed.

"I'm sorry."

"Officer," he murmured. She heard a growl in his voice, the beast in him pacing at the bars to its cage. "You're forgiven." He laughed and brought his face to her ear, and just when she expected him to speak, his head dipped and his lips touched her throat. "In you, it's spice." He still held her nape, but one finger followed a line from her navel to between her breasts. Claudia could hardly breathe from wondering at his intention. "Delicious spice," he repeated.

His mouth opened over her throat, a soft kiss, butterfly-delicate. His fingers spread over her breast, and his tongue flicked over the pulse of her throat. Gently, very gently, he nipped at her, but with his front teeth only. "May I?"

She nodded. He had to. He couldn't help her save Holly if she didn't let him feed. That was what she told herself; not that she wanted it.

He held her tight, so tight she couldn't move her head. Her body thrummed. She felt his tongue on her skin. Warmth coursed through her, between them, catching her up. His upper teeth pressed into her flesh. She bucked because the sting was a thousand times worse than what she'd felt in her elbow. His body went rigid. He held her close, tight against him. His lower mouth pressed upward, moving against her. It hurt. It hurt, *it hurt*, and then—it didn't anymore.

With clinical detachment, she knew what was happening to her: razor-sharp teeth were puncturing the epidermis, through the subcutaneous layer, sliding into the carotid artery; the downward force of his canines, the upward pressure of his lower teeth, the flow of her blood into his mouth. The sting faded because the mental connection between a feeding vampire and his victim released endorphins. She felt . . . needed. Wanted. Beloved.

He withdrew, and she didn't have the strength to do anything but cling to him, to let her head loll against the arm bracing her shoulders. His cheek wasn't completely healed, but the gash was closed, almost gone. "That couldn't have been enough, Korzha," she said.

"Tiberiu. Or Tiber—whichever you prefer."

"This was not enough to heal you. Not enough."

"Hush, dear-heart. I've had my fill for the moment."

"You have to be well. To get Holly, you have to be well."

"I will be soon. Trust me." He held her easily and walked to the bench where her clothes lay. With a sweep of his hand he cleared it, scattering her clothes. He sat with her straddling him. The punctures in his upper arm were little more than fading bumps. He held her gaze and touched her between her legs. "Now, Claudia? Will you let me love you now?"

"Yes," she said, but to her ears, her voice sounded thick. He wasn't circumcised. The head of his cock emerged from its fold of skin. She hadn't ever seen an uncircumcised penis before. He was large and hard, and she felt as if her belly were hollow.

His hands traveled up and down her spine, then around her rib cage to her breasts. He stroked her. "You're lovelier than I remember. But this time, this time I'll do it right. I'll spoil you for all other men. You'll never want anyone but me. No lover will touch you but me."

She felt the sizzle of his fingers straight to her toes. He leaned forward and kissed her nipple. The inside of his mouth was cooler than she expected, but then, her only experience was with men. And a demon. Every now and then, she felt his mind reaching out; a reflex, she thought. He'd long ago touched her mind with his, and she'd feel a pulse of his mental energy in time with hers. But then he'd withdraw, as if he hadn't meant to, was trying not to as though he couldn't help himself. He transferred his mouth to her other breast—feasting, she thought. She knew men liked bodies like hers. She couldn't help the size of her chest in proportion to everything else, a shape directly inherited from her mother. They had the same figure. She waited for the next pulse of his mind in hers, the reflexive twitch of withdrawal, and when it happened, she whispered, "No, don't."

His eyes flew open, his mind still connected with her. "Whatever you want," he murmured. And he stayed, seemingly pleased. Soon he was touching her mind, soothing, caressing. Sharing his arousal with her. Claudia reached between them and stroked a fingertip along his sex. She felt him surge into her hand, and in her head emotion surged, too. A rush of sensation.

Beautiful. Exquisite. Claudia. Yes. Touch me like that.

"Do you want me inside you here, too?" he asked, touching her deeply.

"Yes," she said. Her head swam. It was like being high, without the narco. Electric. "Yes, I do."

From beneath lowered lashes, she watched his face, still pale but now touched with color, as he brought her to straddle him. He was healthier and beautiful to look at. She lifted a hand and touched the place where he'd been injured. His cheek was whole, and his gauntness was filling out. He slid his cock into her. He did it slow, like a man savoring a fine wine. She arched back because he continued to stretch her, to fill her, and she wasn't used to that. There hadn't been all that many men for her. Hardly any. And she hadn't ever been with someone constructed quite on his scale or with his patience. She didn't expect, either, to feel so enthralled with the sensation of him easing into her, of her enfolding him. She caught the tail edge of his sensation, of having his forward and inward motion draw down his foreskin and expose the head of his cock to the pressure of her heat and dampness. To him, she was sizzling hot.

He leaned against the wall and put his hands around her waist. "Vampires," he said with a wicked, soft smile, "are bigger, better, faster, and we do it longer."

Her entire body shivered with approaching climax. He was in her head still. *Not yet,* he said. *Not yet.* Beneath his arousal, she felt his hunger, his near overwhelming desire to plunge his teeth into her and take until he was full and warm and drunk on her. He raged with lust for the tang of her blood. She was crazy to trust him, but she did anyway.

She'd adjusted to him, to his size, and she rocked her hips. His eyes widened, glittering. Such pale skin, but faintly pink. Up until now, she'd been afraid she didn't really like sex or maybe even only kind of liked men. And her experience in Orcus certainly had not seemed like that would change. But she'd been wrong. So wrong. Until now, sex often felt good, but she'd never been completely absorbed by her partners. They'd always been more eager than she, and she'd ended up feeling there must be something wrong with her.

Not this time.

Across his side, over his kidney he had a jagged, irregular white scar. And another across his shoulder. He stood up, holding her, still inside her, and walked, glided or whatever it was vamps did, to the bed of pillows and laid her down. She watched him lazily, dreamily, appreciatively—and with a sense of detachment, as if she weren't Claudia Donovan anymore but another woman, a more exciting, desirable woman.

The kind of woman who made love with a gorgeous vampire and had no worries. When he was beside her again, one leg over hers, she touched him, raised up to kiss his nipples, traced the ripple of his chest muscle. "You're gorgeous, Korzha. What were you when you got made?"

"I was a soldier when I died," he said. His hands were on her hips, pulling her toward him, getting himself even tighter inside her, going deeper. "So you see, I was already an experienced killer before I became what I am."

She touched the scar on his shoulder. "This isn't a bullet wound."

"Hand-to-hand."

"No wonder you're a"—she gasped—"twisted son of a bitch." She laughed with joy.

His mouth twitched, and she saw the tip of one fang. Pleasure blossomed in him; she could feel it. "No more jokes. Time to concentrate on this, Officer," he said. He thrust into her, and really, she decided, she liked sex. Loved it. She loved sex with Korzha more than anything in the world.

Chapter Twenty-six

Claudia lay in Tiber's arms, still-wet hair and all, thinking about what she'd done and how she'd felt doing it. She'd made love to a vampire, and it had been pretty damn good. For the first time since she'd known him well enough to know his usual physical state, his skin felt warm. And her body felt replete. Sated. She liked that Tiber kept his arms around her. It made her feel wanted, whether he meant it to or not; like it wasn't just sex for him. Probably it was, even if he'd given her that "making love" line, but it didn't feel like that right now, and she was more than content to leave things that way. Besides, she was too tired to move out of his embrace; and, besides again, his arms felt good. So good. She didn't even have to worry about unprotected sex because she wasn't going to live long enough to get pregnant. It didn't matter that there wasn't any drugstore for a supply of condoms or a morning-after pill.

Korzha stirred. His hair, which had dried untidily, brushed her shoulder. Claudia braced herself. He'd roll away now, get dressed, or maybe just turn his back to her and do whatever it was vamps did after sex. Only, he didn't. His arm tightened around her waist, and he nipped her ear. He didn't break the skin. "Well, Officer Donovan," he murmured. It sounded nice, the way he said that. "Another fine mess you've gotten us into."

"F-you," she whispered back. He couldn't see her smile.

"Again? Already?"

"Nah," she said, because she didn't want him to think she wanted it if he didn't, and everyone knew vamps weren't shy about taking what they wanted. Particularly sex. Claudia rolled onto her back, taking a pillow with her and positioning it over her bosom. She threw one arm over her eyes and prepared herself for the we-really-shouldn't-have-done-that awkwardness. Oddly enough, she wasn't sorry. Nervous and worried, but not sorry.

To her surprise, Korzha said in a low and honeyed voice, "Mm, no. Stay close." He grabbed the pillow and hurled it against the wall, then curled his body around her. "Humans are so warm," he said. "I adore how warm you are. It's almost—*almost*—the best part of making love to one."

She turned her head and found her gaze locked with his. Again, it was kind of a shock how green his eyes were. The tips of his thick lashes were slightly brown, his irises, streaked with kelly green. The whites of his eyes were startlingly white, and they turned the green deeper. Desire stirred even though she had no idea if he'd ever want her again. "What is the best part?"

"Of you?"

"Of sex with a human."

He smiled. "That's easy. When you are a vampire, sex is . . . different. I feel things humans can't. I adore orgasm with a heart pounding in my ears, the surrender of a body, a mind and a will, of life pulsing away beneath me." He splayed his hand on her belly. After a bit, he added, "I was close to the edge with you. It's a rush when it's like that. Not always, but often. To be hungry, close to starving, and then to feed and have sex with a human. We are most alive when we've just fed, and to swing so hard, the connection is a thousand times more intense. Some vamps do it on purpose, go days between feeding just to walk that edge of control."

"What happens if you lose control?"

"Usually the human dies."

"Has that ever happened?"

"That . . ." His voice fell. "That is a rush, too." He shifted his torso over hers and drew a hand from her knee to her thigh. "Best-looking cop on the force. How lucky for me that your precinct is so near. I always watched for you whenever someone questioned my innocence, existed in the wretched hope that you might one day question me."

"Like you were ever innocent," she said. His mouth, she thought lazily, was drop-dead sexy. He had a well-defined mouth, with a full lower lip. And that gorgeous mouth had kissed her.

"It's a liability, you know. In my job, anyway," she added after a moment.

"What?"

"Looking good to men."

"Really? I'd have thought just the opposite."

She hadn't seen him enough with his hair down. He seemed much less civilized. The look suited him. "No. It seems like everyone wonders who's banging me, or wondering if they can, or thinking I got promoted because I give the captain good head."

"Do you?"

She made a feeble attempt at slapping him, but he ducked, and she didn't bother pursuing the matter. "Most cops are decent, good people, but not all of them. Sometimes I get treated better because of how I look, and sometimes I get treated worse. It all depends on whether they think I'm a babe or a bitch."

"Well, Officer, I think you're a babe." He tightened the circle of his arms around her. "But if you give me good head, I'll promote you to whatever you want."

She snorted. Korzha trailed a hand over her stomach. Their intimacy felt a little uncomfortable now. She didn't see how matters could have turned out any differently, but that didn't make this a good thing. "I need to know something."

He hesitated. "Yes?"

"Are you completely healed?"

He laughed softly. "In time, dear-heart."

"Then you're not. How much do you need to be at full strength?"

"More than I've had so far."

She looked into his eyes, and, quite unexpectedly, she felt as if she were standing on a cliff looking at the distant bottom. "You can have more. You have to."

"Oh, dear-heart," he whispered. "You think you are so tough."

"I am tough, Korzha."

His eyebrows lifted. "Not where it matters."

She suppressed bitterness. "Fang, you don't know shit about being tough."

Korzha moved over her, propping himself up with his hands just over her shoulders. His eyes glittered. "And you don't know the first thing about my life."

She pushed against his chest. "You're a vamp."

"How observant of you."

"It's not like you would have wanted me in L.A." She made a face at him. "Well, okay. So we were thrown together and it happened. We did it. So what?"

"It was good, wasn't it?" He laughed. "Worth the wait?"

"You can *not* out-tough me. I don't give a rat's ass who or what you are, Tiberiu Korzha."

"Which is?" He lowered his head. Oh, yeah, the post-coital glow was definitely gone.

"A Korzha. You're Upper, through and through. Get off me."

They stared at each other.

"No," he said.

"You don't know shit," she whispered. It wouldn't work. Human and vamp? Never. "Now get off."

"Let's do it," he said. He got a leg between hers. "Let's fuck while you think you hate me." His brilliant eyes did something fluttery to her stomach, and she could tell he knew it. His mouth curved into a smile. He shifted his body and pressed into her, hard and smooth. And because his body was cool compared to hers, she felt hot inside, surrounding him.

"Get off. I *do* hate you." There wasn't any mistaking him for human right now. He was naked, and so was she, and he wasn't warm. She just couldn't fool herself that he was anything like normal. Trying to budge him was like trying to lift a boulder. It couldn't be done. Terror flashed over her as the realization came home, a startle-response flood of adrenaline that sent her heart pounding against her ribs. And at that exact moment, he rocked himself forward and made a small sound in the back of his throat. She felt the pull of that clear down to her toes. She liked sex with him. She loved sex with him. How had she forgotten? She wrapped her arms around him, and then her legs. His hand slid to her backside, pulling her up while he kept his thrust deep.

"Jesus, Donovan," he said. His hair fell over his shoulders, and that put his face in shadow and softened his high, pale cheeks. She threw back her head, straining toward him, trying to find a way to take more of him inside her. He pressed her pelvis against him and circled his hips over her. A mental pulse from him curled around her, inside her, intensifying everything, drawing her in. "Do you like that?" he asked. "Tough enough for you?"

She came hard, harder than she'd ever come in her life. Korzha, the bastard, laughed. She heard him laugh while she threw out a hand, trying to find something to anchor her so she wouldn't just fly apart, and couldn't. He moved, pulling her with him, higher on a mound of pillows so that she slid toward him. She couldn't breathe for a moment because she hadn't ever in her life had anyone do this to her. Mind and body at the same time—she wanted him both ways. The back of her hand hit the wall. She cried out at the sharp pain of her knuckles hitting the surface.

Korzha's head snapped up. But for the sound of her breathing, the room went eerily quiet. He reached for her hand. She'd broken the skin, and blood trickled down her finger, filling the creases across her knuckle. A shiver rippled across him. Hunger, she thought. He was still hungry. His pupils dilated until only a narrow ring was left of the brilliant green irises.

Her heart thundered in her chest, in her head, and she rushed toward some spectacular unknown. "Do it," she said.

He reached for her hand and licked the blood from

her knuckle. He wrapped her legs around his waist, then with the other hand gripped the back of her head, twisting a little so that the side of her neck was exposed.

He snarled once, then bit her, harder than before. It hurt more, but the pain faded faster. The rush of his thoughts and emotions into her sent her whirling off the top of a cliff. She strained toward him, bending one knee so that the inside of her thigh pressed his hip. Her pulse echoed in her ears, rapid at first, then slower, then in time with his heart, then in time with the rhythmic sucking of his mouth. He was still inside her, still hard and pressing inward. After a while, he loosened his hold on her. His teeth disengaged, in itself a sensation that sent her spine arching in counter-action. But his mouth stayed pressed to her throat, still in rhythm; his tongue still lapped, and then his hips moved—a slow slide out, quick in, slowly out, quickly in. His impressions slid into her head, a jumble of feelings. Heat. The tang of blood, a thirst so vast he still wanted more. Soft skin against his, the scent of not-quite-roses, her scent. Warmth around his cock, the growing urgency. Bellies meeting. Wanting her. Beautiful.

She held him when he came. Held him still when her breathing slowed. She took a deep breath and spoke quickly before she lost her head again and let Korzha start all over with her. "Promise me something?" she said.

His eyebrows lifted. "We've only just made love for the second time." He hesitated, then said, "And you just told me you hate me. It's a little silly to be extracting promises from me, isn't it?"

"It's about Lath."

"No promises," he said. "Not yet. But," he added,

and she couldn't tell if he was serious or not, "I said it before—I am not inclined to share you. With anyone. For any time. Isn't that enough?"

"That's not what I meant." As long as she didn't move, she felt okay. If she did move, she'd see speckles in front of her eyes. "If he finds me, and if it looks like I can't get away or you can't stop me from running to him . . ." She pushed at his shoulder. "This is important, Tiber."

He sat up, curling an arm around his upraised knee. His dark hair, such a rich brown, tumbled past his shoulders, not anywhere near as neat and tidy as usual. She liked the wildness much better, and found it much more appealing than the always perfect Tiberiu Korzha of Crimson City.

"What is it?" he asked.

Her breath rattled on the way out.

"Will you be Holly's guardian?" She wiped her cheek, the tears there. "Tiber, please. I've got money set aside. Not much, but enough for someone else to raise her. Plus, there's insurance. Get her back to Crimson City, Tiber. You could be her guardian. You *could*. You wouldn't have to see her, just take care of everything. I know you can."

He threaded his fingers through her hair. "Why ask that of me when there are things you might ask instead? When we might dare to try other things that—"

"Promise me."

He shook his head. "You're too resourceful not to think of something else." It was as if he refused to believe.

"I believe in contingency planning."

"So practical." He stroked his fingers through her hair.

"Please?"

He sighed. "Yes, Claudia. I will. For you."

"Thank you." She put her arms around his neck. "Thank you, thank you, thank you."

With catlike grace, he lay next to her, grabbing her and pulling her underneath him. He raised his head and concentrated now on their joined bodies. His hair fell forward, past his cheeks, framing his face. From the shadows, his eyes glittered. "I like this part, too," he said. "With a woman like you, when I've fed this deeply. I like to make love against dark sheets, a dark mattress so I can see how pale she's become." He pressed himself against her, rocking. "When we're home, I'm going to make love to you in my bed—on black silk, so I can see you like this, all pale and delicate. All the way to the edge." He stretched out one of her arms. "We're at the edge now, Claudia. If I took any more from you, you'd start to slip away, and I could do anything to you I want. Anything at all." He rolled over, taking her with him and settling her astride him. Her thighs pressed against either side of his body. Claudia's head swam, and, even though her eyes weren't closed, she saw black sparkles. The only thing that kept her upright was his hands around her waist. Her heart beat hard and slow in her chest.

"Tiber—"

"The demon blood in you makes the edge razor-thin. It's addicting." He ran his hands over her belly and upward to her breasts. "*Jesu*, Claudia, *Jesu*, you bedazzle me."

"I feel dizzy," she said. Speaking took too much effort.

"Yes." He dropped a hand to her sex, sliding a finger between them. "But wait till I've made you come again, lovely, pale as snow Claudia. There's nothing between you and orgasm but more exquisite pleasure."

All sensation turned liquid, hot, urgent. Shattering.

She felt his orgasm, too, soon afterward, shattering them both. She reached the edge and fell long and hard.

Later, he shook his head and touched the pattern on her hip. "I don't know much about dark demons and their magic," he said in a low voice. "But I hate that you're bound somehow. I *hate* it. I don't care how much time you have, I don't want to share. I'm too selfish."

She pried open her eyes and looked at him. Korzha lay sprawled across her, his head on her belly. He had a fabulous ass—musta been one hell of a foot soldier. Maybe a knight. "Is that as bad as you make it sound?"

"Worse." He kissed her stomach. "Now, come closer, Officer, and make one of my old fantasies come true. Show me how the Los Angeles Police Department interrogates wanted criminals." His cool hands cupped her backside. "This time, you'll be the good cop. I'll be the heartless vampire rogue."

Chapter Twenty-seven

Tiber was surprised by Claudia's ready agreement to his suggestion that she stay in the snare while he went after Holly. She just nodded and said, "I'll be in the way. I want you concentrating on keeping her safe." Before he left, she threw her arms around him and said, "You be careful, Tiber, please? I want both of you back safe and sound."

He kissed her. Getting past the portal guards wasn't going to be easy, but he was at full strength now; and in the portal room, the fact that magic was dangerous gave him a good chance of neutralizing the guards. "Just be ready to go when we get back."

In Biirkma Palace, he melted into the shadows and considered his options. Speed was important, but so was success. Identifying Holly was no trouble. She sat alone, separated from five human-looking demon children of roughly the same age. In this setting, without the confusion of the portal, he sensed her identity easily enough. She rocked with her arms tight around her shins, and her chin pressed to the tops of her knees.

Her face retained a hint of childish roundness, but the promise of her mother's beauty was there in the curve of her mouth, the sweep of cheek and the set of her eyes, which were large and pale brown. Her chestnut hair hung in a single braid down her back. He was shocked by the pang of seeing so strong an echo of Claudia's face in the child.

Despite her parentage, in a room of demons, Holly reeked of humanness, and unhappiness and the warm blood beneath her skin. She looked healthy, but thin. She had spindly arms and legs, an indication she would be taller than her mother. Apart as she was, making off with her wouldn't be a challenge. Plainly, the adult demons in attendance weren't worried about kidnapping. They sat on benches against the wall, talking or reading. One napped, but the others looked up now and again if the noise level varied. A black mink-like creature with a pointed snout and pale yellow eyes washed itself at Holly's feet.

Unseen or sensed, Korzha ascended the stone interior wall, spiderlike, until he reached the deeper shadow of the inset window. He opened the window a crack. Enough to make a quick exit. Below, guards patrolled the perimeter of the exterior courtyard. A sharp cry brought his attention back to the room where he'd sat so long a watch. One of the demon children tossed her ball at Holly, knowing she would not respond. All Holly did was, too late, lift a hand to ward off the hurled object. The mink hissed. Korzha saw the girl's eyes quite clearly: shadowed brown. Pale, pale brown.

He tightened his mental focus. The napping adult demon stirred, and Korzha melted into shadow until he felt the demon's mind relax toward sleep. He launched himself into the air, above the center of the room, and then dropped straight down to land in front of Holly. He looked straight into her pale eyes and said, "Polka dots."

Holly's eyes went wide as she registered that Korzha had given her the secret phrase that meant Claudia had sent him. He smiled at the child. "Come, Holly, I'll take you to your mother."

"Whiskers!" The girl bent for the mink, which clambered into her arms and up to balance on her shoulder. Tiber scooped the child into his embraces.

"Hold tight."

The adult demons were on their feet now, gathering the children. One of them ran for the door while another lunged at Korzha. He hissed, showing his fangs, and the demon stopped. Holly, having been at the edge of the group and farthest from the adults was too far away for the late intervention to matter. Korzha soared up and out the window into the crisp night air. Holly and the mink clinging to him, he raced back toward Claudia.

Even before he and Holly entered the area that had once been the snare that contained Vasile, he knew demons were there. The resonance of nullity that had been the snare had begun to evaporate, and curious demons had come to investigate and reclaim the streets. Korzha's now indelible imprint of Claudia thundered in him. She was in danger, in mortal danger and frightened.

Inside the house, just past the entrance, he went to the right at top speed, straight to the columned inner courtyard. A few of the columns had toppled over, while others no longer had the connecting arches and reached to nowhere. A portion of the northwest wall had fallen in. What he saw made his heart sink. A demon sprawled on the flagstones, its neck at an odd angle. It was dead. Claudia stood in a corner of the destroyed wall, surrounded by more than a dozen foes. Two demons were mentally susceptible, and Korzha killed them with a ruthless blast of mental energy that stopped their hearts. The other demons weren't attacking Claudia because she had one by the neck, the blade of her knife pressed tight against its throat. Her eyes flicked to him.

"Get Holly out of here," she shouted.

Behind him, he felt the air pulse. He whirled and cursed himself for a fool. The black-haired Bak-Faru Lath walked through the doorway with a self-satisfied grin that advertised his presence here was no accident. He'd followed Korzha. In the meantime, the effect of the lone Bak-Faru on the other demons was like electricity in water. One vaulted for the sidewall only to be caught by a blast of fire. Another, more confident demon, muttered a series of syllables that he finished off with a gesture that turned the air thick and damp. Korzha watched the ripple head for Lath, gathering energy, spinning with a laser's edge of water.

The Bak-Faru demon stood his ground. Moments before the blast ought to have hit him, Lath lifted a hand. Steam hissed in the air. His eyes swept the courtyard and stopped on Claudia. He moved toward her, speaking as he did with low and guttural syllables following so close on each other not even Korzha could separate the words. Another of the demons roared, a sound that rang from the walls. None of the demons attacking Claudia moved, and from their horrified expressions, Korzha assumed Lath had managed to immobilize them. But for how long? Lath walked toward Claudia. He gestured, a sinuous dance of his hand in the direction of the demon Claudia still held at knifepoint. A flash of light tinged purple at the edges hit her hostage square in the chest. Then, like a fencer making a touch, Lath thrust out a hand. The motion ended in a blur of crimson at the other's chest.

"The human female is mine," he growled.

He glanced once at the tight knot of paralyzed demons, then lifted his hand in the air, his fist crimson with blood. Heat radiated from him in pulsing waves. Lath opened his fingers. The heart fell wetly to the floor beside its body. The blood on Lath's hand flaked off his skin. He smiled, and dimples danced in his cheeks. The platinum thread in his hair shimmered. "No one touches her but me."

Claudia let go of her hostage; the demon's knees crumpled, then he toppled over. Eyes fixed on Lath, Claudia retreated until her back was to one of the huge blocks of stone that had once formed the wall. Blood smeared her shirt, but it wasn't hers. Lath whirled and sent a pulse of light speeding toward the ones he'd frozen in place. It hit them with a blaze of purple-white light. Half of their number vanished. As for the rest, Lath smiled and spoke a single word, and they were gone, too. The smell of burnt air rose. All that remained of the demons who'd surrounded Claudia was a lilac fog dissipating in the air.

More demons appeared in the arched doorway. Lath laughed, a sound of delight. "More of you?" he said to the newcomers. "Come, come." He gestured with two hands. "I am *en*-Lath of the Bak-Faru. Come. I will kill you all."

With this new threat, Korzha and Holly were directly in the line of fire. Korzha folded his arms around the child and darted upward. He landed on top of a free-standing column, a position that gave him a view of Lath surrounded by a glow of light. Claudia took one look at Lath, another at Korzha and her daughter, and started scrambling up the collapsed wall. She too was heading up to relative safety. A line of sweat tracked down her cheek and dampened the back of her shirt. Knife in hand, she hauled herself upward. Two jumps and then she, too, landed on top of a column, well above the demons. Behind her the moon rose huge and red-tinged. Korzha resettled Holly in his arms and with a hop, he landed on a column nearer Claudia.

They watched as, with chilling proficiency, Lath cut down the other demons. One dashed free of the carnage and transformed to gargoyle shape. A blast of purple fire caught it mid-flight, and sent the creature whirling through the air. A streaking, turning ball of orange fire erupted from it and headed straight for Korzha at blinding speed. The blast, meant for Lath, was too close and too fast to miss Korzha and Holly. Claudia's horrified scream echoed in Korzha's ears. He turned his back, shielding Holly, and let the fire hit him between the shoulder blades. Pain embraced him, took his breath and ripped through him. He tumbled off the column, falling downward with one thought in his head: He couldn't let go of Holly. Claudia would never forgive him if something happened to Holly.

Chapter Twenty-eight

For a life-stopping moment, Claudia thought she was going to watch her daughter die. Korzha tumbled groundward, but he didn't let go of Holly. He hit the ground on his knees with Holly safe against his chest. Claudia could smell the burning air. The vampire collapsed to the flagstones. The back of his shirt had been burnt away and exposed a hideous injury. Though he wasn't moving, neither was he turning to ash, the only sure sign a vampire wasn't coming back. By the time Claudia made it to the ground, Holly stood at the vampire's side clutching a black mink in her arms. The animal's nose twitched, and it wiggled out of her arms to curl around Holly's neck.

Claudia held her daughter again. At last. "Oh, my God, Holly. Sweetpea." Tears welled up, burst over her, a wave of all the horrible things that could have happened; all the awful things she'd imagined. She pulled her daughter tight against her, touching her everywhere. My God, Holly was thin. Too thin. Claudia pushed her back to stare into her face, drinking her in. Holly looked pale. Her eyes were big in her face, the skin beneath them blue. The mink chittered softly. "He knew the word, Mom."

"You did good. You did exactly what you were supposed to." Claudia kept running her hands over her daughter—arms, face, stomach—rememorizing her daughter, assuring herself Holly wasn't physically injured. "Are you all right?"

From behind her, she heard a sound. "Claudia-*tes*."

Claudia whirled and got Holly behind her. The minklike creature arched its back and hissed. The demon Lath walked to her, hand extended. Two more Bak-Faru stood behind him. Lath's eyes fixed on her, razor-sharp. His black hair gleamed blue in the light. He didn't look dangerous. He didn't even have a weapon, for cripes sake. Not that he needed one.

He put his hands on her shoulders. "*Tes*," he said to her softly. "You are safe now." With a quick look over his shoulder at the Bak-Faru who waited at the entrance to the courtyard, he ordered: "No one comes in."

When he faced Claudia again, he stroked her hair, winding a lock around his finger. "I do not want you," he said softly. His eyes flashed red again. "To have the vishtau with a human is worse than to have no mate at all."

She lifted her hands, palm upward. "If you hate me so much, why don't you let us go? Me, Holly and Tiber."

The demon stared at her and almost smiled. His dimples winked in and out in his cheeks. "I have the vishtau with you," he said gently. "I can do nothing about that."

"Take us to the portal. Let us go home. You'll never see us again."

"The Bak-Faru will come to the Overworld, Claudia

Donovan." A growl rumbled in his throat. "Humans will pay. I will find the ones who summoned the Bak-Faru, and kill them for what they did."

She studied Lath's face. How interesting that even though she felt desire for the demon, the sensation paled in comparison to what she felt for Tiber. "I can't imagine anyone making you do something you don't want to."

"Claudia," he whispered. His fingers trembled as they moved along her shoulders. "A human who knows the magic to summon demons binds us to that magic. We can do nothing but what the magic demands."

"Have humans summoned *you*?"

Lath shook his head, but Claudia wasn't sure if he meant that as a denial or a refusal. "They will die. Every one of them." He nodded in the direction of the Bak-Faru guards. "We must speak without listening ears, Claudia-*tes*." He pointed to an archway that to her diurnal eyesight seemed nothing but shadow. Lath addressed Holly. "Holly Donovan. Please attend to your pet." He smiled at the child. "We will go to the Overworld soon and your pet must be calm." In a softer voice, he soothed Claudia's instinctive reaction against being separated from Holly. "My Bak-Faru will not allow harm to come to your daughter. And we will not be far. Just there." He pointed. "Only a short distance."

In the anteroom, Lath did something and soft blue light glowed from the wall sconces. He stayed close to her. Too close. "You are human," he said after a moment's deep silence. "I do not know if you can understand the vishtau. It is the business of demons." He brushed a fingertip along her cheek. "When you left me, when you left with the vampire, I felt the loss *here*." He touched his chest and then sighed. "Some things you must know even though you are human. I wish you to understand what has happened to me."

She had to tilt her head back a long way to look into his face. "I'm listening."

"Then hear me, Claudia-*tes*. Understand. Demons cannot choose the vishtau. When it happens. . . ." He paced, three short steps away and then back, frustration and indecision in every step he took. When he stood before her again, he took her hands in his and, leaning toward her, intertwined their fingers. A portion of his ponytail fell over his chest. He left the wrist-thick shank where it fell. "We do not know in advance who will be our mate. If it happens, we cannot choose. The vishtau chooses for us."

"Why me? Why a human?"

"*Tes*. I cannot answer." He let go of her hands and drew a deep breath. "It sometimes happens between a human and a demon. So it has happened between us. The vishtau is always stronger for males because we must protect our mates. I felt you before I saw you. I wanted to deny you. I tried, but I have failed. You are not demon, so I believe you do not feel what a demon female would." His eyes filled with sadness. "A demon female would love me. She would feel the vishtau and want me to protect her. Claudia. *Tes*. I must protect you. I cannot let you die."

He reached up and untied the braids that held back his hair. With long, delicate fingers, he pulled one of the platinum strands from the plait. The material glittered, a rainbow of colors refracting from the thread. He spoke as he worked the strand into her hair. "Long ago, *tes*, when I was in the Overworld, I saw many beautiful human women. They were weak. I did not want to mate with any of them." She felt the strand heat then settle into her hair. "But I want to mate with you."

His fingers touched the side of her head. The demon leaned over her and caught her face between his hands. His hair fell around them like a veil of black. Arousal shot through her like a fire. The air around her heated. Claudia felt sure, was certain he meant to kill her despite his protestations otherwise. She waited, frozen, holding her breath. The air got hotter. It glowed around him, a corona of lilac haze. Claudia's head spun. Flashes of the demon echoed in her head. And then it was like all the air in the world disappeared. The sudden change in pressure felt like a tap on her eardrums. On her hip, the mark Aslet had made flared up, burned her, paralyzed her, suffocated her.

Thwip.

In a rush, the air came back. The fullness in her head pulsed like a light from a lighthouse. She gasped. "What did you just do?"

The Bak-Faru said, "You are marked now, as the female of a Bak-Faru. No demon will dare harm you." He kissed her forehead. "There is one thing more we must do."

"What?" Their eyes stayed locked. Such lovely, lovely lilac eyes in his Aztec face. He knew damn well he was beautiful. He oozed beauty from his pores.

"We must finish what I have begun." He spoke more in a low voice, syllables and words that made no sense yet sounded as if they must mean something, and something important. She stared at his mouth, listening as hard as she could because she felt that if she listened hard enough she'd know what he was saying.

"Claudia," he said in his dark velvet voice, and she was lost in it, lost in the lilac depths of his eyes. "You must say my name."

"Lath."

"I am called Lath, Claudia Donovan, but that is not my name."

"Ur-Kashev-Ghan. You are named Ur-Kashev-Ghan." Claudia felt his spirit flowing into her, spreading through her like a fever. "Ur-Kashev-Ghan is your heart and your life."

"Claudia Donovan, you are my life and my heart. They belong to you and only you. Now, say this. Exactly as I do." Slowly he repeated the words, patiently correcting her when she stumbled. An odd pressure built in her chest as she repeated the sounds, and she felt dizzy.

"It is done," he said when she finished. He touched her forehead. "We have the vishtau. We are for life. For me, there is you. Only you. It does not matter if I hate one human, ten dozen or all of them." Fire danced in his eyes. His fingers traced her lower lip, and his dimples flashed again. "We will mate, *tes*." He tugged on her hands. "Come. Come. You will give me children to love."

"No!" Claudia said, and it cost her nearly everything to deny him. She touched his cheek. He turned his head to one side and kissed her hand. His hair fell across her arm, a wickedly black veil.

"To save you, I have bound you to me for life. There will never be another female for me. To have the vishtau with a human female chokes me; my heart is dust to feel it with you." His fingers followed the line of either side of her jaw, a light touch, a caress. "I have no choice. Because you are my vishtau mate, I will protect you. With you, only you. I must mate with you. The vishtau compels me. For more than pleasure. Not only for pleasure but for children. I would have a female child with you as beautiful as Holly Donovan. Sons, too." Smoke and velvet flowed into his voice. "But we will have pleasure. Much pleasure, because you are beautiful."

She leaned back, but Lath followed. "If you don't want me, send us home, and you just stay here."

He slid his fingers down her spine and then inside her pants, along the dip in the small of her back. "But *tes*, I want to mate with you. I will always want to mate with you. And you will always feel how I want you. This cannot be undone. You and I have said the words. We are bound for our lives. There will never be any female for me but you." Both his hands curved over her bottom. His voice fell. "I would give my life for you. And for Holly Donovan, too. For you, because of the vishtau, I will protect her, too. With my life."

From the courtyard, a scream shattered the air. Not a demon. Korzha. He must have recovered from his injuries, and now the other Bak-Faru were attacking him. A flash of light lit the doorway. She darted toward the door. "Korzha!" Lath held her hand, and it was like trying to drag a Humvee. She whirled to him, heart in her throat. "They're going to kill him, aren't they?"

He shrugged. "The vampire is not my business."

She looked directly into his eyes. "I'll make a deal with you, Lath."

The spark of his quizzical interest leapt between them. "Yes, Claudia-*tes*?"

"Whatever they're doing to him, make them stop." Her voice broke. "Don't let anything happen to him. Don't let him die." She slid a hand down his chest. "Promise me you won't kill him."

"In return for?"

She swallowed hard. "I'll never tell you no when you want me."

For a moment, he hesitated. But then he said, "Claudia Donovan, it is done."

Chapter Twenty-nine

Heart pounding in her chest, Claudia followed Lath back to the courtyard where two of the other Bak-Faru had Korzha cornered. A single word from Lath brought the attack to a halt. Claudia was fiercely glad to see that one of the Bak-Faru had a deep slash across his back and shoulder. Even a weakened Korzha was to be reckoned with. A purple bruise fading to yellow marred his cheek, another purple-blue abrasion at his temple, and he looked gaunt. Hard-used. She felt the connection between them flare up. "You okay, Tiber?"

"Yes," came his reply. His attention darted to Holly and then to Lath, and lastly to her hair, to the platinum strand woven into it.

"Thank you," Claudia said. "Thank you for saving Holly."

Lath stood next to her and curved an arm around her waist to keep her from going to Korzha. It was a gesture intended to make a point. He slipped two fingers under her chin and tipped her head to his. She saw the demon look at Tiber first, making sure he had the vampire's attention. He did. Then, his mouth brushed over hers, and from the back of his throat came a low growl. He kissed her—a surprisingly tender touch—and she felt the heat of his desire. She wanted Korzha, cared about the vampire, but she kissed Lath. The demon drew back with a soft sigh. "What would you do if I said I wanted you now?" he whispered.

"I'd go with you," she replied. She had promised.

"This is good." He touched a finger to her lips. "Are you ready, Claudia-*tes*? Ready to open the portal and return to the Overworld?"

She nodded and tried to catch Tiber's eye again, but he wasn't looking at her. Did he think she'd betrayed him? Did he believe she'd left him for the demon? Tension curled unpleasantly in her chest. One of the other Bak-Faru pushed Tiber's shoulder. Probably he would have looked at her if the demon hadn't done that. But he had, and the moment was lost. She had no idea what he thought of anything. Her stomach fluttered with unpleasant anxiety.

Lath's hand flashed out, fingers down. One of the Bak-Faru took Holly's mink and put it in a satchel. The demon crouched with a friendly smile to show Holly the animal was fine. When he'd closed the satchel, and slung the strap across his chest, the demon touched Holly's cheek. "I will keep your pet safe, Holly Donovan," the Bak-Faru said.

The six dark demons fell into position around Lath. Claudia picked up her daughter. "I'm ready. Korzha." She held out a hand, ignoring Lath's frown.

"*Tes*," he said.

"I didn't promise to leave him here, Lath."

Walking through the streets of Biirkma with seven Bak-Faru as escort made for an interesting experience.

No one challenged them. The demons they saw were simply too old to get out of the way fast enough, or not powerful enough to sense them until it was too late. Lath stayed at the head of the group, exchanging a remark or two with the brown-haired Bak-Faru who carried Holly's mink, now dubbed Whiskers. Before long, Claudia's left biceps screamed in piercing protest at bearing Holly's weight. She was about to put the child down when Korzha reached over and took her. "Thank you," she said.

He gave her a cockeyed grin. "You'd have taken my heart for sure if I'd let anything happen to her."

She grinned back. "Damn straight, fang."

The Bak-Faru came to a stop. Howls rose from within: the Elismal guards sensing the Bak-Faru. Lath motioned to two of his fellows. The air shimmered around them and they vanished. From inside the portal room something howled, then silence. Lath smiled, and they all went in. The two Bak-Faru stood in the middle of the empty room. They bowed to Lath. Claudia caught an unsettling scent of burnt air. All seven of the dark demons in one tiny room. The air practically ignignted.

Lath held out his arms for Holly. "Come, child." He gave Tiber a look. "My life is hers, vampire. She will be safe with me. She will always be safest with demons."

Korzha looked to Claudia, who nodded. The vampire would have refused, she realized. If she hadn't agreed with Lath, he'd been prepared to refuse to give Holly over—even if it meant enraging a demon more than capable of killing him.

Lath stood at the head of his Bak-Faru, Holly in his arms. The demon with Whiskers patted the side of his satchel and then winked one pale brown eye at the child. The six gathered in the door that led to the street. They spoke as one, in a low, communal voice that made Claudia's skin crawl. Around them the air heated, glittered. Foolishly, she assumed the other Bak-Faru were to stay behind.

"Claudia-*tes*." Lath turned to Claudia. "You must hold open the portal."

She nodded. Before she did as directed, she bent for her PD-issue pack, abandoned here all this time. She looked over her shoulder to be sure Tiber followed. Within a foot of the portal, she felt the pulse of energy. This time she knew what to expect and didn't relish the experience. Gingerly she touched the surface of the door. Electricity zinged through her, caught her off balance. The portal felt different; she felt its energy pulsing. She pushed, and her hand moved through the door along with a bitter-cold pain. "Like the saying goes," she muttered, "just do it." And she stepped through.

Claudia pressed herself into the middle of the portal, trapped in the swirling pattern that pulled at her from the inside out. The mark on her hip started to burn, and her head throbbed. On the Orcus side, Lath faced the other Bak-Faru and made a gesture that encompassed the entire room. Around the other demons, the air quivered, heated, and then the wall . . . vanished. Instead of fitted blocks of stone, she saw scores of Bak-Faru moving into the portal room. Lath stepped through the swirling, waltzing air of the portal, Holly in his arms, and into Crimson City.

In Orcus, another demon lifted a hand and moved forward, toward and then through the portal. A blink of an eye later the rest of the Bak-Faru streamed through like marathoners in mid-race pace. It was done. The Bak-Faru invasion had begun.

Behind her, Claudia heard a shout. Sound bent

oddly in the portal. Was that Korzha's voice? The portal held her, was tearing her apart. She saw Lath standing in the Crimson City corridor next to Holly. She turned her head and saw Korzha in Orcus, standing to one side while the Bak-Faru warriors flowed past. Beyond him, past the vampire's shoulder, she saw Aslet, his eyes red with flame.

Forever. It took forever for all the Bak-Faru to go through. One hundred and seven dark demons, she counted. And when it was done, when the last had gone through, the outside wall was just a wall again. Claudia held out a hand to Korzha, but looked into Crimson City. Lath stood in the grimy corridor, Holly next to him. The child clutched the satchel to her chest. On the floor by Lath's foot was a weapon one of the B-Ops commandos had dropped when he went through the portal to his death.

Claudia glanced back at Tiber. "Come on," she said. She held out her hand. Pain rippled through her. Aslet roared.

And then she was pulled forward, into Los Angeles with a bone-numbing jolt. She whipped her head toward Lath, already shouting a demand to know what the hell he thought he was doing. The portal closed, with Korzha on the other side.

Chapter Thirty

"Tiber!" Claudia lay on her back, head turned toward the now opaque portal. Horror flashed through her at the sight of the battered wooden door. Her head throbbed like someone was pounding nails into the back of her skull. She flipped over, shouting at Lath. "You left Tiber!"

Lath and his six Bak-Faru waited in the corridor. Behind them in the light cast by the single bulb swinging from the ceiling, the warriors flowed outward, some in human form, others in manifestations of animal or monster. The building groaned with the energy of demons flooding outward toward the streets of Crimson City. Dark demons, the darkest of the dark. She'd let an army of dark demons into Crimson City.

"The portal is dangerous for you." Lath stood with his arms crossed over his chest. He cocked his head at her, quirking one corner of his mouth. A dimple appeared in his cheek. "The vampire is no longer my responsibility. My promise to him is fulfilled, as is my promise to you. I did not allow my demons to kill him.

He will be safe in Orcus." He smiled again. "If you wanted more, *tes*, you should have asked."

Claudia pushed herself to her knees and threw herself at the portal. One arm passed through, but Lath caught her other arm and stopped her momentum toward the door. She twisted toward him and kicked, but missed badly.

"Claudia-*tes*," he said in reasonable tones. But his eyes flashed red. Her hip burned, felt like it was on fire. She reacted without thinking, using Lath's strength as leverage. She swung her leg toward the portal, hard. At last, she surprised him. He let go of her arm, and she dropped like a sack of dead rats. She rolled toward the portal.

As she moved, her left hand landed on the abandoned B-Ops gun. She felt its weight and figured she had half a clip left at least. She was damn lucky it hadn't gone off and killed her. Weapon in hand, she threw herself at the portal again. Her right side hit first. The barrier gave way, and her body elongated, stretched, began to tear. A thousand needle-sticks. She got herself upright and jammed one leg on the opposite side of the door frame. Head back, she looked into Orcus. Electricity shivered through her body. With effort, she stretched her hand upward. "Korzha!" she shouted. "Tiber!"

In her head, her shout made no noise, but he heard, because he whipped toward the opening. On the Crimson City side, something grabbed her ankle and pulled. She increased the pressure of her foot against the frame. She wasn't going to be able to hold much longer. Impressions flew at her, hitting her from all around.

Through the quivering barrier of the portal, she saw Lath bending over her. Behind him, Holly crouched on the ground, hands over her satchel. In Orcus, Korzha's hand curled around hers. At the same time, she got the fingers of her left hand on the trigger of her gun. If she could stand the pain, she had a clear shot at Lath. Lath didn't understand human weapons, not really, so when she aimed at the demon's chest, he laughed at her. She was going to blow his heart out his back. But something ripped at her. How could she kill him? No. He had to die. She wanted to be free of him. Free of all the demons in her head.

The air in-between them heated, searing her lungs. Korzha launched himself at the portal. The impact wrenched her arm, but Claudia held on. On the L.A. side, she lifted the gun and took aim. Her body threatened to come apart. Her sense of where she was in space distorted. Everything in the portal quivered and shook. Matter was about to rip. She fired at the demon. . . .

Nothing happened. She moved her arm and re-sighted. Her limb elongated, stretched as she broke the plane of the portal. Sparks flew around her, popping, deafening, searing. Her arm quivered and shook, her muscles involuntarily contracting and releasing. Her fingers sprang open. Her gun fired, but upward, into the portal void. Fire erupted from her weapon. All air vanished. Her body threatened to fly apart. Her lungs insisted on oxygen, but there wasn't anything to breathe.

She could see the Crimson City hallway like she was looking through a kaleidoscope spinning at top speed. Tiber still hurtled for the opening. Timing it perfectly, Lath, murder in his eyes, moved to intercept the vampire. She pulled the trigger again. Again, nothing. A streak of blue light arced over her head from the Orcus side and bounced around inside the portal as

Tiber's body pierced the veil of the seal. His momentum into Crimson City pulled her out of the portal and into the decrepit building.

Like a cork coming free of a bottle, there was an enormous rush of energy and then a high, keening, deafening shriek as they both landed in L.A. Claudia scrambled forward as the sound grew to deafening volume. The fire that had erupted from the gun collided with the blue flames.

Claudia threw her body over Holly, covered her ears and then her head. Light filled the room, a burst of white light, and then—

Nothing else. Absolutely nothing happened. Except for the smell of charred wood in the air, the room felt completely normal.

"Officer," said a familiar voice. Tiber. He pulled her to her feet. He caught Holly in his arms and gently took the bulging, wiggling satchel from her. Behind the vampire, Lath's lilac eyes flickered with exultation. Why the hell wasn't he attacking? His six Bak-Faru stared at the portal.

Claudia glanced at the opening. Only, it wasn't there anymore—or, rather, where the battered door had been now remained only a quiver of air. She stretched out a hand, extending a tentative finger. Nothing. No sparks, no zing of electricity, no sensation of building energy, no sense of elongation. The gun she'd had in her hand lay on the threshold, a smoking wreckage of melted, charred parts. She saw Aslet clear as day, and she knew from Korzha's expression that so did he.

Aslet stood in the tiny anteroom in Orcus, staring into Crimson City. His eyes stared past her, disbelieving, triumphant at the irony. His promise to protect Tiber had compelled him to unleash a magical attack against Lath that blasted the portal at the same time

Claudia's weapon fired. Wind caught his hair and blew silver strands across his cheek. That same breeze crossed into Crimson City. Exultation flared in his impossibly blue eyes. The demon lifted a hand and said something in a low voice. Then, with a deep breath, he stepped through the portal by himself.

Lath bowed, hand over fist. "The Bak-Faru welcome you to the Overworld, *Nir*-Aslet," the demon said.

Aslet returned the bow. "*En*-Lath.

And then Tiber scooped up Holly, the satchel and Claudia, and bolted.

Chapter Thirty-one

"Where are we?" Claudia whispered when she and Tiber landed on the roof of a flat-topped concrete building. She turned in a circle, trying to get her bearings. They'd outrun the demons, for now.

Korzha pointed to a dark area across from them. "That's Athens Park."

They were south of the city center. That was Highway 110 behind them, but the structure was eerily silent, and that just wasn't right. From this height, which wasn't even all that high, her stomach did a little flip-flop and her knees went watery when she glanced over the edge at West El Segundo Boulevard. South to Compton. North to the city proper. She had no head for heights whatsoever. She pulled Holly several steps back, brushed her hair from her face, and when her fingers touched the thread Lath had woven into her hair, her anxiety grew.

To the west, toward the Pacific, the sky was pale charcoal, aglow with the lights from the city. To the northeast, past the portal, the city sparkled and danced, unaware of the menace. Claudia exchanged a long and silent look with Korzha. "I guess we hope like heck the Bak-Faru and the Elismal don't decide to get along."

A breeze blew through Korzha's hair. The satchel containing Whiskers bulged and a low-pitched chatter came from inside. Far away and far overhead, Strata +1 glittered. Tiberiu Korzha's world. The Upper. Her world was down below, on the streets in Strata 0. In the heart of the chaos to come.

She slipped her hand into his, completely without thinking, and he didn't pull away. In L.A., things were different. He could go anywhere he wanted. Be with anyone he wanted. Did he want her? She stared at him, at the gorgeous face with the hint of shadowy stubble, a few coffee-bean-colored curls around his ears. Of course he'd go back to being the cold and perfect vamp she'd known before. He was Upper. She was Lower. Vamp and human. It couldn't work. Could it?

With her free hand, see fished her cell phone out of her P.D. pack. Korzha let go of her while she waited to see if the damn thing would explode or something. It didn't. The cell phone screen informed her she'd missed one hundred and fifty-seven calls. "We have to warn them demons are here."

"There you go again, Officer." He crossed his arms over his chest, while she punched numbers on the phone. His smile felt painfully familiar now, and sent a pang of regret through her heart. She missed it already. The phone on the other end rang. "Thinking you have to save humanity."

"Everyone," she said. "I meant we have to warn *everyone*. Shit!" She disconnected from voicemail and dialed again. "The Bak-Faru won't discriminate. They're equal-opportunity haters."

"All by yourself?"

She sang, "Here she comes to save the day. . . ."

Korzha didn't laugh.

"Doesn't someone have to?" She gave the phone a shake. "Come on. Pick up." At last the sleepy voice of the P.D.'s liaison to Internal Operations answered. "Parsons? That you? Donovan here. Yeah, I know. Fine. Listen. No—Don't say another freaking word until I'm finished."

When she was done and had hung up, she slumped against a ventilation duct and got poked by a piece of bent flashing. The roof smelled like tar. Must have been hot in L.A. today. "Parsons is a good guy. Those were freaking dark demons, Korzha. Save the day? Right." She shoved her phone in her pants pocket. "Great job so far, huh? They're here because of me. I let them in. Shit. Lath has a freaking list of the people he intends to kill. What's going to happen to the city with a hundred and seven Bak-Faru demons on the loose?"

"The Bak-Faru intended this all along."

"Yeah, but *I* opened the door." She laughed, but not very convincingly. "I'm going to spend the rest of my life filling out the paperwork on this one."

"Demons may be here." He cocked his head. "But not for the first time. And they won't be, I feel compelled to point out, without opposition. Much as Aslet resents, it, he and his Elismal are allied with me." He laughed. "Who knows—maybe they'll fit right in."

"Right."

"Are demons so different from everyone else here?" he asked. "Really, Donovan. Vampires and werewolves live in Crimson City. Why not demons?"

"Because they can't be trusted!"

He smiled. "Since when does trust occur between

species? Vampires exist. Werewolves exist. Humans exist. We all distrust each other. We even distrust members of our own species. Now demons exist here. Nothing is new if we distrust them, too."

Claudia straightened. "You've seen what they can do, Korzha."

The vampire's eyes shuttered. "Why should humans decide who lives here and who—or what—does not?"

"They're evil." But Claudia remembered Siath and her lost son, and Lath's outrage that humans summoned demons and forced them to acts they abhorred. She thought of all the demons who hadn't bothered her in Orcus, and she couldn't speak with conviction. The whole world was changed. Time was, she didn't trust any vamps.

"So must the cat seem evil to the mouse," Tiber said. He slipped an arm around her. "There isn't anyplace where bad things don't happen, and no species that does no evil from someone's point of view. Perhaps humanity's point of view isn't the only one worth considering."

"Humans are the underdog, Korzha. We don't have any special powers."

"Dear-heart, you underestimate your species."

Her heart sped up. She felt a nice little thrill at the endearment, followed by a flash of guilty despair. He didn't know. He didn't know she wasn't going to die. Maybe that was why he was so matter-of-fact. "Do you think it's possible for demons to fit in?" She asked, incredulous.

He pressed his mouth to the top of her head. "Instead of holding on to the past, let's look forward."

"Tiberiu Korzha, *philosophe*."

He brushed his dangling curls behind an ear, but his attention, like hers, turned to the horizon. "The passing of an age requires a certain degree of philosophy," was his response.

"Philosophy, shmilosophy. Can you get us off the roof?" She didn't like the way Holly hadn't spoken. She wanted to sleep in her own bed and wear her own clothes. To take a long, hot shower and figure out what her life was going to look like from now on. "My car's not far from here. I'd like to take my daughter home," she said.

Tiber nodded and gathered her and Holly up. They landed at the corner of the park. Interesting, how Holly pressed herself against Tiber. "Well," Claudia said in the awkward silence that followed.

"Well." Tiber held Holly's hand, and he still wore the satchel with the mink.

"Need a ride?" Oh, for cripes's sake. A vampire didn't need a ride anywhere; they could fly. "Car's that way." She pointed. So, was this the end? Would they just shake hands and say good-bye? She felt like crying, and when she tried to swallow the lump in her throat, she couldn't. Korzha took her elbow and they started walking. Half a block from where she'd left her car, she stopped at a silver Lexus SUV.

"Nice car," Tiber said.

"Sure is." She sighed. "Too bad it isn't mine." She sighed again and dug in her pack for her keys. She pressed the button on the fob, but there wasn't any responding beep from any of the other cars along the block. "Shoot."

"Maybe farther down the street?"

"Yeah. Maybe." She cleared her throat. "Korzha," she whispered with a quick look at Holly. "We have to talk."

The vampire scanned the street. "What do you drive?" he asked.

"A green car."

"Green." The satchel bulged again, but Holly whispered to it and the movement stopped. Strange, that there was so little traffic. And nobody was on the street.

"Dark green."

"An immense help, thank you. No green cars here."

"A Saturn. It runs. Hardly anything goes wrong with it. Usually.

"I think I got towed."

He tilted his head, and she wondered if he'd start cutting his hair again now that he was back in L.A. Holly still held his hand. "Pity," he said.

"I'm a cop. They'll give it back. So I guess we'll walk home. It's not that far." She looked at Holly. "You okay with walking, sweetie? Not too tired?" The girl shook her head. Claudia glanced down the street, taking Holly's other hand, aware that her daughter hadn't let go of the vampire. Was she so chickenshit?

"You coming, Tiber?" she asked. Three words, not even the dangerous ones, and Claudia felt like she'd just put her entire life on the line. "You can if you want."

"I want," he said.

Her heart went pit-a-pat. "That's good," she replied. Until he found out she wasn't going to die, right? That would change everything. Then he would stop feeling sorry for her and leave her. "Really good," she added.

They walked without speaking, Holly between them, holding both their hands. It was full dark now. Somewhere in the distance a siren blared. An IRAS chopper hummed through the air to the southwest, toward the Lower. The streets were empty, and that seemed strange. There were no people out, and the only vehicle trolling the streets was a tow truck. Traffic lights changed colors for no good reason since there weren't any cars at the intersections. At the corner store where she shopped between big grocery trips, she stopped to read a photocopied notice taped to the window.

Curfew
Closing 9:00 P.M. nightly until further notice
by order of Crimson City Internal Operations.
No exceptions.
Executive Order 1995 §3045(b)

A cop car turned the corner as they were reading the sign. Lights flashed and the prowler headed toward them.

"What time do you figure it is?" Claudia asked.

"Eleven-seventeen," Tiber answered.

"We'd better get off the street."

"It might be safer if went to Strata +1."

The Upper. Claudia let out a breath.

Korzha put his arms around her and said right into her head as the cop car came closer, "Come home with me."

She nodded, then they went up, right in front of the patrol car. She and Holly were shivering with cold by the time he stopped at an exterior landing platform. They went in a window, not a door. Or maybe it was just that the door looked like a window.

"No way," she said, when her knees stopped shaking from her one unfortunate glimpse outward from the platform. The street was a hell of a long way down.

"Way," he replied, and walked in. He pressed a button on the wall, and light suffused the room.

This was no stinky-carpeted hallway of triple-deadlocked doors that would have made her feel right at home, but a single expanse of a room that belonged on the cover of *Architectural Digest*. He had a hard-wood floor, the real deal there, a rug of indigo and olive and in a pattern that looked like something from a book on Nepalese temple art, antique furniture, gilt-framed paintings on the walls—she was lost in Paris without a map, and not a word of French at her command. And all the natives knew she didn't belong.

Tiber faced her. "Welcome to my home, Officer Donovan. Holly."

"Wow," said the little girl.

At the far end of the room another arched doorway with stairs led upward. To Claudia's right was an elevator. "Now, this," she said, "this is life in the Upper."

Tiber leaned in and kissed her forehead. "Dear-heart. I haven't lived this long without picking up a few things along the way."

"I should have expected," she said. But the truth was, there was no way she could have been prepared for the reality of Korzha's life. "I don't know why I'm surprised," she said.

Tiber handed the satchel to Holly and leaned one hip against a carved rosewood table. "I'm a Korzha," was his reply. "Most would agree that I'm *the* Korzha."

"Right," she whispered.

"You can stay here as long as . . ." He lifted an eyebrow. "Holly, keep the satchel closed, please."

Holly took one look at Korzha and froze, her hands on the buckled strap. Claudia heard the noise, too—a creak in the hallway from a door about a thousand miles past his shoulder. Well, okay, it was about two of her apartments away, and someone was knocking on the other side of what looked like a conventional door. Except there were no deadbolts. Well, why bother, right?

"Tiberiu?" a voice called.

Korzha said nothing.

"It's Jon, Tiber. Open the door. I know you're in there."

When Korzha opened the door, a man with walnut skin and black hair slipped inside. His eyes darted to Claudia, who stood near the window with her arm around Holly. "Fleur wants a word with you, Tiber. About Laura Masters, among other things." His eyes darted to Claudia. "Like the cop you hit." He looked at Claudia again. "And," he added, shifting his attention to Holly, "her missing daughter. The baby-sitter was reduced to gibbering nonsense about monsters and fire. Where the hell have you been, Tiber?"

Korzha walked back to Claudia. "I went after a rogue."

In the blink of an eye, Jon was at Korzha's side. Kind of unnerving, that ability to move in between the space of a breath. Claudia watched the new vampire's dark eyes travel up and down her, pausing at her neck. "And?" he prompted Tiber.

"Do forgive my lack of manners," Korzha said. He slipped an arm around her shoulders. "Claudia, may I present Jon Dumont of Family Dumont? Jon, this is Officer Claudia Donovan of our city's finest—and this is her daughter Holly. Both, you will notice, are very much alive."

Jon didn't take his eyes off Korzha. Unlike Korzha, Jon filed his teeth. Passing as human, then. "And the rogue?"

"Is not."

Jon rounded on Claudia, looked like he meant to say something but thought better of it. He whirled back to Tiber. "I don't know what's going on, Tiber, but my advice is get the hell out of here. Now. The Strata's not safe. Not for you. They've sent the Vendix after you."

Korzha laughed. "I appreciate the warning, but Fleur's about to find out she has bigger fish to fry than Tiberiu Korzha."

"Hardly," Dumont said with a snarl. "I'm taking a risk just coming here. You're believed to be a triple-murderer. The cop and her daughter, Laura Masters—"

"Councilwoman Masters?" Korzha's eyes went wide and innocent. "Has something happened to her?"

"Don't play innocent with me, Tiber."

Korzha shrugged.

"Right now, Tiber, my friend, you're a flounder stinking up Fleur's house. She's out for spring cleaning, and the rest of Family Korzha isn't objecting." Jon shoved his hands into his pants pockets. "I'll visit you at Lompoc. When are visiting hours, do you suppose?"

Korzha laughed. "The portal's open," he replied. "And there are demons in Crimson City."

Dumont scrubbed his hands through his dark hair. "I hope to hell you don't mean that."

"Believe me as you like, Dumont. You'll know the truth soon enough. The whole city will."

"Oh, shit," the vamp whispered.

"Tell Fleur I'll explain everything as soon as she calls off the Vendix and not a minute before."

Dumont nodded. "In the meantime, if you want to live to make your explanations, you better get the hell out of Dodge."

"I'll be in touch." Korzha snatched up Holly and then Claudia, and crossed the room faster than she could take a breath. He ducked onto the exterior landing. In the back of her head, like it was really far away, pressure built. Demons.

"My place," she said.

Korzha nodded. He gathered himself and leapt into the air with Claudia burying her head against his chest and hanging on to Holly for dear life. It took a long time to get to the ground, and his shoes made a soft *ka-thuck* when he landed on the pavement across the street from her apartment.

Chapter Thirty-two

Claudia lived in a dump. Compared to Korzha's place, anything else was a dump, but her apartment was especially bad. She lived maybe three miles from the derelict structure where the portal now stood wide open. Her four-story stucco building had been charming for about five minutes in the 1960s, after which its appeal plunged like a boulder shoved off a cliff. The most recent coat of paint was peeling down to the previous layer of putrid green. Gaps in the reddish-orange roof tile exposed a ripped and weathered membrane and missing flashing. Bars covered all the street-facing windows, and in one of the upper windows, a sheet served as a window blind.

Korzha did something and the gate in the arched doorway clicked open. Never mind fishing out her keys again. The trio climbed the cracked cement steps to the front landing. The glass cover over the exterior light was broken. Moths beat themselves against the exposed bulb. Winged bodies littered the peeling surface of the entrance step. The metal-flashed entry door looked as if someone had kicked it pretty hard about a dozen times. About fifty years ago there'd been a pane of glass in the now-boarded-over porthole.

With a bit more of his voodoo, Tiber opened the main door and headed for the elevator—the kind with a creaky iron-gated door. The foyer was about ten feet square, and littered with junkmail and cigarette butts. On the opposite wall, both the bank of mailboxes and the door to the stairwell had dents the size of jack-boots. Claudia found a bent nail on the floor and used it to jimmy her mailbox. She tugged out her accumulated snail mail.

"What floor are you on?" Tiber asked from the elevator.

She stuffed most of her mail in the overflowing trash. Holly yawned, and that made Claudia yawn, too. Jeez, she was tired. Exhausted. And hungry. And Tiber had no business still looking so beautiful. She kicked aside the newspapers piled on the floor. You'd think someone would steal them just to keep things tidy. "Fourth floor, but it's safer to take the stairs."

"As you like," Korzha agreed. He went ahead of them in the stairwell, and held open the door when they got to the appropriate level. At her door, apartment 413, she stuffed her mail into her pack and sighed. Keys. While she rummaged for them, the door opposite hers opened.

"Claudia?"

She turned to see her neighbor peering at her from the crack in the doorway. "Hey, Ruth."

Ruth Wells peeked through the gap allowed by the inside chain. You couldn't tell right now but Ruth was a petite brunette with neon-blue eyes who'd fought off a coke habit and had supermodel looks on a five-foot-one-inch frame. "You aren't dead."

"Nope."

"Holly okay? Where you been, girl?" The door closed. From the other side the chair rattled, and the door opened wider. Claudia watched Korzha's reaction when her neighbor emerged wearing a short wrap-around robe of lime-green satin.

"Yes, Holly's okay. We're not dead. We've been on vacation. Kind of unexpected," said Claudia. Tiber smiled politely. "You still clean, Ruth?"

The woman's attention was riveted on Tiber. "Nine months, three weeks, two days. I didn't tell them anything," she said.

Tiber bowed. "Thank you."

Ruth stuck a hand out at him. "Hi, there. I'm Ruth." Her voice dropped to an on-the-prowl purr. "And you are?"

"Completely charmed. Ruth."

Her eyes opened wide. "Damn."

"I'm delighted to meet one of Claudia's friends."

"I'm supposed to call if I hear from you," Ruth said.

Tiber stared into the woman's face. Suddenly the hallway felt a lot narrower. "You have heard nothing, of course."

Ruth goggled, and Korzha faced Claudia's door. A moment later, the locks clicked. Claudia was pretty sure Ruth didn't notice that nobody had keys. With one arm draped around Claudia's shoulder, Tiber pushed open the door and went inside.

"Later," Ruth called.

Claudia flipped the light switch and looked over her shoulder. A grinning Ruth gave her two thumbs up. She smiled back at her friend, then closed the door. Home. Home at last. The harsh glow of the electric light startled her. She'd gotten used to the softer illuminations in Orcus.

"Holy sh—cripes," said Claudia. Holly looked around. Claudia's heart sank through the floor. "This sucks." The apartment was thoroughly tossed. A disaster. Plants were unpotted, cushions thrown off the couch, and all her books were off the shelves.

Tiber surveyed the living room with her. "I wouldn't have pegged you for such a slob, Donovan." He put an arm around her shoulder, and she leaned against him, just as if they were a couple. Tears welled up in her eyes. From somewhere inside, she found the strength to pretend she wasn't devastated. "If it's any consolation, there's no one here," he said. "Human, demon, dog or fang—no one stuck around to collect you."

She swallowed the lump in her throat. "B-Ops. This has B-Ops written all over it."

"A fair conclusion," he said.

"Can I let Whiskers out now?" Holly asked, holding up the satchel.

"Yes, sweetpea."

Holly bent down and released the mink. The animal wound itself around the girl's legs, tail twitching. Its yellow eyes gleamed. "Well . . ." Claudia looked at Korzha. "I guess we'll get something to eat, take showers and get her to bed while I clean up." She put her arms around her daughter and hugged her. "I'll be right back, okay?" The last part she directed at Tiber. She went back to Ruth's, and ten minutes later came back with two cans of cat food and a change of clothes for Tiber. Ruth's on-again off-again boyfriend was about his size. She found Tiber and Holly in the kitchen. The room had been tidied, the drawers closed, pots put away, and the dishes were stacked on the counter. Holly sat at the table, watching Tiber chop an onion. The edge of his knife flashed like he was an Iron Chef. "I got you a change of clothes," Claudia said.

He twisted his upper body toward her. "You and Holly shower, I'll cook."

"You know how to cook?" she asked.

"Shower," he replied, with a glance at Holly. "Go. Shower. Both of you."

When Claudia came back from putting the bathroom into decent enough shape for her daughter to use, she sat in Holly's chair. Thank goodness she'd stocked up in that hotel bathroom, because B-Ops had emptied everything, every bottle and tube. She watched him study the contents of the fridge and check the expiration dates. He took out half a dozen eggs and a hunk of old Parmesan.

"Do you have a whisk?" he asked. He looked good in his Orcus clothes.

Claudia got up, pulled open the silverware drawer and handed him a fork, daring him to comment.

Korzha stared at it a moment, then set the utensil aside. "Sometime back, I got bored and enrolled at the CIA," he said.

She opened a can of cat food. "What, you're a spy?"

"Certified executive chef." He brandished his knife. "The Culinary Institute of America. St. Helena, Napa County, Cal-i-for-ni-ay."

"Gee," Claudia laughed. Whiskers sniffed, then deigned to eat what was placed before him. "I didn't know you knew how to speak rube."

"While I was there, I bought a winery in Sonoma. We'll have to go there one day."

"Right." Why was he teasing her like this? They couldn't be anything. She stared at him and just couldn't stand to think of him driving north up the coast without her. He was cooking. For a guy who didn't eat real food, the vampire knew his way around a kitchen. He'd found her stash of spaghetti and was bringing the water to a boil before putting the noodles in to soften up. She never waited. She figured noodles were done when they were twice as big as when they went in. He picked up a piece of sprouted garlic and twisted off the yellow-green top. He peeled it and then his knife flashed and Claudia smelled the spicy odor. Probably now was not a good time to tell him she wasn't going to die, or about her promise to Lath. She ignored the rock that formed in her stomach. "I think I'll go clean something," she said.

He winked. "I'll call you when I'm done."

Holly came out of the shower while Claudia was putting the last plant back in its pot. The girl sniffed the air and went straight to the kitchen. Claudia followed, and insisted Korzha take his shower next, with a warning that he had twelve minutes before auto shut-off. He turned down the boiling water and the skillet, and came out of the bathroom fifteen minutes later wearing the new clothes Claudia had scrounged for him: loose-fitting pants, a white tank top and a pair of black, Chinese-style shoes. The scar on his shoulder gleamed a paler white than the rest of his skin. Damp hair curled around his face. Claudia showered next, and discovered that the demon's thread in her hair wouldn't come out. It was fused into her hair and impervious to scissors.

When she was done with her shower and back in the kitchen, Korzha fed them cheese omelettes and Parmesan noodles with a hint of peanut sauce. Holly ate everything on her plate and asked for seconds on the noodles, which, as it happened, were not twice the size they'd been when they went in. Everything was delicious.

Claudia took her time putting Holly to bed and sat for a long while watching her daughter sleep. Whiskers curled up on the pillow next to Holly, its sharp nose near her ear. Claudia had Tiberiu Korzha to thank for this moment. Tears burned behind her eyes. Unless she got a grip on herself, she was building up to a pretty huge breakdown. Everything was supposed to be all better now that they were back in L.A., but it wasn't. She didn't wander back into the kitchen until the evidence of her tears had faded and she had a pocket stuffed with toilet paper in case they welled up again.

Tiber faced her when she came in. He'd cleaned up in the kitchen and was just putting away the last dish. His hair had dried, but he still hadn't fastened it back. She didn't have any idea what to say.

"In case you're wondering," he said. He draped the dishtowel over the oven handle, then tugged once on the collar of her bathrobe. "I've put our clothes—yours, mine and Holly's—in the wash."

"The wash?"

He glanced at the wall clock. "They'll be ready for the dryer in about twenty minutes."

She felt like she was meeting a whole different vampire. "You do laundry? Where'd you get the quarters?"

"I have a way with machinery. But don't be surprised if one of your socks disappears." He grinned at her. "And yes, I separated the colors. Your brassiere will not come out pink."

"Thanks. And thanks for cooking, too." She felt like she was in another world. A good one, this time.

"Later," he said, stepping close. Her heart felt like it wanted out of her chest. For cripe's sake, she was giddy as a teenager on her first date.

She let out a breath. "We have to talk, Korzha."

"Tiber," he reminded her. He moved closer, just inches away. "Tiberiu. Whichever you prefer, *draga in-*

ima, but my first name. And, let's talk *later*, shall we?" His fingers stroked her throat.

"Why are you doing this? All this cooking and cleaning and taking care of me? We're in Crimson City. Home. You can have anybody you want, any way you want them."

He went still. Vamp still. "At the portal," he said at last, "I was surprised you came after me."

"Why?"

"I thought you chose Lath." He touched her hair, fingering the thread that no amount of washing could remove. "Have you chosen him now?"

"No."

"I thought I'd lost you." He ran his fingers through his hair. "When you and I finally met, you weren't what I imagined or expected. Not at all. And . . . I thought you'd chosen him. With my reputation now . . ." He shook his head. "At the moment, I am a wanted vamp and under a sentence of death, and I thought—"

"I didn't choose him. It's you I want, Tiber." She put her hands on his shoulders. "When he was with me, I never once stopped thinking about you and everything you've done for me, and he knows it. He knows I want you. You make me feel safe." With a choked sob, she moved into his arms. "He's still in my head. He's still there, and I don't think he's ever going away."

"But you are here with me." Slowly he stroked her back. "With me."

"Yes."

"This is what you wish? Me."

"Yeah, Tiber. It is."

Tiber stroked her back, and, after a bit, his arms tightened around her. "Holly is asleep?" he asked.

She nodded.

He scooped her up and said, "Your room?" She

pointed, and he walked there. She'd managed to neaten the worst of the mess, but she still felt a surge of embarrassment at the disorder. Korzha laid her on the bed, seemingly unperturbed. "I only want you," he said. "No woman but you. No *anything* but you. For as long as we have." He lay beside her, but Claudia stuck out her arms, stopping him.

"I'm not going to die," she blurted out. She told him about Lath and what he'd done to her. Now her closeness with Korzha would be gone. He'd be horrified by her agreement with the demon and he'd leave her and she'd be alone again. And she didn't want to be alone anymore. Starting completely over, but knowing what she wanted . . . "Lath did something to me, and now he says I'm not going to die."

His eyes glittered in the semidark. "Then I owe him a debt."

"Korzha, this isn't a joke." Her heart turned over in her chest.

"I'm not joking." He leaned over her, using his forward movement to recline them both on the mattress. He put his mouth near her ear, then nuzzled her throat. "May I?"

"Stop that." But she threw her arms around him, pulling his shirt up and off, slipped her hands along his stomach.

"Only a little," he whispered when he'd thrown his borrowed shirt to the side. Claudia stared at his chest. Jeez, he was hot. The vampire reached out and touched the side of her head, running his finger along the thread in her hair. "I need a taste," he said, "of my beautiful Claudia."

Hours later, she awoke. Korzha slept next to her, arms around her. How about that? She was used to his motionless, cool body next to hers. She brushed a lock of hair from his forehead and then rose to find clean underwear, a pair of jeans and a tee-shirt. Her bedside clock flashed 12:00 p.m. but she figured it was more like eight or nine. After she'd dressed, she wandered into the kitchen for a snack of stale bread. Yuck. But then she found an orange and an apple that looked to be in relatively safe shape. Fruit in hand, she went to the living room and booted up her computer. While she waited, she peeled the orange.

Holy cripes! Her insides went cold.

She and Korzha had never used any birth control. Ever. Including last night. The thought had never entered her mind.

The computer booted up. It took her about twenty minutes to eliminate the key-logger, spyware, malware and various trackers courtesy of B-Ops. She was pretty certain they hadn't found her other partition. A normal startup took her to the main OS with the typical mail reader and Internet access, but on boot-up if she hit a specific keystroke, up came the Linux partition. Slash dot. Ah, yes. Apache Tomcat server on Red Hat. Darknet on Linux was a wonderful thing. On her salary, all she could afford was one gig down, half a gig up and darknet from the same terminal. Risky, but she knew how to hide her tracks.

The first thing she did after she changed her IP address was check her e-mail, starting with the anonymized account she didn't give to anyone. She checked the logs she'd routed to the account. Shit. One of her B-Ops rootkits had been discovered, but the rest were still there. After that, she checked her log from the P.D. e-mail server. As expected, the virtual private network password had been recently rotated. Her scripts filtered all the e-mails to tech support. Lots of people hadn't read any of the warnings about the VPN password change. It didn't take but half a minute to find one with the new password in it and an officer's log-in. Some people never learned. The guy probably taped his bank log-in to his squad-car laptop, and she'd bet money he used his badge number as his network password.

And, what do you know, she was right. She logged into the L.A.P.D. VPN and authenticated without a hitch. From there, she logged into the mail server with a default sys admin ID no one had bothered to change. She started checking e-mail accounts, starting with her boss's. She'd been declared missing, feared dead at the hands of the vampire Tiberiu Korzha. Family Korzha had promised their utmost cooperation while the matter remained unresolved.

The most recent message was from B-Ops. Short and sweet, B-Ops demanded to deal with any and all incidents involving unexplained paranormal activity or, and here it got interesting, with anything regarding Claudia Donovan or her daughter. Another e-mail alert advised that B-Ops 911 access had been activated. That meant B-Ops monitored all 911 traffic in the city and could intercept calls and send them directly to their headquarters with P.D. dispatch none the wiser. And then she found a surprising thread for Laura Masters. She printed the exchange to show to Tiber later.

She logged off the VPN and brought up the B-Ops web server gateway. She had the router admin account because one of the B-Ops Cisco engineers had been trying to get laid and, in the course of complaining about being underpaid and subject to the dominion of his idiot boss, talked a bit too much. Never underestimate the power of social engineering. By the end of his third beer she had the log-in, password and the port knocking sequence. One at a time, she got onto her rootkitted servers. She ate the last of the apple while she studied logs, ran queries and dumped the results onto her hard drive.

"A little cracking, dear-heart?" Tiber's voice rose behind her, enveloping and sweet.

She didn't jump, because though he had approached with absolute silence, she'd seen his shadow on the monitor. Heart thudding, she sanitized the log entries for her server access so they looked like routine sys monitor events. "You're a wanted man, Tiber Korzha," she said.

"No surprise."

"Too bad I never saw that there's a no-stop APB on you. I'd have to call you in, otherwise."

"Which means?"

"Any cop who sees you notifies B-Ops ASAP. But there's no stopping you. No questions. They're just to advise of your location." She glanced over her shoulder at him. "If I were you, I'd be looking to find out what your Primary Assembly thinks about all this."

"I already know what they think. They've sicced the Vendix on me.

"What's a Vendix?" she asked. She'd heard the term last night but had been too tired to inquire.

"A sort of executioner, if you will."

She threw her apple at the wastebasket. "That sucks," she said.

He laughed. "A misunderstanding that needs to be cleared up sooner rather than later."

She swiveled on her chair. "Are you absolutely sure that Laura Masters is dead?"

"Yes."

"What if it doesn't work the same in Orcus? Is that possible?"

"Why do you ask, Claudia?"

"You better sit down."

"Because?"

"Last week, this picture was on the front page of every paper in the city." She handed him a photo of Laura Masters. Despite the bite marks on her neck, she looked very much alive.

Chapter Thirty-three

"Masters *is* dead," Tiber said. Of that he was certain. "There's no way she's not."

"Last time I saw her, she looked dead to me too. But if she is, how do you explain that?" She pointed at the photo. Claudia brushed her hair behind her ears, gave a little shiver when her fingers brushed the platinum thread there, then turned back to the monitor. "Aslet dumped her body at the wharf. Leroux wolf territory." Her slender fingers tapped on the keyboard. A screenful of data appeared, text in black on white. Tiber read what he could understand. "M.E. called her at 8:24:02 p.m., PDT. Got her body-bagged and headed for an autopsy."

Tiber frowned. The people he killed stayed that way. If Masters wasn't dead, if she'd become a vampire, his chances of clearing himself with Fleur Dumont weren't good. The Primary Assembly didn't look kindly on conversions. A rogue Masters, if she was sane, wasn't likely to say he'd done her a favor. "Only dead people get autopsied."

"There was no autopsy, Tiber," Claudia said.

Despite the subject matter of the discussion, he liked this new side of her: relaxed, confident, intensely concentrated on the facts. It was a whole new Claudia to fall in love with. Love. It was an odd thought. "Explain, if you will."

"The body never arrived." She reached behind her and with a forefinger tapped the LCD panel at the spot she meant. "Somewhere between the wharf and the M.E.'s office, Laura Masters disappeared." She tilted her head and smiled at him. "Dead people rarely get up and walk away by themselves—unless they're vamps or wolves."

Korzha pulled up another chair and sat on it backward, his arms propped on the back. "Shit."

Together, they stared at the monitor. "The dogs were plenty pissed that Masters got dumped in their territory, I bet. Within twenty-four hours after that picture hit the papers, random vampire-killing incidents spiked."

Tiber was fascinated by her facility on the machine. "Interested in a little consulting work on the side, Donovan?"

"Hmm?" She was staring at the monitor and wasn't listening. She clicked a link. A multi-colored chart rendered on the screen, graphing deaths by date, time, cause and victim. "Forty-eight hours later, dog deaths show a similar spike." She tapped the screen again.

"Retaliation?"

"In spades, Tiber. Watch this." She limited results to non-natural deaths, then eliminated humans from the data set. The upward slope increased. "There's been little sign of slowing since. And here's the projection over the next seventy-two hours." The graphic re-rendered. "With Masters running around and demons in town, if you want my guess, we'll be looking at a near vertical slope before the end of the month. Which means, shoot, that I lost that pool. I bet that jerk Benson wins." She was trying to be flip, but he could see she was upset. "This is exactly what Jaise hoped would happen. Demons won't need to start a war if we do it for them. We'll be too busy killing each other to bother with them."

"If Masters has risen, and I'm not saying she has," Korzha said, with a sick feeling in the pit of his stomach, "she's likely rogue. Dangerous."

"Watch this." Claudia changed her query again and pulled a result set of human deaths where cause of death was paranormal-suspected over the last forty-eight hours, plotted by the half hour. "23:17 p.m. PDT yesterday," she said. She pointed at the base of a precipitous spike. "That's midnight. The Bak-Faru didn't really get going until then. At least I assume it's them." Claudia pressed a few more keys. "Sorted by zip-plus-four. Fifteen in the Lower. And there shouldn't be any, because no one reports from the Lower. Things must be pretty tense there if they're letting B-Ops in there."

"So, where is she now?"

"That, Tiber, is a very good question." She tapped some more on the keyboard.

"Probably I won't find it," she muttered. "I stuck my comm unit on her when we were in the portal room, but you never know." Her fingers flew. *Tap. Rattle, rattle, tap.* "It's worth a check. Got you, sucker. Well, okay, look at this." She peered at the screen, tapped more keys, and sat back, hands on top of her head. "Fricking video card is too slow. And here we are." She leaned forward. "That can*not* be right."

"What?"

More tapping, more muttering. Twenty seconds later

she looked at Tiber and said, "It's in the Lower. My old neighborhood. Now, how the hell did it end up there?"

"We should find out, yes?"

Claudia leapt up and was nonstop action. In less than an hour, she had Holly up, dressed and fed, and was over to Ruth's apartment to arrange for sitting, and had come back from shopping carrying three plastic bags that said *Goodwill Global Industries* on the side. With a grin, she said, "Do you have any cash on you? I owe Ruth twenty bucks."

Korzha stared down when Claudia put the bags at his feet. "Goodwill?"

"It's not safe to use my plastic, and we sure as hell can't use yours. And, you cannot go into the Lower looking like that." She looked him up and down, but without that little gleam of appreciation he liked catching in her eyes when she usually did that. He'd forgotten how good it felt to be in love. And it seemed he had it bad.

"Like what?" he asked.

She rolled her eyes. "Like a refugee from a Jet Li movie." She bent down and pulled a pair of faded blue jeans from the bag. "Keep the tee-shirt, it's good, but put this on. Don't button it." She pulled out a shirt with palm trees, monkeys and coconuts in orange, chartreuse and pink.

"You must be joking! Please, tell me you're joking."

"Shoes." She handed him a pair of black boots with silver buckles at the sides. "Socks."

"They're red."

"I should have gotten you pink?"

"Splendid," he said. He took the jeans from her, too. He already owned a pair of jeans, bought on a lark, worn exactly never.

"Change."

She threw a box of condoms on the bed. His eyebrows rose. "I don't get STDs, Claudia. If that's what you're worried about."

"What about swimmers?"

"Swimmers?"

Her eyebrows drew together. "Are you fertile, Tiber?"

Now that surprised him. The question about took his breath away. "Not very."

"I hope that's nothing like *not very* pregnant," she said slowly.

"It means," he said, "that I am fecund. But vampire fertility rates are low. *Very* low." The idea of an unplanned pregnancy ought to send him into a panic, but it didn't. He was vaguely pleased by the thought. "Aren't you on anything?" Hell, he didn't even know if vampires and humans could conceive. Why had he never checked that out?

She took a deep breath. "I can't afford it at my benefits level. And I don't sleep around, so it just wasn't an issue."

"Claudia—"

"Get dressed." Her mouth was tight. "There's nothing I can do about it now."

He changed. He didn't know whether to be pleased or dismayed that she turned pink when he shucked his borrowed pants. The new jeans were a tight fit. When she spoke, she said, "Too bad you don't have a bullet wound. Still, if you can show off your scars, do." Her eyes zipped up and down, from his head to his feet. Ah, Korzha thought with intense satisfaction. There it was—that little gleam in her eyes. "You look good," she said.

"Thank you."

Claudia went up on tiptoe and pulled the scrunchie from his hair. She ran her fingers through his curls. Her torso pressed against his. If she'd do that more often, he'd keep his hair long just for her. "There." She took a step back and frowned at him.

"What?"

"You're too pale. They'll know you're a vamp the minute they set eyes on you. You're going to have to feed, Tiber."

It was his turn to frown. "I'll take care of it," he said. He probably could find a supply . . .

Her face fell, only for a moment, and then she had a smile in place. Well, well, well. She was jealous. The idea took hold in him and blossomed. She thought he was going to go out and find someone else to feed on, and she didn't like it. Despite feeling like a damn fool, he grinned. If possible, her face fell further. "Donovan," he said. "I'm a vampire."

"Sex and all," she said.

"You'd have to arrest me if I went out and bit some random other woman."

"Like you care."

He put an arm around her waist and kissed the top of her head. He knew what it cost her to come so close to complaining. They needed to formalize this relationship. *He* needed to. He wanted to. But not when she was distracted by all this. "Dear-heart. Claudia," he said. "I promise, no sex with anyone but you." And he meant it. "There are places where even a vamp such as I am may discreetly fulfill his needs. Without sex and without breaking the law."

"Okay, then." Her tight mouth spoiled the effect of her nonchalant reply. "Do whatever you need to. I'm fine with it. Just fine."

He folded his arms around her and breathed in her scent. "Claudia, dear-heart. There's no one else but you. No one," he assured her.

When he returned, fed and with a healthy color, Claudia took Holly and the mink to Ruth's apartment and made sure they knew not to open the door for any reason. When kisses and admonishments were complete, she and Tiber left. She had two windows in her apartment: one opened onto an interior stairwell to the garbage cans and looked across to apartment 415, and another in the living room. They soared into the sky from there.

They touched down half a mile from the coordinates Claudia had, but before they walked into the Lower, she handed him a gun. "Put it in your waistband—of course that's stupid," she said when his eyebrows rose. "The point is to make it obvious you're packing."

"Yes, Officer," Tiber said.

"Don't call me that. In the Lower, that could get us killed. *Me* killed." Her fingers lingered on his stomach, and his body reacted in predictable fashion. As far as he was concerned, the gun was unnecessary; but then, humans did need to show off their toys, and if he was going to try to pass as a mortal thug, he might as well have one.

Claudia grabbed his hand. "Let's go."

She had her own clothes from Goodwill and looked suitably disreputable and completely delicious. Jeans with a hole in one knee. A tee-shirt a size too small, which on her was more than a little distracting. Boots. No jacket. He made a note to take her shopping. Rodeo Drive. Something slinky.

The smell here was less than inviting: human excrement, vermin, and from the mouth of every alley they passed, rotting garbage. He smelled werewolf now and

again, and motor oil everywhere. Human riffraff with
pit bulls or some equally fierce dog at their feet,
slumped in doorways clutching paper-wrapped bottles
or else lolling mindlessly under the effects of narco.
The ones coming down from a high held out twitching
hands for money or another fix.

"Sense anything?" she asked.

"A few rogues. Wolves. There's a demon here. At
least one. Possibly more."

"Bak-Faru?"

"I'm not sure."

They saw anxious faces, wary and assessing, on humans of all colors—from dark as night to pale as a
vamp on the edge. Narco dealers stood on corners
with whores who ranged from unconscionably young
to gray-haired crones. Dilapidated buildings lined the
streets, with boarded-up windows and metal-sheeted
doors. All the store fronts were barred, and the propri-
etors sat behind Plexiglas booths.

Gang tags covered every surface, wild and colorful,
inventive even. Most of the street lamps were broken,
and those that worked dimmed, buzzed and bright-
ened in the uneven cycle characteristic of an illegal
power grid connection. Not everyone looked down
and out; every now and then, Tiber caught a glimpse of
a well-dressed human. Once or twice he saw or felt a
vamp. One of them was rogue. The other was not.
Korzha stuck close to Donovan. The flare of neon
signs flickered in and out with the fluctuating power.

"This way," she whispered, nudging him. "Should be
in here."

Korzha's sense of the demon vanished. Was it gone?
Or just hiding?

"In here" was an Internet café called Jumpin' Beans,
the signage of which some tagger had amended to

Humpin' Beans, with suitable and imaginative artwork underneath. A neon sign flashed the words *Net Café* by turns virulent blue and purple. Underneath was a placard with a hemp-leaf watermark that read *Medicinal Marijuana, Rx and ID Required.*

The choice of music was decidedly retro. Alan Jackson. The room reeked of smoke from Gaulois with an undercurrent of Humboldt weed. There were posters of smiling footballers, each holding a beer and with a svelte blonde on his arm. In one corner a near-life-sized cardboard cutout of the latest NASCAR champion held a brew. His cardboard arm supported a cardboard blonde in a red dress. Someone had tagged the beer and obscured the brand name.

A pot-bellied man with a finger-thin braid dangling to mid-shoulder played pool on a table with torn felt in the center of the room. A woman in a too-short dress and track lines up her arm leaned against the man, waiting to take her shot. Other customers slouched over drinks or smokes or both. At the last stool, a skinny man with stringy blond hair stared into an LCD panel and nursed a glass of whatever beer was on tap. He smelled like a werewolf. An espresso machine took up the left half of the bar. Dusty magazines and newspapers covered the top of it, and a barista lounged nearby, ready to make coffee for any customer ready to pay. As if they really served coffee here.

At his side, Claudia tensed. Tiber could feel her fear. The barista looked them up and down, his attention lingering on Korzha before he looked at Claudia. "Well, well, well," the man said. "Long time no see, babe."

"How ya doin', Rabin?" Claudia said.

"I'm doin'."

Cameras in each corner of the room caught every

movement. Korzha heard the whir of one of the lenses repositioning. Rabin went back to staring at Tiber and scratched his sandy goatee. "I can guess what she's doing here, but what about you? You slumming?" he asked.

Claudia gave Rabin the finger. Her walk had changed into a kind of slouching roll of her hips. Her salute didn't seem to offend anyone. Chances had never been good they'd find Masters or her body, and since this place seemed an unlikely spot for a corpse or a vampire, Tiber assumed they come to find Claudia's comm unit. It'd be interesting to know how it ended up here. From somewhere in the back of the building, he heard a high-pitched chirruping and the soft hum of motors. Odd.

"What can I do ya for?" Rabin asked.

She glanced at the espresso machine. "Quad nonfat macchiato?"

Rabin smiled. "Fuck off, bitch."

"You first."

"T'sing Tao's on tap. If you got a doc's scrip, the weed's behind the counter."

Claudia stuck her hands deep in her pockets and rocked back on her heels. "So, is Fly-Low here?" she asked. Her voice sounded different, Tiber noticed— the same slurred cadence as Rabin. She fit right in. He didn't like the change.

Rabin looked her up and down, paused at her chest in her too-tight shirt; then, after a quick look at Korzha, he jerked a thumb toward a door at the back. "You know the drill. Weapons go in there." He pointed to a battered cardboard box at the end of the bar. Some wag had labeled the box *hardware, software & deadware*. "The metal detector will make noise if you don't unpack it all, and then this guy"—he jerked a thumb in the direction of the blond—"will have to hurt you."

"Really?" Claudia said. "He don't look like much to me."

The blonde's eyes sidled away from the LCD. "If I have to hurt you, you won't like it," he warned.

"Knock once," said Rabin.

When they'd put their guns in the box, and after Claudia, with a show of hands and fingers, pulled two knives from her sleeve and another from her boot, Tiber watched her take a deep breath. He felt the anxiety rolling off her. He leaned into her. "Who the hell is Fly-Low?" he asked.

"After you vamps, he's probably the most powerful person in Crimson City," she said. She knocked once and put her hand on the doorknob. "I knew him a long time ago."

The chirruping stopped the moment she knocked. The hum of the electric motor continued. Damp air hit Tiber in the face when she opened the door. He smelled dirt. Terrariums from fifty- to a hundred-gallon size lined the entire back wall. The air was so wet it felt like rain. Diffuse light shone on the tanks. Tiber closed the door and cut off Jackson singing "If French Fries Were Fat Free." In one corner, a vidscreen showed the bar. The werewolf stared into the camera.

A man turned from his contemplation of one of the tanks. He wore khakis and a dark green tee-shirt with #006633 printed in light gray lettering across the chest. A homemade tattoo around his upper arm looked like a band of connected knives. He had short brown hair, and dark blue eyes all wrong for his olive complexion. Acne had scarred his cheeks, but hadn't diminished his physical appeal in the least. He studied

Claudia, his attention fixed on the metallic thread in her hair. He spared a glance for Korzha, but went back to staring at Claudia.

He looked thirty-five, maybe the young side of forty. The chirruping started again, two distinct calls, one a ululating chirp, the other a more fluid, rolling two-toned tattoo. He tightened the mesh-ventilated lid on a container he held in one hand. He found space for it on a table crowded with soil, bags of pebbles, plant cuttings, brass tongs and stoppered vials. A brazier at one end exuded heat. The setup looked like a large and expensive way to smoke crack and OD fast, but the smell was wrong and the smoldering mass on the platform above the embers looked vaguely animal-like.

"*Bonita.*" His voice lilted with the vocalized vowels of the Southern hemisphere. An attractive accent. He smiled. "I always wondered what happened to you."

"Fly-Low," she said. "Good to see you. Is G around?"

"Yeah," he said. "G's around." His mouth twitched. "You going to introduce me to your new boyfriend?"

"Tiber, Fly-Low. Fly-Low, Tiber."

Another smirk appeared on Fly-Low's mouth. "Peace, Tiberiu Korzha."

"Fly-Low," he said softly. But he didn't say it in anything like a friendly manner. The man's eyebrows lifted.

Claudia nodded at the terrariums. "You got them to breed."

Fly-Low glanced at the tanks behind him and then back at Tiber. His pupils were huge. "I started out with *Phyllobates Terribilis*—those are the yellow ones," he said to Korzha. "Now I have *Dendrobates*, *Epipedobates* and *Minyobates*, too. Blue, green, red—you name it, I got them. I got them all now."

"Congratulations, Fly-Low," Claudia said.

He touched the container on the table. Korzha heard something moving inside. Fly-Low picked up a pair of thick, rubberized gloves. "I still feed them drosophila . . ." His eyes flicked to Claudia, shifted to Korzha. "She used to help me feed my goldens. I've been able to expand their diet, and that's made all the difference." He gestured behind him. "Along with the better tanks. Helps when you can afford the finest, isn't that right, Tiberiu?" He turned to one of the plant-filled terrariums. At one end of the tank, a branch emerged from a shallow pool, a bridge from water to shoal. At the other end, bromelids and dense foliage rose toward the top of the tank. From there, mist showered down. Korzha caught a glimpse of a tiny golden-yellow frog clinging to a damp leaf.

"Hey, that's great," Claudia said.

"They're shy," Fly-Low said. "But if I'm quiet, they let me see them. I like to listen to them sing. When they're breeding, sometimes I sit for hours and listen to them sing." He looked over his shoulder. "The common name is Poison Dart Frog, but it's the ants that make them poisonous. Gotta have the ants or it's no good. They like termites, too, but it's the ants they need. I airfreight them in from South America every Wednesday. They love the ants. Eat 'em like candy."

"So, Fly-Low," said Claudia. "You know anything about Laura Masters?"

Fly-Low turned. He smirked. "Where you been, baby?" He looked at Tiber and touched the side of his neck. "Masters got converted. Everybody knows."

"You sure about that?" she asked.

"Oh, *bonita.*" Fly-Low exaggerated his accent and looked her up and down. "You turned out fine. No wonder G was on you like he was." To Korzha he said in a manner calculated to offend, "She was skinny when I knew her. But real, real sweet. I guess that's why G liked her so much."

"I heard Masters is dead," Claudia said.

"Don't know how that could be." Fly-Low's smile broadened. "Though, come to think of it, I got a necro-wolf takes care of whatever I ask as long as every now and then I get him what he likes best. Gotta keep the help happy." He laughed. "Not to worry, fang. Claudia's not my dog's type. He likes to eat blondes been dead a while." He slipped on gloves and used a thin metal rod to stir the smoldering mass over the brazier. A tiny webbed leg popped up. "Necro-werewolf, he like everything, down to the marrow. When he's done, the only thing left is gonna be a few cracked bones."

"So is Masters dead or what, Fly-Low?"

"What do you think?"

Claudia shifted her weight from foot to foot. "How'd you get the body?"

"I fucking own this city. There ain't nothing happens here without me hearing about it. And that includes your business, fang. I own fifteen percent of TK Enterprises, Inc." He stared at Korzha. "She has a talent for comm mods. Back in the day, she used to make me a lot of money."

"I've seen her work," Korzha replied.

"She coulda made me a whole lot more. She making you money like that?" When Korzha didn't answer, Fly-Low shrugged. "If you two have hooked up, maybe I ought to increase my holdings. Too bad things didn't work out of us. Did they, baby?"

"Laura Masters," Claudia said again.

Fly-Low walked to a side door and knocked once with the back of his hand. "Hey, got a minute in there? I need you to meet somebody." He returned to the brazier and stirred the material again. "It's tradition for me, you know? She knows that." He tilted his head in Claudia's direction. "Don't you, *bonita*?"

"Yeah, Fly-Low, I know that," she agreed.

Fly-Low put his hands down and let his gloves slip off. From a drawer on his side of the table, he took out a wooden case. "Take a look at this, fang." He opened the case and lifted a wooden tube to the light. "The native people of Colombia made poison arrows and darts. I'm a big believer in tradition." From the case, he produced a feathered dart the size of his pinky. He smeared some of the material from his brass rod on the sharpened wooden tip. "It's the old ways for me." He smiled. "Do you believe in tradition, vampire?"

"Depends on the tradition."

Fly-Low held the tiny dart in a beam of light. "Interesting fact. There's enough poison on just the tip of this to kill ten people. Phyllos are the most toxic creature known to man, dog or fang. Take a vamp down long enough to kill him, if you chop his head off." He rotated the dart. "What do you think, fang? Could this kill a demon?"

Then, the side door opened and Laura Masters walked in.

Chapter Thirty-four

Ice slid down Claudia's back. A layer of makeup covered Masters's exposed skin, but up close, it didn't hide the fact that she wasn't a vampire or even a dog. She was just dead. She walked slowly, but then she had to; the room was getting crowded. She stopped behind Fly-Low, arms crossed over her chest. "Tiberiu Korzha." Her voice sounded hoarse.

"Soon as the Primary Assembly takes you down for converting her," Fly-Low said, "I'll give her to the necro. Just the way he likes them. And when she disappears again, I think the Primary Assembly's gonna crack wide open." Slowly, he turned and stared at Claudia. "G knows about the kid."

Claudia had known Fly-Low forever. For as long as she could remember. There'd been a time when she'd thought of him as the only family she had, but she thought better of that as he slid his dart into the wooden tube. "He didn't care, Fly-Low. You know that."

"Oh, *bonita*," he said in his old voice. "You think

that, you don't know anything about him. You don't have any idea what he can do."

"I bet I do," she said.

"Watch this." He put the tube to his mouth, then took it away when Claudia and Korzha both flinched. "What?" He grinned. "You thought I was gonna shoot one of you? No way, man. I don't want to kill anyone by accident. I'm going to shoot it at the wall there." He pointed to a spot covered by dozens of blackened holes. "Target practice. Gotta practice the old ways, right?" Just before he put the tube to his mouth, staring at the wall he asked, "She even know who her daddy is?"

"No," Claudia said.

"That's just not right. You should have told her." He puffed out his cheeks and blew. The dart penetrated the wall with a *thik*. The feather quivered. Fly-low nodded and reloaded his blowgun. "Is she a good kid? Good in school?"

"Yeah, to both."

"That's good to hear." He put down the blowgun. "That'll make G happy."

Over Masters's head, a smoky yellow mist thickened. Claudia smelled burnt air and felt the pressure billowing out. At her side, Korzha turned toward Masters. The air shimmered. With a fatalistic resignation, she watched the yellow mist take shape. Masters's body collapsed to the floor and in her place stood a tall male form. For a moment he was naked, and then he uttered a low word and he wore a pair of jeans and not a damn thing else. Two thin braids held back his long brown hair. Metallic green thread glittered in one of the braids. His eyes were pale, smoky yellow.

"Hello, Garath," Claudia said. Even in his demon form, she recognized him. She'd been barely fifteen, and he'd convinced her she loved him.

"Claudia Donovan." The demon Garath clasped one hand over his fist and bowed.

"Did I tell you to leave the body?" Fly-Low said.

Claudia felt sickened by the realization that Fly-Low must have managed to do the very thing that had earned humans Lath's undying hatred: bind Garath to his will. Tiber took a step closer to her, and that made her feel safer. His fingers touched her back in a gentle reminder of his presence. "Let him go, Fly-Low," she said.

"I got a demon doing whatever I say." Fly-Low laughed. "I've been patient, Claudia. More patient than you can imagine. Never going too far, never drawing too much attention to my organization. I'm so close now I can taste it, so, no, I'm not going to let him go. With a little more help from him, before much longer I'm gonna be running this city. Me and the demons."

Claudia turned to Garath. "What did he promise you?"

Fly-Low laughed again and then answered for the Bak-Faru. "We made a solid deal if I do say so myself." His eyes darkened. "G here killed the people who were with me when we summoned them. Man, I've never seen anything like what he did to then. He was fucking free in Crimson City, but he couldn't get home on account of the portal is sealed. But we came to an understanding, didn't we, G? I gave him the other demon we summoned."

"He died well," Garath growled.

"Thing is, Claudia," Fly-Low said, "he needed a half-demon to get through the portal so he can go home. So I gave him you, too." Fly-Low smiled. "Your girl's what, ten? We figure in about five years or so, when I'm running Crimson City, she can take her daddy home."

Korzha had an arm around Claudia's waist, but now, he turned to Garath. "What was his exact promise?"

"That I would do his bidding until I am able to go home," Garath said.

"You can go home right now," Claudia said.

The demon cocked his head. "I hear you."

"It's true. The portal's open," she added. "I met Siath in Orcus, Garath. She wants you to come home."

Garath's puzzled expression transformed into a smile, and then the air started to heat. Fly-Low shouted. Behind her and Tiber, the door slammed open and the stringy-haired blond barreled in. The air around the demon Garath jumped and danced, rattling the glass in the terrariums. The frogs fell silent. Fly-Low darted forward and snatched the blowgun off the table. He lifted it to his mouth. His cheeks puffed out and the dart flew toward Garath.

At the same time, Garath said a word and Claudia's skin crawled. She smelled smoke. Wind rippled out to catch the dart, whirling it through the air, a wild, out-of-control high-speed spin. By the time Claudia realized the dart was going to hit her, it was far too late—Korzha was in front of her. She heard the dart hit him. He pushed her down, so her view of what happened next was skewed.

Fly-Low laughed. "Kill them," he said to the wolf. "All of them."

The blonde's human shoulders heaved, and Claudia heard the distinctive crackle of bone and sinew reshaping. She heard a canine growl, a hair-raising vibration.

Korzha wavered on his feet.

Light flashed in the room. She heard Fly-Low scream, but the sound strangled before it reached a crescendo. Garath had a hand around Fly-Low's throat and a chilling smile on his face. The blonde leapt before his transformation was complete.

Claudia front-kicked, felt the blonde's wrist break and followed through with a spinning hook kick that caught her foe in the back and took him to his knees. His moan ended with a lupine snarl. She figured she had about two seconds to get the hell out before she found out whether the necro-wolf was any good at eating live prey. She pulled Tiber out the door, on her way out ducking down to grab weapons from the box. She aimed one at Rabin and shoved the other down the front of Tiber's pants before they hauled ass for the street.

She didn't know if the poison would kill him, but whatever the effect, Tiber wasn't in good shape; and here in the Lower, that meant he was in trouble. He wasn't steady on his legs. Another roar came from the bar, and in chorus with that, a howl as they escaped to the street. They made it around a corner just as Tiber's knees gave way. She caught him as he fell to the ground, but his weight pulled her down until she ended up on the pavement with his torso across her lap. His pupils contracted to pinpricks of black. It was like looking into solid green.

She heard the wolf howling, the sound of people screaming, and someone fired a gun. Silence. Overhead, the streetlights surged and dimmed. She tightened her arms around Tiber. The wolf bounded around the corner and slid to a four-footed stop. The beast's breath stirred the small hairs on Claudia's face, and its growl felt like a semi idling in her head.

The necro was bigger than she'd expected, at least four feet high at the shoulder. The wolf bared its teeth and took a step forward, hackles raised. With a rumbling snarl, it jumped, and there wasn't much she could do. She threw herself away from Tiber and hit the ground hard. Her gun went spinning down the sidewalk. The wolf twisted in midair and landed on Tiber. He straight-armed the dog. The necro's mouth opened. . . .

With the toe of her boot, Claudia kicked up hard, while at the same time she levered forward and crashed both elbows down onto the wolf's muzzle. It shook its massive head, momentarily stunned. Claudia grabbed the gun sticking out the waistband of Tiber's pants. She flicked off the safety and pressed the barrel behind the necro-wolf's ear. "It's loaded with silver," she lied. "I'm a cop, dog. They aren't gonna arrest me for putting some silver in your brain. Now back off."

"I can handle him," Tiber said.

"Like hell." His body was still fighting off the poison.

The dog quivered. Claudia tightened her finger on the trigger while the air around them heated and condensed in a single spot. All of a sudden the werewolf shuddered, shrieked, and somersaulted away as if tossed by an invisible hand. It slid several feet, re-transforming as it went. By the time it came to a halt, it was a sandy-haired man again. He stood, shook himself like he thought he was still a dog, then took one look at Claudia and her gun, and ran like hell.

She looked to her left.

Aslet stood with his arms crossed on his bare chest. He wore B-Ops black: black cargo pants, black boots and a black shirt. A pair of shades hung from the neck of his shirt. The semi-automatic weapon slung across his chest had more than a few dings, like he'd been using it in an Op or two since he came to Crimson City. The demon clasped one hand over his fist and bowed. His boiling blue eyes flicked to Korzha.

"He isn't dead," she snapped.

"I wish the poison had killed him. Then we would be released from our promise."

"Yeah. Well, I guess that's too bad for you." Claudia bent over Tiber and took his hand, twining her fingers with his.

She felt the air change when Aslet left, but she didn't look. Shit. She was going to have to warn somebody in B-Ops that they'd been royally compromised.

Tiber twitched. She touched his mouth. "Do you need to feed?"

He got to his feet like someone who'd had six beers too many. When he stood, he didn't ask, and she didn't object. His lower body pressed hard against her, pinning her to the wall hard enough that she needed an extra breath.

The air got thick, and for once it had nothing to do with Lath or any of the freaky shit that had kept happening to them in Orcus. From the light that flared in Korzha's eyes, he felt it, too. His mouth brushed hers once, then dropped to her throat. She felt the pain of his fangs sliding into her neck, her reflexive recoil. He fed quickly, holding her tight, mouth working at her neck. She collapsed against him. Fast. She felt weak so fast, her brain was spinning.

With a low hum, Korzha grabbed her around the waist and took to the air. He moved so fast her head spun, and her stomach just about flipped inside-out. Air whistled past her ears. About the time she decided she was going to puke, he came down on the roof of her building. But there Tiber's knees buckled. She threw an arm around him and stumbled for the stairwell.

One-handed, she tried to open the service door from the roof, but it was locked. "Fuck!" she said under her breath. Tiber's arms slid free of her, and he staggered a little. He snarled, and like that, the door was open.

She got him down the stairs to her apartment. Holly would have to stay with Ruth a little longer. Claudia kicked her door shut and put her hands on Tiber's cheeks. His pupils were still pinpricks. "Do I need to call a doctor or something? You going to be all right?" she asked.

"Soon," he promised. He got them to her bedroom. Her bed. He threw aside the duvet, exposing the sheets. He sat on the bed and pulled her down to him. With his free hand, he delved beneath her shirt until his hand covered her breast, swept over the sensitive nipple. Her belly quivered, and when she felt his fingers scrabbling at the fastening to her jeans, she rose toward him to help. Tiber bent to her, angling himself into her.

She was soon free of her pants, and then Korzha slid into her. *Sweet. You taste and feel so sweet,* she heard. Whether the words were spoken or thought, she had no idea. Her world blossomed all over again. Tiber moved inside her, filling her, stretching her. She tilted her hips toward him, helping him slide deeper. Behind her closed eyes, she saw him and felt him take on her passion, a world of dark and velvet love.

Both his hands came between them, sliding the rest of her clothes up and off. His palms covered her breasts while he moved in her. Claudia rocked her hips along with his. Pleasure roared through her. The connection bowled her over. His mind slipped around hers, and she let it. She wanted him so badly, she felt tears in the back of her eyes, hot and burning. A low sound came from Korzha—a growl, a moan. Their bodies slid along each other. Then his mouth went to her throat again, but, this time his teeth found her jugular. She wondered if she would survive this.

Pressure, harder than normal on her neck, and then, Jesus. *Jesus.* Razor-sharp teeth found the pulse of her, and she thought she'd come apart. Tiber's pelvis rocked into her and his orgasm blended into hers, melted her; and then he reached for something else. Something more.

She could feel his teeth still in her, felt his lower teeth pressing up, him taking in her blood. She felt his body react to hers, the exultation of his passion, the tang of the blood he craved. Her heart pounded, thudded, slowed, struggled to beat, and then didn't. It paused, for a moment was like his. He was old, centuries old. So long ago he'd been a young man, born into what he now was, through violence. Like music too beautiful to bear hearing, he touched her; and she listened.

She knew Tiber didn't want to stop. He wanted all of her—everything there was to have. She wasn't ready. Not yet. But she wanted to be with him forever. She'd die if he stopped and she'd die if he didn't. But he did stop. Even when he'd withdrawn his teeth, when he'd stopped taking her blood, their hearts continued to beat in concert. He stayed deep in her head and deep in her body. Claudia curled herself around him while he licked her throat. He threw back his head, fangs bared, moss-colored eyes lit with passion. His civilized semblance had vanished. Even flush with blood—warm with it, pink and healthy with it—he looked about as human as a wolf. A drop of crimson fell to her chest. He bent his head and licked it away.

Wherever he was in Crimson City, and inside her, Lath rose howling.

"Claudia," Tiber said. "You are mine."

Chapter Thirty-five

"Good evening." Tiber bent his head and kissed Claudia's ear. She smelled of roses—real roses this time. Her daughter was asleep in another room, and, at last he had her to himself. They had a great deal to talk about. Holly's status as half-demon was long settled and of no importance to him. He didn't give a damn what Fly-low and Garath had done ten years ago. Not unless it affected her today.

Claudia wore an overlong tee-shirt and a pair of gray socks. He still hadn't taken her shopping—there hadn't been time for that yet. He'd bought a few things online, the essentials, which he considered to be anything silk, slinky and not very big. He hoped she was at least wearing the underwear. She looked up from her book and raised her chin for another kiss. He was more than happy to oblige.

"How'd it go with the Primary Assembly?" she asked. Her hand curled around his neck, holding him close for another kiss. "Did they call off the Vendix?"

"Yes."

"What about Laura Masters? Did you explain? They gonna defang you for her?"

"Yes, I explained. No, they will not defang me."

"That's good news." She snaked an arm around his waist and under his shirt. Her palm felt warm against his skin. Was he angry? He didn't think so. He knew why she'd been hiding what she was hiding from him.

"We discussed the demon situation," he said.

"And?"

"We continue to . . . negotiate."

"Do they know about you and the Elismal?"

"I have explained that, too." He laughed softly. "There was more concern over B-Ops's denial that demons have infiltrated them." In fact, so far Internal Operations categorically denied the possibility that a demon could successfully impersonate a human. "Fleur is in possession of strong evidence that B-Ops is gearing up for some major action, so who knows what humans intend."

"The P.D. went on high alert yesterday," Claudia said.

Tiber sat down. He leaned an elbow on the table and faced his fear. "You know, don't you, Claudia, that I love you?"

She bit her lower lip. "Do you?"

"Yes." He set a plastic wand on the table before her. "I found this in the bathroom wastebasket."

Her body went still. After a bit, she shrugged.

"At first, I took it for a thermometer. One of the many disruptions of cohabiting with a youngster, yes? Fevers. Agues and the like. Vid games in the web-caster. Radios turned to stations that play atrocious music."

"Sorry."

"This, however, is not a thermometer." A pink plus-sign glowed in the receptacle at the wide end of the stick. "There were, in fact, two more of the devices in the wastebasket. All in a similar condition."

"A new kind of HemoStrip," she said. "I was testing them on myself. You know, to check for paranormals."

"Really?" He leaned toward her, feeling immensely sorry that he hadn't yet made her understand his feelings. "Have you one to test on me?"

"No."

"Are they accurate?"

She hung her head. "Yeah," she said. She touched the wand and gave it a spin. "Yeah, they're pretty freaking accurate."

"Have you been to a doctor yet?"

The corners of her mouth twitched down. "Not yet."

"Allow me to re-state. Has a doctor confirmed your pregnancy?"

Claudia shook her head and then admitted everything, looking at him from beneath her lashes. "I've been pregnant before, Korzha. I recognize the signs." She sighed. "I'm not asking you to do anything about it, okay?"

He spun the wand himself. "I ought to be insulted by that. In fact, Claudia, I am insulted."

"I don't even know if it's yours." Her eyes filled with tears. Sorrow was such human emotion. It tore him apart to see her crying. How many years since he'd been this close to a human? Centuries. Yet he didn't want to live without her. "I don't want to do this alone again. I did that once, and it was really, really hard. I mean, the first time I had no idea what I was getting into, but now I do, and I just don't think I can do it again. Not by myself."

He took her hand, but her fingers stayed inert in his

grip. "Claudia." She was crying so hard, he wasn't sure she heard. "It doesn't matter," he said.

"You don't get it, do you? Things were different when you had children of your own. The world was different."

"Women get pregnant the same way. Then as now. Nothing's changed."

"That wasn't what I mean."

"You're pregnant, is that what you mean?" He smiled. "I think I get that."

"If it isn't yours, Korzha—which probably maybe it isn't—then it has to be Lath's."

"I understand that as well."

"A *demon*."

"Yes."

"Which makes the baby a demon, too."

"Technically, a half-demon."

She threw up her hands. "Half-demon, half-human. Half-vampire. Who cares, Korzha?" Her voice trembled. "I'm supposed to be dead by now. Lath wanted me to die and then didn't let me, and now—oh, hell, Tiber." She snatched up the EPT. "I didn't even know it was possible for this to happen. I wasn't supposed to live and I wasn't supposed to get knocked up."

"I am not Fly-Low. Or Garath," Tiber said.

Her eyes were liquid. "What's that supposed to mean?"

"That means you aren't on your own." He grabbed her shoulders. "I'm not giving you any ultimatums, performing rituals or asking you to do anything except stay with me. I mean, come live with me and be my love in Strata plus-one, Claudia. It means I don't care who the father is." He frowned because she looked at him like he'd just complimented her on her charming second head. "I hope it's mine, but if it isn't, *I don't care.* We'll keep trying, yes? Our circumstances are extraordinary, Claudia; surely you appreciate that?"

"Oh, I appreciate it all right." She sounded bitter.

He left his hands on her shoulders. "The times ahead are uncertain at best. Demons are here. War may be upon us, whether our species stand together or fracture irreparably. There's very little certain now, but there's one thing I know without question."

"Yeah?"

"*I* don't change, Claudia." He pushed her back and put his hands on either side of her face. "I'm this way forever. What's to become of me if I have to watch you grow old and die? I don't want to live without you. I want the woman I love at my side forever."

"You said I'd turn rogue," she said.

"That was before there was us." He frowned. "When your desire to convert was not your own. It is more dangerous that way." He touched the EPT wand and then her cheek again. "I love you, Claudia. I want you with me, but not if you don't want it as much as I do. We can wait until after the baby comes, then I'll make you if you'll let me."

"Won't that get you into trouble with the Primary Assembly?"

Tiber smiled. "Your capacity for going straight to the legalities is part of what I love about you." He stopped smiling. "I asked for and received official sanction."

She looked at him for a long time.

"You don't have to decide now. I'm willing to wait. Nine months. Longer, if need be."

"Do you have any idea what it's like to live with a pregnant woman? I'm going to get fat and bitchy. You won't want me anymore," she said.

He took her hand in his. "I made love to my wife when she was pregnant. Those were some of our closest moments, Claudia. I would treasure the same experience with you."

Her eyes opened wide. She let go of his hand, but stayed in his embrace. He held her until he felt her breathing settle. "I was afraid you'd never want anything to do with me again."

"I'm afraid I'll lose you to that demon."

"No," she said.

Tiber shook his head and sighed. "He isn't going to go away. Not Garath, and not Lath. Neither of them."

"True."

He brought her hand to his chest.

"Maybe they won't win, Korzha. Maybe we'll get the portal sealed again," she said. She leaned the side of her face against him. "There's going to be some sort of military offensive, Tiber. I can feel it. Maybe he'll be killed."

"It's no good thinking that." He kissed the top of her head once more. "The portal's open, Claudia. Wide open. Lath and his demons are here in Crimson City. We need to live with right now, not what might be."

"For as long as we survive."

"At least agree to live with me. Anywhere you want. Here or in Strata plus-one."

"Humans and half-demons living in the Upper?"

"Why not?"

"Are you freaking insane?"

He pulled her back into his embrace. "All right, then. I'll buy this building and we'll renovate. Evict everyone and just take over the whole damn building."

"You can't evict Ruth."

"She can keep a small flat. If you wish. But she must pay rent."

Claudia stared at the EPT. "You *are* a good cook," she mused, half seriously.

"And I do laundry," he added.

"Yeah, but have you ever changed a diaper?"

"I can learn."

Claudia leaned back and smiled. "You? I can't wait to see that, Tiber."

Chapter Thirty-six

Claudia was reading the news on the webcaster when someone knocked on the door. There wasn't much good news to be had. There was still no official confirmation from any species that demons were in Crimson City, despite dozens of blogs from humans, fangs, dogs or other sources. None of the information she'd given to Internal-Operations had leaked to the press, and whether B-Ops was cleaning house was anybody's guess. The Net was rife with rumor. Demon-sightings, clandestine negotiations, and summonings gone awry. One site posted photos that, unless you knew what a Bak-Faru looked like, didn't prove anything except some guy had long hair and a great body. More than a few postings contained descriptions of what sounded a hell of a lot like full-out skirmishes. B-Ops wasn't winning, but they weren't telling the cops what was going on, either.

Someone knocked again.

Claudia unfurled herself from her chair. She didn't have to be back on shift for another four hours. This time of night, there weren't many visitors in the neighborhood, so she expected it to be Ruth. Tiber was out, attending an emergency meeting of the Primary Assembly—though he ought to be back any minute. Holly had school the next day, so she'd been in bed since eight. She and Ruth could have a nice visit. Barefoot, she padded to the intercom. She swallowed to clear her ears. Her head felt stuffed full. Freaking allergies. She stared at the door, and her heart fell to her toes. It wasn't Ruth. She opened the stairwell door.

He wore black; black pants, a black shirt. A light black jacket. He took off his sunglasses. His lilac eyes were as beautiful as ever. "Claudia-*tes*."

"Lath."

His eyes settled on her with a gentleness that curled in her belly. Like the athlete he was, his movements to reach her were all power and grace. His arms slid around her waist. A low rumble came from his chest, a purring growl of satisfaction. "My business is done for the moment. He moved closer. "Now we will mate, Claudia Donovan."

"There's no point," she said. B-Ops black made his eyes shimmer. How could anyone look at him and think him human?

His arms tightened around her. One palm splayed over her back. "You are my vishtau mate," he said through a growl. "And I cannot be without you. My heart has been cold without you, Claudia Donovan."

"I'm pregnant."

His dimples flashed. He put his hands on either side of her face, cradling her head in his hands. "You must not worry. I accept this. The Bak-Faru accept this."

The connection between them tugged inexorably. She could feel the compulsion to step fully into his embrace, but in her heart, she only wanted Tiber. Her green-eyed vampire—Tiberiu Korzha. "This is my home," she told the demon. "You're not welcome here. You shouldn't be here."

Lath's mouth thinned. "Your promise to me should not be undone, *tes*. We are bound." He growled again, and his hands, though they remained gentle, tightened. "I belong to you."

"I'm not telling you no. I'm telling you not here." Behind her she heard the stairwell-landing window slide open. The demon's attention slid up and away. He didn't bother to disguise his reaction, nor the hatred nor the glitter of bloodlust in his eyes. She saw the anticipation of engagement with the enemy, and she knew why Lath had really come. Even before she felt him gather his power, she knew he hadn't come for her. He'd come to stake his territory. He'd come to kill Tiber.

She pushed him in the chest, hard, with the heels of her palms. Pain billowed through her wrists and zinged up her arms. The demon took a step back and cast his spell. Power rippled outward, pulsing through the air, crackling in her hair. A violet streak flashed up, searing the ceiling as he staggered. A table along the wall quivered and vanished. The vase sitting on it shattered with an ear-splitting fracture. The landing window gaped open. Where was Tiber?

Claudia stumbled toward the landing, but Lath's arm whipped around her, pulling her against his chest. She elbowed backward, hand clasped over her fist to put her weight into the jab. The hard tip of her bone connected with the demon's solar plexus. He let out a soft *ouf* and let go. She let the velocity of her elbow-strike carry her into a turn. All around her the air shimmered violet. She put her weight into a reverse jab. With the stench of burnt air choking her, she flipped her arm up, bringing the opposite side of her forearm up to slam into Lath's jaw, except he was too tall for the maneuver and she barely grazed him. Momentum carried her past him.

Hearing movement in the hall, Claudia ducked the threat in the doorway and turned to the sound. Holy cripes. From bad to worse. There were two demons now. Aslet. She wished she could be sure which side he was on. A hairline ring of blue surrounded the fire in his eyes. He'd cut his hair to a pale blond buzz. He had a weapon slung across his back. Like Lath, he wore black, and if she hadn't known him for what he was, she'd have believed he was B-Ops come to save the day.

More movement, this time from her left. Her breath whooshed out, and there he was. Thank God, Tiber was alive. Lath hadn't killed him. Korzha's eyes glittered a furious green. His hair settled around his shoulders as he flexed into a crouch from his drop to the floor. The vampire's rage echoed off the walls. Blood splattered to the floor from a wickedly deep gash on his rib cage.

"Get out, Tiber!" she cried. Tension made her almost weep. An injury like that wasn't going to kill him, not permanently, but bad things could happen to an incapacitated vamp. And demons were fast. Blindingly so. "For God's sake, get out of here!" She raised her voice because with the ringing in her ears she could hardly hear herself. "I'll go with you, you promised me. You promised you wouldn't kill him. Just let him be."

"Dear-heart," Korzha whispered. He spoke in her head. Damn voodoo head stuff. "That is not necessary."

"I don't want anything to happen to you. I can't live without you, Tiber," she said.

Tiber bared his elongated fangs. The sound that came from his throat made the skin on the back of her neck prickle up. Another flash of light shot through him, spinning him around. She saw him fall, heard the sound of his body hitting the ground. Behind her she heard the *shick-tak* of a semiautomatic weapon loading. She swept around, facing the two demons. Aslet stood with feet shoulder-width apart, weapon in hand like he was born to it. Lath laughed out loud and pulled a modified Browning from his waistband. Her heart thudded, shaking her to her toes. The Browning was UV-enabled, and Lath's stance told her that in the short time he'd been in Crimson City he'd learned to use human technology.

"*En*-Lath," Aslet said with a bow in the Bak-Faru's direction. "I cannot allow you to kill the vampire. I have given my promise. The Elismal are promised to him."

Lath clicked off the safety, primed the UV chamber and aimed his gun at Tiber. His eyes flared orange-red. She watched his index finger squeeze, and knew she couldn't possibly move fast enough. "Interfere, Elismal demon," Lath said, "and I will kill you, too. The human woman is mine. The Bak-Faru do not share their vishtau mates."

"Then you must try to kill me," Aslet said.

Lath did something with his hand, and a flash of violet light filled the room, heading away from Korzha. It was a strike at Aslet. Claudia dashed for Tiber, forcing her body through thick, hot air. The concussion blew Aslet off his feet. She saw the demon's body rise and slam against the stairwell.

At Tiber's side, Claudia dropped to her knees. She faced the Bak-Faru. "You'll have to kill me first, Lath," she said.

Aslet hit the ground and rolled to his feet, muttering

words, syllables she didn't understand. Lath glanced at the Elismal demon and laughed. He pointed the Browning at Aslet and shot him. White light seared Claudia's eyes. Aslet howled. When she could see again, Aslet lay upon the banister. He wasn't moving.

Shick-tak. Lath chambered another UV shot.

"No, Lath, you can't. You can't kill him."

"If I don't, you will leave him?"

"Yes."

Lath took a step toward her, his gun pointed down. He was an arm's-length away. "You are lying, *tes*," he said. His eyes were sad. "You are my vishtau mate, but you want the vampire before me." He took aim again. "This cannot be."

"Kill the vampire and she's dead." Aslet again stood in the doorway. The right upper half of his shirt was gone, burned away by UV. His flash-exposed arm hung useless at his side. In his left hand, he clutched his B-Ops issue semiautomatic and pointed it at Claudia's chest. He couldn't miss.

She'd die for Tiber. No doubt about it. If she had to, she would. Just like Tiber would die for her. But she didn't think she needed to. God help them all if she was wrong. Lath moved so fast she didn't see anything but a blur of black. She met Aslet's searing blue eyes and stood her ground even when she saw him press the trigger. Everything happened fast. Tiber shouted. The air pulsed hot and electric.

Lath collided with her and shoved her away. Hard. She slid halfway down the hall, away from the spray of bullets. The UV-loaded Browning popped from Lath's hand. His body spun around once. Blood and bullets spattered the wall behind him. But the Bak-Faru stayed on his feet, chanting again. Claudia's heart froze in her chest. Lath had been in Crimson City long enough to learn about UV, and more than long enough to learn how to kill a vampire without it.

She scrambled for the gun, got her palm burned by the UV mod unit, and flipped it around. Lath knelt at Tiber's side, gripping a black-handled knife, and he was putting magic behind it. The mod unit drew the Browning's balance off, but she leveled it at Lath and prayed like hell the kickback wouldn't make her miss. He turned his head and looked at her. She could see the sadness in his eyes, and it just about broke her heart.

"Don't make me kill you, Lath."

His lilac eyes stayed on her face, sad, a cavern of sorrow. Slowly, he shook his head. "You are mine. I love you before all others. With everything that I am. And you will always love the vampire before me."

"Yes."

"Lath is not my name."

"Your name is Ur-Kashev-Ghan." The moment she said his name, she felt their connection even more strongly. The demon nodded. "Ur-Kashev-Ghan," she said, "if you kill Tiber, my heart would break. I could never love you. Never."

"I would die for you."

"Please, Lath, don't do this."

"Claudia Donovan, without your heart, I am already dead." His knife started a downstroke.

She pulled the trigger.

The flash almost blinded her, and the kickback knocked her on her butt. When she opened her eyes, she didn't see Lath, and for half a heartbeat she thought she'd missed. But she hadn't. The Bak-Faru lay unmoving on the floor, a smoking hole in his chest the size of a volleyball.

With shaking hands she unloaded the bullets. All of

them. And then she unfastened the UV mod and threw it across the room. When she looked up, Aslet was watching her from the doorway. Half his face was reddened from the blast he'd taken. Blood dripped down his arm from a slash there. From over his shoulder, she saw a hole in the wall from Lath's second shot. This was going to cost a fortune to repair.

"You need the paramedics," she told the demon.

Aslet nodded toward Tiber. "The vampire?"

"Sorry, man. You're still on the hook. He'll be dancing a jig in a minute." And he'd be hungry as hell.

Back to the wall, she slid down until she sat next to Korzha. She nodded toward the interior of her apartment and said to the demon, "Put some QuikSeal on that cut before you bleed all over my new bamboo floors. Down the hall, second door on the right. There's a first-aid kit in the cabinet. Help yourself."

Aslet's blue eyes stayed on her. "I am sorry your vishtau mate is dead."

"Yeah, well." She was glad she was sitting down, because otherwise she would have collapsed.

"For a human female, you are brave."

"Thanks." She touched the diminishing wound in Tiber's shoulder. It was nearly healed, though he was unconscious. Aslet walked past her. "You're a good aim," she called after him. "For a demon."

The demon's laughter stayed in her ears when Tiber opened his eyes. "Hey," she said, stroking her fingers through his hair. The sight of his gorgeous green eyes made her heart flutter. Sometimes, a thing was just right, and so you went with it. "Up and at 'em, fang. We've got another mess to clean up."

He sat up, took in the damage to the room and touched a finger to her cheek. "Such a lovely smile, dear-heart. It's always nice to wake to." He looked around the room—at the damage, at Lath's body—and his head dipped toward hers and Claudia felt a shiver of anticipation. "Is it finally all for me?"

"Yeah, Tiber. It is." She nodded as she twined her arms around his neck and pulled him to her. "After the baby's born, I'm yours for as long as you can stand it."

"Forever," he said. "Forever sounds perfect to me."

She put her mouth by his ear and whispered, "Forever sounds good to me, too."

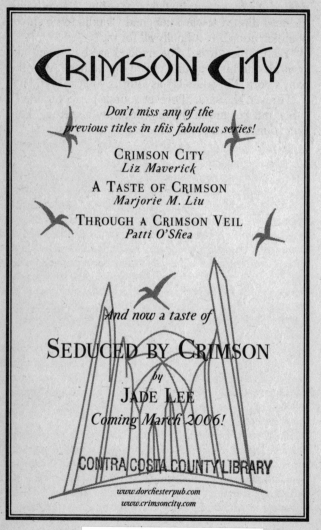

CRIMSON CITY

Don't miss any of the previous titles in this fabulous series!

CRIMSON CITY
Liz Maverick

A TASTE OF CRIMSON
Marjorie M. Liu

THROUGH A CRIMSON VEIL
Patti O'Shea

And now a taste of

SEDUCED BY CRIMSON

by

JADE LEE

Coming March 2006!

www.dorchesterpub.com
www.crimsoncity.com

A man can get tunnel vision during battle. He fixates on the sight of blood spurting from a white throat or the smell of charred flesh. If he's trained, he can still fight the demons, the black-hearted Bak-Faru he'd likely only seen in a book, but a large part of his mind still fixates on one hideous thing. For Patrick Lewis, it was the taste in the air: blood and bile. Metallic and bitter, it made his throat close and his chest heave. But he had enough training to fight even if he was coming late to the battle.

The screams reached him first. He was in the San Bernadino Botanical Garden, so the sound could travel far, especially at night. He was running full-tilt for the grove when the smell hit him, the smell and that taste in the air.

He didn't even stumble: that's how well trained he was. But his mind was so caught up in not retching that he almost missed the sight of his first live Bak-Faru. The thing was humanlike. Large and dark-haired, it had eyes that glowed bright lavender in the night. Patrick's mother had told him the demon gate was being used, and indeed, attuned as he was to nature, he'd felt each and every tremor as something passed through. Still, he hadn't actually believed such disaster was possible until now, seeing one, two…no, make that four of the creatures walking away. Two sported wounds—jagged flesh that bled dark down their naked torsos. But they didn't seem to be slowed.

Patrick didn't think. He had seven ceremonial knives with him and began throwing. Score. The closest demon clutched his neck and stumbled, but didn't fall. The monster's companions barely even glanced around, even when Patrick's second knife lodged in one of their shoulder blades. They were intent on escape.

Patrick wanted to pursue. He even took a step forward, but the need to find his parents burned hotter. He had to get to the grove. Especially since his mother's screams were growing weaker. Yet he had to go slowly. Much though it burned his gut, Patrick shifted from battle to stealth; it wouldn't help his parents if he stumbled blindly into more of these creatures.

He slipped around a redwood and peered into the grove, where his tunnel vision returned with full force. His mind registered each sensation as a disparate element: the taste of blood in the air, the smell of death, and the clenching of his gut. He refused to look for long, searched the bodies on the ground with as much speed as he could manage.

He found his father first, with only one shoulder and half his chest; the rest was burnt to oblivion. It was as if a rocket had burst through him. Numbness seeped into Patrick's spirit. At least he hadn't felt any pain.

He stumbled, scanning the rest of the bodies. He found his mother. She wasn't as lucky. She'd been gutted by a short blade, or more specifically, by long claws. Blood and bowel poured relentlessly from her into the ground where she lay. She was still alive.

Patrick skidded to a halt in the dirt beside her, but there was nothing for him to do; too much of her was spilled across the ground. His hands hovered uselessly above her torn belly. What could he do? He dialed 9-1-1 and stammered out details. The operator was speaking to him, but he didn't hear her because his mother opened her eyes. The phone left his ear as he leaned forward. He opened his mouth to reassure her. He was going to lie, to say that she'd be just fine, but all that came out was a single word:

"Mom?"

She focused on him and her expression softened. She struggled to speak, her voice a bare whisper, and Patrick lowered his head as close to her mouth as he dared.

"Run," she said.

He straightened enough to look into her eyes. "They're gone. The…" He couldn't bring himself to name the monsters, the creatures of nightmare that had at last returned to his world. "They've left."

His mother swallowed, and he was sure he saw relief in her gaze. He grabbed her hands, his mind scrambling for something to do. "Hang on," he said.

"Find her," she said. "Close…the gate." She was fading; he could see it. Her eyes were growing more distant, and her hands were like ice. He wanted to strip off his shirt to cover her, but he would have missed her next words.

"Draig-uisge," she said. It shocked him to hear his druidic name spoken with such command. "Find her…the Phoenix Tear. Close the gate. Permanently." Then she closed her eyes and was gone forever….